RHAPSODY
IN A
MINOR MODE

Also by Elaine Kozak

Root Causes

The Lighthouse

RHAPSODY
IN A
MINOR MODE

ELAINE KOZAK

Rhapsody in a Minor Mode
Copyright © 2023 by Elaine Kozak
Author photo by Howard Fry

All rights reserved. No part of this publication may be reproduced, distributed, or transmitted in any form or by any means, including photocopying, recording, or other electronic or mechanical methods, without the prior written permission of the author, except in the case of brief quotations embodied in critical reviews and certain other non-commercial uses permitted by copyright law.

Tellwell Talent
www.tellwell.ca

ISBN
978-0-2288-9101-7 (Hardcover)
978-0-2288-9100-0 (Paperback)
978-0-2288-9102-4 (eBook)

In memory of all whom I have lost

PART I

Chapter 1

"IF BRAD ACTUALLY *IS* your father, Niels," Rebecca said. Rebecca was the sister of the long-deceased man whom I had recently discovered to be my biological father. I had just told her how happy I was to finally meet his family.

"Pardon me?" I said.

She regarded me over the rim of her martini glass. Rebecca was, I judged, in her late-thirties, and making the most of her unremarkable features and chunky body with a well-cut black dress, flattering hairstyle, and skillfully applied makeup. She had returned home to Vancouver from Dubai, where she now lived, to spend the holidays with her parents, and I had come to their New Year's Eve party to meet her.

"I would have insisted on a DNA test, but Mom said she saw a family resemblance and didn't need one. Don't see it myself." Rebecca shrugged. "Okay, the hair, maybe, but is that enough? Mom was just so glad to think Brad left something behind that she took Leah at her word. I would have made you do the test."

"I'd think in the circumstances my mother's word would be enough," I said stiffly.

Rebecca's lips twitched. "The thing is, Leah doesn't really know who your father is. There were three of them."

"What do you mean, three of them?"

"Three guys."

"My mother? Three guys? No way," I sputtered.

"Yes, well, they put something in her drink. But your dad could have been any of them."

I stepped back and held up my palm, warding off Rebecca's words. My mind reeled with the implication of what she had said. She smiled at someone over my shoulder and began to walk away. I grabbed her arm.

"Wait! The other two—who are they?"

Rebecca looked back at me, her expression unreadable. "Best to let it go, Niels." She disengaged her arm and left.

I stared after her, breathless with disbelief, then stumbled through the crowd to where my girlfriend Aude was talking to an older man. "We have to leave, Aude," I said, cutting in. The man gave me a cool, dismissive look. I returned it with one I hoped said that he was too old to be flirting with a twenty-year-old woman.

"Really, Niels," Aude said reproachfully and, observing the strict *politesse* her French parents had instilled in her, introduced us. We exchanged a brief handshake.

"I'll leave you two lovebirds alone," he said and sauntered away.

I set my glass of wine on a nearby table. "Let's go."

"What's the rush?"

"I need to leave. I'll get our coats."

Aude followed me as I unsteadily tracked the perimeter of the room to the den by the entrance where a rack had been placed for the guests' coats. I found ours and helped Aude put hers on before struggling into my own, my arms as limp as noodles. She pulled her long, glossy hair free of her collar and gave me a puzzled look.

"What's up, Niels?"

My head spun. I closed my eyes and braced myself against the coat rack.

"Are you okay?"

I shook my head, straightened up, and headed for the front door.

Aude caught my arm. "Niels, we can't go without properly taking our leave."

I knew better than to argue and trailed her as she searched for Don and Yvonne, my presumed grandparents. We found them amidst the caterers and serving staff in the kitchen, arguing in low hisses. Aude paused, uncertain. Don caught sight of us and placed a restraining hand on his wife's arm.

"Sorry to interrupt, but we're leaving," Aude said.

Don's face smoothed into lines of cordiality. "Are you now?"

"Yes, and we wanted to say goodbye and thank you."

Don bared his teeth in a banker's smile. "I'm sure you have more exciting things to do on New Year's Eve than hang out with a bunch of old farts."

Yvonne stepped forward, all violet and platinum elegance. A tall woman, she rested her cheek against mine when she pulled me into an embrace. Stepping back, she held my shoulders lightly. "Thank you so much for coming. Do keep in touch."

I nodded automatically, not meeting her eyes.

She pressed Aude's hand. "And perhaps we'll see you again too?"

"That would be nice."

Don hovered to the side. He wasn't as comfortable with me as Yvonne was, not quite as accepting. "If your family wasn't already rich, I'd have to wonder whether you were maybe after my money," he had said once when we were alone. Seeing my startled look, he had slapped me on the back and laughed. "It was a joke, son, a joke." But I wondered. Now he shook my hand and flashed his trademark smile. His perfect, pearl-white teeth were vaguely sinister. I pulled out of his grip and, with a last goodbye, we left.

The streetlamps rhythmically washed the interior of the car with bronzed light as we drove home.

"Your grandparents seem nice," Aude said.

I touched my cheek where a trace of Yvonne's face powder lingered. The scent filled the car.

"I guess."

Aude fell silent, perhaps sensing my mood. I was driving my maternal grandfather Fin's electric sedan and wishing there was more car noise than the discrete hum of the motor and slurp of tires on the rain-slicked Vancouver street to fill the quiet. Instead of heading to Fin's house in the Shaughnessy neighborhood as intended, I turned on West Sixteenth in the direction of the apartment Aude shared with a college friend. She started and leaned towards me.

"I thought we were going to your place?"

It was to have been our first night together. Fin and his second wife Dominique—my grandmother Alexandra had died twelve years previously—were away, and I had the house to myself. Fresh sheets were on the bed in the room I had occupied since birth. An unopened box of condoms that I had bought, red-faced, earlier in the day were in the drawer of my nightstand. A bouquet of irises, Aude's favorite, graced the dresser. A half-bottle of French champagne chilled in the fridge, and I had made a special trip to the French bakery on Granville Island for the brioche Aude had once said she preferred to croissants for breakfast.

"Sorry, Aude, I can't tonight."

"Is something wrong?"

Oh, yes, something is very wrong, I wanted to shout. "I don't feel well."

"Something you ate, maybe?"

"Maybe."

I pulled up to the entrance of her apartment building and turned off the car. My parents had taught me manners too, and they included seeing a girl safely home. I got out and walked around the car, but Aude wasn't one to wait to be handed out of a vehicle and had already emerged.

"My bag," she said.

I opened the rear door and took out a tote with the things she had brought for the night.

"I'm sorry to spoil your New Year's, Aude," I said as we headed to the entrance of her building.

"It's okay. I'm sorry you're not feeling well." At the door she turned to me. "You don't have to come in. You should get home."

I glanced up to noise coming from one of the apartments. "Are you sure?"

"It's only the Sinclairs. They're having a party tonight."

"Okay."

She took her bag and regarded me for a moment. My heart fluttered with uncertainty and regret. Tonight had been intended to crown years of loving each other. Despite living far apart and meeting only occasionally, a bond we had formed as children had evolved over the years to the conviction that we were meant to be together. Aude had grown from a feisty, bespectacled little girl through a coltish adolescence to become a lovely, statuesque woman. The overhead light burnished her auburn hair and sparked off the small diamond at her throat, my Christmas gift.

"I hope you feel better soon. Will I see you tomorrow?" Aude said.

"Yeah, maybe."

"Take care." She leaned towards me. I accepted her kiss gingerly.

She unlocked the door with her keycard. I held it open for her to pass through and watched her walk to the elevator. Inside, she turned and gave me a little wave.

"Bye."

The elevator doors closed and I stared at them for a moment. "Goodbye," I said.

At Fin's house I shed my overcoat and suit jacket and slumped into an armchair. Within the refuge of the cone of light cast by the lamp on the side table, I grappled with Rebecca's shocking revelation. When I was growing up, no one had ever spoken about my biological father, and I hadn't been sufficiently aware to ask my mother about him until I was eleven. She had regarded me—sadly, I recall—for several moments before replying.

"Your father is dead, Niels."

Squirming with discomfort and confused emotions, I had dropped the matter and slipped away. I had thought about him from time to time with a formless regret, not having anything material around which to shape it. At one point I realized I didn't even know his name. So when my mother asked me what I would like for my sixteenth birthday, I replied that I wanted to find out about my real father. Pain had flashed through her eyes. I thought at the time that it was because of my unintentional slighting of her husband, Theo, but realized now there may have been more.

"I'll see what I can do," she said.

Nothing happened for several months. One night, my mother drew me to the side after dinner to say that she had been in touch with my biological father's family and, if I still wanted to, they would like to meet me. It was only then that I learned his name was Brad. "Of course I still want to," I said. I wondered now by what process my mother had chosen Brad from the three guys and how, without a DNA test, she had convinced Brad's parents that I was their grandson.

Two weeks later, Mom, Theo, and I sat down to coffee with Don and Yvonne at their house in the endowment lands next to the University of British Columbia. My heart beat out an erratic rhythm and I wiped sweaty palms on my wool-clad thighs while they quizzed me on my interests and plans. In response to my own stumbling questions, I learned that Brad had excelled at skiing and sailing, he loved Thai food, New York was his favorite place to visit, and he had completed one year of law school when he died in a boating accident. When I left, Yvonne had pressed a framed graduation photo of him into my hands. The manifestation of what to that point had been a phantom inexplicably unnerved me, and rather than taking it home I left it on the dresser of my bedroom in Fin's house, where it still stood.

I arose from the armchair, went upstairs to my bedroom, picked up the photo, and studied Brad's face. There was little to suggest we were related. He was fair, I'm dark; he had a snub nose, mine is aquiline; his lips were fleshy, mine are . . . I don't know, just straight-forward lips; his jaw was rounded, mine is square. Okay, his hair grew up in a wave off his forehead like mine. This was the resemblance everyone seemed to fix on, but, as Rebecca said, was it enough? I sighed and was about to set the photo back down when I noticed his eyes. They also were different from mine, and contained in their depths an icy arrogance I had not noticed before.

Shivering suddenly, I carried the photo down to the kitchen and slid it under the refuse already in the garbage can. Still chilled, I turned on the espresso machine, made myself an americano, and took it back to the armchair. My head felt like it was full of bees. I wanted answers, and if my mother had not been somewhere in the air I would have called her there and then. The family had all gathered at Counter Point, our estate near Victoria on Vancouver Island, for Christmas. Mom, Theo, and Theo's parents, Papa Luke and Mama Ris, lived there. Fin and Dominique had come from Vancouver, and my stepbrother Fox and I flew in from Melbourne and Toronto, respectively, where we were attending university. After the holiday we had scattered. Fox had left after only three days—despite travelling so far, he rarely stayed longer on his visits, always claiming that an obligation required him to go right back home. I had driven Fin and Dominque to the airport on their way to Singapore the day before, and my parents, Papa Luke, and Mama Ris had departed for Miami en route to Bolivia only a few hours ago.

I thought about my mother, or tried to. My mind lurched away from imagining what had happened to her. She had explained that Brad was the brother of a friend, and I had assumed I was the product of a teenage romance. But what had happened was obviously rape—my mother would never have consented to sex with three guys, especially not at fifteen. Had it been reported? Nothing anyone had ever said or done indicated that it had become a police matter, or even that it had happened. How did Rebecca know? Or did everybody know and had agreed to be silent?

My mother was a dignified and sensitive woman. How did she, or any woman, get over such a degrading and destructive experience? Perhaps she never had. Mom had been absent during the first nine years of my life. Now I understood why—what an awful reminder I would have been. And maybe still was.

And then there was my biological father, whichever of those three guys it had been. At the thought that the blood of that man flowed through me, my skin crawled and my gorge rose. I swallowed hard, fighting it down. I set my coffee on the side table, buried my face in my hands, and regarded my life through a new, awful prism. I had been neither planned nor wanted. Why did I even exist? Rising shakily, I looked around. I had spent much of my childhood in this house, but it suddenly felt alien. Like I was an impostor with no claim to its shelter. I needed to go, to get away, to try to figure out what this new and horrifying truth meant.

I tidied up the kitchen, put the brioche in the freezer, and left the bottle of champagne in the refrigerator for my grandfather to make of it what he would. Up in my room I changed into jeans and a sweater and put some clothing, my shaving kit, and computer in my backpack. An autobiography of Philip Glass my mother had given me for Christmas sat on the bedside table. I picked it up but set it down again. I had brought the garbage bag from the kitchen up and took it to the bathroom to collect the trash there. Back in my room, I looked around and saw the vase of irises on my dresser.

Aude. I shook my head. I couldn't deal with her. Not here, not now.

I grabbed the flowers and stuffed them into the garbage bag. Their spiky blueness among the trash seemed like shrieks of despair. "I'm sorry, I'm sorry!" I said. I yanked them out, put them back in the vase, and stared at them for a moment. Left alone, they would wilt and rot and the water would turn swampy and stink. I put aside the garbage bag, carried the vase downstairs and outside, and placed it on the edge of the terrace where the irises might catch some rain. "Be happy," I said and returned to the house.

Back upstairs, I scanned the bedroom again for other rubbish and remembered the box of condoms in my nightstand. I removed it from the drawer and thrust it to the bottom of the bag next to Brad's photo. Turning, I noticed Meredith, the three-quarter cello I had used as a pre-teen, on her stand in the corner. Her clear, bright voice had kept me company through many long hours. When I had outgrown her, Fin had given me a full-size Peresson cello. I had not brought it home on this trip to avoid unnecessary wear, renting one instead for the local Christmas concert in which I had performed. Although I no longer played Meredith, I had insisted on keeping her. *Was it wrong to deny the instrument a chance to fulfill its purpose?* I shook my head—a question for another time. I picked up my pack and the bag of garbage and, after one last glance around the room, turned off the light and left.

Chapter 2

"HEY, NIELIE, TIME TO get up, no? It's five days now you're in bed," Jax said.

I coughed deeply, throatily, and without exaggeration. I had left my grandfather's house in the early hours of New Year's Day, and the wait for a taxi was so long that I had set off on foot for the airport, hoping to flag one down on the way. I did, eventually, but not before an insistent drizzle soaked me. At the airport I exchanged my return ticket for an early flight to Toronto, arriving mid-afternoon to a blizzard. In my rush to leave Vancouver I had forgotten that I would be re-entering real winter, and my damp clothing was a poor defense against the cutting cold. The walk home from the subway against driving snow froze me to the marrow, and I wasn't surprised to wake the next morning with a razor-raw throat.

"Still sick," I said.

Jax sat on the edge of the bed, leaned forward, and placed a hand on my forehead, causing her right breast to rest on my arm. She often wandered around the house braless in a singlet or light T-shirt, thinking, perhaps, that because she was not interested in men they were indifferent to her femaleness. Not that I had feelings for her in that way, but her breasts were particularly nice and hard to ignore pressing against me.

"Do you maybe need to see a doctor?"

I shook my head.

She straightened up. "Don't want you to get pneumonia."

"It's just a cold."

"Okay, big boy. Let me know if you need anything." She rose and left the room.

My choice of university had been one of several matters of contention between my grandfather and mother about my schooling, activities, and plans over the years. Fin, known professionally as Gabriel Finley Larsen, was a composer of note and had steered me hard into a life of music. One of my first memories was sitting on his lap at the piano. "This is middle C, and the next one D, and then E," he had said, guiding my tiny fingers over the keys. He no doubt had hoped I would be a musical prodigy. I was not. Still, my life was built around music—lessons, camps, masterclasses, performances with youth orchestras, trips with Fin to hear and meet celebrated performers, and endless practice. And there was no question that after high school I would continue my studies to make music a career.

The question was where. Fin had pumped for Juilliard or Berklee College, or even schools in London or Vienna where he knew the cello instructors. With my reasonably solid credentials and his connections, I would have no difficulty getting in anywhere. My mother argued for UBC. The COVID pandemic was still going strong, and she thought it better if I were close to home. But Granddad was adamant that I go elsewhere to be exposed to different instructors and styles and music scenes.

"Excuse me, don't I have a say?" I had said.

They conceded that I did. After a year and a half of pandemic restrictions I wanted to get away—but not too far. I chose the University of Toronto, which offered well-known instructors and a different scene but was only a five-hour flight from home. Living in residence didn't appeal, so I found a full-service apartment within walking distant of the campus.

The first couple of weeks were exhilarating as I explored my new environment and tested independent living. With pandemic restrictions, however, classes were a mix of online and on-site instruction, and social interaction was difficult. Anonymous behind their masks, people moved singly or in clutches of two or three, and there were few if any opportunities to do more than exchange greetings. As the fall progressed I found myself alone most of the time, holed up in my apartment with my laptop as the main portal to the world, and only my cello for company.

One afternoon I was walking down a hallway in the Faculty of Music when I saw a woman standing in front of a bulletin board. I had noticed her before: stocky with heavy-framed glasses and short hair crowned by a crest of dark curls, and invariably dressed in jeans topped with a man's vintage suit jacket, dress shirt, and colorful tie. Today the jacket was black with a wide chalk-stripe, and the tie featured palm trees on a beach. She was juggling a violin case, satchel, file folder, and clear plastic box. Both the folder and the box fell, scattering sheets of paper and multi-colored push pins on the floor.

"Fuck!" she said, the word ballooning her mask.

I hurried forward and helped her pick the items up.

"Thanks!" Behind the glasses, dark-brown doe eyes crinkled in a smile.

"No problem. Why don't I hold something?"

"Sure."

She handed me the violin case and satchel, selected a sheet from the folder, and pinned it to the bulletin board. Taking the satchel back, she shoved the folder and pin box inside, then held out her hand. I put the handle of the violin case into it. She hesitated and accepted it.

"I was going to shake your hand," she said with a laugh.

"Oh! Sorry."

"I'm Jax, by the way."

"I'm Niels."

"Thanks again. See you around, Niels." She gave me another eye smile and continued up the hall.

Warmed by the bit of human contact, I gazed after her then glanced at what she had posted on the board: ROOM FOR RENT, followed by details. I stared at the notice for a moment.

"Jax, wait!" I said and hurried after her.

Knuckles rapped sharply on the table. It was the beginning of the third week of the new semester and I was in my Philosophy of Perception class. I turned away from contemplating the snow swirling outside the window in response to the sound. The balding man sitting at the table's head eyed me with a raised eyebrow over the reading glasses perched on the end of his nose.

"Would you kindly do us the courtesy of attending to the discussion?" he said.

I glanced at the other students seated around the table. Everyone was looking at me.

"Or perhaps you'd prefer to be elsewhere?" the professor continued.

"Actually, yeah." I rose and picked up my computer, backpack, and jacket. Mouths fell open. Someone snickered. In the corridor, I stuffed my computer in my pack and shrugged on my jacket.

That's a bridge burned. I didn't care. I exited the building and set off for home, toeing runnels through the fallen snow. Forty minutes later I shook the snow off my shoulders, stamped my feet on the porch mat, and let myself into Jax's narrow brick house, my home for over three years. Jax glanced up from where she was working at the dining room table. Piles of books and papers covered the surface. She had finished the coursework for her doctorate and was deep into the research for her thesis.

"Nielie! I thought you had a class this afternoon."

I hung my jacket and scarf on pegs in the entrance and stood at the door to the dining room.

"I walked out."

"Was there a problem?"

"Yeah, couldn't get into it. Prof basically told me to leave." She frowned. "What?"

"Look, I don't want to disturb your work." I turned to head to my room upstairs.

She stretched and rubbed the back of her neck. "I was about to take a break. Let's have a coffee and you can tell me about it."

In the kitchen she filled and turned on the coffee maker. While it dripped and emitted plumes of aromatic steam, she leaned with folded arms against the counter.

"So, what's up?"

I set my pack on the floor by the table, sat down in a chair, and sighed. "Can't focus, can't concentrate, not interested."

Jax eyed me with concern. "What's that all about?" The coffee maker hissed and blew to signal completion of the brew. "Hang on." She filled a couple of cups, slid one in front of me, and sat down across the table with her own. "You've been broody ever since you got back. What's going on?"

"It's too awful to talk about."

Jax leaned forward. "It's me, Nielie. You can tell me anything."

I had thought I'd never speak of what Rebecca had said about my parentage to anyone, but found myself pouring it all out.

Jax leaned back in her chair. "Oh, fuck."

"Yes, exactly. I feel sick. It's like something foreign and disgusting has entered me." I shuddered. "Creeps me out. I'd hoped that coming back here would leave it all behind, but it's stuck to me like slime. It's the first thing on my mind in the morning and it crowds out everything else all day. Nothing helps."

"Maybe you need to talk to somebody."

"I'm talking to you."

"I mean someone professional."

I shook my head. "Nothing they'd say would change the reality of it."

We went around in this vein for a while, Jax telling me to get help and me saying no. Darkness fell and Toru, a Japanese flautist and Jax's other tenant, shuffled into the kitchen, bobbed his head in greeting, and began to prepare a variation of the noodles he regularly ate for dinner.

Jax rose and said, "I'm going to order us a pizza. You dig out a bottle of that wine your family sends you and let's fix this."

The pizza arrived and we took it and the wine to the living room. I gnawed on a slice to please Jax. She gave up coaxing me to eat and took what remained to the refrigerator. I shared out the rest of the wine, buzzing slightly from what I had already consumed. Jax returned and picked up her glass.

"What do your parents think about all this?"

"I haven't discussed it with them."

"Why ever not?"

"Can't face them, especially my mother. Besides, they're way the hell out in some remote part of the Andes."

Jax shook her head, swallowed the last of her wine, and set her glass down. "So, what are you going to do with this, Nielie?"

I released a long, exhausted breath. "I have absolutely no idea. I honestly don't think I can continue with school."

"Come on. It's your last semester."

I grimaced. "Yeah, but I just can't *attend*. Almost three weeks in and I can't remember anything from the lectures, I haven't done any reading, I've missed assignments, and I've barely practiced. Besides, I'm not even sure anymore that music is what I want to do with my life. I'd just like a time-out, you know? A breather so I can make sense of it all."

Jax took off her glasses and rubbed her eyes. "Look, I'm totally wiped. I need some sleep and so do you. It'll look different in the morning, you'll see."

But it didn't look different when I woke the next day. If anything, talking about it had given what I was going through some form, and indicated a path.

"Feeling better today?" Jax said, joining me at the kitchen table.

"No, but I've decided what to do. I need to cut my losses. It's still early enough to withdraw from school without penalties."

"That's pretty radical."

"It's better than failing, which I'm on track to do. The other thing is that I can't just mope around here. I want to go away, somewhere far, and do something completely different for a while."

She took a sip of coffee. "What did you have in mind?"

My shoulders sagged. "I don't know. Not a place where I know anyone and have to explain myself, but not totally strange either, like Niger or Uzbekistan or somewhere like that. A place where I can find work of some kind."

"So how long do you see yourself staying in this place, and what do you expect to accomplish?"

"Again, I don't know," I said crossly. "Planning it all ahead of time would defeat the purpose, and the whole point is to be free of having to accomplish anything."

Jax made a *calm down* gesture with her hand. "Okay, okay. So, basically you just want to step out of your life for a while."

I leaned forward. "Yes, that's it exactly. I want to give myself some space and see what happens. Everything in my life has been so structured, so *purposed* to this point that I haven't had a chance to think, to breathe even, and see if it's taking me where I really want to go."

"And that is?"

"Well, I don't know yet, do I. And honestly, I really don't know who I am anymore. If I ever did. Didn't you ever feel that way?"

Jax folded her arms and smiled. "Yes, I did. After I got married."

My eyes popped out of my head. "You were married? Like, to a guy?"

Her smile broadened. "Oh, yes. And then I fell in love with his sister." She shook her head. "What a mess that all was."

Still agog, I studied Jax, trying to incorporate this new information into my sense of her. She was lost in thought and didn't notice my scrutiny.

"Why don't you go stay with your brother? The one with the funny name," she said.

"Fox—it's a contraction of Forrest Xavier."

"That's a mouthful, all right. Isn't he in Australia? That's pretty far away."

I shook my head. "I couldn't face him if he knows. And if he doesn't, well, I don't want to tell him. Besides, we're not really that close." Although almost a year younger than me, Fox had blazed into manhood, vivid and charismatic, and left me in his shadow.

Jax straightened up. "How about *my* brother then? Is Halifax far enough? Like me, Steve used the money our auntie left us to put a down payment on a house, and rented out rooms to help pay the rest. He's got a family now, and when I called at Christmas he mentioned that he's paid off his mortgage and stopped taking in tenants." She made a face. "He did it a lot more quickly there than I'll be able to here in Toronto. Anyway, you could go and stay with him."

"Are you sure? It sounds like he doesn't want renters anymore."

"Oh, he really didn't mind having them. The house is big

and the rental suite is quite separate from their space. Anyhow, he'll do it if I ask."

I considered this for a moment. I had never met Steve, but Jax spoke about him often. It would be different enough but not too strange. "Yeah, okay, if he'll have me. But I don't want to leave you in the lurch, Jax. I'll pay my rent until the end of term, or you find someone else." I quickly calculated how it would affect my finances—I would definitely need to find work.

Jax's forehead knitted in thought. "It may not come to that. Do you remember Polly?"

"Ah, yeah," I said. I had met her a few days after moving into Jax's house. Assuming I was alone, I had been singing along to music streaming through my earbuds while cooking dinner when I sensed another presence, and turned from the stove to see Jax and a willowy woman with light brown hair, high cheekbones, and striking black-rimmed silvery-blue eyes grinning at me.

I plucked out the earbuds, my face burning with embarrassment. "Sorry!"

"Hey, there can never be too much music." Jax turned to the other woman. "This is Niels Larsen. He just moved in. Niels, this is Polina Fedoryk."

"Call me Polly," she said, extending her hand. "What are you making? It smells wonderful."

I ladled in more stock and gave the rice mixture in the saucepan a quick stir. "It's risotto."

"Risotto!" they said.

Jax set a bag of groceries on the counter and glanced over. "With asparagus, no less. Where do you get asparagus at this time of year?"

"The greengrocer on the Avenue had it. It's spring in Peru."

Polly came up on the other side. "And prawns too!"

I had made enough for leftovers. "Would you, ah, maybe like to join me for dinner?"

"What do you think, Polly? Beats spaghetti. I've got a baguette and stuff for salad." Jax emptied the bag and began washing the greens.

Polly chatted with me while I finished cooking the risotto. She worked as an assistant to the vice president of a bank in the city but had grown up, as I did, near Victoria. We compared notes on neighborhoods, hangouts, and restaurants. When all was ready and the table set, we sat down to the meal in the dining room.

"Where'd you learn how to cook?" Jax said, helping herself to risotto.

"My mother signed me and my stepbrother up for cooking classes when I was thirteen. She said she didn't want to raise useless men."

"A wise woman," Polly said.

We conversed lightly as the meal progressed. Glancing up at one point, I saw Polly tuck a lock of hair behind her ear and gaze up at Jax through her lashes and realized that they were on a date. One could infer Jax's inclinations from her appearance and apparel, but Polly? Her shoulder-length bob, pencil skirt, lace-knit sweater, and pearl necklace were nothing if not feminine. I scarfed down the rest of my food, mumbled an excuse, and made myself scarce.

Polly and Jax were together for a few months until the man for whom Polly worked was hired as the president of a bank in Dallas, Texas. The promotion he had offered her was too good to pass up and she had followed him there.

"Polly's in the picture again?" I said.

"Maybe. We've kept in touch. When I talked to her over Christmas she said she's had enough of the heat and politics in Texas and wants to come back to Canada. I told her she'd be welcome to take Toru's room when he goes back to Japan in the spring. If yours becomes available, she might come back sooner. I'll ask her."

"That would be good." *And a relief for me.*

"You definitely want to do this, Nielie? Sure you can't hang in until you finish your degree?"

"Yes, absolutely sure." In my mind the disconnect from my studies was now so complete that going back was inconceivable.

"Okay." Jax slapped her thighs and stood up. "Let me call Steve and see what he says."

She called her brother, confirmed he had time to talk, and outlined the situation. "I'm sure I've mentioned Niels before. He's been with me for over three years. Yeah, another music guy. No, don't worry, he's not the party type. Yeah, he's clean. No, I don't know for how long, does it matter? Okay. No, don't worry about that, he can manage." She glanced at me. "In fact, he's a very good cook." She put the phone against her chest. "When do you think you'll be there?"

I blinked. "Ah, later this week maybe?" There was no point in hanging around now that I had decided to leave.

"Soon," Jax said into the phone. "We'll call with a specific date. Great, and thanks, Steve." She ended the call and turned to me. "Well, there it is, Nielie."

I struggled to breathe. All the talk, the drama, had been like bubbles in the air before. This was real now. My heart dribbled around my chest. *What the hell did I just do?*

The decision to leave pulled me out of the misery and inertia in which I had been mired. Arrangements had to be made, actions taken. The next day I went to the faculty administration and withdrew from all my classes. The form asked for a reason, and I wrote, "Need to deal with a family matter." I arranged my flight to Halifax, wincing at the bite it took out of my funds—my parents or Fin had always paid for my airfare—and began to pack. Over three years I had accumulated a surprising amount of stuff. I put the books, music scores, and bits of memorabilia I wanted to keep in a box to store in Jax's basement and hauled the rest to a local charity. Jax stopped me as I was descending the basement stairs with my cello.

"You're not taking Celeste?" she said with raised eyebrows.

I had named the Peresson "Celeste" for its haunting, otherworldly tone.

"Why do you always give your cellos women's names?" Fox had asked. "Why not Morris, or Stanley?"

I had run my hands down the curves of Celeste's body. "Don't see many men shaped like this."

"No, I'm not taking her," I said to Jax. "Is it okay if I leave her with the other stuff?"

"Of course." She frowned. "Are you sure, Nielie? Isn't this going too far? What will you do for music?"

"I want a break from music. I'm not sure it's what I'm meant to do."

"But all the time you've invested in study . . ."

"Yeah, it's consumed my whole life. All the more reason to stop now."

"Have you told your family what you're doing?" Jax said on the eve of my flight to Halifax.

I shrugged.

She sighed in exasperation. "Nielie, you have to. They'll worry about you."

"I doubt it."

"Come on. If you don't tell them, they'll be after me. I don't want to be the one having to explain all this."

"Okay," I finally said.

My family didn't share the details of our daily lives on social media as others did, saving discussions of where we had been, what we had done, and our thoughts about the world for when we could speak. My mother had sent Fox and me an email the previous week saying that they had arrived safely in Bolivia and were visiting the first of the projects in South America that the family's charitable foundation supported. I had not replied. I stared at the screen. What to say? After typing and retyping for half an hour, I settled on an email that said:

> *I have discovered that the basis of my life is false and I'm going away to try to figure out who I am and what my life should be. I need to do this alone. I'll be fine. Take care.*

I also had to write to Aude. Before leaving Vancouver I had sent her a text from the airport saying that I unexpectedly had to return to Toronto. I don't know if she answered because, for reasons I can't even explain to myself, I had placed my cellphone on the floor and ground it with my heel into a mangled mess, which I threw into a garbage bin. Aude had, however, sent me several emails since then, each more apprehensive than the last. The most recent one said, "You're scaring me." I rested my elbows on my desk and ground my palms into my eyes. How to reply?

Chapter 3

IF THERE WERE ANYONE I should have been able to talk to about what Rebecca said, it was Aude. I had known her for over half of my life and there was little we didn't share. We had met at summer music camp in Vancouver when I was eleven and she was three months short of ten. Arriving at the stage where we were about to rehearse for the final performance with the full student ensemble, I noticed a ruckus in the back corner. Two boys were taunting a girl who sat beside a small lever harp. Red-faced with hands fisted on her hips, she was replying in kind. I leaned my cello against my chair and went over to investigate.

"Why are you bothering her?" I said.

The boys turned and stepped back.

"She talks funny," one of them said.

The girl blew out a puff of disgust.

"Well, maybe you sound funny to her too," I said. "Anyhow, the concertmaster's going to be here soon."

The boys slunk off, mumbling. I regarded the girl. She was dressed in a skirt, blouse, and sweater despite the heat. and her chin-length auburn hair was so thick it stood out horizontally. Green-rimmed glasses sat at an angle on a lightly freckled nose.

"Are you okay?" I said.

"Yes. *Merci*." She thrust out a small hand with long, blunt fingers and introduced herself.

I frowned, trying to understand the name she had given. In addition to having an accent, her voice was unusually low and throaty for a child.

"You mean Ode, like a poem?" I said.

She scowled. "What is this poem? No, Aude is my name. Aude Langevin."

"How do you spell it?"

She tsked. "A-U-D-E."

"Ah," I said. "Where are you from?"

"I live here now, in Nelson, but I come from France it is two years."

The noise level had risen in the room. I glanced around. Most of the performers had taken their places. "I should go."

"And who are you?"

"Niels."

"I am enchanted to meet you, Niels," she said, baring crooked teeth in a wide grin.

Aude often sought me out at camp the next summer, flashing her crooked smile and chattering about almost anything. Her hair had grown and was constrained in braids as thick as ropes, but she still wore the green glasses and prim little outfits. I didn't mind her attention because she was a bright, funny little thing.

I learned that Aude's father was a ski instructor and the family ran a holiday lodge in Nelson. She had a brother, Maxime, who was two years older, an orange cat named Minou, and a black dog named Gilet because he had a white patch like a vest on his chest. She had wanted to study the harp since she was five after hearing one played in a church, but started lessons only after they moved to Canada.

In turn, I told her that I had been raised in Vancouver by my scientist grandmother and musician grandfather and had started piano lessons when I was five but switched to cello when I was eight. That after my grandmother died, my mother came to take care of me. That she recently married, giving me a father and a brother, and we now lived near Victoria.

The third summer we spent most of our free time together. Aude had narrowed and lengthened, and suspicious little nubs disturbed the smoothness of her stylish cotton tops. Her accent had softened and she spoke idiomatically. "Niels has a girlfriend," the guys snickered. I didn't mind. On the last day of camp, our mothers met.

Aude's mother, Valérie, was a pert-faced woman with the same rich coloring and thick wavy hair as her daughter. "So, this is the boy I hear so much about," she said.

My mother glanced at me, eyebrows raised. I had never mentioned Aude.

I didn't return to the music camp after that. The next summer I attended the Berklee School of Music's youth program. One afternoon in early September, my mother came to my room.

"Valérie Langevin just called."

It took me a moment to remember this was Aude's mother. "Oh, yes?" I said, sitting up.

"They will be in Victoria with a business delegation late next week. Aude will be with them and apparently wants very much to see you. She asked if they could drop by to visit."

"Well, say yes!"

Leah smiled. "I have. They'll come on Saturday afternoon."

"No problem finding us?" Theo said when Aude and her family arrived at Counter Point.

"No, your directions were good," said Aude's father Denis.

Tall with strong features and dark close-cropped hair, he struck me as a man who could be stern if the occasion warranted it.

My parents, Fox, and I had gathered at the front door of the Big House, the soaring cedar, stone, and glass structure at Counter Point in which we lived, to greet Aude and her family. My parents drew hers away with offers of coffee or wine. Aude and I studied each other. She would have seen a fourteen-year-old who was several inches taller than the boy she had known, had a scattering of pimples on his face, and never knew what his voice would do when he spoke. Aude had also grown, and the nubs on her chest had blossomed into intriguing bumps. Her long hair was tied back with a bow and the tortoiseshell glasses that had replaced the green ones made her look older than her—I did a quick calculation—almost thirteen years. She smiled broadly, displaying braces at work.

"Let's go," I said, taking her hand.

I led her to a glassed-in breezeway that connected the main house to the original guest wing which Fox and I now occupied. The breezeway offered a view of the ocean and served as a lounge with armchairs, TV, small fridge, bar sink, and snack cupboard. Aude accepted the offer of a soft drink. Fox had bobbed along behind us, so I took three cans out of the fridge and poured potato chips into a bowl. Aude and I talked about this and that, but mostly sat and grinned at each other. Fox tried to insinuate himself into the conversation, but when Aude ignored him he pouted and began a noisy game on his tablet.

"I'm going to marry her," I said to Fox when Aude and her family had left.

His eyes grew round. "Right away?"

"No, goof. But some day."

With the Salish Sea and several mountain ranges separating us, Aude and I rarely saw each other in the following years. I had judged her father correctly—he controlled her life closely and restricted her presence on social media. We kept in touch by email, but sporadically. Our lives were busy outside of school, Aude's with competitive skiing and helping out at the family's lodge as well as her music, and mine with Fin's close and activity-packed programming of my music education. This now included piano, in which, he insisted, I needed competency at an advanced grade to enter the better music schools. Late one summer, Aude wrote to say that she would be performing with her school orchestra at a youth music festival in Victoria on the Thanksgiving weekend, and billets were being sought for participants.

"Can Aude stay with us?" I asked my mother.

Leah frowned. "Yes, of course, but it's a forty-five-minute drive from here to the festival."

"Now that I have my license, I can drive her—if you lend me your car."

She considered for a moment. "I'll call Valérie."

Aude had just turned fifteen and I barely recognized the leggy female who strode towards me when I went to pick her up. The tortoiseshell glasses were gone, revealing eyes that were amber shot with green, and no wires caged her smile. Her throaty voice had acquired a deep, smoky timbre. She would have seen an almost-man close to six feet tall, with short, neat hair and a hardening jaw from which he had to scrape peach fuzz with growing frequency.

Aude spent four days with us, a perfect guest, thoughtful and well-mannered. On the drives to and from the concert hall we talked endlessly about our lives, dreams, and plans. When I took her to join the rest of her orchestra for the trip home, Aude kissed me on the lips. It wasn't my first kiss—a movie date with Tamsin, a school friend, had ended with some exploratory pecking—but Aude's carried a certain promise, even possession.

After that our paths rarely crossed. The pandemic struck the winter after Aude's Thanksgiving visit and kept us both close to home, and I moved to Toronto in the fall of the following year. Aude entered the music program at UBC a year later. I saw her occasionally on my visits home, but only in passing, as she typically spent school breaks away, competing with the university ski team or working back in Nelson. During that time we kept in touch by phone or email, not constantly but in bursts of intense exchanges. *When we're together . . .* we would often say. Such plans we had. Then weeks and even months might pass until we connected again. This didn't bother me—ours was a relationship that didn't need constant affirmation.

It was Aude's idea that we arrange to perform at the same holiday pageant in Vancouver this past, fateful Christmas. I contacted the concertmaster and secured a spot in the orchestra. When Aude and I met up I saw a poised, shapely woman. Apart from filling out and shaving regularly I had not changed much, but judging from her greeting, whatever Aude saw seemed to please her. Something had subtly changed between us—it was only later that I recognized it as a sexual spark. On stage I had to fight not to glance back to where she sat at the harp—in her emerald-green velvet dress, her lustrous hair cascading down her back, she was breathtaking. We planned our New Year's Eve together as we would have a wedding night.

I stared at the computer screen. How to explain to Aude what I was going through? That I wasn't the guy she thought she knew, but a creature of abhorrent origins. That, born of violence, I feared I carried within me its seed, and wasn't sure I could trust myself with her, or any woman. That I needed time to reconcile myself to this new reality, to test all the uncertainties, to redefine myself.

Dear Aude, I finally wrote. *Something has happened that has changed my life. I don't understand what it means yet and I'm going away for a while to figure it out. I need to do this on my own. I'll be in touch when I've got it all straight.* After I pressed the send button, I lay my head down on my folded arms and cried.

Chapter 4

"YOU'RE NOT GOING TO cut me off like you've done your family," Jax said as we stood by her car in an awkward moment of farewell. Despite the painfully early departure time of my flight, she had insisted on driving me to the airport.

"No, of course not." As a final step to completely dissociate myself from the life I had led and person I had been before Rebecca's bombshell, I had erased my presence from all my digital platforms. "I'll be in touch when I have a new email address and phone."

"You know you can come back if this doesn't work."

"But Polly will be in my room."

"We'll work something out." Jax rested a hand against my cheek. "I'll always have a place for you, Nielie."

We hugged long and hard. I picked up my luggage and headed into the terminal. At the door I turned back to wave, but Jax was pulling away from the curb and didn't see.

Even without the sign displaying my name misspelled on a cardboard flap, I would have recognized Steve. He had the same solid, stocky build and round, brown eyes as his sister.

"You Niels?" he said, lowering the sign when I approached him.

"Yes," I said, shaking his hand. "I appreciate your picking me up, but you really didn't have to. I could have found my way."

"Not a problem. Here, let me take your bag."

Before I could object he grabbed it and led me out to the parking garage. Down the second row in he stopped and clicked a fob. A white van painted with STEVE REDDIE ELECTRICIAN, with the added note that he was ALWAYS READY, responded with a beep. He hauled my bag into the back of the van and we got in.

"So, you're a musician too?" Steve said as we exited the airport parking lot and headed to the highway that the road signs said would take us to the city.

"I guess so."

"Is Jacqueline any good?"

It took me a moment to realize he was referring to Jax. "Yes, of course. She's doing her PhD, after all."

Steve grunted. "Don't know where that came from. Family were just fisherfolk. No one went to university." He rubbed his chin. "Our grandpa played the fiddle, but it was country music. Don't know how Jacqueline got into the fancy stuff." He gave me a sidelong glance. "And I really don't know where that other business came from. Probably good she moved away. Rest of the family don't get it but . . ." He shrugged. "She's my little sister."

Steve turned into the narrow driveway of a tall house with white wood siding and forest-green trim. The shake roof bristled with gables.

"Here we are," he said.

"Great," I said with relief. I had been up long before dawn to catch the early flight and struggled to stay awake on the drive into town.

Steve went ahead and I humped my bag down the walk along the side of the house after him. The yard sloped down, allowing for a ground-level entrance to the basement. Steve unlocked the door and led me into a short, dark hall. With the flick of a switch, several lights sprang to life, illuminating a large space with a galley kitchen on one side and a wall unit with bookshelves and a television on the other. A chrome dining set and two mismatched armchairs floated in between. Two doors were set in the far wall. Steve opened the one on the left.

"You can use this room," he said, motioning me in.

I entered and heaved my bag on the single bed with a huff. A high window provided a modicum of light, and a bedside table, desk, chest of drawers, and small wooden armchair completed the furniture in the room.

Steve led me to a door beside the kitchen and opened it. "The bathroom's in here. Laundry too," he said, indicating a stacked washer-dryer in the corner. He closed the bathroom door and gestured to the refrigerator. "You don't have to worry about getting groceries today. Sheila—that's my wife—put some stuff in there for your breakfast, and she'll bring you something hot for supper."

"Oh, thanks. That's really thoughtful."

"Not a problem. So, what are your plans? Jacqueline didn't say."

"I need to find a job, so I'll start looking right away."

"What are you looking for?"

"Just about anything."

"Okay, I'll ask around. Some of the guys need a hand from time to time." He glanced at his watch. "I should get back to work." He pulled a business card from his pocket and handed it to me. "Call if you got any questions. The cell number—I always have that with me."

I took the card. "Steve . . . thanks so much for, first of all, letting me come and stay, and for picking me up and the food and all. I really appreciate it."

"Well, Jacqueline said to take good care of you." He sketched a salute in farewell and left.

I missed Jax desperately. It felt like days, weeks even, since I had seen her, although it was only that morning. Sighing, I went to my room and began to unpack.

The next morning I wandered around my new neighborhood, locating bus stops, supermarket, pharmacy, liquor store, and bank. I withdrew a quantity of cash and, chilled by an icy wind, entered a nearby coffee shop. It was in a vintage building and poorly lit, so after ordering a coffee I waited to claim one of the tables near the window—which were being vacated with excruciating slowness—to have enough light to read a copy of the local daily I had bought. The newspaper was thin, and thumbing through the pages quickly brought me to the employment ads. There were few jobs on offer: convenience store clerk, laundromat attendant, carpet cleaner. I closed the paper and offered it to a bewhiskered old-timer at the next table who had been rubbernecking as I read. The internet or government employment center would be better bets.

When I returned my cup to the bus pan by the counter, I asked the barista if there was an electronics shop nearby. He directed me to one a couple of blocks away, where I purchased a cheap phone with a prepaid plan. On the way back to Steve's house I picked up groceries and a bottle of the rum Jax said he favored. After a ham-sandwich lunch, I trawled employment sites on the internet and half-heartedly made a list of possible leads to follow up. My lack of enthusiasm was not from an unwillingness to work but a realization that I had nothing to offer—beyond musical gigs I had never held a job before. As it was now late afternoon I decided to wait until the morning to make my calls.

Around five-thirty I heard a vehicle drive up and its door slam. Assuming it was Steve, I waited a few minutes then went out and knocked on his kitchen door. When he opened it I handed him the rent money and bottle of rum.

"The rum is to say thanks for everything."

His face lit up with pleasure. "Not necessary, but much appreciated." He held up a finger. "And I've got something for you." He disappeared into the kitchen and returned with a slip of paper. "Ran into a buddy today, has a café. Said one of his cooks just up and quit on him. Needs help right away. Jacqueline said you were good in the kitchen."

I accepted the paper on which a name, number, and address were scribbled. "I, well . . . yes, I can cook. But I've never worked in a restaurant."

Steve made a dismissive gesture. "Don't worry, it's not a fancy place. And Rick's a good guy. Give him a call."

As it wasn't yet evening I called Rick right away. The cooking classes I had taken as an adolescent and Steve's referral seemed to be sufficient to qualify me for the job.

"You'll pick up the rest when you get here. Can you start tomorrow?"

"Ah, yeah, sure."

"Come by around eleven," he said and gave me the address.

The café, named the Sea Shack, was a small, steamy clapboard building near the Halifax Harbour. The exterior was daffodil yellow, and it had blue and white gingham half-curtains on the windows; a well-trodden, wide-planked floor; and eight tables with chairs, all painted bright blue. There were a handful of people at the tables, and a lanky man in his forties with faded red hair and a pleasant weather-worn face rose from one when I entered.

"You Niels?"

I confirmed that I was and we shook hands.

"Rick. I'll work today's shift with you, but I thought it would help if I went over the drill first."

He picked up a menu and ran his fingers down the list of offerings. They were basic: all-day breakfast, fish and chips, soup, sandwiches, and burgers. He explained that the clientele was mostly people working in the area, but the café also drew in visitors wandering around the waterfront. Half of the business was take-out. He led me through swinging doors into a small and crowded kitchen. After introductions, he motioned me into a storage room at the back that also served as office. We sat down on scuffed metal chairs and Rick explained how things worked.

Billy, a short, wiry man in his fifties, arrived at five in the morning with pastries fresh from a local bakery and opened for coffee. Adam, a paunchy guy in his forties with thick brown hair and a lumpy nose, came in at six to start hot breakfasts. Between them they dealt with food service, supply deliveries, and preparation of the daily soup, coleslaw, and ingredients for burgers and sandwiches. Before leaving at noon, Billy took stock and ordered supplies. I would start at eleven-thirty to help Adam with the lunch rush, then carry the kitchen on my own after he left at two. When my eyebrows rose in alarm, Rick reassured me that traffic dropped off considerably in the afternoon. It bumped up over dinner, but nowhere near the level of earlier in the day. The restaurant closed at eight and I would have to clean up before heading home. Saturdays were quieter without the working crowd. The café opened at nine, and Rick's cousin Marge covered the entire day on her own. The café was closed on Sundays.

Billy told us he needed the storage room for dealing with supplies, so Rick and I put on hairnets and aprons and went to work. In the small kitchen I was constantly moving out of his or Adam's way while trying to pay attention to what they were doing. It got easier after Adam left, and by dinner I was handling orders by myself.

A server and dishwasher supported the cooks. Kerry—a plump woman in her forties with curly black hair and rosy cheeks and who called everyone "Honey"—worked my shift. The dishwasher, Jordan, was the kind of guy many would cross the road to avoid. Of medium height and stringy build, he had an acne-scarred face, shaved head, and arms inked to the shoulders with wildlife tattoos, on full display thanks to a T-shirt whose sleeves had been cut off. He spoke little, and when he did it was with a sinister sibilance. He scared me.

The cooking part of the job was not complicated, and when Adam left me alone on my second day on the job I felt confident about carrying on alone. I found, however, that working multiple orders, assembling the separate components of a dish, and plating or boxing the food required a familiarity with the kitchen set-up and sequencing of steps that I had not yet acquired. But at critical moments, when I was frantically searching for sliced tomatoes, a soup ladle, mayonnaise bottle, or take-out box, Jordan would slip whatever I needed in front of me or indicate where to look with a word. After we had closed and cleaned up, I handed him the bills and change that Kerry said were my share of the tips.

"Here," I said. "I couldn't have gotten through the day without your help."

Jordan waved it away. "Nah. You can buy me a beer sometime." He pulled on an army jacket that was wholly inadequate for the weather and fished a hand-rolled cigarette from the breast pocket. "See you tomorrow," he said and left.

I offered to buy Jordan the beer after work one day the following week. He led me to a small bar called the Broken Mast, three blocks away. Entering it, we could have stepped back half a century. It had a pressed-tin ceiling darkened from decades of cigarette smoke, faded beige walls, chipped dark-brown wainscotting, worn wooden tables, hard metal chairs, and the smell of lost hope. Jordan nodded to a few people as we made our way to the zinc-fronted bar. I got us a couple of draft beer and followed Jordan to an empty table. We sat and he sucked back half of his beer in one swallow. I sipped mine and wondered what to talk about.

Jordan wiped his mouth with the back of his hand and said, "So, what are you doing here, anyway?"

"Me?" I ran my finger through the ring of condensation my glass had left on the table. "It's a long story. Something happened in my life and I needed to get away."

Jordan nodded sagely. "Yeah, sometimes you just gotta leave."

"How about you? Are you from here?"

"Cape Breton. Left home when I was sixteen. My pa was a real hard case. Fist like a hammer. Eight of us kids, so they didn't need me." A side of Jordan's mouth twitched. "Came here green as anything. Got in with a bad bunch. Drugs. Did some time in prison." He eyed me closely but I nodded without comment. "Done probation next year."

"Is it hard? I mean, getting back on your feet after prison."

He took an orange plastic lighter from his pocket and turned it end over end on the table. "Yeah, but tough as it gets, it's better than where I was before. Prison saved my life." He glanced up, his expression shy and proud. "Been clean now for almost four years."

I opened my mouth, hesitated, then spoke. "You seem to know as much as Billy or Adam about how the café works. You could have taken over the cooking."

"Nah. Happy where I am."

"But you work hard, and from what I've seen you're pretty capable. I'd think you could do better than washing dishes."

Jordan drew back his lips in a grimace, exposing several gaps in his teeth. "Would you want to have to look at this? Nah. Better out of sight."

"Can't you get them fixed?"

"Ha! Know what that costs?"

"Could your family maybe help?"

He shook his head. "Family don't want to know me."

Work at the Sea Shack took over my life, for which I was grateful. Mornings were spent getting ready to go, and I arrived home at night too late to do anything more than clean up and go to bed. In all but the worst weather, when I took the bus, I walked to and from the café, a half-hour each way. I especially liked the night walks, the freshness of the air after the oily fug of the kitchen, the squares of lit windows revealing some vignette of domestic life along the way, the exchange of greetings with complete strangers I passed. Back home I stripped and had a shower to get rid of the deep-fried smell that permeated my clothes and hair. I recalled a scene from an old movie my parents had watched once, where a woman who worked in an oyster bar squeezed fresh lemon juice on her hands and arms to get rid of the fishy smell. Seventeen at the time, it had struck me as extraordinarily sensuous. I settled for lemon-scented soap.

Occasionally I came in early to cover for Billy or Adam if they needed to be elsewhere. I had weekends off, but once did a Saturday on my own when Marge was sick. Without Jordan the day dragged. The dishwasher was a seventeen-year-old student who spent every free moment glued to his phone and provided neither help nor company. In my off time I did laundry, got groceries, or explored the city.

Through this all, the upheaval wrought by the New Year's revelation always—*always*—shadowed my thoughts. When it threatened to draw me down too much, in long stretches when I was alone or when I woke in the night, I would play through a piece of music in my head. The effort of concentrating on each note crowded out other thoughts. Sometimes a little prelude or sonatina was enough to pull me out, other times it took a whole symphony. It helped in other ways because, despite what I had said to Jax, I missed music like a lost limb, the discipline of practice having for so long defined my days. Occasionally I'd feel the weight of a ghost bow in my right hand or the fingers of my left would stop imaginary strings. I dreamed music too: playing the cello with a bare branch that began to sprout leaves instead of a bow; arriving onstage for a performance in a large hall where the ranged seats receded into a darkened distance, wearing only a blue-striped pajama top and a pair of black socks; playing to an audience that morphed into cacti. No doubt all highly symbolic. But abandoning my cello also brought an element of relief, like what I expected one would feel after the necessary breakup of a loving but problematic marriage.

Steve and Sheila invited me upstairs for dinner a couple of times. With the peremptory demands of their four-year-old and toddler—both boys—proper conversations were impossible. I didn't mind—it saved me having to talk too much about myself. The bustle and casual interactions of the Sea Shack kept me from feeling lonely. An odd but easy camaraderie developed between Jordan and me. He proved to be a keen observer of life, and his sibilant asides revealed wit and intelligence and often had us both laughing helplessly. I despaired for his future but he seemed to be, if not content with, then accepting of the limitations of his life.

Chapter 5

ONE SATURDAY IN LATE February, I opened my door to a knock.

"You're going to have some company," Steve said. "Hope you don't mind." He explained that Sheila's brother, Alistair, would be moving in the following week for a couple of months. "He works on a container ship and his contract is ending. He wants to do a course here before he goes out again. He's a nice guy."

"Yeah, no problem," I said, although I didn't at all welcome the intrusion into my comfortable solitude. But Alistair—or Al, as he asked to be called—proved to be reserved to the point of rudeness. He was a big man in his late twenties, sandy-haired like his sister, but with a heavy jaw, broad chest, muscled forearms, and large-palmed hands. Next to him I looked like an undernourished plant.

A few days into his stay, Al began to disappear every morning just as I was rising. The following weekend when we were both knocking around the kitchen getting our breakfasts, I made an effort at conversation.

"Steve said you work on a container ship."

"Yup," he said without looking up from the toast he was buttering.

"Have you been doing it for a while?"

"Two years."

"What exactly do you do there?"

Al carried his toast and a jar of apricot jam to the table and sat down. "Work as a deckhand. Training as a mechanic. Want to get my master technician certification."

I took the chair across from him. "What's it like, being on those ships? How long do you usually spend on it in one go?"

He swallowed the toast he had been chewing. "Contracts are usually six or eight months, then a few months off if you want." He shrugged. "I like it."

I took a sip of my coffee. "I guess you need special training."

"For the really technical jobs, yeah, but for support work like in the galley or as a steward or basic deckhand, no. Just a certificate in basic seamanship. You know, how things work on those rigs, safety and survival stuff, especially. The crew is all on its own out there in case of an emergency and everyone has to know how to handle themselves."

I sat up in my chair. "Galley—that's kitchen work, right?"

"Yeah."

"How do you get one of those basic certificates?"

"Different places offer them here." Al eyed me curiously. "You interested?"

An internet search after breakfast turned up a good introduction to working on a container ship. I leaned back and thrust my fingers through my hair. My mind buzzed. Wandering around the oceans could be just what I needed, particularly if it came with work and a bed to sleep in. Imagine the places I'd go, the things I'd see. I bent back to the keyboard. One of the community colleges in the city offered the course Al had said was necessary: certification in basic seamanship by the International Convention on Standards of Training, Certification and Watchkeeping for Seafarers. I peered closely at the screen—a class was starting in April. After giving the matter all of three minutes' thought, I clicked on the link to register.

"See if you can get Marge to cover for you," Rick said when I asked him for the time off to take the classes. After some grumbling, Marge agreed to cover my afternoons if came back to do dinner and clean-up and worked three of her Saturdays. When I told Rick about the arrangement, he said, "Fine, but I'm going to lose you, aren't I?"

Could he really have thought that I'd make a career out of frying fish and chips? "Not right away," I said.

"Just give me as much notice as you can."

I also signed up for a course on food handling and safety but was able to do it online.

The seamanship certification classes were like nothing I had experienced before, full of blue-jeaned, narrow-eyed, no-nonsense men with a handful of equally serious, focused women and run with tight, military order. We covered marine hazards and possible emergency situations and the various equipment, systems, and practices for dealing with them. We learned how to fight fires, launch lifeboats and effect marine rescues, protect ourselves and each other, perform basic first aid—essentially how to survive in extreme circumstances. We did practical training exercises in the college swimming pool and put out a real fire in a ship mockup. We also learned about life on board, different roles and operations, team dynamics, and social cohesion.

"I'm never going to remember all that stuff," I despaired to Jordan after the third day on the course.

"Nah, you will."

"I don't know. I'm not sure I'll even pass." But when I wrote the exams for the different components the answers came when I needed them, and in due course the STCW certificate arrived, signed, sealed, and stamped, with a mugshot of me looking like a startled guinea pig stuck on a bottom corner. With the certificate and other credentials in hand, I registered with a maritime crewing agency.

I had hoped to pump Al for information about container ship life, but he had connected with an old girlfriend and all but moved out. When he left in May I knew him little better than when he arrived.

Chapter 6

"I UNDERSTAND THAT NIELS Larsen works here."

On hearing the voice of my grandfather I started, and the knife with which I had been cutting onions slipped and sliced the ball of my left thumb. Blood oozed onto the cutting board.

"Shit!" I held my hand up and frantically looked around for something to staunch the blood.

"Jeez!" Jordan lurched to the sink and grabbed a handful of paper towels.

Kelly pushed through the swinging doors that separated the kitchen from the dining area. "Someone to—" Her eyes widened and her mouth fell open. "Oh my god. What happened?"

I sucked air through my teeth as Jordan wound paper towel tightly around the wound. It reddened quickly.

"Just a cut," I said.

Kelly came forward. "Just a cut, maybe, but we can't have you bleeding in here. You need a proper bandage." She hurried to the storage room and returned with the first aid kit. After struggling with the clasp she opened it, poked through the contents, and pulled out a tube of ointment and a large adhesive bandage. She cleaned the wound with an alcohol wipe, tutting when she saw its length, smeared it with ointment, and bound it with the bandage. "That's a pretty big cut," she said. "You may need stitches." She cocked her head in the direction of the dining room. "Anyway, there's someone to see you out there."

"I heard."

"Someone you know?"

"Yeah."

"You go. I'll clean up," Jordan said.

I pushed through into the dining room. Fin was seated at a table by the window, gazing at the raindrops speckling the glass. He turned as I approached the table.

"Granddad?"

"Niels."

Fin rose slowly from his chair, his craggy face, thick white hair, and black trench coat creating the impression of an eagle about to take flight. Heads turned in our direction.

"How did you find me?"

"Your friend Jax." Fin studied me for a moment. "We have to talk."

"I'm working."

"Well, how about when you're done?"

"I don't finish until nine."

"My flight is just after eight. I stopped here on the way home from New York. Surely you can take a coffee break."

I glanced in the direction of the kitchen. Kelly and Jordan's faces disappeared from the serving hatch. Turning back to Fin, I said, "Let me check."

When I entered the kitchen, Jordan was busily wiping the counter while Kelly straightened a stack of plates. They turned faces bright with curiosity to me.

"It's my grandfather. Could you cover for me for a little while?"

"Sure, no problem," Jordan said.

"Thanks." I got my jacket from the storage room and pulled it on. "Shouldn't be more than half an hour or so."

"We're cool. Take your time," Jordan said.

"Appreciate it."

I went back to the dining room. "There's a coffee house just around the corner. We can go there."

We walked the short distance in silence, our heads and shoulders delicately wetted by the uncertain rain. I held open the door and followed Fin in. It was a local place, not one of the chains, and the decor ran to dated event posters and vinyl record covers that hadn't seen a duster in a while. Coffee-scented steam and the pleasant buzz of voices greeted us.

"Why don't you find a table and I'll get the coffee," I said. "Double espresso, right?"

Fin nodded and headed towards a vacant table in a quiet corner. The coffee house was run by an aging couple who seemed to draw from the same wardrobe of worn jeans and plaid shirts, and whose hair was braided into similar long gray strands. The male of the pair greeted me with the extra-wide smile reserved for regular customers. I carried the coffees back with some difficulty, my injured thumb declining to oppose the other fingers around the cup handle.

"What happened to your hand?" Fin said when I gave him his cup.

"Cut it. Occupational hazard." I rested the wounded hand in my lap and took a sip of coffee. "So why are you here?"

Fin leaned back in his chair and studied me for a moment. "Leah said that we should respect your wishes to be left alone . . ."

"But?"

My grandfather blew out an exasperated breath. "Really, Niels, you expect to abandon your studies to bugger off to . . ." He made a cutting gesture in the direction of the Sea Shack. "To work in a cheap restaurant without any explanation?"

"Yes, I do, actually."

"Come on."

"Look, I'm old enough to vote and drink and join the army

if I wanted to, so I think I can make decisions about my own life."

Fin grimaced. "Okay, but can you at least walk me through all the life-changing decisions you've made in the last few months? I mean, to have abandoned your studies, and in your last year with only a few months to go. Do you know what that means for your future in music?"

"Yeah, well, I'm not sure that's where my future lies. I'm an okay cellist, but that's it, isn't it. I'll never be a Rostropovich, or Casals, or du Pré, or Yo-Yo Ma. I expect that you hoped I'd match your greatness, but really, Granddad, I'm just a garden-variety musician."

"But music . . ." Fin made a helpless gesture. "The years you've committed to it, and to walk away now?"

"Music's all I've ever done, it's all you've ever let me do. I honestly don't know how I feel about music, or anything else, for that matter. I need to step away to find out."

"And you're going to find out by, what, peeling potatoes, washing dishes?"

"I'm actually the cook," I said, not without pride.

Fin opened his mouth to say something then stopped. We stared at each other without speaking, our coffees forgotten. I broke off first to glance at my injured thumb. A circle of blood was slowly growing on the bandage.

"So you plan to work at this restaurant until you arrive at some kind of understanding about how you feel about things?"

"No, I plan to join the merchant marine as soon as I can get a placement on a vessel."

Fin's eyes widened comically and I suppressed a smile—he would not appreciate being laughed at.

"The merchant marine? Good god! What on earth do you know about working in the merchant marine? Surely it requires some kind of training."

"I've taken some. The essentials for working as a seaman.

Not in operations—obviously you need more specialized training for that. But to work in a support role, in the galley."

"So you're going to be a cook on a boat then?"

"No, that takes more experience than I have. I'll be an assistant to the cook."

Fin shook his head. "What exactly do you think you'll accomplish?"

"I'm tired of always having to accomplish something. That's been the story of my life, hasn't it. All the lessons and masterclasses and summers in music camp. Hours of practice. Every day. Never time for anything else." I took a fortifying breath, wishing myself anywhere but in this hopeless conversation. "I just need a break, Granddad. Working on ship, it's straightforward, gives me a place to live, and I can see something of the world."

Fin leaned forward. "If it's travel you want, we can arrange that. You don't have to work. I can give you the money for it. But come back. Come home."

"I'm not sure I can ever come home."

His forehead wrinkled with incomprehension. "What do you mean you can't come home? That's nonsense. Of course you can."

My thumb throbbed with pain. "Did you know that my biological father raped my mother?" I said sharply. "Of course you did. How could you not?"

Fin reared back as though I had struck him and stared at me, speechless.

I leaned forward, remorseful. "Sorry, Granddad, I shouldn't have said it like that."

He closed his eyes and drew a quavering hand down a face as white as his hair. I reached out. "Are you okay?"

He took a long, deep breath and opened his eyes. "How did you find out?"

"From Rebecca Grisham, my supposed aunt."

He started to say a word that sounded a lot like *fuck* but bit it off. "You weren't ever to know. So this is why you've . . . ?" He made a sweeping gesture to encompass me and my actions.

"Yes. Knowing that has changed things. Like, I wasn't wanted or needed, and I ruined my mother's life. God only knows how she was damaged by what happened to her. I mean, that's the reason she wasn't around until I was almost ten, right? Did you insist she come back then, to face up to her responsibilities after Gran died?"

Fin shook his head. "It wasn't like that."

"Whatever. Anyhow, knowing what I do now, I can't face Mom or any of the rest of the family. Not now, maybe not ever."

We sat in silence for several minutes, Fin gazing off into the distance. He sighed heavily and turned back to me.

"You need time to come to terms with things. I see that now."

"Yes. I want to figure out who I really am and what I'm intended to do with my life."

Fin regarded me with a half-smile. "By running away to sea?"

Put that way, it did seem a bit naive. My cheeks reddened.

Fin made a placating gesture. "Never mind. How long do you expect to be doing this merchant marine thing?"

"I don't know, Granddad. I don't have a specific plan. I'm just going to take things as they come, see where they take me."

"Okay, fine. But please, don't completely lose touch. Not like Leah did when she left. Those ten years she was away, we didn't know if she was even alive. Let me know how you're doing from time to time."

"I will." I pushed back my chair and stood. "I need to get my hand seen to."

Fin glanced at it. "Yes, you should. Look, do you need money?"

"No, I'm okay." An idea stuck me. "Wait. Could you maybe give me . . ." I thought rapidly. "Five thousand dollars?"

"Yes, certainly. Can I ask what you need it for?"

"It's not for me, it's for a friend. He's having a rough time in life in part because he's missing a bunch of teeth and can't afford to get them fixed."

Fin raised his eyebrows but said, "All right, I'll transfer it to your account. It's the same as before?"

"Yes, and thanks, Granddad." I shuffled my feet. "I'm glad you came."

He regarded me for a long time. "I hope you find what you're looking for, Niels."

I nodded. "Goodbye," I said and turned away quickly to hide the emotion in my face. I took a couple of steps then turned back. Fin was slumped in his chair like a spent force. He had taken off his glasses and was rubbing his eyes.

"I love you, Granddad," I said.

He smiled faintly and raised his hand. It may just have been a gesture of acknowledgement, but I took it as a benediction.

Chapter 7

"HOW ARE YOU DOING, Niels?"

I glanced up from scrubbing the stainless-steel counter at Birgit, my new boss. She leaned against the giant stove, her chef jacket unbuttoned over a ribbed singlet, her arms folded across her chest. She was a natural blonde, her features so fair they were almost indistinct. A touch of lipstick and mascara would have brought her face to life, even made her pretty, but the context didn't warrant such embellishment.

I straightened up and my stomach rolled with nausea. "I'm fine."

"It will pass." Her English was clipped and she pronounced *will* with a *v*. "I leave now, yes? Otto has two hours before his watch," she said, referring to her husband, the first officer.

I nodded. "And thanks, Birgit. You've been really patient."

"It's okay."

When she left I returned to my scrubbing with a sigh. Another wave of nausea hit me, emanating from a point somewhere between my solar plexus and gut. I grimaced and fought it down. Although the vessel was remarkably stable, my body had tuned in to the deep, subtle vibration that ran through it and rebelled. I managed through the endless hours of duties and drills with a cocktail of medication to keep the nausea down, coffee to keep me awake, and cola for energy. My last solid meal was over three days ago; just the thought of it made me want to vomit. I smiled grimly—one benefit of the experience was that the soft roll of flesh that had formed around my waist from one too many Sea Shack dinners had melted away. Would the nausea pass as Birgit said? I plunged the sponge into a pan of hot soapy water and slapped it, dripping, on the next section of counter. If it didn't, and soon, my seafaring days could be numbered.

I had received the call informing me of a position in the galley of a container ship operated by a Danish shipping line in early June. I accepted immediately and was told to report for work at the terminal in Houston, Texas, in twelve days.

"You did warn me," Rick said when I gave him notice. "At least it shouldn't be too hard to find someone, this being almost summer."

"Why not Jordan? He can do it as well as I can."

Rick's eyes narrowed. "He's been in prison, you know."

"Yes, but he isn't now, and in all the time I've spent with him he's been steady. Works hard, always ready to lend a hand. And from what I've seen he's honest too, if that's what you're worried about."

"Humph," Rick said. "I'll think about it."

When I closed the Sea Shack for the night a couple of days later, Jordan hovered at the door.

"Rick offered me your job. Said you recommended me."

"Great! You're going to do it, aren't you?"

"Yeah, figure I'll give it a shot. Just need to keep my mouth shut." He laughed. "For more reasons than one."

Jordan took me out for a beer on my last night of work. I had been to the Broken Mast several times with him and was now greeted familiarly. After, we stood outside in the fall of light cast by the bar's ancient neon sign.

"Was good to work with you," Jordan said.

"Yeah, likewise." I took a fat envelope from the pocket of my jacket and held it out. "For you."

He glanced at the envelope then at me. "What's this?"

"It's for your teeth, so you can fix them."

"What?"

"Take it."

Jordan hesitantly accepted the envelope, opened the flap, and drew out one of the fifty one-hundred-dollar bills in it. "Shit," he said, his eyes widening. He thrust the envelope back at me. "I can't take your money. You're going to need it."

I held up my palm. "It's not my money, it's my grandfather's, and he's got lots. I don't know how much it'll cost to fix your teeth, but hopefully this will help. Take it."

He drew back the envelope and ran his finger along the edges of the bills. "Son of a bitch."

Would he use it to fix his teeth? Or would he spend it on drugs or women or more tattoos? I didn't care. I held out my hand. "Good luck with everything."

Jordan gripped it hard. "You, too, man," he said, his voice thick. He waved the envelope and shook his head. "All you've done. Wish I could do something more than say thanks."

"Thanks is enough," I said, and with a small wave turned and headed home.

The night before my flight to Houston I sat in the state of suspension that exists when you are all packed and ready to go somewhere but haven't yet left. I made one last call to Jax. I needed to smooth things between us—our last conversation had been testy.

"I had specifically asked you not to let my family know where I was," I had said.

"Look, when your grandfather asked I wasn't about to tell him to take a hike," she replied. "Gabriel Larsen isn't someone

I can afford to piss off, you know. All he'd have to do is make a couple of phone calls and my music career would be finished."

"He'd never do that."

"I remember you saying once that he could be fierce. Besides, I thought you should talk to someone in your family."

I wanted to tell her to mind her own damn business but made do with a cool goodbye. I dialed her number now with some trepidation, but when she answered her voice had its usual warmth, and we had a long, cozy chat that ended with my promising to keep her posted on all my adventures.

Well, this is one adventure that might end before it begins, I thought as I lowered myself carefully onto my bunk. The nausea medication had not kicked in yet, and I closed my eyes and lay perfectly still. So far we had only sailed to ports along the U.S. coast. There was one more stop before we headed into open ocean to cross the Atlantic. *I can't continue like this*, I thought despairingly. *I'll have to talk to someone about leaving.*

While showering the next morning I realized that the nausea was gone. Shampoo suds filled my mouth as I let out a great whoop. I quickly rinsed off, toweled dry, and pulled on my clothes.

"It's stopped!" I said, bursting into the galley.

Birgit looked up from tying the strings of her apron. "Yes. Like I said."

"And I am absolutely famished."

"So wash hands and bring me breakfast things from the cooler. I make you nice egg."

On my first day on the container ship, the introductory tour of the vessel left me with the impression of a behemoth of such complexity that it was a wonder only twenty-odd souls could make it function. Everything was big: the tower, the chains, the engine—an enormous insect with its pipes and lines and metal carapace—and the vast stacks of containers, rising precariously high at the edges of the deck. Positioned vertically the ship would have rivalled a skyscraper in height. All the surfaces were hard and wanting badly to rust. You were in some steampunk fantasy until you entered the bridge and time-warped into a starship. But that was not where I spent my time.

The galley, from the perspective of the person responsible for its daily cleaning, seemed like nothing more than a sea of stainless steel and tile. Otherwise it was a typical commercial kitchen with burners, ovens, sinks, trays, shelves, drawers, and all manner of pots, pans, and utensils hanging about. Without portholes to offer natural light and vistas, it was a world onto itself. My day started at six and I worked with little or no break until lunch was completed, then had a few hours off until dinner preparations started. That and cleanup kept me going until around eight in the evening. Regular fire and safety drills were obligatory and cut into the free time I had.

I apparently had not been paying attention to discussions of working conditions during my research into jobs on container ships, because the twelve-hour days with no days off—ever—caught me by surprise. And as for the notion of seeing the world: our route circled to the same ports on either side of the Atlantic but all I saw of the cities was their skylines. Whenever I could I went out on deck to watch the ship enter port: the slow waltz with a tug guiding it into its berth, the wildcat shrieks and groans as it was moored, the precise movements of the giant gantry cranes as they delicately lifted the containers and conveyed them to land and then reversed the process to load up again. But stays were usually only for as long as it took to unload and reload. Most of the ports were large and difficult to traverse on foot, and the security was tight. Occasionally a shuttle was available to get out to the immediate neighborhood, but it was usually far from the city center and more often than not I was required to load and stock provisions, and everyone still needed to be fed. In the six months I spent on that vessel I got off only five times.

It didn't bother me at first. I quickly discovered that a stint as a short-order cook didn't prepare one for turning out three meals a day with constantly changing menus. Fortunately, Birgit's instructions were patient and clear. Learning the routines of onboard work and life took time as well. A few weeks in, however, I had enough and grumped through my daily tasks, placing pots down on the counter and dropping utensils into the sink with more noise than necessary. Birgit regarded this protest with a raised eyebrow but said nothing. At the end of the day, after I had knotted up and disposed of the last bag of garbage, I surveyed my stainless-steel cage and wondered how I was going to make it to the end of my contract.

Despite being on my feet most of the time, I walked the outside stairs and decks to shake the sense of confinement. When the weather was bad I used the treadmill in the exercise room. It was a poor substitute but still provided a sense of movement and freedom. One of the regular users of the room was a stocky blond man whose coarse-featured face was transformed by eyes of such an intense blue they beamed like headlights. His pecs and biceps strained the thin fabric of his T-shirt and he did sit-ups on the training bench, zipped back and forth on the rowing machine, and lifted dumbbells without effort.

"You make it seem so easy," I said one day when he had completed his routine.

"What is hard for you?" he said, wiping his face.

I laughed dryly. "Pretty well everything. I don't even know where to start."

He looked me up and down with a practiced eye. "I can show you."

I raised palms in protest. "Oh, I don't want to bother you."

"It's okay. I am Marko." He added that he was the third engineer on the ship.

I introduced myself, but it was to his back because he had turned to rummage in the gym bag he had brought. "Hah," he said, pulling out a notebook with a narrow pen clipped to the coils. He opened it and began to write. I stood awkwardly by, not knowing what exactly was happening. After a few minutes he ripped out three pages and handed them to me. They were covered with bulleted points describing exercises, with and without equipment. Some were illustrated with stickman drawings. He indicated the five-pound dumbbell.

"You start with these then we work up to the fifty."

"Ah, okay," I said, wondering what I had gotten into.

Marko slung his towel around his neck and picked up his gym bag. "I will come and check."

I had never worked out before, never even considered it. *Round of cheek and soft of belly*, Fox had said once, poking a finger into my side. He was the athlete in the family, advancing to competitive junior tennis, his grace, power, and discipline on the court belying his typically anarchic approach to things. Marko's instructions were clear, but the exercises required focus and commitment. At the end of my second session I was ready to quit. Marko came in just as I was finishing up.

"Good, fine," I said when he asked me how it was going, manly pride preventing me from admitting how awkward and uncomfortable the exercises were.

He slapped my back in approval. Before I knew it we had arranged to have him supervise my next session.

I had never given much thought to my body. With each bend and stretch, each squat, lunge, pushup, press, and curl, I became acquainted with my muscles and limbs and joints, my heartbeats and breath, their capabilities and limits, what they liked to do, where they needed to go. The aches and fatigue after a session were almost a religious experience. In time I not only looked forward to the workouts, but began to need them. I moved differently, more compactly, and with a certain authority. As I was stretching to reach a container on a high shelf in the kitchen one morning, a button on my shirt popped.

"I don't know if it's your food or the laundry, but my clothes have gotten tight," I said to Birgit.

She smiled and flexed her bicep. "I think you are getting muscles," she said.

Frustrated though I was by the unrelenting work schedule, it had the benefit of distracting me from my woes. After the long hours and vigorous exercise program, sleep came easily. What remained of my free time was spent by myself. I ate hurriedly and usually alone. The social distance between officers and the crew went beyond their separate quarters, dining room, and lounge. My interactions with the rest of the crew were limited to everyday pleasantries. Most were Filipino or South Asian seamen who, although friendly, preferred to spend time with their own countrymen.

I was accustomed to a solitary life, however. The environment in my grandparents' house, where I had spent my early years, had been rarefied, even austere. A succession of young nannies saw to my daily care, but I quickly learned that my older, cerebral grandparents were the people who mattered. I valued every second of their attention, and knew that to keep in their favor I needed to be still and quiet, and never to mumble, blubber, or whine. When my grandmother, Alexandra, worked at home, she would often say, "Bring your book and sit with me," and I would rush to find one and tuck myself into the armchair in the corner of her study. She would glance up from time to time and ask how I was doing or remark on something from whatever she was reading or writing as though I would understand. Fin always worked in his studio when he was home, which was only half of the time. If invited, I would sit at the coffee table by his sofa with a book or schoolwork and watch him draw music out of the air with awe. When my grandparents' friends visited I was brought out to meet them and, with my little paw lost in the hand of some eminent scientist or musician, expected to exchange a few words in conversation.

I drowned in books and music, but my screen time was restricted to musical performances we watched on the television in Fin's studio. "We don't want your brain turning to mush," he said. There were no playdates or sleepovers with children my own age, no birthday balloons or bouncy castles, no trips to Disneyland. So different were my experiences from those of my schoolmates that I could have come from another planet. But I was not unhappy then. It was, after all, the only reality I knew, and I learned to occupy myself and be comfortable with solitude.

On the ship, the books and music I had loaded on my computer and movies that played for the crew were my only entertainment. At sea, Wi-Fi was unreliable and expensive, so I only went online in ports where it was free. Mostly it was to catch up on news. Jax apparently had not shared my new email address, and the only messages I received that were not junk were from her. To these I replied with anecdotes wrung out of the demanding and repetitive nature of my life on the ship. In one I recounted the feud between Birgit and Viraj, a grizzled Sri Lankan, who helped serve the meals and kept the common areas and staterooms clean. Early in the voyage Birgit had asked him to take off the grubby knitted cap he wore when handling food. He had replied that, in their three previous tours together, the captain had never told him to remove the cap and he certainly wasn't going to do it for her. A civil war ensued, with much insolence on Viraj's part and huffs and eyerolls on Birgit's. After sending the note I decided to begin documenting my experiences on the ship. For what purpose was not immediately clear, but many of the people, situations, and occurrences were unique enough to be worth remembering.

That night I created a file titled *Journal* on my computer. I had no fear of the blank screen—my mother was a writer and words were always in play at home. I typed *July 31* at the top of the page then thought for a moment. *Time is all straight, hard edges here*, I wrote, *the day demarcated into large chunks of work, small chunks of non-work, and sleep.* I looked around my small stateroom with its narrow bunk, fitted wood-veneer cupboards and desk, industrial carpet, slatted ceiling, and square salt-stained portholes and added: *I live in a cell inside a metal hive.* Well pleased with these profundities I saved the file, adding new notes from time to time.

> *August 4: So hot today the dinner buns rose too quickly and collapsed in the oven.*

> *August 6: Birgit knocked over the pan rack. The noise brought the captain down.*

> *August 11: Bananas overripe so lots of banana bread again.*

As time passed the entries became more abstract.

> *August 21: Strange how despite being big and open and empty, the sea and sky looked two-dimensional, like a painted screen.*

> *September 14: Was fascinated by the ocean today, seemed as cold and hard as molten glass.*

And, alarmingly,

> *September 28: Stood on second deck from the top and felt an almost irresistible force trying to pull me over the rail.*

In time the entries veered into the past. There was enough distance from the New Year's revelations now for me to probe my memories without my throat closing and my heart racing. Inexplicably, I brooded over my grandmother Alexandra's death.

> *October 5: Why hadn't I realized sooner that she was so sick?*

It was only after two strange women moved into the guest rooms to nurse her that I had become aware of Alexandra's declining health.

"Your grandmother's not well," Fin had explained.

"But she's going to get better, right?"

He placed his hand on my shoulder and regarded me with weary, deeply shadowed eyes. "I don't think so, Niels."

The atmosphere in the house grew heavy with a dismal inevitability. I felt split in two: the boy who ate and slept and went to school, and a sack of confusion enclosing an emotion for which I had no reference then but now recognize as dread. That was when I insisted on abandoning piano to learn the cello. I had never stood up to Fin before, but after some debate and a stubbornness on my part that surprised us both, he got me a half-size cello and arranged for lessons. "Lily," I called the cello, whispering the name into the point on the scroll where I thought her ear must be. Holding her human-like body and drawing out her sweet voice brought me comfort. I spent hours at practice, trying to drown out the silence of my grandmother's dying. Lily had soaked up so much sadness, however, that when

I needed a larger instrument and Meredith came into my life, I let the little cello go without regret.

When I had finished writing out what I remembered of the time, it occurred to me that my preoccupation with Alexandra's death was probably because it had brought my mother into my life. I tentatively began recording what I remembered of our first encounter.

October 8: Mom didn't look any older than Jennie Liu, I wrote, referring to a high school student who had lived three doors down from us in Vancouver. *I had expected someone stout and gray, like Mrs. Oleksa the housekeeper. We had stared at each other, Mom shivering in the cold. The scarf she wore was periwinkle blue and her eyes were very dark.*

With a child's logic I had assumed that, with my grandmother dead, my mother had come to take care of me. I felt a sudden sympathy for her. How hard it must have been to face me, what awful memories I would have reawakened. But she had done her duty. I saved the file and put my computer aside. She would not be burdened with me anymore.

After four months on the ship I entered a peculiar state of grace. The routines had become soothing rather than tedious, the cocoon of defined duties and packaged hours paradoxically liberating—less freedom reduced personal responsibility, and with that came a certain lightness. One night I wrote in my journal:

> *October 26: It must be what life in a monastery is like, relinquishing one's will to some higher purpose.*

And later:

> *November 11: Time seems to be telescoping into itself but the space in my head is infinite.*

At the end of my contract I disembarked in Rotterdam with six months' pay and no particular plans beyond hanging out in Europe for a while. I hopped a train to Amsterdam and set up in a funky hotel in the university district. The city was busy and bright with Christmas preparations. I got new clothes, toured museums, took in a concert, and drank beer and chatted with people in pubs. I sent out a gift box of treats to Jax and a postcard to Fin wishing him a merry Christmas and telling him I was okay.

I woke on my eighth day in Amsterdam to deep winter darkness and a spatter of rain against the window, feeling alone and desolate. *I need sun*, I thought. I checked out of the hotel and headed for the train station, where I bought a ticket to Paris with the vague idea of continuing farther south from there. On the train I watched the countryside flashing by, my thoughts in a muddle. The stop in Rotterdam was announced and, on impulse, I grabbed my bag, got off the train, and headed to the office of the shipping line for whom I had previously worked. It took some time to identify the right person and for them to be available, but I was eventually ushered into the woman's office.

"Would you have an opening on a ship for someone to work in the galley, or as a steward?" I said.

The woman was nonplussed; this is not how things were usually done.

"Well, I can check, of course, but it might take some time and I am not sure what might be available on such short notice," she said. I had given up my cellphone so we arranged that I would report back at the end of the next day. "You should be prepared to wait," she said in parting. "Usually these things are arranged well in advance."

I checked into a seedy hotel in the neighborhood and went in search of a meal—I had eaten nothing all day. I downed the first beer in a couple of gulps. *You're completely mad*, I thought, but returning to the order and encapsulation of a working ship was inexplicably appealing.

The next day the woman at the shipping line greeted me with a wide smile.

"It is luck, maybe, for both of us that you are here. There is a ship to arrive tomorrow and they need someone in the galley. The assistant has fallen ill, and this close before Christmas it is hard to find someone on short notice, so if you want I can assign you there."

The ship would be going to Asia via the Suez Canal, which pleased me immensely. I completed the necessary paperwork and went to join the ship the following afternoon. After going through security I went to the waiting room for the shuttle that would take me to the vessel. Several members of the crew had already gathered. Most were Filipinos chatting among themselves in Tagalog. Two were older Slavic-sounding men. The last was a young man with curly black hair and a fine-boned, expressive face. Like me, he carried baggage and was apparently just joining the ship, which may have accounted for the apparent alarm with which he regarded his future shipmates. When his large dark eyes rested on me he smiled hesitantly. I went over and extended my hand.

"Hello, I'm Niels."

He clasped my hand and shook it. "Hello, I am happy to meet you, Niels." His English was careful and Spanish-accented. "I am Daniel."

Chapter 8

"SO, YOU'RE THE GUY who kept my nephew from going crazy these past six months?" Daniel's uncle Emilio said. He was a barrel of a man with penetrating eyes; a broad, sensuous face; and dark hair graying at the temples. Daniel had explained that his uncle had given him a home when, at sixteen, he had fallen out with his widowed mother's new husband.

"Yes, I guess so," I said, shaking the hand Emilio offered. We spoke in Spanish, mine dredged up from the pocket in my brain where I had stashed what I had learned in school, and bolstered by practice with Daniel on the ship—we had conversed in English and Spanish on alternate days to improve our fluency in the other's language.

Daniel had signed on to the container ship as a deck cadet, a junior role that included helping to clean and maintain the ship structure and equipment, cast off and berth the ship at port, and move cargo. It was his first contract, and he quickly discovered that the career direction it offered wasn't of interest. I helped him adjust to life at sea and we became friends. When he invited me go home with him when our contracts ended, I gladly accepted. After disembarking the ship in Rotterdam we had made our way to Spain, arriving late this afternoon at his uncle's tavern in the Triana neighborhood of Seville.

Daniel shook his head. "Can you believe that Niels signed up for a second contract right after finishing his first?"

I laughed. "It wasn't so bad, but I'm done now."

Emilio gave his nephew's shoulder an affectionate squeeze. "We missed you, Dani. So, does this mean you've given up on the sea?"

Daniel shook his head. "No, just on the merchant marine. I've applied for the officer-training program with the navy."

Emilio threw up his hands. "Where this obsession with the water comes from, I don't know. I'd hoped you would take over this tavern for me."

"You know that Julia plans to, *Tio*. How's she doing, by the way?" He looked around. "Is she here today?"

Emilio shook his head. "The baby is coming soon and she was starting to find it hard. I told her she needs to rest if she's going to deliver my first grandson without any problems."

"It's going to be a boy, then?"

Emilio lifted massive shoulders sheepishly. "Julia didn't want to know ahead of time. But after my three girls, I think it's time for a boy, no?"

Daniel laughed. "I don't know—your girls are forces to reckon with. I'm glad you are here. I didn't expect to see you."

"Marietta has come down with a cold." He opened out his hands in mock enquiry. "Who gets a cold in summer? Anyhow, no time to find someone else for the bar, so here I am."

"I can help, *Tio*."

Emilio gestured at our luggage. "You just got here. You must be tired."

"Not really. We've been sitting on the train all day." Daniel turned to me. "You don't mind, do you?"

"Not at all."

He picked up his bag. "I'll unpack and take a shower. Half an hour, maybe?"

"Take your time." Emilio cocked his head at the handful

of patrons in the tavern. It was a rectangular space enclosed by dressed-stone walls, with French doors along one folded back to extend the room into a courtyard. The high wood-slatted ceiling was supported by what looked like ancient, smoke-darkened beams. "It's still early."

I followed Daniel through full-height swinging doors hidden behind the back wall of the tavern's long mahogany bar. They opened to a corridor with two closed doors on the left and short swinging doors leading to the kitchen on the right. This part of the tavern was briskly modern, in contrast to the antiquated body of the dining area. Daniel pushed into the kitchen. Five people dressed in typical kitchen uniforms of white jacket, black and white striped aprons, and skull caps were busy at the counters. My mouth watered painfully at the heady smells of garlic and peppers sizzling in oil. Daniel called out a greeting. A woman wielding a skillet waved and two men came over to shake his hand. He introduced me and they spoke excitedly over each other for a few minutes.

"I have to get ready for work," Daniel said with a wave. We left the kitchen and continued down the corridor to a heavy-duty double door, which opened to a back courtyard enclosed by a fence with tall lancet-shaped wrought-iron pickets. The tavern sat on a corner and a closed gate in the fence gave access to a side street, presumably for service and delivery vehicles. Facing us was a stone outbuilding of similar vintage to the old part of the tavern. A dark-blue late-model sedan was parked in one of its two bays. The rest of the ground floor was enclosed, the door leading to it secured by a fist-sized padlock.

Daniel headed to an iron staircase ascending the right side of the outbuilding. At the base he gestured back towards the main building. "It used to be a foundry. *Tío* Emilio refurbished it and made it into a restaurant. He'd always wanted one. This building used to be the stables. I live upstairs."

I followed him up the staircase, our arms brushing against

the narrow silvery leaves of an olive tree that grew nearby. At the top, Daniel rummaged in his bag, withdrew a ring of keys, and fitted one into the lock of a heavy wooden door.

"Fooof!" he said, stepping inside. He dropped his bag on the floor, continued on, and unlatched the windows of two dormers that bumped out of the sloped ceiling. "Leave the door open so we can get a breeze." He turned back to me. "Anyway, *bienvenido*."

The space was about twenty feet long and, like the tavern, had thick stone walls. The beamed gable ceiling sloped from around ten feet in the center to the outside wall, which was about five feet high. A low stand between the dormer windows held a television and some audio equipment. Four beanbag chairs formed a half circle in front of them. To the side was a small dining table and chairs. An interior wall ran the length of the room a few feet off the center. A short kitchen counter with a single burner and small sink on top and a compact refrigerator and cupboard tucked underneath was fitted between two doors opening off the interior wall.

Daniel indicated the first door on the right. "This is my bedroom. The other's the bathroom." He strode down the room and swept aside a heavy unbleached cotton curtain to reveal an alcove bracketed by the interior wall and what appeared to be a storage cupboard. A single bed covered with a woven tribal blanket sat within the alcove under a small four-paned window. An upended wooden crate holding a gooseneck lamp at the head of the bed and a set of deep shelves on the opposite wall completed the furnishings.

"You sleep here. It's not much, but it works when friends visit and it's late and they don't want to drive home. Even *Tío Emilio* uses it sometimes."

I dropped my bag on the floor by the bed. "It's perfect."

Daniel went to the bathroom and returned with towels, which he set on my bed. "Make yourself comfortable."

I unpacked while Daniel showered and dressed. Twenty minutes later he emerged from his room wearing a crisp white shirt and black slacks. "When you're ready, come and have a meal," he said on his way out.

I showered, dressed in my freshest clothes, and returned to the tavern through the back door. There were two more men in the kitchen now, one of whom was waving his arms and speaking excitedly. Unlike the others, he wore a white apron and a tall toque on his head. The boss, I figured. I continued to the front. Daniel was behind the bar drawing a draft beer and chatting with Emilio, who sat at the counter sipping a glass of wine. I slid onto a stool a couple over from him.

"So, you are settled in, Niels?" Emilio said.

"Yes, thank you." I was commenting on the beauty of the tavern and stable buildings when the agitated chef with the toque interrupted. He and Emilio conversed in short, rapid bursts.

"*Mierda*," Emilio said after the chef stormed away.

Daniel finished serving a customer and came over. "What's wrong, *Tio*?"

"Pablo says Linda didn't come in again, and we have a party of sixteen at ten o'clock. And of course it's Friday night." Emilio shook his head. "After all I've done for that girl."

"Does Linda work in the kitchen?" I said.

"Yes," Emilio said.

"Maybe I could help."

Daniel's eyebrows shot up. "Do you miss it already?"

Emilio studied me. "Yes, I remember Dani saying you worked in the kitchen on that boat. But you are our guest."

I shrugged. "I don't mind. I'd just be sitting around anyway."

Emilio's face lightened. "If you're sure, let's go talk to Pablo."

He and I went to the kitchen. Still deep in his indignation,

Pablo initially waved away the suggestion, but after consideration asked me what I could do. I sketched out my experience, searching for many of the Spanish words.

"*Bueno*, we'll give it a try." Pablo beckoned to one of the women I had seen earlier. "Ana, get him dressed." He regarded my hair, curling on my shoulders after a year without a barber. "And make sure to cover his hair. He'll work the cold station."

He waved us away and turned to speak to another of the staff. I followed Ana to the back, put on a jacket, apron, and skull cap, and washed my hands. Indicating each on the menu, Ana explained the composition of the dishes I would be responsible for and showed me where to find the vegetables, cold meats, olives, cheese, seafood, and garnishes I would need. I made what sense I could of it. Pablo came over once, told me not to be so generous, and ignored me for the rest of the evening.

The night eventually wound down. When the restaurant closed, Emilio came over to me.

"Have you eaten anything?"

"No." I had noticed others snatching a bite or a drink, but nothing had been offered to me and, it being a strange kitchen, I didn't ask.

Emilio waved his hand imperiously. "Get this boy some food, and for Dani as well!"

Ana filled two bowls with chicken and rice and brought them over. We carried the food and a basket of bread out to the bar. Daniel looked up from rinsing the sink.

"Fantastic! I'm starving."

He came around and we sat at the counter, spooning up the savory dish.

Emilio looked at me over his shoulder as he drew two large glasses of lager. "So, friend of Dani, I want to thank you for helping out in the kitchen tonight."

"I was glad to, *Señor* Navarro."

Emilio set a glass down in front of me. "You can call me *Tio*," he said.

Time passed agreeably in Seville. I drifted through the days, reveling in the sun and heat, energy and bustle, rich Mediterranean colors, earthy textures, and timeless quality of the city, so different from the hard metal container ships, monochromatic oceans, and constant movement of the previous year.

"I'm not, ah, overstaying my welcome, am I?" I said to Daniel over coffee one morning three weeks later.

"*No hay problema.* Stay the summer."

"That would be really nice, but are you sure? I don't want to impose on either you or your uncle."

"Not an imposition—you're no trouble. Besides, *Tio* Emilio approves of you. He's not that keen on some of my friends."

"Can I at least help with the rent?"

"There's no rent. *No te preocupes.*"

Daniel and I rubbed along well together. A few months older than me, he was a clear-eyed realist with an upright, steady bearing and resolute, purposeful manner. His company seemed to draw out the same qualities in me. I don't know what Daniel would have made of the earnest, over-sensitive, naive young man I had once been. That person had gotten lost somewhere on the high seas. The year living among strangers had toughened me up and effected a certain detachment from my past life and the circumstances that had caused me to step out of it. The facts of my parentage—when I thought of them—still caused a small ache under my heart, but not the burning shame and anguish I had felt in the first few months. It seemed that, in the same way working out had packaged my soft, unformed body with muscle, time had encased all that confusion and pain in emotional scar tissue. Paradoxically this saddened me, as though I had lost touch with something vital in my being.

Daniel took over the bar and front-of-house work previously done by his cousin Julia—who delivered a baby girl Emilio promptly fell in love with—sharing the day and evening shifts with Marietta, a woman in her fifties with honey-blond hair twisted into an knot, a trim figure, and stylish cat-eye glasses. She was a relative of Emilio's, as many of the staff seemed to be. "*Tio* Emilio has a big heart," Daniel said when I remarked on the fact. "Too big sometimes. But he can be pretty tough if he needs to."

The absent Linda was another relative, the daughter of a second cousin. She showed up, sullenly apologetic, the day after the missed shift I had covered. When another of the kitchen staff called in sick the following week, I stepped in again.

"Do you want a job?" Pablo said at the end of that night.

"I, ah, don't have a work permit."

Pablo shrugged. This was obviously a trifling concern.

"And I don't know how long I will be here. But while I am, I'm happy to help."

Pablo shamelessly took advantage of this offer and I found myself doing two or three shifts a week.

"Are you sure you don't mind?" Emilio asked me on the third occasion.

"I haven't anything else to do while Daniel's working, and it's a way of repaying your hospitality."

I began to fill in for absent servers as well. Working in the tavern was fun and a shift always included a hot meal. Despite my refusal of pay for this work, Emilio occasionally pressed a folded hundred-Euro banknote into my hand, saying that young men always needed money.

It was not all work, of course. Daniel introduced me to his city, careening through the streets on his moped with me riding pillion. On free evenings we joined up with his friends for drinks or meals. On two occasions we rented a car and explored the surrounding Andalusian countryside. One time we caught the ferry to Morocco and spent a couple of days wandering around Tangiers.

Among Daniel's friends were several beauties with flashing eyes and inviting smiles. I had not been around young women for a year and a half. Meeting them invariably involved *dos besos*, the cheek-kissing by which Spaniards greet each other, and I could not help but react to the soft pressure of their bodies against mine, the brush of hair against my face, and their spicy scents. The intensity of my response was alarming—I still feared that my father's propensity for violence might be coded in my DNA. It also was confusing: Aude was the one I loved.

For all our closeness, there were aspects of my life, like my parentage and details of my background, that I kept from Daniel, as I expected there were things he didn't share with me. But I did tell him about Aude, how we had known each other since childhood, had a special understanding, and would marry in time.

"Ah," he had said with a knowing smile. "*Un amor escrito en las estrellas.*"

One evening a woman in the group we were out with had one glass of wine too many and moved in on me. When I removed her hand from my thigh for the third time, Daniel shook his finger and said, "Lay off, Carmen. Niels has a fiancée."

That night he hooked up with one of the other women, leaving me to walk home on my own. His intervention with Carmen had made me miss Aude acutely. I didn't think of her often—not that my commitment to her had diminished, she was simply not part of my current reality. I pulled the cheap cellphone I had bought for my stay in Spain from my pocket to call her but put it back without dialing—the prepaid plan didn't cover overseas calls.

Back at Daniel's place I signed on to my computer and composed an email.

> *Aude, I miss you terribly. It's been a while, I know, but I've been dealing with something. Hard to write about so I won't start but I really want to talk to you.*

I paused my tapping. I would explain everything, all the sordid details, and I would accept her judgement, whatever it was. Hopefully she would understand and not think the worst of me. I continued:

> *I'm in Spain now, part of what is a very long story. Let me know a good time to call. Will figure out time difference. Look forward very much to hearing your voice again.*

I re-read the message and pressed send. I was about to shut down the computer when a beep indicated an incoming email. *That was fast.* Too fast, as it turned out—a message informed me that Aude's email address was no longer valid. I frowned at this but didn't worry. In my mind, Aude remained frozen where I had left her at her door, dressed in her green velvet gown, hair cascading down her back, my diamond winking at her throat. But her life would have carried on. She would have graduated by now and her email address had been tied to the university. It didn't matter—I would probably go home soon. I had no other plans, and facing my family was inevitable.

News came in late July that Daniel had been accepted into the Spanish navy's officer program, with instructions to report to the training academy in northwestern Spain in September.

One afternoon in late August, Emilio drew me to the side when I arrived for a shift in the kitchen.

"With Dani going, can you stay until Christmas? Julia said she might come back then."

"Ah, yeah, maybe. Let me talk to Daniel."

"It would help *Tío*, and you're welcome to stay on at my place," Daniel said when I spoke to him. "But it's up to you."

"Isn't there a ninety-day limit to my stay in Spain?"

"*Tío* will figure it out."

Emilio made a few calls, I filled out some forms, and a couple of weeks later I was granted a long-stay visa. Emilio also started the process to get me a work permit. Until that was in place, we agreed that I would receive room and board and a small stipend in exchange for work at the tavern. I missed Daniel after he left, but my days were full with work, sessions at the gym, and thrice-weekly attendance at an intermediate course in Spanish—my knowledge of the language grew daily but I needed formal instruction to consolidate it.

I was relieved to delay returning home.

Chapter 9

ONE DAY AFTER CROSSING the Guadalquivir River on the way home from my Spanish language class in Seville's old town, I decided to pick up something to eat in the Mercado de Triana. Just outside, a guitar player sat on a bench in the shade of a tree, hunched over a guitar propped on a crossed leg. The piece he was playing was slow and sad. I had seen the old man busking at various locations in the neighborhood before but never stopped to listen. For some reason I did now, straining to hear through the market and traffic noises. After a few minutes I gave up and dropped a few Euro coins into the hat he had set on the ground. He neither raised his head nor acknowledged me or my coins in any way.

The following week I had an afternoon free of work and classes. Restless, I wandered around the neighborhood and came upon the old guitarist seated on a low wall bordering a small park. The spot was quieter than the one near the Mercado and his music was clear. The tune he was picking out was bright and cheerful. When I stopped to listen, he looked up and smiled. I nodded in return and sat down on the wall a short distance away. His guitar was well used, the veneer on the surface worn down in parts. Yet its sound was rich and resonant. The man and his instrument were obviously old friends, and I felt a momentary pang for Celeste and the feel of her wooden body between my thighs. The rhythm of the music he was playing eluded me, jumping from one pattern to another, but still integrated.

"That's flamenco you're playing, right?" I said when he had finished the piece.

"*Sí,* of course." A certain flatness in his Spanish vowels suggested that he came from a different part of the country.

"I can't quite get the rhythm."

"It is a *buleria.* This is the *compás.*" He beat out a rhythm on the guitar body with his fingers.

"I don't understand."

A few raindrops speckled our faces. Within seconds they thickened into a dense rain. The guitarist jumped up and thrust his guitar into its battered case. I glanced around for shelter.

"There's a café across the street. Let's go there," I said.

The guitarist emptied his hat of the few coins it contained and slapped it on his head. We crossed the street, dodging cars, and entered the café. It was an upmarket coffee house with colorful tiles, delicate wrought-iron furniture, blown-glass pendant lights, and a long counter featuring an array of fancy cakes and pastries. The customers were mostly women. They glanced at us—two wet and scruffy men—and dropped their eyes. We found an empty table and sat down. I thought of the handful of coins in the guitarist's pocket.

"Can I get you something—coffee? Or tea?"

"*Café, sí.*"

I headed to the counter to order. The old man leaned his guitar case against the wall next to our table and followed me.

"What kind of coffee would you like?"

He moved his hands apart. "A big one."

"Two americanos," I said to the young woman at the till. I turned back to the guitarist. "And how about something to eat? Anything appeal to you?"

He nodded eagerly and pointed to a slice of fudgy cake

covered in a dusting of icing sugar. "That one." He indicated a creamy confection crusted with almonds. "That one too."

I paid for the order, including in it a custard tart for myself. We returned to our table, and a few moments later the server brought over our coffee and pastries. The guitarist grasped a fork, cut into the fudgy cake, and shoved a piece into his mouth. I studied him while he ate. He was a couple of inches shorter than me, sturdily built but thin. His face was structured around high, prominent cheekbones, with a generous mouth; slightly warped nose with finely cut, flared nostrils; and dark brown eyes. He would have been a handsome man in his youth. A day's worth of stubble shadowed his cheeks, and shaggy salt and pepper hair hid his brow and caught on his collar. By the coarse texture of his skin and sunburst of wrinkles around his eyes, I put him at well over sixty. *Maybe even older*, I thought, observing his knotted knuckles. The neck of his gray sweater sagged and the collar of the blue shirt he wore underneath was frayed, but the clothes were clean.

He glanced up, perhaps feeling my scrutiny, and grinned, revealing uneven smoke-darkened teeth. "*Bueno*," he said. He pushed aside the empty plate and started on the almond cake. When that was finished, he picked up his cup and took a long swallow of coffee. "Ahhh," he said, setting his cup down. He passed the back of his hand across his mouth then held it out to me.

"I am Tiago."

I shook his hand. "Niels."

Tiago repeated my name, testing the pronunciation, then wiggled his eyebrows as though to say, *Well, I guess we can't do too much about that, can we?*

"When it started raining you were explaining the rhythm of that piece you had played. You tapped it out on your guitar. I'm a musician . . ." I paused. It was the first time since abandoning my studies that I had identified myself as one. "Anyhow, I'd like to understand."

Tiago's eyes brightened. "You are a musician?"

"Yes."

"*Guitarra*?"

"No, cello."

"Okay. It was *buleria* and this is the *compás*." He tapped out the rhythm again on the table. I concentrated hard: twelve beats but irregular accents. He tapped it out again, exaggerating the accents.

"Third . . . sixth . . . eighth . . . tenth . . . twelfth," I said. "Ha!"

Tiago grinned and tapped it out once more for good measure. "Other *palos* have different *compás*."

"*Palos*?"

"Different kinds of flamenco." Tiago glanced up. "The rain has stopped. I will go now." He stood, picked up his guitar case, and slung the strap over his shoulder. I rose as well and accompanied him outside.

"*Adiós*," he said and headed up the street. It was the direction I intended to go as well but I hung back, not wanting to crowd him. When he disappeared round the corner, I followed slowly. To that point I had not paid much attention to flamenco, despite, or perhaps because of, its ubiquity in the city. Most of what I had encountered was kitschy, flouncy, tourist stuff in bars and restaurants. At the tavern another of Emilio's indigent relatives strummed away on weekends, his playing increasingly sloppy as the night wore on and his empty wine glasses piled up. Nothing in what he offered held any interest for me.

Tiago's music felt different, in its simplicity perhaps, and the business of *compás* intrigued me. When I got home I opened my computer and began to research flamenco. After reading a couple of entries I split the screen, opened my journal, and began to make notes.

Flamenco, it turned out, is many things: a philosophy, an emotional state, a world view, even a way of life. It has been laid claim to, not without controversy, by the Romany people of Spain who are called *gitanos*—some in the country refer to them contemptuously as "Spanish Gypsies." Flamenco music, song, and dance are the creative expression of it. The powerful emotional state of heightened passion, spirit, and inspiration associated with flamenco is known as *duende*. I watched a video, then another, then more, of performances throbbing with color and passion by heralded masters.

It was midnight when I finally sat back and shut down my computer. Cramped and aching, my body called for sleep but my mind vibrated as though newly awoken.

On my next day off I set out in search of Tiago. I was anxious to quiz him further on the complex taxonomy of flamenco styles, or *palos*, as he had called them, which organized the music by its rhythmic structure—*compás*, harmony, and theme. He was nowhere to be found. By the time I returned home that afternoon I could have sketched out a street map of Triana. I resumed the search a few days later and found him almost immediately, set up on the wide stone base of a statue of some former dignitary on the edge of a small square only a few blocks from the tavern. A cigarette dangled from the corner of his mouth while he idly picked at a loose button on his threadbare suit jacket.

"Niels!" he said when he caught sight of me.

"Hello, Tiago. You are well?"

He pursed his lips. "*Sí*, of course." He patted a section of the stone base on which he was perched in invitation and I sat down.

"Since I last saw you, I've been reading up on flamenco. When did you learn to play guitar?"

Tiago dropped his cigarette butt and ground it into the dirt. "I don't remember."

"Didn't you take lessons?"

"No, I just watched and listened." He shrugged. "There was always flamenco."

"So, I think I understand *compás* now."

Tiago raised his eyebrows and smiled.

"I mean, I understand the concept of it, like how a *solea* has the same *compás* as a *buleria* but is not so fast, and how although the *siguiriya* also has a twelve-beat *compás* the accents are different. And about the different fandangos and tangos." The flamenco names were spicy in my mouth. "The *malagueñas* were familiar."

"Ah, *sí*." Tiago launched into a short riff on his guitar, illustrating its distinctive melodic phrasing.

"And I recognized the rhumba too."

"Not traditional—from Cuba," Tiago said, but it didn't prevent him from dashing off a lively, bouncy melody, his fingers swarming the guitar like octopus legs.

We continued talking about the various flamenco *palos*, Tiago playing examples of the different musical forms. I bent towards him, trying to tease out the distinctions between them. He explained that there is a type of flamenco that is *jondo*—solemn and profound—and played an example. The melancholy notes hung like memories in the air. An old wizened couple, the man bent over a cane, the woman clutching his arm with bird claw hands, stopped and listened, and when it ended the man dashed a tear from his eye. The woman fumbled with her purse but Tiago raised his hand with a smile, and she nodded and put it away.

"Now flamenco *chico*—happy music." Tiago's fingers picked out a light, lively melody. The old couple listened for a few more minutes then slowly moved away.

Glancing at my watch, I was startled to see that two hours

had passed. "I didn't mean to occupy so much of your time, Tiago, but this has been great." I rose and drew some money from my pocket, selected a twenty-Euro banknote, and dropped it in the hat. Tiago's eyes lit up. He scooped up the money, slapped the hat on his head, and placed his guitar in its case.

"Come," he said, rising.

"Me? Where?"

He set off swiftly, gesturing for me to follow.

I caught up and fell into step beside him. "Where are we going?"

"Not far."

We wound our way through the streets to a busy avenue where Tiago led me into a fast food restaurant. At the counter, he turned to me and gestured to the posted menu.

"What do you like?"

I understood that hospitality was being returned and chose a small burger and coffee. Tiago placed my order and requested chicken nuggets and a large cola for himself. After some spirited discussion about dipping sauces—the last time they had mistakenly given him something other than the mustard sauce he had requested—he paid with the bill I had given him. When our order was ready I picked up the tray and followed Tiago to a table. He sat down and propped his guitar against one of the spare chairs.

We ate without speaking, Tiago with considerable relish. When the food was gone we piled the wrappings onto the tray, transferred it to an empty table, and concentrated on our drinks.

"Your guitar." I gestured to the instrument case. "It's different from others I've seen. Smaller, I think."

"Yes, flamenco guitar." Tiago reached over and opened the case.

"I didn't mean . . ." I said, but he already had taken the guitar out.

"Here." He handed it to me.

I reached for the instrument's neck, but when my fingers touched it a shock jolted my arm. I jerked it back. "Ah! What was that?"

Tiago stared at me for a long moment and held the guitar out again. "Here."

I accepted it cautiously but the shock was not repeated. It was the first musical instrument I had held in almost two years, and it felt both awkward and familiar. I turned sideways in the chair, crossed my right knee over my left, and positioned the guitar as Tiago had done. It settled intimately on my thigh. I touched the strings over the sound hole lightly and slid my left hand up and down the neck, forming a few chords. My fingers tingled. I glanced up at Tiago. He was regarding me intently, a small smile curving his mouth.

"Will you teach me how to play?"

Tiago pursed his lips and shook his head. He held his hand out for the guitar. I yielded it reluctantly.

"No?"

He returned the guitar to its case, lowered the lid, and snapped the locks. "You learn how to play and then you come to see me." He rose and picked up the case. "I am going now."

I followed him dumbly, collecting myself sufficiently outside to thank him for the meal. "Tiago, how can I find you? You know, so I don't have to wander around looking. Could I get your telephone number?"

He shook his head. "No telephone."

"Do you have a plan or schedule or something for where you're going to play?"

"Ah, no." The idea amused him. "I live here." He rattled off a street name and number. I quickly pulled out my phone, asked him to repeat the address, and sent it to myself in a text.

"*Adiós*," he said and left. I gazed after him, lost in thought.

Chapter 10

"*TIO*, WHERE IS THE best place to learn how to play flamenco guitar?" I asked Emilio.

He had other business interests, a chain of auto parts and tire stores, but dropped by the tavern regularly, partly to keep an eye on things but also because, as he once said, "I am surrounded by women and need to escape." I had grown fond of Daniel's uncle and enjoyed his visits.

"Suddenly you want to learn flamenco?" he said.

"I guess it is a bit sudden." I didn't know how to explain the spell Tiago seemed to have cast over me. "But I studied music once, and since I'm here I thought I'd like to learn the music of this region."

Emilio raised his eyebrows. "You're a musician?"

I had not revealed this part of my life to Daniel or Emilio, so distant had I grown from it. "I was once," I said.

Emilio didn't seem overly curious about this admission. "Okay, I'll ask around."

He had a short list for me the following week. "This guy is apparently the best," he said, pointing to the first name, "but it may be hard to get time with him. The other ones are pretty good too."

I checked out the instructors on the list. As Emilio had said, the top-ranked teacher was taking no new students, but his office took down my name in case the situation changed. It being late November, the others also had no openings for private lessons until the new year. I didn't sign up immediately. I had planned to leave Seville when Emilio's daughter Julia resumed work at the tavern, but with visas no longer an issue—Emilio had arranged a work permit for me and I was on the payroll now—I considered staying on for a few more months.

"Would you still have some use for me when Julia comes back?" I asked Emilio the next time I saw him. "I can't start guitar lessons until January and it would be good to have some work while I'm taking them. Even a couple of shifts a week would help." I had squirreled away most of my container-ship earnings and preferred not to burn them up if I didn't have to. I also didn't want to move—Daniel's apartment suited me well.

Emilio opened out his hands in a gesture of delight. "Yes, yes, of course. You know, Julia, she is not so ready to leave that baby of hers. She said maybe she will start slowly, a day here and there to see what it's like. Yes, it would be good if you stay."

I began to look for an instrument. After researching how to choose a guitar I checked a couple of stores but was overwhelmed by the options and often contrary information from the sales staff. I had not seen Tiago in a while and decided to seek his advice. The address he had given me was on the floor above a law office on a commercial street. I pressed the buzzer on the side of the door.

"Niels!" Tiago said when he opened the door.

"Yes, hello, Tiago," I said awkwardly. "I hope you don't mind my coming to see you. Is this a good time?"

He motioned me in. "*Sí, sí.*"

I followed him as he puffed up the stairs. At the top he entered the first of two doors on a short corridor, stood to the side, and waved me in. He closed the door and indicated the carrier bag in my hand.

"What is this?"

I drew out two orders of chicken nuggets from the fast food restaurant he had taken me to. "Here, these are for you. I hope I got the right dipping sauce."

Tiago's eyes lit up with pleasure. "*Sí, bueno.*"

I emptied the bag of the remaining items: a bottle of cola and some apples. While Tiago rinsed a plate at the sink, I looked around the room. A narrow, unmade bed was tucked into one corner with a small table at its side. A wooden armoire with ornate doors sat against the wall across from the bed. Articles of clothing were strewn at its base. I could see the edge of a bathroom sink through the open door in the wall between them. An armchair at the foot of the bed faced a television set perched on a dresser next to the armoire. Tiago's guitar leaned against the armchair. A counter began a few feet on this side of the chair and ran to the far wall. In it was a sink filled with dirty dishes. On top was a single-burner hotplate, a microwave, and a clutter of pots and utensils. Two open shelves above the counter held dishware and an assortment of cans and food packages. A small refrigerator was tucked underneath. A table with two chairs sat against the outside wall under the only window in the room. Tiago pushed aside an overflowing ashtray resting on it—the air reeked of cold ash and stale smoke—and tipped the nuggets from their container onto the plate.

"But what are you going to eat?" he said, correctly assuming that he was not intended to share the chicken nuggets.

"I'll have an apple. They've come all the way here from close to my home in Canada."

He picked an apple out of the carrier bag, one of the glossy, ridiculously expensive McIntoshes I had found in a greengrocer on the way, studied it, and set it down. "You are from Canada?"

I gave Tiago a short geography lesson while washing an apple and joined him at the table with it and a small knife I had found and rinsed. Between bites of apple I told him about signing up for lessons in flamenco guitar.

"I need a guitar but don't know how to choose one. Would you help me?"

Tiago stopped eating, his interest engaged. He was about to speak when someone knocked sharply on the door. A woman carrying a large plastic bag entered. She looked to be around thirty, with a narrow face; long, straight nose; deep-set hazel eyes; and dark hair parted in the middle and gathered into a knot at her neck. She wore a plain white shirt open at the neck under a gray suit jacket. The matching trousers covered narrow hips and slender legs. A delicate chain necklace with a small gold cross and a chunky watch were her only accessories.

"Ah, Paula," Tiago said.

"*Abuelo.*" Paula turned to me. "Who's this?"

I rose and extended my hand. "I am Niels. I've asked Tiago to help me buy a guitar."

Her eyes flashed. "He's in no position to help you buy a guitar." Her Spanish was crisper and more polished than her grandfather's.

I lowered my hand, unshaken, and sat down. "Oh, no, sorry, I didn't mean help with money, just advice in choosing one."

Paula relaxed fractionally and pointed her chin at what remained of the chicken nuggets. "What's that you're eating?"

Tiago pursed his lips and shrugged.

She huffed and moved to the bed, dropping the bag beside it. Tiago winked at me and bit into another nugget.

"So, you need a guitar," he said through the mush in his mouth. "Have you looked at any yet?"

I reviewed what I had learned from reading and my visits to the music stores, talking over the noise Paula was making. She had removed her jacket and rolled up her sleeves, and was stripping and remaking the bed with linens from her bag. That done, she nudged the discarded clothing on the floor to join the used linen piled there and placed clean folded clothing from her bag into the armoire and dresser. After stowing the dirty laundry in the plastic bag, she went into the bathroom. An exclamation of disgust was followed by sounds of running water and splashing. This completed, she came to the small kitchen area and regarded it with her hands on her hips.

"You could at least wash your dishes!" she said, cutting me off.

We didn't try to talk over the rush of water and clatter of china and cutlery. When Tiago finished eating his last nugget, a hand snaked across the table and picked up the plate. The dishwashing completed, Paula pulled the bag of garbage from its container under the sink. I reached out to tip my apple core and the contents of the loaded ashtray in as well. She gave me a brisk nod in acknowledgement.

"You smoke too much, *Abuelo*," she said.

Tiago pursed his lips and shrugged.

She knotted the garbage bag closed, put on her jacket, and picked up the bag of dirty laundry. "I didn't have time to get food today. I'll bring it tomorrow," she said and left, closing the door firmly behind her.

Tiago shook his head. "Just like her mother."

"Do you have other children?"

"A son." He shifted in his chair. "So, we need to find you a guitar."

"I don't like this shop," Tiago said. "Let's go to another one."

We were in one of the stores I had previously visited. The two staff members had regarded us superciliously and responded to our questions in an offhand and dismissive manner. "*Gitanos*," I heard one of them mutter. Tiago certainly looked the part, with his rugged face, ancient suit jacket, fraying scarf, and battered hat. By association I appeared to have been taken for one as well.

The salesman at the next store also regarded us warily, but after listening to Tiago's explanation of what we were looking for he brought five guitars for consideration. Tiago held each one up and examined the bridges.

"The strings must be low to play fast," he said to me.

He fiddled with the guitars' tuning pegs then tapped and strummed them, holding his ear close to the sound hole. He engaged the salesman in an animated discussion on the guitars' structure, and the thickness and density of the different woods from which they were made. Many of the Spanish words were new to me and I followed as best I could.

Tiago set the last of the lot aside. "Do you have any others?"

"Yes, but they cost more," the salesman said.

Tiago shrugged and made a *bring them on* gesture with his fingers. I shifted uncomfortably beside him. I had not fixed a budget for this purchase but didn't expect to spend more than a few hundred Euros.

The salesman went around the store and brought back three more guitars for consideration. They were beautiful instruments, the lines clean, the wooden bodies gleaming and clearly superior to the previous ones. I adjusted my expectations. Tiago liked them better as well, murmuring as he turned each this way and that. As with the previous ones, he quizzed the salesman on construction and materials and tapped, strummed, and even smelled one. He turned to me and indicated two.

"These, maybe?"

I picked each up in turn. They were surprisingly light, the strings inviting under my fingers. Tiago watched me intently as I handled them.

"Do they speak to you?" he asked.

"Speak?" I thought of Celeste, Meredith, and Lily. Had they spoken to me? "I can't say. What should I look for?"

"Any others?" Tiago asked the salesman.

The salesman started to shake his head then held up a finger.

"There is one, but it's used. Came in yesterday on consignment. Let me see if I can find it." He disappeared into a backroom. I picked up the two guitars again, straining to feel something, anything. I had the terrible sense of falling short somehow. The salesman returned and handed the used guitar to Tiago, who asked the usual questions. I was concentrating on communicating with the other two instruments and didn't listen.

"Niels!" I looked up. He was grinning. "This guitar has cedar from Canada."

"Really?"

I set the guitar I had been holding aside and took the used one from him. It didn't have the hard, polished look of the new ones, the wood more mellow, a patina acquired with use, perhaps. The rest of it was exquisite: the sides and back of rosewood that seemed to glow with a low fire, an ebony fretboard and bridge, a rosette made of a fine mosaic with a leaf motif. The neck was warm and smooth in my hand. Despite needing tuning, the guitar's tone was rich and darker than that of the others I had tried, as though it were coming from deep inside the instrument's throat.

I glanced up at Tiago. He was watching me with a gleam in his eye. "It's a fine guitar," he said. He turned to the salesman. "Whose was it?"

"An old man's—I don't know his name. His daughter brought it in. She was selling off his things."

"What do you think, Niels?"

The guitar seemed to pulse softly in my hands. "I, ah, yes, it feels different from the others."

"It carries a trace of the man's spirit, maybe."

"Is that good?"

"Not good or bad, but you may hear an echo when you play sometimes. How much?" he asked the salesman.

The salesman's attention had been caught by a well-dressed

woman and adolescent boy who had entered the store. "Ah, twelve hundred Euros."

Tiago puffed out his disbelief and argued that, being second-hand, the guitar should be less than a new one.

The salesman folded his arms and shook his head. "Not with that kind of quality. The daughter said it was custom-made for her father."

Tiago pursed his lips and looked at me. Was the salesman leveraging my interest in the piece, or just trying to get rid of us? Twelve hundred Euros was three times what I had expected to pay, but I wanted the guitar and had passed the point of caring. I set it down on the counter and pulled out my credit card.

The salesman looked at the proffered card skeptically. He finally took it from my hand and scrutinized it.

"Is this your card?"

"Yes, of course."

"Do you have identification?"

I patted my pockets. "No, not with me."

"I don't think this is your card."

"What?"

"The name—I don't think it is you."

"Of course it's me."

He thrust the card at me. Open-mouthed, I accepted it. I glanced down at my name and then up at him. "What—you think I should be blond or something?"

"You want the guitar, you pay cash."

"I don't carry that kind of cash."

He shrugged. "Too bad."

I stuffed my card back into my wallet. "Let's go," I said to Tiago.

Outside we stopped and I spluttered with outrage. Tiago put his hand in his pocket and pulled out a few Euro bills and some coins and offered them to me. "Here."

"Oh, Tiago, no," I said, moved by his generosity. "Thank

you, but it's okay. I have the money. I just think he treated us badly."

"Yes, he did. Will you still get the guitar?"

I sucked in a deep breath. A bit of humiliation—was that too great a price? I could look for another guitar elsewhere, but there was something about that one . . . "Do you really believe what you said about the guitar speaking to me?"

His eyes crinkled in a smile. "Did it?"

I exhaled sharply, part laugh, part exasperation. "I think so."

"*Bueno.*" Tiago slapped me on the back. "Let's go and get something to eat."

I returned to the store the next day with my passport for identification. A different salesman was present and occupied with a customer. While waiting, I wandered around the store and found my guitar on display. I picked it up; it fit into my hands like it belonged there. A price tag dangled from the neck: eight hundred and fifty Euros.

Free now, the salesman came up to me. "Looking for a guitar?"

I held up the tag. "Is this how much it costs?"

"Yes, but it's not new, so maybe I can do a bit better."

"I'd appreciate that. I'm a student and every little bit helps."

"How about eight hundred?"

"That would be great."

At the counter, I handed over my credit card and opened my passport to the page with my photo. "Here's some identification."

He gave the passport a cursory glance and rang the purchase through. When it was completed I realized I needed a case and accepted the one the salesman recommended. I bought extra strings as well. All this for three hundred Euros less than what I would have paid if my card had not been rejected the previous day, in the company of my new *gitano* friend.

Chapter 11

AS CHRISTMAS APPROACHED THE tavern grew busier, and I worked most days. Daniel came home on a two-week leave and we had a boisterous reunion. We had kept in touch while he was away but there was always more to tell, and we spent a couple of late and wine-soaked nights catching up.

"You're taller and straighter than before, if that's possible," I said to him. He had acquired a kind of sheen as well, a combination of pride and confidence.

Emilio refused Daniel's offer to help in the tavern, saying that his holidays would be limited from now on and he should enjoy them while he could. While I worked, he reconnected with other friends and went down to Cadiz to visit his mother. When the tavern closed over Christmas, Emilio folded me into his family's celebrations. I had met his wife, an elegant woman named Mía, and Julia previously, but not his other daughters. The eldest, Ava, reminded me of Tiago's granddaughter Paula, with the same slim, dark looks and serious bearing. A college professor, she was edging into a career in politics and spoke in pronouncements full of import. The youngest, Sierra, was icily beautiful, clothes, hair, makeup perfect as befit the media celebrity that she was. Even within her family she held court. She had just become engaged to the scion of a Madrid banking family and gestured often to show off her outsized engagement ring. Julia was plainer than her sisters, but I liked her best for her unaffected cheerfulness and soft roundness. One could lose themselves in those plump thighs and pillowy breasts.

I had not seen Tiago since our guitar shopping expedition. On a free afternoon between Christmas and New Year's, I headed to his place with a basket filled with ham, cheese, and other delicacies. As I passed the law office over which his rooms were located, I glanced in the window and saw Paula speaking to the woman at the reception desk. I stopped in surprise. She looked up and, seeing me, came and opened the door.

"Are you here to see *Abuelo*?"

"Yes." I held up the basket. "I have a gift for him."

She considered me for a minute. "I have a few minutes free. Can I offer you a coffee?" She smiled faintly. "You're unlikely to get one from him."

"Ah, thank you."

I followed Paula into her office and sat down in the visitor chair she indicated. She went to a credenza on the side wall, made a cup of coffee with the small automatic machine on it, and handed it to me. She made another for herself and sat down on the business side of the desk.

"I want to apologize for my behavior when we last met," she said.

"There's no need."

"No, I was rude. I had a bad day but that was no reason to take it out on you."

"It's okay, really."

She took a sip of her coffee. "But I would like to know what you want with my *abuelo*."

"What I want with Tiago? I don't want anything with him. We're just friends."

She studied me over her cup. "Why are you friends?"

Although she was doing so pleasantly, I resented being grilled. "Is it necessary that there be a *why* in friendship?"

"Look, I care for my *abuelo*." She gestured to the ceiling. "And I keep an eye on him. So when something unusual like your unlikely friendship happens I want to understand what is going on."

I set my untouched coffee on the edge of her desk. "I encountered him"—I searched for the correct word in Spanish—"busking, and became interested in flamenco music. I've decided to learn how to play it."

Paula's eyebrows shot up. "*Abuelo* is going to teach you?"

"No, he told me not to bother him until I knew how to play."

She threw back her head and laughed. "That sounds more like it."

"Look, I like Tiago. I enjoy his company and talking to him. I would never do anything to . . . anything bad to him."

Her eyes softened. "Okay. I had to ask."

"I understand. Do you know if he's home?"

"Yes."

"Why don't you get him a phone? It would be a lot easier to keep in touch. For you too, I'd expect."

She opened her hands out in a helpless gesture. "I got him two. He lost them both."

I rose and picked up the gift basket. "Thanks for the coffee."

She rose, too, and held out her hand. "Friends?"

"Of course," I said and shook it.

Chapter 12

JANUARY CAME AND I began private lessons twice a week with Oscar, a kindly man in his fifties with a coffee-colored skin and short, tightly curled gray hair. If I was free, I also attended his drop-in workshop on Saturdays. With my previous years of study I easily grasped the theory behind the music, the different influences that shaped it, and its unusual scale in the minor mode. Having played cello, my left hand was familiar with its job on the frets. But most of the action involved the right hand. Before anything else, I learned the correct way to hold the guitar and the position and angle in which to place my right hand and thumb. The care of nails and how they affected power and tone received considerable attention—I grew the ones on my right hand and shaped them regularly. There were demonstrations and drills for the string-plucking *picados*, the flowing arpeggios, the strumming *rasqueados*, and the basic chords that give flamenco its distinctive sound. I fumbled through these intricate workings, my fingers like a team of horses all wanting to go in different directions. It was humbling.

"Slowly, slowly," Oscar would say. "It will come."

Determined to master these basics, I spent most of my free time on practice. One afternoon, after an hour of what felt like torture, I set my guitar aside with a grunt of disgust and decided to check in on Tiago. His fingers engaged the strings with speed and precision beyond thought, it seemed. Maybe he could advise me.

As I came to the street door for his building a woman wearing a pale-blue hijab and thick-lensed glasses, and carrying a cloth bag bulging with groceries, approached from the other direction. She stopped at the door, set down her bag, and blinked up at me.

"Hello," I said. "I'm here to see Tiago."

"I do not know if he is home." Her Spanish was thickly accented.

"Would you mind if I checked?"

She studied me for a moment, considering.

"I am a friend of Tiago. My name is Niels."

"Okay. I am Fatiha." She extracted a key from her purse, unlocked the door, and pushed it open.

"Here, let me help you," I said as she bent to pick up her groceries.

She hesitated but let me carry her bag up the stairs. At the top she turned and held out her hand. "I will take it now."

I gave her the bag and knocked on Tiago's door. Footsteps approached and the door opened. Paula stood inside, but unlike previous times she was dressed casually in jeans and a mauve crewneck sweater. Her hair had been clipped into a pixie cut that curled around her ears and forehead and molded to her head.

"You've cut your hair!" I blurted.

"Ah." She smiled. "You think I'm Paula. I am Paloma. You must be *Abuelo*'s young friend. Paula told me about you." She held out her hand and I shook it, then followed her into the room.

"Sorry, but you look just like her."

She glanced over her shoulder. "We are twins. Look here, *Abuelo*, your friend has come to see you."

Tiago was sitting in the armchair, a throw over his lap. He

grinned and raised a hand in greeting, his eyes lighting up when he spotted the greasy bag I held. I placed it nonchalantly on the kitchen counter, hoping Paloma would not see it.

"How are you, Tiago?" I said, approaching the chair.

"Not as well as we would like," Paloma said.

Tiago dismissed the comment with a wave of his hand. It was a feeble movement and I noticed his hollow cheeks and pallor.

I turned to Paloma. She was stashing a stethoscope in an oxblood leather case.

"You're a doctor?"

"Yes."

"Is something wrong with Tiago?"

"He's recovering from pneumonia." She brushed hair out of his eyes with a gentle finger.

He pushed her hand away. "You talk like I'm not here."

"I didn't mean to." She looked at me. "We're trying to get him to stop smoking. Please don't buy him cigarettes if he asks."

Tiago growled. I noticed then that the room was free of its usual fug of stale cigarette smoke. Paloma slipped on a black leather jacket. "I can't come tomorrow, but Paula will check on you." She pointed to two vials of pills on the kitchen counter. "Remember to take those tonight and in the morning."

Tiago waved a hand dismissively. "*Sí, sí.*"

"Nice to meet you," Paloma said and left.

Tiago put aside the throw and tried to push himself up. His arms trembled with the effort.

"Hey, Tiago, why don't you stay there and I'll bring the food to you."

He nodded and sank back into the chair. I rinsed and dried a plate that was in the sink—Paloma's care apparently didn't extend to housekeeping—and put the chicken nuggets and sauce I had brought onto it.

"Here," I said, setting the plate on Tiago's knees.

"What are you going to have?" I had learned it was important that Tiago not eat alone and pulled a bar of nut-studded chocolate from my jacket pocket. "Ah, *bueno*," he said and picked up a nugget.

As we ate I described my guitar studies, what I had learned, my practice routines. "But the fingering is really hard."

"It will come. Don't watch your hands."

When I got up to leave, Tiago again tried to rise.

I made a *stay* motion with my hand. "No, not necessary."

He cocked his head in the direction of the bathroom. "*Sí*, necessary."

"Okay." I gave him a hand up. "I'll come back to see you soon."

He shuffled to the bathroom. Turning at the door, he pointed to the window ledge on which rested a small, brightly colored ceramic bowl. "There are keys. Take them."

I visited Tiago every few days, and each time he appeared stronger. One day the stench of smoke billowed out of the door when he opened it to my knock.

"I guess you can manage the stairs now," I said.

He waved the cigarette he was holding and grinned. "Don't tell."

"I won't." With the smoke smell permeating the room there wouldn't be any need to.

The following week I came across him perched on the bench near the Mercado de Triana, playing a languid piece on his guitar.

"How about a coffee?" I said.

"*Sí, sí!*"

I got two coffees and some churros at the market and we sat in the sun enjoying them. After, I saw him home and up the stairs to his apartment. When I came back down Paula was standing outside her office, arms folded, talking to a thick-set, floridly handsome man in a black cashmere overcoat. Behind him, a bald, muscular man in a dark suit and shirt leaned against a large black sedan and examined his nails. Both men could have come from central casting for a gangster movie. Conscious of staring, I was about to walk away when Mister Cashmere Coat spoke briefly to his sidekick. The bald man straightened up, helped his boss into the back of the car, and got in on the driver's side. As the car drew away, Paula lifted a hand in farewell.

"Hello, Paula," I called.

She glanced at me, a frown creasing her forehead. "Oh, Niels."

I gestured in the direction of the departed car. "A tough client?"

Her forehead cleared and she laughed. "Worse than that. He's my *tio*. How are you?"

"Well, thanks. Just brought Tiago home. He was busking by the market. Seems much better."

"Yes, thank goodness. Look, would you like to come in for a drink? I could use one."

"Sure."

I followed her into her office, where she opened a door in the credenza and pulled out a bottle of liquor.

"Is brandy okay?"

I nodded. She poured some into two coffee cups and handed me one, and we sat down.

"Your uncle—would he be Tiago's son?"

"If you can believe it."

I sipped the brandy, curious but hesitant to pursue the subject. "I met your sister," I said instead.

"Yes, Paloma mentioned it. We very much appreciate your visiting *Abuelo*. These last few weeks have been hard on him, and I know he enjoys it when you come."

"So, Paloma became a doctor and you became a lawyer? That's pretty impressive."

"Perhaps." Paula set her cup down, laced her fingers across her stomach, and smiled faintly. "You know, life for us, for *gitanos*, is difficult here. There's a lot of prejudice."

"Yes, I've seen that."

She nodded. "For women it's even worse. Apart from a lack of trust and opportunities, we're also constrained by our own culture, our traditions, beliefs, and fears. My mother was a very strong woman . . ." She looked away for a moment. "We lost her to COVID. Anyway, she had received some education and was quite forward thinking. She made sure that Paloma and I went to and stayed in school, and that we thought about our futures. When we were sixteen we decided to pursue professions that would let us help our community. A doctor and a lawyer, we figured. We drew lots to decide who would do which one."

Paula pantomimed making the draw.

"I thought I had been given the easier path." She smiled faintly. "Paloma's studies were longer and more arduous, but her work is straightforward and rarely morally ambiguous." She reached for the bottle. "Would you like more?"

I shook my head. "I should be getting home." I thanked her for the drink and, after some parting words, got up and left.

Chapter 13

FLAMENCO TOOK OVER MY life that winter and spring. I practiced scales until my hands cramped and my fingers ached. The guitar lessons progressed to the meat of flamenco—the *compás* and moods of the different *palos*—and I began to learn some simple phrases. Chords swirled like smoke through my mind as I drifted into sleep, and I rose each morning with a rush of anticipation. In time my fingers gained dexterity and intelligence. My guitar was male, I decided. Unlike my cellos, which had relaxed into my body and yielded to my fingers and bow, the guitar sparred with me, bucking and biting, sometimes drawing blood. And it resisted being named—it didn't need me to tell it who it was. When I wasn't playing I soaked up what I could from videos, recordings, or occasional live performances by flamenco artists.

    I shared all this with Tiago, whom I visited every few days. If it were in the evening I brought a bottle of wine along with the chicken nuggets—I tried other food but they were his favorite. While Tiago listened with interest to my experiences learning flamenco, he offered only occasional cryptic remarks. He had more to say about the flamenco greats I admired, sharp observations that I didn't always understand. When I tried to draw him out about his own background and past, he wasn't forthcoming. All I learned was that he was one of six or maybe seven children—he thought there was one who died as a baby when he was still very young—that his father traded in horses, the family moved around a lot in the area near Jerez de la Frontera and Cadiz, and he had worked on a ranch.

I continued the practice of documenting anything of interest—instructions, observations, experiences, facts, details, and any advice Tiago offered—and my journal grew to several hundred pages.

After one of my evening visits to Tiago, I took an alley between buildings that connected two main streets to shorten the route home by a few minutes. Halfway down the narrow passage a dark figure detached itself from the shadows. When I turned to retreat, a second figure blocked the exit and advanced toward me.

"Let's have your wallet," the first figure, a skinny boy in his teens, said. A knife flashed, its point aimed at my nose.

I had continued my regular workouts in the gym and briefly considered taking them on. Later, I would look back at that moment as a measure of the distance I had come in the two and a half years since leaving Canada—the thought would never have entered my mind before. But caution prevailed.

"No wallet." Reaching into my pocket, I pulled out the few Euros I was carrying and held them out. "Here's all the money I have."

"Ah, come on," the second kid said and started to slap my other pockets.

I gritted my teeth but held my arms away from my body. The kid found my phone and handed it to the first guy. He clicked it on and the screen reflected in the glitter of his eyes.

"Naw, it's a piece of shit," he said, thrusting it back at me.

I accepted the phone and slid it back into my pocket, hoping they would now leave me alone. They shifted from foot to foot, not happy with the slim pickings.

"Your watch!" the first kid said, thrusting his palm out.

I hesitated briefly. "It's just a watch."

"Don't matter." His fingers wiggled.

I slowly undid the buckle of the leather strap and removed it. There was a noise at the entrance to the alley. "*Vamos!*" the first kid said. I had started to pull the watch back but he snatched it and they took off.

I stood for a long time, my wrist cool and light. It was not *just* a watch, of course. It was a classic piece from a prestige jeweler that Papa Luke and Mama Ris gave me when I graduated from high school. I had worn it every day since. Papa Luke had been a monk once, leaving the order after he had met and fallen in love with Mama Ris. A deeply spiritual man, he had spent his life building a multi-dimensional mission to help people make sense of and come to terms with their lives. I thought of him now, the gentle, caring man who always seemed to sense when you needed to be asked how you were doing, who listened even to the most confused blather and puerile whingeing without judgement, who always came up with just the right words to make you feel better. The watch had been like a circle of his calm and kindness around my wrist and I felt exposed without it. I continued home, sadness slowing my steps. Papa Luke was possibly the one person who could have helped when everything fell apart that New Year's Eve. If he had been at home, if he had not been so far away in South America, I might have turned to him. And if I had, what a different course my life would have taken.

Chapter 14

ONE AFTERNOON IN JULY I was sitting in the shade of the olive tree, trying to escape the stifling heat that had built up in the apartment. The tavern kitchen door opened and Jana, one of the servers, stuck her head out.

"Someone at the restaurant wants to say hello."

"Who?"

"*No sé*," Jana said and went back inside.

I had made several acquaintances since arriving in Seville and assumed it was one of them. I went up to the apartment, put my guitar away, combed my hair, and went to the tavern. Jana indicated a couple sitting at a table on the terrace. The man had his back to me. I took two steps and froze, my heart aflutter. *It can't be.* I completed the distance in a few more steps and dropped my hand on the man's shoulder.

"Fox!"

Fox glanced up and began to rise, then stopped and gaped at me. "Jesus Christ, Niels, what the hell's happened to you?"

I grinned. "Quite a bit. But, man, Fox, it's so good to see you." I would have hugged him but he had sunk back into his seat, still staring at me, so I pulled out the chair beside him and sat down. "How on earth did you find me?"

Fox dismissed the question with a wave. "Everybody knows where you are. That woman you lived with let Fin know. But they're keeping their distance. That's what you wanted, right?" He had a way of smiling when he didn't mean it, a quick twitch of the left corner of his mouth. He gave me one now. "But you know me: I never do what people want."

"Well, today I'm awfully glad of that. So, what brings you to Spain? You can't have come all this way just to see me."

"We're out on our winter break, a group of us." He gestured to the woman seated across the table. "This is Belinda. Belinda, Niels."

Belinda was pretty—big, round cerulean blue eyes; pert nose; soft, full lips; long, sun-streaked hair pulled back into a ponytail—but she had the vapid presence of an activated android. I returned her limp handshake and turned back to Fox.

"So how the heck are you?"

Jana appeared at the table with their food before Fox could reply. Belinda started when a plate of salad was placed before her.

"But I didn't want olives!" She turned to Fox. "I thought you told them."

"I thought I did too, but my Spanish is a bit rusty."

"Do you want to send it back?" I said.

"There aren't that many, Belinda. Just pick them out," Fox said, his voice edged with impatience. Belinda pouted and pointedly forked the four offending olives to the side of the plate.

Fox had ordered the seafood stew and I quietly reveled in his presence while he took the first few bites. His hair was stylishly cut and his sculpted features lean and tanned. Wearing a pale-blue polo shirt with a fine-knit, lemon-yellow sweater draped over his shoulders, he could have been a model in a glossy ad for a designer label. Despite his vibrant youth and apparent well-being, however, his eyes had a desolate look.

"Everything going okay?" I said.

He shrugged. "I guess so. No complaints, really."

"You said you're on your winter break. So, still in school?" I frowned, calculating. "Thought you'd be done by now."

"I kind of shifted gears. Doing microbiology now. Still have a year to go."

"Microbiology! Wow. Never imagined you a science guy."

His lip twitched in another half-smile. "Yeah, me neither, but here I am."

"Are you still playing tennis?"

"Yeah, but not competitively. Never made it to the top leagues." He tapped his right thigh, the site of an injury he had suffered at nine when it was impaled on the tines of a pitchfork. "Couldn't get past the weakness in my leg."

"Sorry to hear that."

"Doesn't matter, really."

I let him get in a few more bites, and said, "Have you, ah, seen Mom and Dad recently?"

"Yeah, they came down for Christmas then went to Tasmania for a few weeks."

"How are they?"

"Fine, I guess. Not much changes there. Dad's continuing with his portrait commissions and your mom's published a new book.

My *mom? She's your mom too.* "Oh? What about?"

"Don't know. You can find out, I'm sure, on the internet." He looked at me curiously. "Don't you check up on them?"

I shrugged and mentally promised myself to do so. "And how are Papa Luke and Mama Ris?"

"I don't know why you still call them by those ridiculous names. I mean, it was one thing when we were kids, but now?"

"Come on, Fox, you know they love those pet names. Anyhow, are they okay?"

"I imagine so, haven't heard otherwise. The great guru on the hill has come out with another book too."

Belinda looked up from poking around her salad. "The great guru?"

"My grandfather. He's this wise old man who writes new-agey self-help books."

My eyes widened in shock at Fox's dismissal of Papa Luke and disparagement of his acclaimed body of work on spirituality. *What's happened to you, Fox*, I thought sadly.

Jana appeared and removed the plates. She frowned at the mess remaining on Belinda's—she had picked out the chicken and tomatoes and left everything else. "Was something wrong?" she asked me in Spanish.

"Maybe she wasn't hungry. Don't worry about it," I replied in kind.

"Look at you, rattling on like a native," Fox said.

Another server brought their desserts. Fox cut into his slice of almond cake. Belinda spooned up some flan, moved it around her mouth, and set down her spoon. "The texture is weird." She picked up her phone and began to fiddle with it.

"And your mother, how is she?" I said, trying to goose along the flagging conversation.

Fox looked up from his cake. "Fine, I guess."

"And your sister? She must be, what, thirteen, fourteen now?"

"Yeah. Don't see them much."

"I see," I said, although I didn't. Fox's reason for going to live and study in Australia had been to get to know his biological mother, Fiona, and half-sister Madeline, but he didn't seem to be particularly close to them. Why, then, was he staying there? His departure for Australia immediately after high school had shocked and saddened our parents, and they would no doubt be happy if he returned home, or to anywhere in North America. I perceived an uprootedness in Fox, a sense of being adrift. I leaned forward, trying to draw him out of himself.

"So what are your plans? How long are you here for?"

Fox put his fork down on the empty plate and pressed a napkin to his mouth. "We leave tomorrow for Granada, a couple of days there then to Barcelona, then back to Madrid."

"Oh, that soon? Can we visit before you go?"

Belinda gave a small cry. "I can't believe it! My phone just shut off. The battery's dead."

"Didn't you plug it in last night?" Fox said.

"I meant to, but I guess not." She looked around, her gaze passing over me like I wasn't there. "Can we go soon? I don't like it here and I want to see more of Seville."

"I guess we'd better go," Fox said.

"Can we get together tonight? I'll come over and meet you at your hotel, or wherever you like."

"Maybe."

"Come on, Fox. I mean, I haven't seen you for ages and don't know when I'll see you again."

"Well, I have to see what the other guys are going to do."

"Here, let me give you my cellphone number." I patted the pockets of my cargo shorts and, finding them empty, got up and fetched pen and paper from the bar. When I returned Jana was presenting Fox with the bill. I touched her arm and took the bill.

"It's on me," I said to Fox.

"Oh. Thanks."

I accompanied them out of the tavern, scribbling my phone number on the piece of paper as I walked. "Here. Give me a call," I said, handing the paper to Fox. "I'd love to have a good visit, get caught up."

He glanced at the number, nodded, and slipped the paper into his pocket. We stood awkwardly, unsure of how to say goodbye. I would have kissed Fox on the cheeks in the Spanish manner but didn't think he'd appreciate the display. I gave a small wave instead.

"So glad you found me."

"Yeah," Fox said with his little half-smile.

I spent the rest of the day exhilarated and distracted. When evening came I showered, dressed in my best clothes, poured myself a beer, and eagerly awaited Fox's call. Around ten o'clock I ate some bread and cheese to quiet my empty stomach. At midnight I undressed, brushed my teeth, and crawled into bed, heavy with disappointment.

I thought back to the awkward lunch and realized that Fox had not once asked me anything about myself: how I was, what I was doing, why I had left everything and gone off. Had he not wanted to get into personal matters with Belinda around? If so, why had he brought her? And he didn't seem particularly happy to see me or enjoy our reunion. Why had he bothered to get in touch? Did I even know this man with whom I had shared a home anymore?

After my mother had come back into my life and married Theo, Fox and I became stepbrothers. We settled in the Big House, the larger residence at Counter Point—Papa Luke and Mama Ris occupied a smaller waterfront cottage on the estate. Our first years as a family were, for me, perfect. Fox and I were inseparable then and I had loved him almost beyond reason.

Although I no longer lived with Fin in Vancouver, he still wielded considerable influence over my life. At his insistence I began serious instruction in the cello. Fox began to play tennis around the same time. When he showed an aptitude for the game, he also began an intense program of training and competition.

Inevitably we were drawn into different crowds, made new friends, and spent less time together. The difference in our dispositions became marked as well. I was a stolid, quiet, studious kind of guy and my school pals were similar geeky types. Despite being younger than me, Fox had a poise beyond his years and a mercurial nature that attracted people. He fell in with a set of arrogant and entitled boys—of which our private school had no shortage—who slouched through the hallways with a kind of world-weary hauteur and treated anyone outside their group with condescension. I recalled painfully an incident when I was sixteen that revealed just how far apart we had grown.

We were killing time outside the school grounds until the bus we took home arrived, Fox sharing a cigarette with a couple of his friends while I stood a short distance away. One of the group was grumbling about his father. A second joined in, calling his mother fat and useless.

"Yeah, my parents are pretty clueless, too," Fox said.

The first boy flicked the spent cigarette into a boxwood hedge. They said goodbye and headed off in their own directions. Fox came towards me, nodded in acknowledgement, and continued past to the stop where our bus was pulling in. When I didn't move, he stopped and looked back.

"Aren't you coming?"

"Fox, don't ever speak about our parents like that again."

He raised his eyebrows in disbelief and his face darkened. "And just who the fuck do you think you are?"

"Your brother."

"You're not my brother." He turned and walked with long, hard strides to the bus.

I was too stunned to follow and the bus left without me. Fox had taken a window seat but turned his face away as the bus drove past. He wasn't home when I finally got there—having dinner at a friend's house, my mother said—and left early the next morning for a tennis lesson. When he came home that afternoon, he tapped on my door and stuck his head in.

"Look, Niels, sorry about yesterday. You know I didn't mean it."

I regarded him warily for a moment. "Yeah."

He flashed me a wide grin. "Great! Any idea what's for dinner? I'm starved."

After, Fox went out of his way to be friendly. But his acid comment had cut deeply and I received his attentions cynically—Fox couldn't afford to be on bad terms with me. He had never grown out of the craziness that drove him to constantly push limits and test boundaries, as he himself had said, rarely doing what was wanted or expected of him. Since we were children he had counted on me to offer him cover or rescue him when things went south. The wing in which our bedrooms were located had its own entrance, and Fox often came and went without our parents' knowledge, speeding off into the night on his bike. Occasionally I'd be woken by a phone call asking me to pick him up or help him out of some bind. Whatever the hour, I'd obligingly crawl out of bed, dress, and head out to get him in the family's small, noiseless electric car, which was conveniently parked in the open carport, not turning on the headlights until I reached the road.

Giving up on sleep, I got out of bed, took a beer out of the refrigerator, and went outside. The summer breeze was light and warm against my bare legs and a few stars were visible above the city's ambient light. I sat down in a chair under the olive tree and popped open the can.

Looking back, Fox's disconnect from our little family probably began during the first great wave of the COVID pandemic, when little was understood about the virus or the threat it posed and everything that was not deemed essential was shut down. Like everyone else, we retreated into our home and limited our outings and contact with others to only what was strictly necessary, like shopping for food. Except for Fox, of course. He had fallen head over heels for Shadi, a gorgeous girl with waist-long black hair and long-lashed, almond-shaped eyes. During spring break, before everything shut down, she had gone to visit relatives in Iran with her parents. Early one afternoon in the second week of the lockdown, I heard the clink of a bicycle chain outside my window and saw Fox speed down the driveway. He returned before dinner. I said nothing about it to him or my parents. Two days later he went off again but returned shortly after.

Theo and I were at the supermarket stocking up on groceries one morning a few days later when his phone rang.

"It's Leah, probably forgot something." As he listened, his forehead drew into a frown. "How the hell . . ." After listening a minute longer, he turned to me. "How do you feel? Are you okay?"

"Yeah, I think so. Why?"

"Leah thinks Fox has COVID. She went to check on him when he didn't show up for breakfast and found him sick in bed. His symptoms match what the reports say."

He exchanged a few more words with Leah, turned off the phone, and studied me for a few moments. "You and Fox have been home for almost three weeks now and that's well past the incubation period for this virus. Have you been going out without our knowledge?"

"I, ah . . ."

Theo sighed. "Look, I know you guys go out now and then without letting us know."

My face became hot and red and I hoped the mask I wore covered it. How stupid to think that our parents were not aware of what was going on—they would have had to be deaf and blind not to have heard or seen our stealthy movements at least once. Since they were neither stupid nor uncaring, they must have allowed us this freedom recognizing that, with Fox's propensity to disobey, hard strictures and punishment would have been counterproductive. I swallowed hard, not knowing what to say.

"Niels, I understand that you two look out for each other, but this is important."

Can't remember when Fox last looked out for me, I thought. "I haven't gone out, but I think Fox maybe did."

"When?"

"Last Thursday, and then I think on Sunday as well."

"Who did he see?"

"I don't know, he didn't say anything to me."

"Shit." Theo glanced around. "You know, if Fox has it we could be infected as well. Let's finish up quickly and get out of here."

Back home we found some articles of my clothing, schoolbooks, computer, and cello heaped on the sofa in the living room.

"No, you can't come in here," Leah said through the French door between the breezeway lounge of our bedroom wing and the rest of the house.

"Jesus, Leah, are you feeling sick too?" Theo said.

"No. Not yet, anyway. But I've been in pretty close contact with Fox this morning so I could well be infected. I'll know in a few days."

"We might be too."

"Yes, you may, in which case we'll reconsider. But in the meantime you two need to stay out of here."

We worked out the logistics for Fox and Leah's quarantine. Theo and I cooked batches of food that we left with medicine and other provisions at the outside door—my mother was adamant that the French door remain closed and locked. Most of our communications were by phone.

Three days later my mother called to say that Fox was up and seemed better.

"Good, I'm coming over to talk to him," Theo said. "No, no, don't worry, it will be through the door."

I followed to say hello as well. Fox stood on the other side of the French door in his pajama bottoms and a loose, wrinkled T-shirt. His face was pale and his hair was a mess, but otherwise he looked fine.

"I am very relieved to hear that you're feeling better," Theo said.

Fox shrugged and grinned like it was no big deal.

"But," Theo continued, "I can't believe that you went out when you knew damn well you weren't supposed to."

"I didn't—"

Theo cut off the denial with a chop of his hand. Fox glowered at me over Theo's shoulder.

"Who did you go to see?"

"Why does it matter?"

"Why does it matter? Don't you realize how serious this is? At the very least we have to let them know that you're sick."

Fox's face reddened. "It was just Shadi," he mumbled.

"Shadi—that's the girl you've been mooning over, right?"

Fox pouted and scuffed the floor with his slippered foot. I started to back away. I didn't need to be part of this reprimand.

"No, you stay here," Theo said to me over his shoulder. "We all need to know what's going on." He turned back to Fox. "She's the one who went to Iran, right?"

"Yeah."

"It's one of the COVID hotspots right now. Have you spoken to her since?"

"No."

"We need to call them, see if they're sick as well."

"You don't have to. I know they are."

"How do you know this?"

"I found out the second time I went. They wouldn't let me see her."

Theo's face set in hard lines. "So, you knew you'd been in close contact with a person who had COVID and you didn't think it was necessary to let the rest of us know?"

"Well, I didn't feel sick then."

Theo drew in a long, slow breath. His mouth was white with anger. "Fox, I honestly don't understand how you could have been so thoughtless, so reckless as to put yourself and all of us at risk. This virus, it's brutal, especially for older people. Think about your grandparents. It could be deadly for Papa Luke with his heart condition. Now we're not going to be able to see them, to help them for who knows how long." He shook his head. "How you could have done this to us, Fox?"

The next morning Theo's phone rang while we were eating breakfast.

"Oh, Jesus, Leah . . ."

I looked up.

"You're sure?" He shook his head. "No, we're fine. My God, Leah . . . yeah, I know. Just tell us what you need, what you want us to do." He shut off the phone and buried his face in his hands.

"Mom's got it, hasn't she?"

He nodded.

"What should we do?"

He dropped his hands and gave me a bleak look. "What can we do? Just ride it out, I guess."

My mother was hit harder by the virus than Fox. Through the French door, Theo urged her to go to the hospital.

"Talked to doctor . . . not yet time . . . for hospital," she said. The words were separated by huge gulps of air and ended in a violent paroxysm of coughing.

Fox had hovered in the background during the exchange. Theo beckoned him forward.

"Listen, Fox, I'm going to bring that fold-up cot we have to the outside door and I want to you to set it up in the lounge where I can see it, and then get Leah to move in there. We need to keep an eye on her. She's pretty sick and may not be able to tell when it's time to go to the hospital."

"Sure, but I'm better now. Can't I come out?"

"Fox, even if you're feeling okay you still may be infectious. And even after, you're not coming out until Leah is completely well. Someone needs to be in there to help her."

"But that could be, like, days!"

"Yeah, could be."

Mom objected to being made to sleep in what she said was a fishbowl, but she was too weak to counter Theo's adamance. With my help he dragged a recliner to our side of the French door. He had spoken to the doctor and described what signs would indicate that Leah needed to be hospitalized. "We'll take turns watching," he said.

Over the next six days one of us was always in the recliner. Even when it was not my shift I usually sat with Theo if I had nowhere else to be, mostly because I didn't want to be alone, but also because I felt the need to bear witness to the extraordinary experience we were living. We passed the time on our computers, reading, or making desultory conversation, our eyes constantly confirming that the blanket over my mother's chest still rose and fell with her breath. Her piteous coughing was the worst to bear. *How are you feeling? Has anything changed? Do you need anything?* we would call out when she stirred. She would shake her head or raise a feeble hand in response, too fatigued to speak.

Fox stayed in his own room, only coming to the lounge when either Theo or I phoned him—occasionally in the middle of the night—to say that Mom needed assistance of some kind. He would help her to the bathroom, tidy up her makeshift bed, keep her water jug filled, and heat up her food and hold the tray steady on her lap as she picked at it. I watched this necessary intimacy with a mix of jealousy and frustration, because I knew

Fox resented his confinement and the obligation of performing these small services.

"Dad's just punishing me," he said when I phoned him once.

"Come on, Fox, this isn't about you."

I was dozing in the recliner early one morning when my mother threw off her covers and got out of bed. Her long hair was tousled and dull, and her pajamas hung as though from sticks.

I leapt up. "Mom! Mom, wait, I'll call Fox."

She gave a dismissive wave but I punched in his number and told him he was needed. He stumbled into the room half-asleep—it wasn't yet six o'clock. They spoke and he helped her out of the room, waving as he went. When she had not returned by six thirty, I called Fox again.

"Ah, geez!" he said when he finally answered. "Don't worry, she's fine. She's had a shower and is drying her hair now. I think she's feeling better."

I called Theo to let him know. He rushed over and we waited for Mom to come back into the lounge. Ten minutes later she walked unsteadily towards where we stood on the other side of the French door, gripping furniture she passed for support. Her long hair streamed behind her and her face, thinned by the days of illness, was radiant.

She touched her fingers to her lips and pressed them to the window in front of Theo's face. "Hello, darling." She turned and touched the glass in front of me. "And how are you, Niels dear?"

"Fine, Mom. I'm just fine," I said, my head light with relief.

After the COVID episode Fox closed in on himself, spending much of his time in his room. At meals his contribution to the conversation was limited to perfunctory responses to questions. When pandemic restrictions relaxed in the summer he spent most of his time away, playing tennis or hanging out with his buddies. In September Fox and I returned to a school environment distorted by controls and restrictions. We wore masks, traveled by car rather than bus, and returned home immediately after classes ended. On four occasions we reverted to online classes after COVID cases were found in our school. Thrust into each other's company by circumstances, we spent more time together, going on walks, watching movies, playing chess and other games. I thought our friendship had been restored. After I left for university in Toronto the following fall we kept in sporadic touch. At the end of my first year I returned home for a long visit before heading to Vienna to attend a cello workshop. While I was there I received a short note from my mother saying that Fox had left for Australia to live with Fiona, and that he planned to attend university there. He had said nothing about these plans when I had seen him two weeks previously, nor, apparently, had he let our parents know until a few days before he left. He neither wrote nor phoned to say goodbye.

Chapter 15

I HAD OTHER VISITORS that summer. Jax and Polly stopped by on their way to Italy, where Jax was participating in a Vivaldi festival. *A busman's honeymoon,* she wrote. *We got married last week. A tiny affair, just Polly's mom and dad, Steve and Sheila, and a handful of friends.* For a wedding gift I got them a room at a small hotel close to the tavern for the four nights they planned to stay. The trip was also a celebration of Jax's receiving her PhD and landing a year-long contract to teach at a junior college in Toronto.

In the arrivals lounge at the airport we greeted each other with whoops and long, hard embraces. They looked much the same as before: Jax in a cream linen jacket, white shirt, and chinos, Polly in a flowery sundress and short-sleeved cardigan. Jax freed herself from my hug and stepped back.

"Good god, Nielie, you've turned into a hunk."

I had taken the days of their visit off work and toured them through the city's attractions, hiding from the fierce sun in galleries, museums, and churches. When the crowds overwhelmed I took them to places I knew off the main path, where we drank cold beer and stuffed ourselves with tapas. On their last night we came back to my place and sat drinking wine under the olive tree.

"I don't know about you guys, but with the heat and the wine I'm exhausted," Polly said.

Jax took her hand. "Honey, I'm not ready to go just yet. Can you hang in a bit longer?"

"Why don't you have a lie down if you're tired?" I said.

"Yeah, okay," Polly said equably.

I led her to the bed in Daniel's room. She curled up, and in the two minutes it took me to find and cover her with a light throw, she fell asleep. I got another bottle of the crisp, slightly fizzy *vino verde* we had been drinking and returned to Jax.

"Thanks for that, Niels. She hasn't been sleeping well, still a bit of jetlag."

I topped up our glasses. "No problem. You two really suit."

"Yeah, she keeps me centered." Jax took a sip of wine. "Now, Nielie, tell me more about the guitar business."

We had taken in a flamenco show and I had mentioned in passing that I was learning how to play. Jax didn't say anything then but obviously had not forgotten.

"It's a bit of a cliché, I know, like going native. But I'm totally in its grip right now." I told her about meeting Tiago, the shock I had when I first touched his guitar, how we found my own, the lessons I was taking.

"Flamenco's not simple. There are so many dimensions. To start, it's based on a different scale than Western music—the fifth harmonic minor mode, you know, what they call Phrygian dominant scale." I described *compás*, the complex finger work, and the different musical forms. "And you don't just play off sheet music. Although there are set structures and pieces, flamenco usually means improvising, or at least providing your own interpretation within the form. But to improvise, even interpret, you really have to know what you're doing. Players who grow up with flamenco seem to absorb it like a language, but for an outsider like me? Learning to play, even with all the music I've done in my life, has been more demanding than I could have imagined."

"So play me something."

"I'm really not very good yet."

"Come on, Nielie, it's me."

I got my guitar, fiddled with the tuning, and played a short, lively *alegría* that I had almost mastered. I made a couple of mistakes but they got lost in the flurry of notes. Jax clapped when it was over and I flushed with pleasure—it was my first performance outside of lessons.

"Do another."

"I'm only just learning these, so there may be some bumps." I played a fandango then finished with a slow, melancholy piece I particularly liked.

"Very nice. So where are you going with this, Nielie?"

I leaned the guitar against my chair and sat back. "I have absolutely no idea," I said.

Chapter 16

"YOU TOLD ME TO come and see you when I learned how to play guitar." I had found Tiago at one of his favorite busking spots, a bench under a large, shady tree. "Can I play for you?"

He smiled and motioned to the bench beside him. "*Sí, sí.*"

I sat down and opened my guitar case, fumbling with the latches. When the guitar was in position on my knee, I hesitated. In all the performances I had ever done, never had I felt so nervous. I flexed my fingers and began, playing the five pieces I had practiced until I could perform them in my sleep. An older woman who had been listening dropped some coins in Tiago's hat before moving on.

He raised an eyebrow. "You have a fan."

I waved away the comment in embarrassment and cleared my throat. "What do you think?"

Tiago studied me for few moments with a slight smile. "You can play guitar, that is good. Maybe you can play flamenco. I don't know yet."

Deflated by Tiago's comments, I slumped in the seat. Despite the months of study and practice I was apparently deficient in some way. He touched me lightly on the hand.

"You come to my house. We'll see."

"Is there any point?" I said testily.

He waggled his head. "Come tonight."

"I can't, I work." *Smarten up*, I thought. It's not like I hadn't been critiqued before. "Maybe Sunday?"

"*Sí, bueno.*" Tiago bent and picked the two coins the old lady who had listened to me play had dropped into the hat and held them out for me.

I waved them away. "No, no." I stood up and slipped my guitar into its case. "See you on Sunday."

"It is not enough to play well or fast," Tiago said. "That is fine, in its way, but without *feeling* it is just showing off."

We were in his apartment, hunched over our guitars. My eyes stung; smoke hung heavy in the air and another cigarette was consuming itself in a saucer on the table. I understood playing with feeling—it was fundamental to musical interpretation.

"So what am I missing?" I tried not to sound petulant.

Tiago reached over and stubbed out the smoldering cigarette. I was relieved when he didn't light another one. He shifted back into his chair and looked at me.

"You are playing with your head." He tapped his crown with a knotted and nicotine-stained finger. He used the same finger to touch his chest. "Flamenco you need to play with your heart, your gut"—his hand made a vague gesture towards his groin—"and your balls."

"Okaaaay."

"To start, you need to loosen up. Don't think so much. Listen to the music inside, to where it's coming from." He tapped his midriff.

I looked at him blankly.

"Here." He settled his guitar into position. "I'm going to play a little bit. Then you play something back."

"You mean, repeat what you played?"

"Not repeat—reply. Like we're talking to each other. But don't change the subject."

"Like improvising?"

"Something like that."

Tiago played a short melody, bright and lively. I closed my eyes and saw children skipping, balls bouncing, heard chatter and laughter. When he stopped I opened my eyes, nodded, and began my own melody. I worked with the *compás* he had laid down and replied with a similar musical line, but introduced some minor chords to describe a bully threatening to disrupt their play. Tiago's eyebrows rose and his reply elaborated on the threats and incorporated more dramatic accents. We went back and forth like this, progressing to an altercation, tears, rescue, punishment, comforting, a darkening sky, pounding rain, and, finally, returning to home and shelter. At least that's how the story unfolded in my mind. When it was over we sat and grinned at each other.

"Now you start the story," Tiago said. "Have you ever been in love?"

"I think so. I mean, I am, yes." I thought for a minute then chose a solemn piece to describe both the connection and the distance between Aude and me.

"She is not here," Tiago said when I was done.

I shook my head.

"Why are you not with her?"

"Do you want to me to tell you in words or in music?"

"Music, of course."

Collecting my thoughts, I began with a storm of chords for the cataclysm that had propelled me out of my life, then tried to describe the journey I was on, ending with a light, uplifting note of hope.

"Something happened?" Tiago said.

"Yes."

Looking at him, I noticed that the lines of his face seemed deeper than usual, the hollows of his eyes darker. "I'm tiring you."

He pursed his lips and waved the comment away.

"Still, I should go." I rose and put my guitar in its case. "Can we do this again?"

Tiago set his own guitar aside. "*Sí*, of course," he said.

I digested the experience for several days before returning to Tiago's. My improvisations had been clumsy at best, but I had felt a spark of something. I could not have articulated what it was, yet I understood it in a formless, inexact way. Like removing the time dimension from music, or coming at it from the inside out. Whatever: the comprehension buzzed subcutaneously, like an itch.

Beyond that I had the sense of having passed some test with Tiago. He was quite capable of telling me to forget it when I had asked to come back, if that was what he thought. When I did return, he took up his guitar cordially, even enthusiastically. We played the dialogue game, or focused on some specific element of playing, or talked about how to approach different flamenco music structures and styles. When he played I watched carefully as his darkened, twisted fingers negotiated with the strings, sometimes delicately, sometimes recklessly, sometimes violently, his taps minor explosions on the skin of the guitar.

Chapter 17

"DO YOU WANT TO go to a wedding?" Tiago said. He was taking a cigarette break during one of our sessions in his apartment.

"One of your granddaughters?"

"No. My friend Paco's grandson."

"But I'd be a stranger. Why would they want me to attend?"

"Because you would bring me."

"Oh. You have no other way to get there?"

Tiago shook his head. "It's at his son's farm, Paco lives there." He carefully drew on the small stub of the cigarette pinched between his fingers, crushed what remained in the saucer, and snorted out twin streams of smoke.

"Where exactly is it?"

"Near Cadiz. I know the way."

"When?"

"Not this weekend but the next."

"So, what? A couple of days away?"

Tiago pursed his lips and shrugged. "Three, maybe four."

The idea appealed. I didn't often have the chance to get out into the country, and a local wedding would be an interesting experience. "Is your friend *gitano*, too?"

"Of course."

"Let me see if I can get the time off."

Paula's office was still open, so I dropped in to say hello as I often did when she was there and free.

"Niels! Nice to see you. How is the flamenco coming?"

"Learning a lot from your grandfather."

"He enjoys it very much, you know."

"Well, he's very patient with me, anyway."

"He says you have *compás*."

"You mean, I have rhythm?"

"It means a bit more than that. Anyway, how are you doing?"

I told her I was fine and mentioned Tiago's invitation to attend the wedding with him.

"Ah. He wants very much to go but neither Paloma nor I have the time to take him. Will you go?"

"If I can. What do I need to know?"

She thought for a moment. "You will have to make your own sleeping arrangements. Will you rent a vehicle?"

I nodded.

"A van big enough to sleep in would be best. Of course you will need pillows and blankets."

"Will there be bathrooms and things like that?" I said, slightly alarmed.

"Oh yes. A bit rustic but good enough. I have been to this farm. They grow olives and raise cattle. *Abuelo* used to work there."

"Yes, he mentioned working on a ranch once." I sat Tiago on a horse in my mind and found it suited him well. "How about food?"

"That's something you won't have to worry about—there's sure to be lots of it. But it's always good to bring wine."

"A *gitano* wedding?" Emilio said when I requested the time off. "Yes, you must go. It is quite an experience. I've been to a couple. My grandmother was a *gitana*, you know, and I still have distant relatives out there."

I quizzed him about this revelation of his ancestry.

"She had been disgraced, somehow—*gitanos* have this complex code they follow. The story goes that my grandfather saw her selling things in the market and somehow got to know of her situation. He rescued her, although it wasn't entirely a selfless act as she was apparently quite beautiful."

"You've never thought to claim that part of your heritage?"

"They don't have an easy time of it, you know." His eyes creased in a big smile. "Although, sometimes when I hear a good flamenco *cante* my blood fizzes a little."

I rented a van with a cargo bay long enough to stretch out in. The thought of sharing the space with Tiago for several nights gave me pause, but I carried on—it was intended to be an adventure, after all. When I picked Tiago up in the early afternoon of our trip he was nattily dressed in a new suit, hat, and scarf. The suit was from another era, with sleeves that dragged on his knuckles and trouser hems that had been inexpertly shortened, but it had seen little wear. He heaved his guitar case and a battered yellow canvas duffel bag into the back of the van.

"Aren't you bringing a blanket or something?" I said.

He shook his head. "Where's your guitar?"

"I didn't think I'd need it."

He got into the passenger seat and made a *go-go* motion with his hand. "Always bring your guitar."

"If you say so."

I returned to the tavern. In addition to my guitar I brought another pillow and more covers. Sharing the cargo bay with Tiago was one thing, sharing my blankets was another.

I had not been outside Seville since my excursions with Daniel the previous summer and enjoyed the drive through the hilly Andalusian landscape, the raw umber soil showing through the parched greenery like scalp through a head of thinning hair. The late August sun beat down fiercely on the van. Tiago insisted that we ride with the windows open rather than using the air conditioner. The wind whistling through the cabin dried my eyes but I blinked rather than argued—it had been hard enough to get him to use his seatbelt. He took in everything around him with a wide grin and patches of color in his cheeks, pointing out places or things of particular interest.

"Turn here!" he said.

I braked abruptly and turned onto a secondary road that led into the hills. When we entered a small town he glanced from side to side then pointed.

"There, that store. We should get wine."

We parked near the store and went in. Tiago got a cart, pushed it to the alcohol section, and, without consulting the prices, chose and placed several bottles of wine into it. On the way to the till I snagged some water and fruit. When it came time to pay, Tiago gave me with a beatific smile and I obligingly pulled out my credit card.

A few miles beyond the town, Tiago directed me to a side road and leaned forward in his seat. "*Aquí, aquí!*" he said as we approached a driveway. We turned in and followed a road through an olive grove, the trees dusty and seemingly fatigued under their burden of hard green fruit. Shortly after we burst into a large compound anchored by a white U-shaped farmhouse whose ends were connected by a wall to create a courtyard. Some distance behind it was what looked like a barn. A few smaller buildings were scattered around, a couple apparently residences, the rest sheds for equipment and supplies. All were white and had shallow gable roofs made of the red tile typical of the region.

A large hand-drawn arrow pointed in the direction of the barn where two men stood: one young, holding a clipboard, the other much older. As we approached, Tiago stuck his head out the window and hollered, "Aye, Paco!" The young man with the clipboard indicated that we should continue on through an open gate into a large fenced corral. There were some vehicles already there, four cars and two camper vans. The occupants of the vehicles milled around, setting up tents, small tables, and folding chairs. As I backed into the space to which we had been directed, the older man waddled over on bowed legs. With his bald head, sun-darkened complexion, and furrowed face, he looked like an ambulant walnut. Tiago was out of the van before I killed the engine. He and the other man hugged and thumped each other on the back. After some chatter they headed in the direction of one of the smaller residences with their arms around each other's shoulders. Unsure of what to do, I went over to the guy with the clipboard. He was about my age, a few inches shorter, and had a dark-complexioned, alert face.

"Is there a toilet anywhere?" I said.

He cocked his head to an area in a pasture beyond the corral, where there was activity around three large semi-trailer trucks. "They're just setting them up. In the meantime, there's one at the other end of the barn you can use."

I followed the perimeter of the building until I found the correct door. When I was done I headed back to the van. Another vehicle had pulled up. The clipboard guy directed it around the barn to another corral where a few cars also were parked. When it pulled away I extended my hand.

"I didn't introduce myself earlier. I'm Niels."

He shook it. "I'm Juan, Rafael's cousin."

"Rafael?"

He looked at me curiously. "The groom."

"Oh! Sorry. I just brought Tiago." I motioned in the direction in which he had disappeared. "I'm kind of an interloper."

Juan smiled. "No problem—glad you did. Are you a relative of his?"

I was flattered that my Spanish, which had steadily improved as I lived and worked in the language, was good enough for him to consider me a native. "No, I'm learning flamenco from him."

Juan's eyebrows rose. "Ah, you must be good then."

I shrugged. "Listen, I don't know anyone and I haven't anything to do. Can I help in some way?"

He started to decline then his eyes brightened. "Yeah, if you don't mind taking over here, there are other things I could be doing." He showed me the clipboard, flipping through the pages. On each was printed a table with three columns. Names were typed in the first column, the other two left empty. Juan had scribbled notes in some of these. "When they show up, ask them if they're camping. If so, tell them to park in the corral you're in. If not, tell them to go around the barn to the other one. Write down where they go and how many are in the party."

"Okay, just let me get my hat." I went to the van, put my hat on, grabbed a bottle of water, and came back.

Juan handed me the clipboard with thanks and headed in the direction of the semis in the pasture. They had unloaded two industrial-looking trailers and eight portable toilets. One of the semis was making rumbling noises preparatory to leaving. A car pulled up and I turned my attention to it.

I spent the remainder of the afternoon directing traffic. Ten more vehicles were added to the camping corral, twenty-two to the other one. The industrial-looking trailers turned out to house showers, wash basins, and toilets and were already in use. Clatter and cooking smells from the farmhouse drifted over to where I stood. I marveled at the logistics and cost required to accommodate the expected guests.

Around seven o'clock, Juan and another guy came over. Juan handed me a beer.

"*Gracias*, Niels. Mateo will take over for a while. There are food and drinks at the house. Could you let the others know?"

I left him explaining the parking setup to Mateo and headed

back to the van, glad of the break. I downed the beer in a few swallows and went around the corral to tell the campers about the food. Among the last were two young women who had come in an older sedan with a Swedish license plate. They were struggling to set up a small tent.

"We can't get the pegs in, the ground is too hard," the taller of the two women said. She had the hardy build, scrubbed face, and strawberry-blond hair of a northerner and spoke Spanish with an accent I didn't recognize.

"It's a corral for cattle so the ground has probably been beaten down," I said.

The other girl, all delicate bones, liquid eyes, and silky black hair, raised her hand to her mouth in alarm. "There aren't any, you know, cow pats around are there?"

"I'm sure they would have cleaned any up before people arrived. I've been around most of it and haven't seen any. Here, let me give you a hand."

The ground was indeed hard but I was able to insert the pegs deep enough to secure the tent.

"*Muchas gracias!* I'm Lisa," the dark girl said.

The strawberry blonde held out her hand. "And I'm Ebba." I shook it and introduced myself.

"Let's finish up and go get something to eat. I'm famished," Ebba said.

Lisa smoothed down her hair. "I need to freshen up."

Ebba gestured impatiently. "Oh, you're fine."

"But it's so dusty."

I left them quibbling about how and where and whether they would be able to wash and dress and returned to the van to find Tiago struggling with the door handle.

"You lock the van! Why do you lock the van? I need my things."

I pressed the key fob and, still muttering, he yanked the back door open and pulled out his guitar case and duffel bag.

Spying the wine, he grabbed three bottles, stuffed them into his bag and turned to leave.

"Wait! Aren't you staying here tonight?"

He looked offended at the idea. "Why would I stay here? I stay with Paco."

"Okay, just so I know where you are."

He *humphed* and walked off. It seemed that, having served my purpose, I didn't merit further consideration, but that suited me fine—I was quite happy to have the van to myself.

Lisa and Ebba came over. "We're going to eat. Do you want to come?"

The food and drinks buffet was set up under a large events tent by the farmhouse, numerous long tables with benches arranged around it. We loaded our plates and carried them to a table where people Lisa knew were sitting. As we introduced ourselves around, Ebba learned I was Canadian. She switched from speaking Spanish to English, saying she knew it better, and cut us off from the others. She was in Spain to research what she called the plight of the *gitanos* for her doctorate from Uppsala University. Lisa was her flat-mate, and through her she had become friends with Sofia, the bride. I told her I was studying flamenco guitar and had accompanied my teacher to the wedding.

While we were eating, Rafael's father and mother, the proprietors of the estate, came around and greeted everyone. Their prosperity was writ large in their handsome faces, proud bearing, and expensive clothes. The bride's parents, somehow smaller and more amorphous, followed in their train, seemingly dazzled by events. It was clear where the advantage of the union lay.

"When will we see the bride and groom?" I asked Lisa.

"Oh, we're unlikely to see them tonight. They're kept separate before the wedding."

By the time we finished eating, night had fallen. We left our dishes at a station in the back to be washed by a group of older women up to their elbows in small tubs of sudsy water. A fire had been lit in a rock-lined pit and chairs arranged four rows deep in an oval around it. We refilled our wineglasses and headed over. A half hour later, Tiago appeared at my elbow.

"Where's your guitar?"

"In the van. Why?"

"Go get it."

He moved off in the direction of a cluster of vacant chairs in a section of the first ring.

I got my guitar and returned to the fire with some misgivings. When he caught sight of me, Tiago beckoned and pointed to the chair to the left and slightly behind him. Two other guitarists had joined him as well as Paco and an older woman he introduced as his sister Maria. *What the hell?* I thought. Did Tiago really expect me to play with these obviously seasoned musicians? Paco and Maria began laying down a rhythm with *palmas*, the flamenco handclapping. One of the guitarists, a young man with soft round features and plump cheeks, nodded and began to play a sprightly *alegría*. He was okay, but not great. He played for several minutes then the other guitarist, a forty-something man with a full mustache and bushy brows, took over and the beat changed to a *bulería*. He had a firmer command of his instrument and played with verve.

After an extended duet they pulled back and nodded to Tiago. He began slowly, an old man playing a melancholy *siguiriya*. It was quickly apparent that Tiago's playing had a crispness, clarity, and depth in timbre that the others lacked. The tone of his music changed and the pace picked up, then picked up again, the tension building. I sat on the edge of my chair, holding my breath. Others were equally rapt. The intermittent shouts of *olé* ceased. Tiago raged on, tearing at the strings of his guitar, his left hand flying up and down the fretboard. He played for over fifteen minutes, ending with a resolution that felt like a small bomb exploding. I fell back in my chair, spent. It was silent for several long seconds, then the crowd erupted in applause and a chorus of *olés*. Tiago waved his hand bashfully. When it had quietened down, people rose to refresh drinks as though it were the intermission of a performance. Several came over to talk to Tiago. I stayed in my chair, wondering what was going to happen next.

After people had returned to their seats the chatter grew lighter and finally ceased, and they turned towards us. Tiago introduced me with a gesture. After a few seconds of scrambled thought I took a deep breath, settled my guitar into place, and launched into a rhumba I knew well. It was a flashy piece but easy to play. The jaunty tune got people nodding and swaying. Some of the younger ones got up and began to dance. I looped through the refrains a couple of times with some variations to extend the piece beyond its three minutes. When I finished, relieved that I had made no major flubs, the applause was enthusiastic if short.

After, the tenor of the music changed. The focus turned to Paco, who sang a traditional flamenco *cante* to Tiago's accompaniment. Accompanying a singer is different from playing solo guitar and I observed closely. When Paco was done, Maria sang with one of the other guitarists. At midnight Juan doused the fire to signal the end of the music and people headed home or to their makeshift beds. At the van I realized that I had not brought any form of lighting. I fumbled a bed together in the dark, undressed, and tried to get comfortable on the metal floor. I still vibrated from the scope and power of Tiago's playing, so much beyond what I had heard from him previously. But this was his real world—a dark night, a fire, an audience of true aficionados—not the Seville streets with their indifferent passersby or the emptiness of his small rooms. *If I could become even half as good*, I thought as I drifted off to sleep. *Even a quarter* . . .

The wedding celebration began in late morning with a service in the church of the village a few miles away. Only immediate family and friends attended because of limited space. While they were gone vehicles arrived steadily, disgorging people before parking in the corral. By noon a large crowd milled around near the farmhouse, the men in formal suits, the women in brightly colored dresses like so many hothouse flowers. I stood on the edge of the crowd feeling decidedly underdressed in my white shirt and black slacks. Ebba came up beside me.

"A bit gaudy, don't you think?"

I glanced at her. Her own dress was a beige linen shift. "Well, it *is* a celebration."

In the early afternoon a convoy of luxury cars swept into the yard. People surged to the first one, from which the bride and groom emerged. They were both dressed in white, but Rafael was eclipsed by Sofia, a vision in a bejeweled headdress and extravagantly ruffled gown whose bodice sparkled in the sunlight from the tiny crystals that encrusted it.

"They're much too young to marry," Ebba said quietly.

"Why do you say that?"

"Sofia's just turned twenty and Rafael's not much older. Neither have really lived yet. But it's the *gitano* way, you know, to marry young."

I ignored her and applauded with the others as the bride and groom swept past into the forecourt of the house. When lunch was announced I found a place at a table on the periphery. Ebba had stayed close and sat down with me. Lisa, looking like a blue-green butterfly in her own party dress, was with a group of other *gitanas*. The meal was lavish, built around the barbequed carcass of a steer. Empty pitchers of wine were quickly replaced by full ones. By mid-afternoon the air was filled with raucous voices, shrieks of laughter, and pungent cigarette smoke.

Clamor in the forecourt of the house brought people to their feet from the tables and rushing towards it. Ebba and I followed. The bride had emerged from the house, surrounded by a group of women who were waving their hands and singing.

"I don't believe it!" Ebba said. "I think they've just done the *pañuelo* ritual."

"What's that?"

She gave an exasperated sigh. "You wouldn't believe it in this day and age, but they verify that the bride is a virgin. It's still very important for *gitanos* that women are virgins when they marry."

"How do they do that?"

Ebba grimaced. "They actually test it physically."

"Good heavens. How?"

"A wise woman is hired for the purpose. There's a special cloth, like a large handkerchief. She wraps it around her finger and, you know . . ." Ebba twirled her index finger in demonstration. "If everything is as it should be, there'll be spots on the cloth."

"Oh."

"And it's not even private—the married women are witnesses. When it's confirmed the cloth is shown to everyone and the women sing a song, *el yeli*, to announce it to the world. I think that's what they're doing now."

People began to shower the couple with something small and brightly colored.

"Is that a kind of confetti?" I said.

"No, it's sugared almonds. Darn! Lisa and I brought some but I forgot them in the tent. Maybe she took them." She glanced around. "You're taller, can you see her anywhere?"

I caught sight of Lisa's butterfly dress among the women surrounding Sofia. "She's with the other women near the bride."

"Then she must have."

A couple of men approached Sofia and lifted her onto their shoulders. Rafael was similarly hoisted up on the shoulders of a giant of a man. The singing swelled as the crowd joined in and people began to sway and dance. Rafael pulled off his jacket and began to remove his shirt.

"Why's he doing that?"

Ebba shrugged. "I don't know, it's just part of the ritual. The groom, too, is supposed to be a virgin but they have more latitude—don't you guys always? They're certainly not subject to an inspection of some kind. In theory they're supposed to remain faithful once they're married. I wonder how many do?"

We watched them for several more minutes. The men dancing around with the bride and groom on their shoulders seemed inexhaustible.

"What happens if the bride doesn't pass the virginity test?"

Ebba's eyebrows rose. "Ah, things can get quite serious and messy then. Bride and her family are disgraced. Lots of shame. Marriage can be annulled." She shook her head. "I can't imagine having to go through all this. And Sofia, she's a modern, educated woman and still she agrees to do this."

"Yeah, it's hard to understand. But if she's modern and educated and still agrees to do it, it must be meaningful to her." I gestured towards where Sofia was laughing and waving as she was danced around the crowd. "She hardly seems unwilling."

Ebba gave me a sharp glance. "So, you agree that women should be treated like this?"

"That's not what I'm saying. I don't think women—or anyone—should be forced to do anything they don't want to do. But some of these practices that are foreign to us, to our way of thinking and behaving, have logic and meaning in their own cultures, and I don't think it's our place to tell them what they should or shouldn't do."

Ebba made a disgusted sound. "So, you think that if a woman is conditioned to believe that female genital mutilation is logical and meaningful, we on the outside should say, hey, go ahead, do that awful thing to your female children?"

I was beginning to feel out of my depth. *What would my*

mother say to this? I remembered a dinner-table discussion many years before on the scope of human rights and who should decide what they cover. "I think the sanctity of the human body and mind is universal and inviolate. I'm not sure how much a test for virginity that a person agrees to abuses it. The notion of virginity at marriage is not in itself necessarily a bad thing, but I agree that it should perhaps be a more private matter."

Ebba gave me an arch look. "Will you be a virgin when you get married?"

"What?" I felt my face reddening.

Ebba laughed. "You're embarrassed! Good god, are you a virgin?"

"How on earth did we arrive here?"

She studied me with a slight smile. "So why don't you sleep with me tonight? That way, if you are a virgin, we can get you over the hump, and if you're not it won't matter. We could make that van of yours really rock."

"I have a girlfriend," I said stiffly.

"She wouldn't know—she's obviously not around. Do you know what *she's* getting up to?"

I changed the subject. "Anyhow, as a researcher, shouldn't you be a bit less judgmental about your subjects?"

Ebba snorted in response and we turned back to watch the *el yeli* celebration.

The rest of the day was a blur of endless food and drink. A flamenco-flavored rock band started up as night began to fall and played until midnight. After the *el yeli* business, Lisa drew Ebba and me into a group of young people with whom we talked and drank and danced. When things finally wound down I headed back to the van with a large bottle of water tucked under my arm to ward off a hangover, and made sure to lock the door in case Ebba chose to remind me of her invitation to have sex.

The next day was more of the same. No one staying at the farm seemed in a rush to leave, and many of the guests from the previous day returned for an enormous buffet lunch. I had had my fill of partying and sought out Tiago to see when we would be heading home.

"Not today!"

"I'm going to have to get back to work soon."

"Okay, okay. Tomorrow, maybe."

Maybe? I sought out Lisa. "How long does this go on for?"

"Hard to say. Ebba and I will be going this afternoon, though."

Many of the other guests departed for good after the evening meal. When night fell, a fire was lit in the rock pit and those remaining pulled chairs around it. Tiago came up to me.

"Where's your guitar?"

"You want me to get it?"

"Of course. We must play."

When I returned to the fire circle with my guitar, Tiago beckoned me over to where he was sitting with Paco and Maria. I looked around, hoping the other two guitarists were still there. They weren't. Apart from Juan and one of his friends, who was tending the fire, the people were older, family and close friends, probably. Tiago started playing a familiar number and nodded at me to follow. An older woman wrapped in a fine, fringed shawl with her white hair pulled back tightly in a bun rose and began dancing, her steps light, her hand movements fluid and expressive. Chairs were pulled back to give her space and another older woman joined her. Paco began a *cante* and I followed Tiago in accompaniment.

The parents of the bridal couple, their children long departed, joined the circle around the fire. People clapped and Maria sang a *cante* of honor and congratulations, which they accepted with gracious nods. Wine continued to flow, my glass never emptying. The fire leapt and crackled, the flames tonguing the darkness. Tiago and I played, Maria and Paco took turns singing light, cheerful, humorous songs. People danced and did *palmas* in accompaniment.

As the night wore on the music slowed and become more somber. People settled into their chairs and grew quiet. Paco sang a melancholy *cante* about a woman who is swept away while crossing a river with her lover and how, try as he might, he couldn't keep her fingers from slipping through his, and her look of longing and loss as the water claimed her. A few people wiped their eyes when he was done. Then Maria uttered a cry of such savage anguish that the hair rose on the back of my neck. The lament that followed was beyond anything I had heard before. It spoke of hardship and heartbreak, of unendurable struggles, of defeat without hope, of a darkness so profound that death was embraced like a lover. Maria's voice slashed at the air, the despair in it a jagged and rusty blade. Her song ripped me open and all the pain and loss and sorrow I had ever felt boiled up and spewed out. I began to weep uncontrollably. Mortified, I buried my face in my hands and swallowed great, gulping sobs. I felt a hand on my shoulder: Tiago. He held it there for several moments then gave a squeeze and returned to playing the guitar.

I don't remember much about the rest of the night. Back at the van I rolled myself up in a blanket without undressing and fell into a deep, dreamless sleep. The next morning a buffet breakfast was set out in the forecourt to the house as on previous mornings, but most of the tables and chairs had been packed away and the semis had arrived to remove the bathhouses and toilets. The dusty, well-trodden grounds had a weary, forlorn look—the party was definitely over.

I found Tiago at a table with Paco finishing their breakfast. "We go this morning?" I said.

Tiago nodded. "I will come soon."

An hour or so later he came to the van with Paco. While

I loaded his guitar case and duffel bag, they exchanged some last words and embraced for a long time. The drive home was a quiet one. Tiago said little beyond giving me directions. When I stopped for gas at the little town where we had bought wine, he took a pillow from the back, tucked it between his head and the window, and fell asleep. The van stank of smoke-saturated clothes and unwashed bodies. I had continued to use the toilet in the barn rather than the overcrowded trailers, but could only manage a superficial wash in the tiny basin and was in need of a long, hot shower. Tiago also had stinted on his personal hygiene. With him leaning against the window I could not lower it, and had to make due with woefully inadequate air vents.

When I stopped in front of his apartment, Tiago woke up irritated and crossly declined my offer to carry his bag and guitar up for him. Once he had opened the entrance door, however, he thrust both back to me and slowly climbed the stairs, his hand gripping the banister. After dropping his stuff off inside his room I started to tell him how much I had enjoyed the wedding, but he waved me away. I descended to the street to find Paula leaning against the van with her hands folded against her chest. She straightened up.

"So, how was it?"

"Quite the experience."

"I can imagine. And *Abuelo*? Did he have a good time?"

"He was very much in his element but is pretty tired right now."

She nodded. "He and Paco tend to misbehave when they get together and they're too old for that now. I don't have anything for the next half hour or so. Would you like a coffee?"

I made a regretful gesture with my hand. "Thanks, but I need to get the van back to the rental office." It wasn't due for a few more hours but I was desperate to be alone. "Not sure you'd want me inside, either," I added. "I'm pretty ripe."

She laughed. "Another time, then. I'd love to hear all about the wedding."

Chapter 18

AFTER RETURNING FROM THE wedding I was eager to discuss what I had experienced during Maria's howl of a *cante* with Tiago, but what with having to take extra shifts for the people who had filled in for me and then spending time with Daniel on his last visit before a three-month deployment on a naval ship in the North Atlantic, it was a couple of weeks before I saw him again. I went to his place on one of my free evenings with a bottle of red wine, the usual offering of food, and my guitar.

"I thought you had forgotten me!" Tiago said when he opened the door to my knock.

I handed him the food and wine. "I could never forget you, Tiago."

He grinned and motioned me to the table. He opened the bottle and poured some wine out in two tumblers he had plucked from the sink and rinsed. I accepted mine, ignoring the greasy fingerprints on the outside. While I munched on the stuffed baguette I had brought, Tiago tucked into the chicken nuggets with his usual relish but only ate a few pieces. He rewrapped the rest and put them into the refrigerator "for tomorrow." When I had finished eating he topped up our wine. I took a large swallow and set down my glass.

"Tiago, your playing that first night at the wedding, it was amazing. I'd never heard you play like that before."

"Well, you know, in the street . . ." He completed the thought with a wave of his hand.

"Do you think I'll ever be able to play guitar as well as you?"

He studied me for a moment. "You play guitar well already. Flamenco?" He shook his head. "You don't want to play like me. How I play is *my* music. You have to find your own."

"How do I get there?"

His eyes widened. "You just keep playing."

"But how can I tell if it's any good?"

He threw up a hand. "*No sé.* You play and see how it feels. But you can't copy. Oh, you can watch and learn things from other players, but then you put it together in your own way."

We took up our guitars and played as we usually did, Tiago starting the conversation, me picking up the theme in reply. We had been going back and forth for a while when he held up a hand to stop me.

"You are too . . ." He fisted his hands and crossed his arms across his body. "Too tight, too controlled." He emptied what was left of the wine into my glass, reached under his sink, pulled out another bottle and added more. "Here, drink. It helps."

I drained the glass. My playing did loosen, my fingers running ahead of my thoughts, often to surprising effect. I wasn't always happy with the result but Tiago waved his hands in encouragement.

"*Bueno, bueno.*"

"I hope this doesn't mean I have to get drunk to play."

"Just to learn how to loosen up."

We continued for a bit longer, then Tiago set his guitar aside. "Enough for tonight."

I put my guitar back in its case. "Can I just sit for a while before I go home? The wine's really gone to my head."

"*Sí, sí,* no rush."

I eased back in the chair. "Tiago, can I ask you something?"

"Of course."

I shifted in my seat. "You know, that last night at the wedding—something happened to me. Maria's singing was amazing, so powerful that I seemed to, I don't know, lose all control or something. Like I was turned inside out. I've never felt anything like it before."

"You were touched by *duende*, I think. It's a gift to feel it. Also to make others feel it."

"But I always thought experiencing *duende* would be more transcendent, not so . . . black. I don't ever want to go there again."

"It tells you something about yourself, I think. What you are afraid of. Who your demons are."

I laughed drily. "Oh, I know who my demons are."

Tiago raised his eyebrows in enquiry.

"Three men."

He bristled like a dog sensing a threat. "Who are these men?"

"My mother was assaulted, violated, by three men when she was young. That's how I was conceived. I only found out recently. It's been . . ." I drew in a long breath and released it slowly. "Devasting. I don't know which one of them was my father and it makes me sick to think that I was made by a man capable of doing that."

Tiago studied me for several moments, his eyes small points of brightness in the dim light.

"*Un hombre tiene muchos padres*," he said.

After returning home that night I lay in bed, unable to sleep. Tiago's words, issuing from a throat abraded by his pungent cigarettes and soaked in rough red wine, echoed in my mind.

A man has many fathers.

I thought of those who could claim that role in my life.

Tiago himself, for the world he had opened up for me. Fin, for shaping the contours of my character and burdening me with the need for music. Theo, for showing me how to be a man. Papa Luke, for illuminating the dark spaces within me. Emilio, for his example of generosity. As for the man who had made me? Measured against these others he was nothing.

Dawn was seeping through the windows before I finally slept, and although I woke only a few hours later it was with a clarity and lightness I hadn't felt for a long time. In this new, fresh frame of mind, I felt ready to face my mother and family. In truth I missed them all terribly.

I also was anxious to reconnect with Aude. Lost in the study of flamenco, I had not thought of her much in the previous year. My encounter with Ebba at the wedding had brought her forcibly to mind. Ebba's casual suggestion of sex made me realize that if *I* could attract such proposals, Aude was probably constantly fending them off. If she, in fact, was. She had gone out with other boys in high school and university, as I had dated other girls, always with the understanding that they were diversions until we would be together. But as my blushes before Ebba attested, I had never gone beyond necking. Had Aude? *Whatever*, I thought stoically. It would all be sorted on my return. Was she missing me as much as I missed her? I assumed that, like my family, she knew where I was and could have reached me if she wanted. That she had not probably meant she was waiting for me to make contact first. Fair enough.

Having come up empty trying her phone number and email previously, I googled Aude's parents' inn. It had changed hands. As my phone contract didn't include overseas calls, I sent the new owners an email requesting contact information for the Langevins. A reply from one of the employees advised that the current owner was in hospital recovering from back surgery and a response would have to wait for their return. Three weeks passed without reply. I went back to the internet and keyed in

Aude's name. The screen was flooded with links concerning Aude's namesake, a fashion mogul in Paris. After scrolling through numerous stories about the woman's fashion shows, style awards, Saint-Jean-Cap-Ferrat villa, two Bouvier dogs, affair with an Italian race car driver, and messy divorce, I gave up. That there was nothing about *my* Aude was not surprising. Following Fin's no-screens policy when I was a child and my parents' exhortations against splashing oneself all over social media, I had limited my digital presence to only what was needed for professional purposes. Aude's parents had been even stricter. It didn't matter. I would be home soon.

"*Tio,* I'm thinking of going home in December." I was covering the bar that night and Emilio and I were having a drink—him beer, me coffee—before it got busy. "That should give you enough time to find someone to replace me."

"Oh." Emilio paused. "I was hoping you would take care of things over Christmas while I'm gone."

"Where are you going?"

"Sierra's wedding—didn't I tell you?"

"You did, but the date didn't register."

"It's just after Christmas. An odd time, I know, but Aarón is Jewish, of course, and having it then is best for them because they have breaks from work and many of their friends will be in Madrid for the holiday and can attend. Mía and I thought we would go to Tenerife after. It's so long since we've had a holiday."

"Oh."

Emilio glanced at me. "But if you can't do it we can come back right away."

"Marietta won't be here?"

"Her sister is not well. It could be her last Christmas and Marietta wants to be with her."

"Okay. Nothing's fixed for me yet. I'll go when you get back."

After Emilio left I absentmindedly tidied up the newspaper he had left on the counter. When I aligned and folded over the sections, a photo leapt off the page: Paula's uncle. The headline above it read, "Murder charge dropped." Then in smaller letters, "Key witness changes testimony." I shivered, remembering the sense of menace that had emanated from the man and the thug attending him, and slid the paper into a recycle bin under the counter.

Chapter 19

MUCH AS I WANTED to go home I was torn about leaving Spain and the friends I had made, especially Tiago. I now visited him two or three times a week, occasionally in the afternoon at one of his busking spots but more often in the evening. Something had changed between us after that drunken evening when we had spoken about *duende* and demons. He honored me by playing with the flash and fire of his performances at the wedding. He also was more generous with his comments and direction regarding my playing. I left each session with some new insight to note in my journal. I would have to find a way to keep in touch with him after I left.

One afternoon in early November I let myself into Tiago's building to find him sitting on a step halfway up the staircase, struggling for breath.

"Tiago!" I hurried up and sat down beside him. "Are you okay?"

"*Sí*, okay," he wheezed.

I started to rise. "I'll call an ambulance,"

He grabbed my sleeve and pulled me down. "No, no ambulance."

"What is it? Your heart?"

He shook his head. "No, just sometimes the stairs are hard."

He grasped the handrail and began to haul himself upright.

I jumped up. "Here, let me help you. I'll carry the guitars." I threaded one arm through the straps of both his and my guitar cases and looped the carrier bag with food and wine I had brought over the wrist. With my other arm around his waist I helped him up the remaining stairs, one at a time. Tiago's hand trembled as he inserted the key into the lock on his door. Inside, he sank into a chair at the table. I set the stuff I was carrying down, filled a glass with water from the kitchen tap, and handed it to him.

"Here."

He drank and his breathing steadied. I sat down across from him.

"You're not well."

"I'm tired, that is all."

"Have something to eat, you'll feel better." I stood up. "I'll go and get you some coffee."

"No, no. Just rest."

I regarded him with concern. Color was slowly returning to his face. "Is there anything I can do for you?"

"I will lie down. Maybe you can come another day."

Tiago stood and unbuttoned his jacket, his fingers fumbling. I helped ease it off his shoulders and slung it over the back of the chair. He moved slowly towards his bed. It was unmade and I sprang forward.

"Here, let me straighten out your bed."

He waited, hand gripping the metal frame at the foot of the bed, while I quickly tidied the sheets and blankets. When it was done he lay down with a sigh.

"I'll put the food away."

He raised a hand in acknowledgement, his eyes already closed. I stashed the bag of food in the refrigerator and the wine under the sink, picked up my guitar case, and went to the door. With a last anxious glance at Tiago, I slipped out and closed it quietly behind me.

Instead of going home I stopped at Paula's office. She was conferring with an older gray-haired man, one of the two other lawyers in her practice. Soledad, Paula's secretary, greeted me with a smile.

"She shouldn't be long."

Paula came out a couple of minutes later with a buff folder in her hand.

"Niels, hello!"

"Yes, hi. Any chance you'd have a few minutes to talk?"

Paula held up a finger. "I have to make a phone call. If you wait, we can have coffee."

I sat down on a chair in the tiny reception area. Paula's voice rose and fell unintelligibly for several minutes. After a short interval of silence she emerged from her office, pulling on a suit jacket.

"Let's go to Toto's," she said, referring to a nearby café. "I haven't had lunch."

We walked the short distance. Inside, Paula called to the server to bring her the day's featured *bocadillo* and a coffee.

"Mineral water for me," I added.

We sat down at a table and exchanged pleasantries for the short time it took for our order to be delivered. Paula bit hungrily into the small baguette stuffed with cheese and ham. I poured the mineral water into a glass and sipped it, waiting for Paula to finish her sandwich. In a few bites she was done. She delicately touched her napkin to her mouth and picked up the demitasse of coffee.

"You wanted to talk to me about something?"

"I'm worried about Tiago. When I arrived today I found him on the steps, out of breath. I had to help him to the top. He was so tired that he lay down right away. And it's not just today. I know he's old, but he seems to have less stamina than even a couple of months ago. And he's always had a smoker's cough, but sometimes it's brutal. Once he almost choked and I had to thump him on the back. He doesn't eat as much as he used to, either. Maybe Paloma should have a look at him."

Paula regarded me for a moment. "*Abuelo*'s got cancer."

A chill ran through me and the glass I was raising to my lips suddenly felt heavy. I lowered it carefully. "Very bad?"

"Yes. In the lungs but Paloma thinks it has spread elsewhere."

"Last winter, when he was sick, was that what it was about?"

"At that time it was pneumonia, but that's how they found out."

I blinked rapidly. "Can something be done? Like chemo?"

Paula sighed deeply. "Yes, maybe, but Paloma isn't an oncologist, and *Abuelo* refuses to see anyone else or go into hospital."

"Does he know what's going on?"

She opened her hand in a gesture of uncertainty. "Paloma has told him he is very sick, but how much he understands, or chooses to understand, I don't know. We both would prefer that he get treatment, of course, but we respect his wish not to."

"So . . . he's just left to die?"

Paula smiled wanly. "Everyone does, in the end."

"Yes, but it just seems, I don't know . . ."

"It's how he wants it to be. Paloma is consulting with colleagues and will make sure he doesn't suffer too much."

I struggled to maintain my composure. Paula laid her hand briefly on mine.

"It means a lot to us that you care for him."

We were silent for several seconds. "Does Paloma have a sense of how long he has?"

Paula raised a shoulder in a helpless shrug. "Not really, but she thinks it's less than a year."

I dreaded my next meeting with Tiago, but when I came upon him busking outside the market by the bridge a few days later he seemed much as he always had.

"Niels!" He waved me over.

I sat down on the bench beside him. "How are you?"

In the unforgiving sunlight the marks of illness on his face were evident: sharpened cheekbones, sunken eyes, dull skin.

"I am fine." He pulled a crushed package of cigarettes from his pocket and lipped one out. I wanted to remonstrate but didn't. He lit the cigarette with a battered lighter and blew out a stream of smoke. "Where is your guitar?" he said.

"I had some business in town."

He gestured up the street. "Go and get it."

"I have to work soon, but I can visit for a while now."

"I'm sorry your teacher is unwell," Emilio said. "It is good of you to want to be with him. You are welcome to stay as long as you like. You are so much part of the family now I'd be happy if you didn't leave at all."

"*Muchas gracias, Tio*," I said. Moved by his kindness, I busied myself wiping the spotless top of the mahogany bar where I was working that evening.

Emilio swallowed the last of his beer and handed me the glass. "I'd better get home, although now, with this wedding, it's all fuss, fuss, fuss. And the cost!" He pushed himself up with a grunt, said goodbye, and left.

With Tiago's approaching death heavy on my mind, I would have preferred to be in the kitchen where I usually worked than in the restaurant where I was obliged to smile and engage with customers. The sense of impending loss was crippling. A couple sat down at the bar and ordered. I absentmindedly poured out a glass of fino sherry and a flute of cava. After setting them before the guests I gazed out at the gathering dusk and wondered how this old and irascible man had come to mean so much to me.

In the weeks that followed I found Tiago better on some days than others, and learned to recognize signs of weakness or weariness and adjust my visits accordingly. At one point three vials of tablets appeared on the counter by the sink. Small, inexorable changes occurred. With climbing the stairs a growing ordeal, Tiago went out to busk less frequently. By Christmas he didn't go out at all. Paula and Paloma engaged Fatiha, Tiago's neighbor, to help with his daily needs.

I visited Tiago most days, if only for a quick coffee, checking with Paula beforehand to see if there was something he needed. The smoke fug in his apartment was heavy. The only thing making it bearable was that it almost masked the odor of illness. When I got home I would have to strip and shower to get rid of the smell.

"How about we open a window?" I said once to Tiago.

"No, no, too cold."

I stuck my head into Paula's office when I left that day. "Now that Tiago can't go out by himself, can't you just stop getting him cigarettes?"

Paula shrugged. "It gives him pleasure and there's not much that does anymore. Besides, it hardly matters now."

If he was up to it, I would take Tiago out to Toto's café or to sit on a bench in the winter sun, supporting him on the slow journey up and down the stairs. Once I rented a car and took him for a drive in the country. When I came in the afternoon I often roused him from sleep. Regardless, he greeted me with such warmth and welcome in his eyes that I wanted to weep. Did he have no other friends? What about that dreadful son of his? Were there no other grandchildren?

"Does Paco know what's going on?" I asked Paula.

"Yes, and he's been to see *Abuelo*. But he doesn't have a car and depends on someone to bring him in, so can't come often."

We played guitar together on most visits. As time passed, the vigor of Tiago's playing lessened and he set his guitar aside sooner and sooner. "No, you play," he would say when I made to follow.

By the end of January the disease had whittled Tiago down to a fraction of himself. The strong bones in his face stood out in stark relief, giving him the look of a martyr. He could no longer sit for more than a few minutes in the hard chair at the table, so I would help him to his armchair and prop his guitar in his arms. He would run his hands gently along the instrument's body and play a few chords, but it was mostly left to me to make music. His ear and mind were still sharp, however, and he was quick with pointed comments on my playing.

In early February I arrived one day to find Paloma and a strange woman in the apartment.

"This is Ximena," Paloma said. "She is one of *Abuelo*'s cousins, from his old village. She is going to take care of him."

Ximena was short and stout with a broad face and shrewd eyes. Her long dark hair was threaded with white and tied back at her neck. The hand I shook was solid and calloused and its grip strong.

"I'm glad someone will be keeping an eye on him," I said.

Tiago glowered at me from his armchair. I sat down on the bed and tried to engage him in conversation. He ignored me and scowled at the women who were shifting the kitchen table over to make room for a cot.

I rose. "Why don't I come back later."

Paloma glanced at her grandfather and nodded. "That might be best."

Chapter 20

THE CALL I HAD been dreading came one afternoon in early March as I was getting ready for my evening shift in the tavern kitchen.

"It's, ah, happening," Paula said. "I thought you would want to know."

A pit opened in my stomach. "I'll arrange for someone to cover for me at work and come right over."

"The thing is, we may not be here."

"Are you taking him to the hospital?"

"No, *Abuelo* was quite adamant that he didn't want to go to hospital. He wants to die in the open, under the sky. We're taking him to a park outside of the city."

I swallowed hard. "I'd like to come, to be there."

"Okay, I think that will be all right, but you have to hurry. We're getting what we need ready, blankets and things. It will be cold, so dress well."

"Can I help somehow?"

"Could you maybe pick up some food? And something to drink? It would save us some time."

"*Sí*. Food I can do."

I hurriedly dressed for outdoors and rushed to the tavern kitchen. When I explained the situation, a couple of the staff agreed to cover my shift. Although I had stood in for them more than once, I felt a rush of gratitude for their understanding. I made some sandwiches, placed the food in a bag, and headed out. On the way to Tiago's apartment I picked up some water and a jug of wine. When I arrived, Paula was placing a heavy jacket on top of a pile of blankets in the cargo area of a small grass-green hatchback that was hiked up on the curb. She was dressed in jeans and a thick knit sweater.

I handed over the carry bag. "Here are the food and drinks."

"Good, thanks." Paula tucked the bag into a corner next to a foam pad that was rolled up and secured by a couple of bungee cords. She straightened and brushed a strand of hair off her forehead. "Paloma is getting some stuff from the hospital."

"This dying under the sky—is it a *gitano* tradition?"

She smiled faintly. "I've never heard of it before, but freedom is important to us." She glanced up at Tiago's window and her smile faded. "I hope we can get there in time."

We went up to Tiago's apartment. Ximena was inside.

"I have washed and dressed him," she said.

Paula rested her hand on the woman's shoulder. "*Gracias.*"

I had grown accustomed to Tiago's diminished state but the change in his appearance in the two days since I had last seen him shocked me. His skin was devoid of color and lay on his bones like a dropped cloth. His half-open eyes were clouded and unfocused.

I took his hand. "Tiago, it's Niels."

His looked at me and his mouth moved, to smile or speak, I could not tell.

Someone knocked softly and Fatiha entered. Seeing us all, she hesitated on the threshold. "I came to see if Ximena wanted a break."

Paula stepped forward and took her hand. "Come in and say goodbye."

Fatiha's hand flew to her mouth. "Oh." She went to the bed,

rested her hand on Tiago's arm, and stood for a few moments with her head bowed. Turning, she nodded at us and slipped out the door, her eyes, magnified by the thick lenses of her glasses, bright with tears.

Shortly after we heard footsteps on the stairs and Paloma came in carrying her physician's bag.

"I have what I need. Are you all ready to go?"

Paula nodded and rose. She glanced at Tiago then back at her sister. "How are we going to get him down the stairs."

"Ah, hadn't thought of that. Maybe put his arms around each of our shoulders and hold him up?"

"But his feet will drag and, anyway, the staircase is so narrow I'm not sure all three of us will fit across."

Paloma looked around the room, considering. "How about we make a sling, put him in it?"

"He's still pretty heavy and I don't think we can lift him high enough to keep him from bumping. How about we put him on the foam pad and slide him down?"

Paloma grimaced. "*Mierda.*"

"I can carry him down," I said.

Two identical faces turned to me, their eyes identically wide with relief.

"Could you?"

"That would be great."

I drew the blanket off Tiago, slid my arms under his back and his knees, and lifted him up. For all his deterioration, his was still a good weight.

"I'm not going to be able to hold on to the banister, so could one of you walk in front of me going down, just in case I get off balance?"

"Of course." Paula turned to Ximena. "I guess this is it."

Ximena came to Tiago and placed her hand on his head. "*Adiós, primo.*"

"Let's go," Paloma said.

She led the way down the stairs with me close behind, feeling for each step and planting my foot firmly before shifting my weight. Halfway down I was struck by the thought that everything I had done to that point—abandoning school and leaving home, cooking at the Sea Shack then on the container ships, working out in the gym there, meeting Daniel and coming with him to Seville—had brought me to this place and time and with the strength to carry a dying man down a flight of stairs to fulfil his final wish. As though reading my thoughts, Tiago raised a finger and touched my cheek. "Good boy," he said.

With some difficulty, we got Tiago into the back seat. Paloma climbed in on the other side, her bag on her lap.

"Wait! We have to bring his guitar," I said.

Paula frowned at me. "I don't think there's room."

"I'll hold it."

I dashed back up the stairs and burst into Tiago's apartment, startling Ximena. Grabbing Tiago's guitar case, I tore back down. The fit was tight but I managed to wedge the case between my knees. In the driver's seat, Paula shook her head but smiled. She started the car and we drove off.

Paula wove through the city, heading to the hills of the Sierra Norte de Sevilla Natural Park. We traveled in silence, like we were holding our collective breath, willing Tiago to hang on until we reached our destination. After nearly an hour we saw the sign for the park. Paula turned into the entrance. The road wound through dramatic rock outcroppings dotted with scrubby bushes and groves of muscular oaks, their bare branches stark in the fading light.

"Where should I stop?" Paula said.

"Just find somewhere flat. It's going to be dark soon," Paloma said.

Paula pulled off the road onto a large grassy patch, bumped to a stop, and turned off the ignition. "Hopefully there won't be much traffic at this time of day." She glanced back at Tiago. "This could be a bit hard to explain."

We unloaded the stuff from the back and unrolled the foam mat on the ground a few feet from the car. I opened the back door and gently maneuvered Tiago into a position from which I could lift him out. As I stood up with him in my arms, his face turned to the sky and he smiled. I walked the short distance to the foam pad, crouched, and set him gently down. His eyes found mine. "*Gracias*," he breathed.

I stood and backed away, fighting tears. The sisters moved in, tucked a pillow under his head and wrapped blankets around him, murmuring as they worked. When they were done we stood gazing down at him for several moments. Paloma stirred.

"I could use a drink. Did I see some wine?"

We settled with cushions and blankets on the ground by the car and I emptied the carrier bag.

"I didn't bring glasses."

Paloma picked up the jug of wine. "*No importa*. From today, Niels, you are one of us." She cracked open the cap, tilted her head back, and took a long swallow. When she was done she wiped the top and handed the bottle to Paula, who took a delicate sip. Though identical in face and figure, the sisters' differences went beyond their hairstyles. Paula's voice and actions had the polish of someone who smoothed and cajoled and made things right. Paloma's, by contrast, were edged with the impatience of someone for whom there was too much to do and never enough time.

Night settled upon us, pierced occasionally by the private noises of birds and small animals. A few stars popped out, followed by more, until the sky looked like an inverted bowl of crushed glass. I had seen many starry skies when I was at sea but, dimmed by the ships' lights, they never had the immediacy and density of the one we huddled under now. The air smelled of soil and sap and the ineffable scent of stone. Tiago lay still on his foam pallet, only his eyes moving. He would open them and stare brightly at the stars. When they slowly closed, he would, with effort, open them again.

Paloma occasionally attended to Tiago, touching his forehead and smoothing his blanket. Once, when he became restless, she filled a hypodermic needle and gave him a shot. After, she sat down and leaned against Paula. "Wake me if you sense a change," she said and fell asleep.

I was slumped against the car, fighting sleep and wondering how much longer we were likely to be there, when I remembered Tiago's guitar. Rising, I took it from its case in the car and carried it to where he lay. I had intended only to place the guitar next to him but, after considering a moment, sat down instead. I rested the guitar on my thigh, remembering the first time I had held it, the charge I had felt, and wondered at the journey it had set me on and the man who had been my guide, now dying at my side. Tiago's eyes followed my movements, glinting in the meager moonlight. I checked the tuning then began to play softly, music light as gossamer, ethereal as a drifting spirit. Tiago's head moved slightly—it could have been a nod—and his eyes slowly closed. My fingers stiffened and my legs cramped. I shifted and wriggled but continued to play.

Paloma woke and she and Paula listened. Lost in the music, I was startled by a movement near me.

"His breathing has changed," Paloma said. She bent over Tiago, her fingers on his wrist. Paula knelt beside her.

"Oh." I raised the guitar to set it to the side.

"No, don't stop," Paula said.

My heart thudding, I began to play again. Tiago's eyes were half open and his left hand scrabbled feebly at the blanket. Suddenly his neck arched back and he opened his mouth wide as though to swallow the sky. A long moment passed. Paloma set down Tiago's hand and placed her own on top.

"It's over."

I played a final chord and stopped, breath knotting in my chest. "I'll leave you alone with him," I said and rose, my legs trembling. I put the guitar back in its case, leaned against the car, and stared up at the spectacle of the stars. I felt nothing, neither cold nor pain nor emotion. I could have been the void in which the stars hung.

"Could you drive?" Paula said.

"Sure," I said.

She and Paloma had wrapped Tiago in blankets like a mummy, and we propped him up in the back seat, tucking the pillow and cushions around to keep him in place. Difficult as it was carrying him when he was alive, it was even harder moving his body.

"It's like breathing gave him buoyancy," I said.

Paloma nodded. "Yes, it's something like that."

We loaded the remaining gear in the back and got into the car, me in the driver's seat, Paloma in the back, and Paula in the passenger seat with the guitar. We slid through the dark, empty roads, the hum of the car the only sound. Checking the rear-view mirror, I'd catch sight of our macabre load—I no longer thought of it as Tiago—and my skin would prickle.

The lights of the city finally thickened along the horizon.

"Where should I go?"

"To the hospital," Paloma said. "I need to certify his death."

She guided me through the streets, and when we were in sight of the complex she took out her cellphone and pressed a button. When the call was answered, she murmured into it. At the hospital she directed me to go around to the back where the morgue was located. A man in pale green scrubs was waiting at a set of double doors with a gurney. He pushed it to the car, and with some effort he and Paloma pulled Tiago's body from the back seat and onto the gurney.

"I'll be about half an hour," Paloma said to Paula before shutting the back door.

"Where to now?" I asked Paula.

"Your place. I'm sure you're ready to get home."

We drove in silence to the tavern and I pulled up beside the gate to backyard. The property was dark and silent.

"Can you get in?" Paula said.

"Yes, I know the lock code." In the light from the streetlamp, Paula's face drooped with exhaustion. "You look really tired. I have an extra room—you're welcome to stay."

She smiled wearily. "*Gracias*, but I have to pick Paloma up."

We got out of the car and met at the front bumper. I handed her the car keys.

"Thanks for letting me be part of this, Paula."

"It's us who should thank you. I don't think we could have done it without your help."

Our farewell cheek kisses expanded into a long hug. I hadn't held a woman close in a long time and savored the feel of her pressing against me and the scent of her hair, still bearing traces of soil and sap and stones, releasing her before things became awkward.

"Will there be a service?"

"Yes. I'll let you know when." With a wave she got into the car, started it up, and drove away.

"Oh, Mr. Niels, hello," Fatiha said, blinking behind her glasses. She was standing outside the entrance to the small church where Tiago's funeral service was about to be held. "I wanted to come, but I don't know what to do."

I offered her my arm. "You can come with me." She smiled shyly and smoothed her hijab. I dropped my arm and made a gesture towards the door. "Here, let's go in."

We entered and slipped into a pew at the back. Candles were lit but the church was otherwise empty except for Paco and Maria, seated near the front, and Ximena a couple of rows behind near the wall. They all glanced back and smiled greetings. A few minutes later, syncopated steps ricocheting off the vaulted ceiling announced the arrival of Paula's uncle, followed by a salon-coiffed woman in a stylish suit and an adolescent girl dressed in torn jeans and a hot pink blouson jacket, with long, straight blond hair showing dark roots. They went to the right front pew, but after some frowning and whispered debate the girl sat down two rows behind her parents and whipped out her phone. It was hard to reconcile these cashmere-coated, couture-clad beings with Tiago and his thrift-store suits and battered hats. The thuggish man whom I had seen lounging against the car in front of Paula's office entered shortly after. He glanced around the church, his narrowed eyes resting briefly on those of us already seated. I involuntarily shrank back under his gaze. Presumably satisfied that there was no threat, he sprawled in a pew two rows up from the entrance.

 Not long after, the priest with a robed boy in attendance appeared from the back and stood expectantly in front of the altar. A small commotion in the entrance announced the arrival of the coffin. Two young men propelled it forward on a trolley. Paula and Paloma walked on either side with their hands resting on the lid. When it was in place at the front they glanced around the church, greeting the few of us there with nods, and took seats in the left front row.

 The priest began to intone the words of the service. I looked around—*Is this it?* I had expected something more dramatic, more *gitano*, like the wedding had been. Women wailing, people tearing their clothes—not this anemic mouthing of ritual. There wasn't even any music, just the rise and fall of the priest's voice. I turned my thoughts inward, remembering Tiago busking in the street with his hat at his feet, dispensing wisdom over tumblers of wine in his apartment, grinning as we sparred musically with our guitars, mesmerizing the crowd around the fire with his blazing guitarwork. Fatiha touched my hand lightly and I started.

"I think it's almost over," she whispered. "I am going."

The slowing cadence and long tones of the priest's voice signaled conclusion. Whatever was planned for after, I had no place in it.

"I'll go with you."

I rose and, with a final glance at the wooden box that contained what was left of my old friend, followed Fatiha out of the church.

Chapter 21

THE DAY AFTER TIAGO'S funeral I was in my apartment trying to cull the belongings that, despite my spartan lifestyle, had accumulated during my stay. After Tiago died I told Emilio that I would be leaving soon. I had made the statement with a sense of detachment, like I was speaking on someone else's behalf, and felt the strangeness of it still. While I had been learning flamenco with Tiago there had been structure and substance to my life in Seville, but with him gone it no longer had purpose here. I had no desire to study with anyone else; I even wondered if the whole flamenco experience had been so closely associated with Tiago that it lacked meaning now. *I am going home*, I had said, but where—and who—was that? My parents? Jax? Aude? The confusion was why I had still not set a date and booked a flight.

I picked up two books and studied them—keep or discard? My mind blanked and I set them both down with a sigh. Footsteps pounded up the stairs and someone hammered on the door.

"Niels! Niels! Open up!"

I was at the door in a few strides and opened it to find Paula, her hair disheveled and her face flushed.

"Paula? What is it?"

"Oh, Niels, you must come quickly. Get your passport and wallet, that's all, but you have to come now."

"What?"

She shook her head with impatience. "There's no time to explain, but trust me that you must leave here now." I hesitated, not comprehending. "Niels! We have to go!" she pleaded.

Propelled by her urgency, I went to the drawer where I kept my passport then the table for my wallet and phone. My laptop was next to them so, without thinking, I grabbed it too. As we ran down the stairs we heard raised voices in the tavern kitchen. Paula grabbed my arm and pulled me towards the back gate.

"You can open the gate, right?" she said.

"Yes, but I—"

"Quickly!"

I juggled the items I was carrying and tapped the numbers of the code on the lock. The gate began to open, agonizingly slowly. A shout sounded at the rear door of the tavern kitchen.

"*Jesús,*" Paula said, glancing back. We squeezed through the widening opening of the gate. "Follow me! Quickly!"

I stumbled after her—the down-at-heel espadrilles that served as my house slippers made running difficult and I was clutching the items I had brought awkwardly to my chest. We turned one corner, then another. Voices and commotion trailed us.

"My car is just up there," she panted over her shoulder. I saw her green hatchback two cars ahead. She clicked her fob as she ran and the locks released audibly.

"Get in!" She dove into the driver's seat and started the car while I ran around to the passenger door. My leg was still outside when Paula accelerated down the street. I quickly drew it in and slammed the door.

"For Christ's sake, Paula, what is going on?"

"Just let me get out of here, then I'll explain."

She drove as quickly as the crowded street allowed, perched

on the edge of her seat, glancing constantly at the side and rearview mirrors. We wove an erratic route through the neighborhood, turning left, then right, slipping down narrow alleys, going in one direction and then its opposite.

"Can I at least ask where we're heading?"

Paula checked the rearview mirror for the umpteenth time. "I'm not sure yet. Out of the city to start, anyway."

Several minutes later, she released a long breath and eased back into her seat.

"I think I've lost them."

"Lost who?"

"My *tio*. Well, that man who works for him, anyway. I don't think *Tio* would actually do anything himself."

My mouth fell open. "Your uncle? What the hell does he want with me?"

Paula glanced over. "Look: we're almost outside the city. I'll find a place to stop and explain. It's too much to start now."

On the city's outskirts we turned onto a minor road and continued for a minute or so. She pulled onto the weedy verge of a narrow country lane that ran through gently undulating meadows covered with the fine green fuzz of spring vegetation, turned off the ignition, leaned back in her seat, and expelled a long breath.

"Well?" I said.

She turned to me. "The short version is that *Abuelo* had a will and left two items to you: his guitar and a metal box." She gestured over her shoulder. "They're in the back."

"All the fuss is about a guitar and a metal box?"

She smiled faintly. "*Tio* thinks the box is full of gold."

"*What?*" I stared at her incredulously. "Tiago didn't live like anyone who was sitting on a bunch of gold."

"I would have thought so too, but *Tio* is convinced it exists. I do remember *Abuelo* taunting *Tio* once about the gold, how he'd never get it while *Abuelo* was alive." She grimaced. "There was no love lost between the two of them. After *Abuelo* died, *Tio* tore his place apart looking for the gold. He didn't find anything. I was mystified about what box *Abuelo* was referring to in his will until Paco brought it in when he came for the funeral. He had been keeping it for *Abuelo* at the ranch. *Tio* found out about the will and the box this morning and figures the gold is in it."

"Is it?"

She shrugged. "Maybe. I haven't opened it. Paco didn't have a key and I couldn't find one among *Abuelo*'s things. When I heard *Tio* was coming after the box, I had to get it and you out of there."

"Why didn't you just give it to him? I sure as hell don't want it."

She gave me a level gaze. "Because it's not his. *Abuelo* was quite specific that it should go to you. Apart from my personal commitment to *Abuelo*, I have a fiduciary duty to see that his expressed wishes are fulfilled. I was surprised that he made a will at all, I didn't think he had anything to leave, but a month ago he asked me to make it legal that you should have the guitar and the box."

"Now that you've done your duty, I should be able to dispose of the stuff anyway I like. I really don't want the box if it's creating all this trouble."

Paula stared out of the window for a moment without speaking. "Niels, whatever that box contains, I think you should honor *Abuelo*'s wish that you have it. And I've gone to a lot of trouble to get it to you." She made a dismissive motion with her hand. "No, ignore that. More to the point, you are no longer safe. It wouldn't be a good idea for you to return to Seville. Even if you were to give *Tio* the box . . ." She shook her head. "He is a complicated man. It's best that you just go away."

I recalled the newspaper headline—MURDER CHARGES

DROPPED—and shuddered. "Okay," I said in a small voice. "But where?"

"Not Madrid. *Tio* will probably be checking the trains and buses and even the airport. I'd say either Faro, in Portugal, or Tarifa for the ferry to Tangier. Tarifa to Morocco may be better. What do you think?"

I nodded numbly, my body tensed with the need to get away, and fast. "Whatever you figure is best."

"*Bueno*. There's a map in the glove compartment, could you get it for me?"

I pulled out the map and handed it to her. She unfolded it and scrutinized it for a couple of minutes.

"We'll take the back roads just in case." She traced the route to follow with her finger. "It will take longer but you should get there in plenty of time to catch the afternoon ferry."

As we set out, I sorted through the implications of my sudden departure. My first concern was the tavern. I phoned Marietta to say that an emergency had taken me out of the city and I wouldn't be able to work the front tonight. I wanted to call Emilio as well, but that conversation was complicated and needed to be private.

The next concern was travel. I drew my passport and wallet out of my pocket and flipped through both for reassurance.

"You should be able to get a flight out of Tangier." Paula glanced at my thin T-shirt, tattered jeans, and worn-down shoes. "And some clothes."

"My guitar . . ."

"I'll get it and your other belongings packed up and shipped. My briefcase is on the back seat. Get it and take out the pad of paper and pen that are inside. Write down an address where I should send your things. And take the file folder out as well. Those papers concern your inheritance. Read them through."

I did as she requested and wrote down Fin's address on the pad. The legal documents said that the terms of Tiago's will had been satisfied and my inheritance had been satisfactorily transferred to me.

Paula glanced at the papers in my hands. "When you're ready, sign where I've indicated."

I scowled at her pointlessly but complied.

We rode in silence for several minutes.

"What I really don't understand is how Tiago could ever have come to accumulate a bunch of gold," I burst out. "If he in fact did."

Paula glanced at me. "What do you know about *Abuelo*?"

"Well, not a lot, really. He didn't talk about himself, said once there wasn't much to say. I asked him from time to time about how it was, well, to be *gitano*. He told me about the history of it mostly, the restrictions and attempts to assimilate your community over the years, and a bit about some of your culture and traditions. And, of course, we talked a lot about flamenco, mostly music, but other aspects of it. But not much about his own life. He mentioned that his father dealt in horses, traded them, and was something of a horse doctor. And I know Tiago worked at the ranch with Paco, but not much else."

"I see." Paula was silent for a moment. "Well, there was definitely more to *Abuelo*'s life than that. As with most of us *gitanos*, *Abuelo*'s family was very poor. His parents scratched together a living with the horse business, and his mother made and sold jewelry. He was one of seven kids, somewhere in the middle of them all. Despite the poverty of the village in which they lived, there was always music. His father was a *cantaor* and his *tio* played guitar. The story goes that somehow the family got a battered guitar and the boys—there were four of them—all learned to play and would fight over it. *Abuelo* was still very young, nine or so, when it became apparent that he was better than the others. His *tio* took him under his wing. By thirteen, he was traveling around, performing with his *tio*."

Paula stopped at a corner and peered through the windshield. "Is this where we turn?"

I consulted the map. "Yes, and we go for another thirty kilometers or so before picking up the next road."

If the trip hadn't been so fraught with anxiety, I would have enjoyed the picturesque Andalusian landscapes we were winding through—the dry hills with patches of silvery olive groves or rows of the barren vines of early spring folding in on each other and punctuated here and there with stone farmhouses, all against the backdrop of a rim of smoky blue hills on the horizon.

"Anyhow, by the time he was twenty, *Abuelo* had started to attract attention farther afield and had acquired a patron, or patrons, I guess, a wealthy couple who introduced him to some important people. He started to appear in high-profile venues and with other important flamenco performers. This was in the late sixties, early seventies, when there was a revival of interest in flamenco." Paula turned and smiled at me. "For a while he was a bit of a rock star."

My forehead wrinkled in puzzlement. "I've been researching flamenco guitarists for over a year. How come I never came across anything about him or his music?"

"Ah. *Abuelo* was nothing if not eccentric. He would not allow his music to be recorded. Something about immediacy and authenticity. I think it added to his mystique. He was in great demand and started to earn money, big money. *Gitanos* aren't as a rule accustomed to being rich, and are not particularly trusting of virtual money, like bank accounts, so the possibility of his keeping it as gold may not be that farfetched."

"But this doesn't square up with the guy I knew. Something must have happened."

Paula sighed. "Yes, something happened." She fell silent for a moment. "*Gitanos* typically marry young."

It seemed like a non sequitur and I wondered if she was

changing the subject. "Yes, I remember that from the wedding last fall. Not you and Paloma, though, it seems." I glanced curiously at her, trying to imagine those two strong, determined women in frothy dresses, submitting to the *pañuelo* ceremony, assuming a secondary position in a household.

She smiled, ruefully I thought. "Yes, well, we've certainly chosen our own paths. Anyhow, *Abuelo* married very young—he may only have been seventeen. It had been set up when he and my grandmother were just children. She was a bit of a shrew, however. Even I remember how difficult and unpleasant she could be. Somehow they managed to produce two children, *Tío* and my mother, but they loathed each other. *Abuelo* was, I think, happy to be away, traveling about and performing. Unfortunately, he tended to forget about supporting them. My mother remembers a feast-or-famine type of atmosphere—occasionally her mother would receive a bunch of money and they'd live high for a short time and then it was gone, and they'd go for weeks, even months, relying on income from odd jobs and handouts from their parents."

We entered a small town at the junction to our next road. Paula pointed to a bar-café. "I could use a washroom and a cup of coffee." Still wary, she parked on a quiet side street. At the café, we ordered coffees and took our turns in the facility. The place sold gray hoodies with the name of the local soccer team stitched in red on the left breast and I bought one, earning us a couple of dry almond biscotti to accompany our drinks.

When we were back on the road, I picked up the story. "You were at where Tiago was always away and didn't send money home regularly."

"Ah, *sí*." She took a sip of her coffee and set the cup down in the holder on the consol. "I don't know much about *Abuelo*'s life when he was performing but I expect he lived quite well. And I doubt he lacked for female company. The followers, you know. There was one, an English girl." She shook her head.

"They'd come over, these privileged, entitled kids, clutter up our beaches and cities, appropriate our culture, play at being *gitanos*. They still do. Anyhow, this girl hooked on to *Abuelo*. I've seen pictures of her—she was beautiful. And *Abuelo*, he was quite striking then as well."

"Even as an old man, he still had presence."

"Yes. They had an affair. She traveled with him, stayed with him in hotels when he performed. This went on for a couple of months. A walk on the wild side, I expect she thought. A little exotic holiday adventure. She didn't realize she was playing with fire. Then suddenly a fiancé showed up. Enough of this, he probably said. You've had your fun. Time to come home."

She fell silent. After a long moment, she glanced at me. "*Abuelo* killed them both, stabbed them."

My stomach lurched. "Tiago? Killed them?"

Paula nodded.

"But it was just a fling."

Paula smiled faintly. "It doesn't work quite that way with us. There was the thwarted love, of course, but also profound insult and betrayal. That's a deadly combination. Then it turned out that both the girl and her fiancé were somebodies, lords and ladies, that kind of thing. The Spanish courts were merciless, judgement was swift, the punishment hard and long. An example had to be made. National standing and pride were at stake: this is not who we are! Of course, much was made of *Abuelo* being *gitano*."

We drove without speaking for several minutes. My thoughts whirled as I tried to reconcile this version of Tiago with the one I knew. Paula gave me a sidelong glance.

"Does it make you think differently of him now?"

I didn't answer immediately. "I honestly don't know. Maybe. I'm glad I didn't know." I paused. "What happened to him after? He must have spent time in prison."

Paula nodded. "Many, many years. It broke him, I think.

And all that talent, his brilliance—never fully realized, lost forever. And all for a—" She bit off whatever word she had planned to say.

"You said Tiago came from a large family, so there still must be nieces and nephews still around, if not his brothers and sisters themselves. Yet there was almost no one at his funeral. Was this why?"

Paula smiled wryly. "Oh, it wasn't the killing that alienated *Abuelo* from everyone. It was the betrayal of his family. Family is everything for *gitanos*. To neglect his wife and children as he did, to be unfaithful to them—with a *payo* no less—was unforgiveable. He was completely shunned, while he was in prison and after he came out. My mother and *Tío* didn't see him for years. The only person who stood by him was Paco, and after prison *Abuelo* went to work at Paco's son's ranch—where the wedding was held—for many years. I didn't meet him until I was around ten, and it wasn't until he was too old to work at the ranch and moved in with my mother that we got to know him. When my mother died, it fell to Paloma and me to take care of him."

"Despite his murky past?"

Paula made a noise in her throat that could have been a laugh. "He was my *abuelo*, and I came to love that old man, stubborn and cranky though he was."

We began to descend into Tarifa. The late afternoon sun slanted down on the port city, turning the white houses encrusting its gentle slopes golden.

"Have you been here before?" Paula said.

"Yes."

"Good. I'll drop you close to the ferry terminal."

Paula wound down towards the port and pulled over on a side street. Indicating the next intersection, she said, "Turn right there and it will take you to the terminal."

We got out of the car and went around to the back. Paula

opened the door to the cargo area. Tiago's guitar case was there, and with it a rectangular gray metal box. I opened the guitar case, slid my laptop under the body of the instrument, and clipped it shut before turning my attention to the box. Built to hold tools or fishing gear, it was secured by two sturdy latches and a hasp lock in which was inserted a chunky padlock with a thick shackle. It dragged on my arm when I lifted it and the contents rattled and shifted.

"So this is it?" I said unnecessarily.

Paula shut the door. "That's it."

We looked at each other for a moment.

"Are you going to be okay? I mean with your uncle. He's not a man I'd want to anger."

"He needs me too much." Paula smiled crookedly. "To keep him out of jail. And *Abuelo* didn't owe him anything. As I said, they despised each other. *Abuelo* had a certain and rather peculiar sense of honor and, despite his own past, didn't think much of what his son had become. He'll be angry all right, but I'll be fine."

"It's not my place to comment, I know, but why do you provide him legal support?"

"He's family."

We fell silent, not knowing how to end the extraordinary escapade we were on.

"Paula, you've gone to an awful lot of trouble for me. I'm not sure I understand why."

"You were important to *Abuelo*."

"He was important to me, too."

"Yes, but you were truly a blessing for him. You redeemed him in a way, I think."

I set down the metal box and we embraced long and hard. I drew back. "Be safe, Paula."

"You too. Let me know where you end up." She headed to the driver's door.

"And say goodbye to Paloma for me."

"I will," she said with a wave.

She got into the car, started it up, and pulled away from the curb. I watched until the car turned left at the intersection and disappeared. Feeling suddenly alone and vulnerable, I pulled the hood of the hoodie over my head and set off to the ferry terminal, the guitar case over my shoulder and the metal box thumping against my leg. I purchased a ticket, passed through the secure gate, and entered the departures area. The next ferry was scheduled to leave in forty minutes. I scanned the people in the room. Apart from casual glances, no one seemed to be interested in me. I found a seat against the wall, slid the box under the seat, and wedged the guitar case out of sight next to the pillar beside it. When I turned on my prepaid phone to call Emilio, I remembered that with everything going on I had forgotten to top up my account and little money remained. I mentally crossed my fingers and keyed in his number.

Emilio answered after one ring.

"It's Niels, *Tio*, and my phone's just about out of money so this may be short."

"Niels! What on earth is going on?"

In a low voice I explained the situation, telling all except Tiago's tragic past. He listened without interrupting except for occasional juicy expletives.

"This is complete bullshit!" he said when I was done. "Are you okay?"

"I think so. Or I will be once I'm on the boat. Look, *Tio*, I am very sorry for leaving in this way—not giving you any notice or saying a proper goodbye."

"*No importa.* I just want you to be safe. Are you sure you don't want me to come and get you?"

"No, I think leaving like this is the best plan. And I'm really sorry about the ruckus in the tavern. I hope the staff weren't too badly affected."

"They were shocked and a bit shaken up. And worried about you." His voice hardened. "No one comes into my place and yells and threatens my people."

"*Tio*, please don't do anything on my account. Those are really, really bad guys."

"I have friends, too."

We spoke a few minutes longer, and Emilio was in the middle of a sentence when my phone died. I gazed at the blank screen feeling like a boat cut from its mooring. A static-ridden recorded message announced the arrival of the ferry. I remained in my seat as it unloaded and the queue of those waiting to load formed, scrutinizing the people joining it from under my hood. A tall, powerfully built man in dark clothing entered the hall and looked around the room with hard eyes. I shrank back into my chair, willing myself into invisibility. The man's face suddenly softened and he raised a hand in greeting to a woman with a young child. I slowly released the breath I had been holding. A uniformed women raised a barrier and held out her hand for tickets. The queue of people began to shuffle past her down a corridor. I waited until most had gone, then joined the final stragglers onto the vessel and what I hoped was safety.

As the Spanish coast faded from view, my apprehension lessened. It jumped again when I lined up to clear Moroccan immigration and customs. How to explain a locked box that I couldn't open? The weary-eyed official with the Zapata mustache who processed me barely glanced at my passport before stamping it and waving me through.

In Tangier I set out for the small, family-run hotel in the medina where Daniel and I had stayed on our previous visit, hoping they still had a room available this late in the day. I made slow progress, my espadrille-clad feet slipping as I climbed the dusty and dimly lit street. The strap of the guitar case chaffed my shoulder and the handle of the metal box cut into my palm.

Looking down at it, the incredulity of it all suddenly stuck me. *Gold? Really?*

As I walked, I thought of what needed to be done tomorrow. Book a flight out of Tangier, of course, final destination Vancouver. But before taking the box on the plane I would have to know the contents. Turning onto the street that led to the hotel, I noticed a small garage on the corner. Lights still burned inside. I crossed the street and went in. A scrawny young man with black caterpillar brows and a pronounced overbite under a bushy mustache leaned against a cluttered counter watching a soccer match on a small television. He nodded to me in greeting. I held up the metal box.

"Can you cut the lock for me?" I said in Spanish, repeating the question in English and clumsy French. He looked from the box to me without comprehension. I set it on the counter and mimed the cutting with my fingers. He grinned toothily and disappeared into the garage's service bay. While he was gone I took a five-Euro bill out of my wallet. The man returned, wielding a set of large metal cutters. Despite their size, it was only after I added my strength to his on the handles that we cut through the hasp. The man's eyes lit up when I handed him the money, and he said a jumble of words. I removed the lock and offered it to him. He bobbed his head in confusion but accepted it. I thanked him again, picked up the box, and carried on.

The reception to the hotel, a small room that fronted the family's living quarters, was still open and lit but vacant. I called out a greeting and a boy of nine or ten peered through a bead curtain, waved, and disappeared. A minute later the boy's father came out, the disturbed beads clacking pleasantly. When he saw me, he smiled.

"You were here with Daniel once, but I don't remember your name." He spoke in accented Spanish.

"Niels," I said, warmed by his recognition. I recalled that Daniel knew the family through a relative who had worked at the tavern. The man's name popped out from some crevasse in my brain. "And you are Kamal, right?"

He nodded, pleased. "Do you need a room?"

"Yes, if you have one."

"There is one, but it is small." He eyed my odd baggage curiously but said nothing.

"No matter, it will be fine." My body sagged with sudden fatigue at the prospect of a safe harbor after the chaos of the day. "Two nights for now. I'll know tomorrow whether I have to stay longer."

We completed the paperwork. Kamal gave me directions to the room and handed over the key. I pulled out my wallet.

He held up his palm. "No, no, you can pay when you leave."

"Okay, thanks. Would it be possible to get something to eat and drink?"

"You know, we only do breakfast, but there is a restaurant up the street."

I drew out a ten-Euro bill and set it on the counter. "Could your boy maybe go and get me a meal and some water?"

"Yes, of course."

I left Kamal instructing his son and went to find my room. It was at the end of the corridor across from the communal bathroom and toilet. Like the rest of the building, the walls were whitewashed and the floor made of faded terracotta tile. A bed covered with a blue and yellow woven cover sat under a small window. The remaining furniture crowded the rest of the space: a rustic table with washbowl and pitcher over which hung a slightly marbled mirror, a narrow chest with three baskets on shelves serving as drawers, and a wooden chair with a rush seat. I leaned the guitar case against the wall and set the box on the chest. Losing the hefty lock had robbed it of its mystery and menace. I studied it for a moment. Opening it could wait until I had cleaned up and eaten.

The boy staggered down the corridor bearing a laden tray

just as I was emerging from the bathroom wearing only a towel around my waist. I opened the door to my room, took the tray from him, and set it on the bed. When I waved away the change he held out in a small, pink-palmed hand, he flashed me a smile missing a middle tooth and scampered away. I plucked a liter bottle of water from the tray and drained half of it. After setting the washbowl and pitcher on the floor I unloaded the rest of the tray onto the table: another bottle of water, a bowl of lamb stewed with chickpeas and apricots, olives, a basket of flatbread glossy with olive oil, a plate of sliced oranges sprinkled with cinnamon, a thick-bottomed glass, and an unmatched fork and spoon. Still wearing only the towel—I had rinsed out my underwear and hung my other clothes up on wall hooks to air—I sat down and dug into the food with my image in the mirror for company.

It wasn't until I had wiped the bowl clean with the last piece of bread and consumed the oranges that I turned my attention to the metal box. I had not invited this article or the complications it had created into my life, and raged briefly at Tiago. In the remoteness of my quiet little hotel room, the likelihood of the box containing gold seemed very low, and Paula's uncle's threats and the drama of my flight from Seville absurd. And if it contained gold? I shook my head. That would be even worse. I rose with a sigh, went to the chest where the box sat, and snapped open the clasps.

I stared at the contents of the box for a long time. There was gold, all right—no bars or wafers, but a great jumble of jewelry. I removed a fistful, mostly chains of various lengths with links of different shapes and sizes, then individual items: necklaces and bracelets, a belt with coins on it like a belly dancer might wear, rings and tie clips and cufflinks. Colored stones winked from some of the items. It all gleamed dully in the dimness of the bare bulb that lit the room. Was any of it real? As I reached into the box again I noticed that the jewelry didn't fill it.

Underneath were three layers of small plastic boxes. It took me a moment to recognize them as cassette tapes. I took one out, then a few others. "Tiago," with dates and place names were scribbled on most of them.

"What the . . . ?" I said.

Chapter 22

I WENT TO SLEEP with my thoughts in a tangle but woke with a plan. Over breakfast I perused the internet on my computer and, on the way back to my room, asked Kamal for paper and pencil. In my room I began a list. Item one was *clothes*, followed by *suitcase, phone, computer charge cord, boxes, tape, pen, market, travel agency, couriers*. On the way out I picked up one of the tourist maps in the hotel reception, which helpfully offered ads for various places to shop.

My first stop was a department store, where I picked up basic toiletries, a shirt, jeans, T-shirt, underwear, socks, and a pair of knockoff sneakers. A leather bomber jacket the color of strong tea caught my fancy and I bought it too. I also got a small wheelie suitcase in which to carry everything. In an electronics store down the street I bought an international pre-paid phone. Back in the hotel I changed into my new clothes, pulled the metal box out from under the bed, and chose a chain with heavy links. Closing the box, I slid it back under the bed.

"Can you recommend a jeweler who might purchase some pieces?" I asked Kamal at the reception desk.

He regarded me in my new clothes, eyes bright with curiosity, then turned to my tourist map and circled a couple of locations. "These, I think. They both speak some Spanish and French, and maybe English too."

I thanked him, took the map and one of the business cards displayed on the counter, and left. I chose the jeweler in the souk because I could purchase the other items I needed there. The jeweler's kiosk was tucked between a barber and a merchant offering large round platters loaded with great cones of richly colored spice. I waited outside while the proprietor, a sleek, suit-clad man with graying hair, helped a woman wearing jeans and four-inch stilettos under her chador complete a purchase. When they were done he walked her to the door, waved her off, and invited me in with a gesture.

"English? *Español?*" I said as we entered the shop.

The man went behind a glass-topped counter. "*El español es mejor*," he said.

"Okay. I have something to sell," I said in Spanish. I drew the gold chain I had brought out of my pocket and placed it and Kamal's card on the counter. "Kamal said you might be interested."

The man glanced at Kamal's card, considered me for a moment with shrewd, dark eyes, and gave a small nod. "Let me have a look." He picked up the chain and went through a bead curtain to a back room. There he lay the chain down on a workbench, switched on a small bright lamp, and bent forward to examine it.

I waited, idly scanning the collection of jewelry displayed on black velvet under the counter. Several minutes later the man returned with the chain resting in a long, velvet-lined box.

"If I may ask, where did you get this?"

I was prepared for the question. "An inheritance from an uncle."

"Yet you want to sell it?"

"I have others."

"I see." He paused. "This is what I can offer." He stated an amount which, after a few seconds calculating dirham exchange rates, I realized amounted to around four hundred Euros. When

I didn't immediately respond, the jeweler added, "I'm sorry, but that's the best I can do. I don't really know you . . ."

I raised my hand. "I understand. That will be fine."

He bowed and withdrew into his back room, bearing the chain. "Geez," I breathed when he was gone. My intent in trying to sell the piece had been to confirm that what I had was in fact real gold, and to get some money for the rest of what I planned. It appeared that I had succeeded on both counts. The man returned and counted out the amount in large-denomination dirham bills.

"You no doubt would prefer Euros, but I cannot do that."

I folded the bills and slipped them into my pocket. "This is fine. Thank you."

He smiled and nodded. "I thank you. It is a beautiful piece."

Which you will no doubt sell for several times what you have paid.

I said goodbye and left.

I made the rest of my purchases in the souk and hurried back to the hotel. On the way I stopped at a travel agency to enquire about flights to Vancouver, and booked one routed through London that left at six o'clock the following morning. At the hotel I asked Kamal to arrange for a driver to pick me up in a couple of hours, and again in the early morning to go to the airport. Back in my room I quickly assembled the five cardboard boxes I had bought, and divided all the gold jewelry among them except for a wide gold band inset with a mosaic of what looked like lapis lazuli for me, and a ring with a dark green stone that was possibly an emerald for Aude. I distributed other items I had bought at the souk among the boxes: souvenir ceramics, glass animals, feathers, scarves, painted wooden plaques, leather change purses, strings of glass beads, necklaces of hammered metal, earrings, and copper bangles. I intermixed these with the gold jewelry in the hope that it would be seen as costume jewelry among the other trinkets by any customs agents who might decide to examine it. Was this camouflage necessary? I didn't know, but thought it worth the trouble.

When all the items were in the boxes I hefted each one, transferred a couple of items to equalize the weight, and taped them securely shut. I wrote out Paula's name and office address on each of the boxes. The car and driver were waiting for me when I came to the reception balancing the five boxes in my arms.

Kamal came out from behind the counter. "Can I give you a hand?"

"Maybe open the door?"

He did and shook his head laughing when I passed through. I would have to have a story to satisfy his curiosity when I returned.

I had worked out the most efficient route to five international courier companies. Sending the packages this way was an excess of caution, perhaps, but I thought there would be fewer questions if they cleared customs separately. At each courier office I completed the necessary paperwork, describing the contents of the boxes as souvenirs. That done I returned to the hotel, where I paid the driver and confirmed the time he would pick me up in the morning.

Back in my room I phoned Paula, but she didn't answer. In the paranoic spirit that seemed to be guiding my actions, I sent her a cryptic text: *I hope you got home safely and that everything with your uncle is okay. You'll be receiving five parcels with stuff you should have. I have kept what I think was meant for me. I'll explain later.*

While waiting at the departures gate at the airport early the next morning, I dialed Fin's cellphone number. Dominique answered.

"Niels! How wonderful to hear your voice."

After we had exchanged pleasantries, I asked to speak to my grandfather.

"Fin's still asleep."

"*Still* asleep?" It was nine o'clock at night in Vancouver. "Is he all right?"

Dominique's laugh sparkled down the line. "You think we're at home. We're in Helsinki, flew in earlier in the week. With the time changes, I'm up early."

"Okay. I'll call again when I can. The main thing is that I'm heading to Vancouver and wondered if I could stay at your place."

"Of course you can. I'll text Astrid, the housekeeper, to alert her—you don't know her, she's new. Here's her number so you can let her know when to expect you."

I scribbled the number down on the back of the previous day's list with Kamal's pencil, both of which were still in my jacket pocket.

"But, oh, Niels, Fin will be thrilled to hear that you are coming home."

Chapter 23

I ARRIVED IN VANCOUVER in late afternoon. Just before flying out of London I had sent Astrid a text with my flight details and the time I was likely to be at my grandfather's house. A slim, forty-something Nordic blonde dressed in jeans and a navy blazer was waiting when my taxi drew up to the door. If I correctly read the tension in her eyes, she was not happy to be called out during what she no doubt thought was a holiday while Fin and Dominique were away. Or it may have been discomfort at dealing with a scruffy, rumpled stranger.

"Sorry for any inconvenience," I said, hauling Tiago's guitar and my wheelie suitcase over the threshold. I had left the metal box with Kamal.

"No problem. How long do you expect to be here and what will you need?"

"I don't need anything. I can take care of myself. Thanks."

She didn't try to hide her relief. "I'll leave you, then. Here is a key. There's some fresh food in the refrigerator and things in the freezer you can heat up."

I took the key and thanked her again. She nodded briskly and left.

My room was much as I had left it over three years previously: Meredith dozing on her stand, the same silver-green leaf-patterned cover on the bed, the book on Philip Glass my mother had given me on the bedside table, and, on the dresser, what was possibly the same box of tissues I had opened the morning I left. Shedding my clothes, I showered, wrapped myself in an old bathrobe I found hanging on a hook, and descended to the kitchen with a load of laundry. After throwing the clothes into the washing machine, I made up a supper of cheese sandwiches which I washed down with a generous measure of Fin's twenty-year-old scotch. After cleaning up I went to bed and slept around the clock.

The next morning I realized that I had not put the laundry into the dryer before going to sleep. After doing so, I rummaged in the dresser and closet in my room for clothing I had left behind. The old shirt I found was too tight, the pair of jeans too loose around the waist. I fixed the latter with a belt and put on a sweatshirt that fit.

Needing light and air, I went out for a walk and stopped at a diner for breakfast. I lingered over coffee, watching people coming and going, the traffic buzzing by, the world I had reentered familiar yet strange. I had intended to return, of course, but not so abruptly. Perhaps it was better this way.

What to do next? I had received an email that morning from Paula in reply to one I had sent from Heathrow with a fuller explanation of the contents of the boxes. It said that she had received them—one had been opened and examined without incident—and remonstrated against my returning the jewelry. She promised to pack up my things at the tavern on the weekend and expedite their delivery. Still, it would be days, even weeks, before they arrived. The only thing I really wanted was my guitar. There was Tiago's, of course, but I was reluctant to play it until I understood what possessing it meant. Nor did I understand what possessing what I assumed were recordings of Tiago playing meant. Fin might be able to advise, but he and Dominque would not be home for two weeks.

There were people to contact: Aude, Jax and Polly, and,

of course, my mother and stepfather. I brooded in a vague and unproductive way over how to reconnect with my parents. A server came and offered to refill my cup. I declined, paid my bill, and left. On the street I stood irresolute for a couple of minutes as people flowed around me. It was a typical March day in Vancouver, overcast with a cool wind bearing the threat of a shower. I drifted to a park edged with a line of cherry trees frothing with blossoms and sat down on a wooden bench with a small plaque dedicating it to a man long dead. The park's deep-green lawn still glistened with dew and the heads of bright yellow daffodils edging the borders nodded in the breeze. I took out my phone and, after a moment's consideration, keyed in my stepfather's number.

Theo answered with a noncommittal "Yes?" He wouldn't have recognized my number.

"It's Niels, Dad."

A pause. "Niels. Fin said you were coming back." His voice was neutral.

Of course Granddad would have let them know. "Yes, got in last night. How are you and Mom?"

"We're well, thanks. And you?"

I rubbed my eyes. We could be strangers exchanging pleasantries. Is this how it was going to be? "I'm fine, a bit jetlagged. I'd like to come and visit, if that's all right."

"Yes, of course. We'd like to see you. When did you have in mind?"

"Tomorrow, if that works for you both."

"Tomorrow is fine, but today works as well," Theo said in the same impersonal tone. "Unless you have something else to do."

I tried to think of a reason to put off going but it was not yet noon and an empty day stretched ahead. "No, I don't. I'll let you know what ferry I'm on."

"Why don't you fly? We'll cover the fare."

"It wouldn't be any quicker. I'll take the ferry." I needed the time to prepare for this reunion.

We exchanged a few more words and I hung up, dazed at the speed with which things were moving.

Theo stood to the back of the people waiting at the ferry terminal arrivals and advanced slowly through the thinning crowd. My mother was not with him. Cool though our telephone conversation had been, his eyes and smile were warm. He clasped me in a hug that was slightly longer than it needed to be. Stepping back, we studied each other. His ash-blond hair, tied back with a leather cord, held more silver now, and the laugh lines around his sea-green eyes had deepened.

"You've become a man," he said.

"What did you expect me to become, a poodle?"

He smiled broadly and clapped me on the back. "Come on, I'm parked a ways back, but by the time we get there most of the other cars should be gone."

On the way to Theo's SUV we talked of inconsequential things: the weather, the route I had flown home, Fin and Dominique's trip. Inside, he turned on the ignition and backed out of the parking space.

"I thought we'd stop for coffee or a beer on the way home," he said. "Any preference?"

"Ah . . ." I said, nonplussed. No doubt I was in for a lecture. "A beer, I think."

Theo merged onto the highway and sped towards Counter Point. Before the junction that led to the estate, he turned into the parking lot of our neighborhood pub, a two-story building striving for old-world charm with leaded windows and decorative half-timber trim. Inside, heads turned as we made our way to an empty table. I was used to this. Even though he was approaching fifty, Theo's striking good looks still drew attention when he entered a room.

We sat and ordered beer. While we waited for it, Theo studied me again.

"You've bulked up."

"I discovered the pleasures of working out."

"You carry it well."

Our beers arrived and we took tentative sips. Who was going to speak first?

"Would you like something to eat?" Theo said.

I shook my head. "No, I'm fine."

"We've followed your travels a bit. Your friend Jax kept Fin up to date. Sounds like you had a few adventures."

"Yes."

"What's finally brought you back?"

"I've been intending to return for a few months, but got delayed and then something happened that ended up in my leaving Spain quickly."

Theo's eyes narrowed. "No trouble, I hope?"

"Not of my making." I made a dismissive motion with my hand. "It's a complicated story that needs time to tell."

"What was your thinking in coming back here? Do you have any plans?"

"So far none beyond seeing you and Mom and connecting with Aude again. The rest I've yet to figure out."

We fell silent. Theo twisted his pint back and forth, studying the patterns of foam the motion formed on its surface. He pushed the glass away and raised his eyes.

"Your leaving that way and not keeping in touch has been pretty hard on us. Especially your mother."

Theo rarely if ever referred to Leah as "your mother". This was going to be heavy going. I steeled myself. "I'm sorry about that."

He smiled wryly. "But Leah and I figure it's poetic justice. Both of us did the same thing when we were young."

I relaxed slightly.

"After Fin saw you in Halifax that spring and we understood what was going on and why, I wanted to go and give you a good shake but Leah said you should be left to work through it in your own way."

"I appreciate that."

"Have you?"

Have I worked through it? I gazed into the distance without answering for several moments. Turning back to Theo, I said, "I'm in a different space than I was then, but it's not something you can ever completely reconcile yourself to."

"Umm." Theo paused. "I'd just like to understand. Why didn't you feel you could discuss it with us?"

I rubbed my eyes, suddenly weary. I should have taken more time to get over the jet lag, to prepare for this inevitable accounting for my actions. I tried to conjure up that younger me who had fallen apart after learning about his shameful origins.

"I was pretty upset and totally confused by what I had learned. And very ashamed. I needed time to sort it all out, and until I did I couldn't face any of you, especially Mom. What a horrible thing to have happened to her. That was the reason she went away after I was born, wasn't it?"

Theo shook his head. "That wasn't why Leah gave you up for adoption."

I froze. My heart felt as though it was caught in a vise. What new hell was this?

"Mom gave me up for adoption?" I choked.

Theo grimaced. "Shit. I guess you didn't know that."

"No."

"She did it because she didn't feel she could take care of you." He sighed heavily. "Leah's the one who should be telling you all this. Look, when you were born she was all alone and didn't have the knowledge, or, for that matter, the means to care for an infant."

I raised my hand, palm out. "Whoa. What do you mean she was all alone? Where was she?"

"She was at home in Vancouver, but both your grandparents were away. Fin was in Europe, I think, and Alexandra off at a conference somewhere."

"But the rest of the family—"

"My mom and dad were at the ranch in New Mexico, Ben was in London, I was . . . I actually don't know where I was, but not around. I didn't even know Leah then."

"I can't believe my grandparents would have left her like that in her condition."

"I doubt it was intentional, but Fin and Alexandra were very important, very busy people, and not particularly practical. Neither of them ever dealt much with everyday matters. Someone else always took care of that stuff. I figure they just thought it would all get done somehow."

"Where was the housekeeper?"

"There wasn't one then, apparently."

"But couldn't someone have helped Mom? I mean, at the hospital?"

"Maybe, but she was only sixteen then, by herself, totally out of her depth, and without any resources. She didn't have any of the stuff you need for a baby—clothes and diapers and such. Not even cab fare home from the hospital. So she left you there with a note saying that she was giving you up for adoption, thinking that, in the circumstances, it was the best thing to do."

I raised my hand again. "I don't understand. Why didn't she have what she needed, or cab fare?"

"Again, Leah really should be the one telling you this. Fin cut off all her funds when she became pregnant. You have to understand, Leah and her dad didn't have a very good relationship when she was young. He was pretty overbearing. Still is, but it was worse then. There's other stuff, but that's another story. He came down pretty hard on her. Stopped her allowance, cancelled her credit card."

I drew back in my seat. "Even after what happened to her, what those guys did? Why?"

"Well, that's the thing. Leah didn't know about the three guys or what had happened to her then."

"How's that possible?"

"She was drugged."

A memory stirred. "That woman, Rebecca, she said they had put something in her drink," I said slowly.

"Yeah. To this day Leah doesn't remember the actual assault. Something to be thankful for, I guess. But at the time Fin wouldn't accept that she didn't know who the father was. Thought she was being stubborn."

I shook my head. "I still can't believe Granddad would have left Mom like that."

"Yeah, well, Fin's mellowed a lot. He was pretty cut up when he found out what had actually happened."

"So . . . why wasn't I adopted? How did I end up with my grandparents?"

"Giving a child up for adoption isn't that simple. Forms need to be filled, papers signed. When Fin and Alexandra found out—I think some agency tracked Leah to their home—they claimed you."

"So if it got sorted out, then what happened to Mom? Why didn't she stay around?"

"Leah went away right after she left you at the hospital, before Fin and Alexandra came home, and she stayed away because she assumed you'd been adopted. She didn't know your grandparents had taken you until she came home after Alexandra died, almost ten years later. And I can tell you that, for Leah, finding you again and being part of your life is nothing short of a miracle."

I buried my face in my hands, trying to process this new information. After a couple of minutes I raised my head.

"Why didn't anyone ever explain this all to me?"

"Niels, it's not something you tell a child."

"If Mom doesn't remember anything about the attack, how did she find out? Or decide that this Brad guy was my father?"

"One day she noticed how your hair grew."

"This fucking hair again," I said, thrusting my fingers into the wave that swept up off my forehead.

Theo raised his eyebrows at my uncharacteristic use of profanity. "Anyhow, it made her think of him. She and the sister, Rebecca, had been friends, and Leah had spent time at their house. She confronted Rebecca and learned what had happened."

"How did Rebecca know?"

"She was an accomplice. Unwilling, maybe, but she helped drug Leah."

I groaned. "And I'm related to these people? And if not the Brad guy, then one of the other two assholes?" I shook my head. "Just the thought makes me sick again."

"Yeah."

"But knowing what happened, why did Mom put me in touch with Brad's parents?"

"Leah realizes now that it was a mistake. At the time she thought it would help normalize things for you after your unusual upbringing. Don and Yvonne seemed nice enough."

"Rebecca said they should have demanded DNA proof."

"Well, they didn't. They were very happy to find you. Yvonne called a couple of times after you left, wondering why they hadn't heard from you." Theo laughed mirthlessly. "Leah finally told them that Rebecca could explain why."

I blew out a long breath. "I don't blame Mom for going and staying away."

We fell silent. After a long moment, I stirred.

"You know, this is actually all my fault."

Theo's eyebrows shot up. "*Your* fault? How's that?"

"I'm the one who insisted on finding out about my biological father."

"It's only natural to want to know."

"Yeah, maybe," I said gruffly. "But you're all anyone could ever hope for in a dad, and I'm really sorry to have thought I needed more."

When we arrived at Counter Point Theo went to his studio, leaving me to meet my mother on my own. I entered through the door to the bedroom wing, dropped off my bag, and headed to the center of the house. From the main hall I caught sight of Leah seated in an armchair in the high-ceilinged living room with the expansive windows looking out to the ocean, working on her laptop. I continued forward, my steps silent on the dense Oriental carpets scattered on the floor. A dog lay at Leah's feet, a new one. River, whom she had rescued from the side of the road after he had been hit by a car, was obviously gone now. I felt a moment's sadness at the old dog's passing. Alerted to my presence, the new dog, a Spitz breed with a black muzzle and alert, upright ears, took my measure with cool, dark-brown eyes. The beginnings of a growl brought Leah's head up from the computer screen. She bent and stroked the dog.

"Hush, Rune."

She took off her reading glasses and set them and her computer to the side, rose, and came to where I stood a few feet away. The dog, still regarding me warily, followed close on her heels. My throat closed at the sight of her, our years apart marked by a different hairstyle and new lines around her mouth and eyes. Her hands rested lightly on my shoulders then cupped my face. Her eyes glistened with tears.

"Niels, my dearest boy, you've come back to me," she said.

PART II

Chapter 24

"GO HOME, NIELS."

Aude's mother stepped backwards over the threshold and began to close the door. I grabbed the edge of it and held on.

"Why are you doing this? I just want to talk to Aude. Where is she?"

"She's not here."

"Yes, you told me that when I phoned. But I don't understand why you won't tell me where she is."

Mrs. Langevin glared at me. Through the new owner of their inn, now recovered from her back problems, I had finally tracked Aude's parents to Whistler, where Mr. Langevin managed the ski instructor and patrol program. Mrs. Langevin had refused to give me Aude's contact information when I had telephoned the previous day, so I had flown to Vancouver and taken the bus to Whistler that morning.

"You should not have come."

"But I have. All I want is her phone number or her email address. Why won't you give them to me? And why are you so angry?"

Her eyes flashed. "Why am I so angry? You leave and there's no word, nothing, for three years. You broke the poor girl's heart. Leave her alone."

"I tried to get in touch with her last year."

She sniffed. "Last year."

"I did. And when I left, I wasn't leaving her, and I told her why I had to go away."

"And then you just expected her to sit and wait? For three years?"

"Well . . ."

She shook her head. "You are a very stupid boy."

"Maybe so. But that is between Aude and me. I need to talk to her and explain."

"You need to leave her alone. Besides, it's too late."

"What do you mean, too late," I said, alarmed. "Is she okay?"

Mrs. Langevin smirked. "Oh, she is very okay. She's married now, to a real man, not to a stupid boy."

"Married?" I gagged on the word. "She can't be."

"Well, she is."

"To whom?"

"You don't know him. He's French. They're in France."

I stood there, my mouth hanging open. "How could she? It was me she was going to marry, we always understood that."

"Whatever you understood, with no word, no contact, it couldn't go on forever." Mrs. Langevin regarded me with something like sympathy. "Go home, Niels," she said again and closed the door.

I staggered back, almost losing my balance on the entrance steps. Breathless from shock, I sank down on the top one. My mind went blank. I could not move, could not even form the thought of moving. Great, fat flakes of snow began to fall, wetting my hair and eyelashes. Mrs. Langevin opened the door behind me, exclaimed in disgust, and closed it again. Shortly after she came out and thrust an open umbrella into my hand.

"I've called a taxi." She went back inside and shut the door with a solid, definitive *thunk*.

In time—it could have been a minute or an hour—a taxi appeared. I got up, closed the umbrella, set it down on the step, and walked like an automaton to the car. At the terminal I waited, damp and shivering, for the next bus back to Vancouver. On the ride I ran the news over and over in my mind, unable to accept what I had heard. How could Aude have done that? And so quickly after I had gone? The Aude I knew would have waited. We had often not seen each other for long stretches and it hadn't affected our relationship before. And she was only twenty-three. What about all the plans she had? We had?

Back at Counter Point I was relieved to find my parents out for the evening, sparing me explanations I was not ready to give. The prepaid phone I had bought in Morocco didn't access the internet, so it was not until then that I could find out more about what had happened. The response to the query *Aude Langevin, marriage, France* predictably included several pages offering links to her namesake, the fashion mogul, but on the fifth page was a link that led me to a clip from a French newspaper. Under a headline that my imperfect knowledge of French translated as *Star Conductor Weds* was a picture of Aude smiling up at a dark, good-looking man gazing at the camera as though gauging its worthiness to capture his image. I struggled through the French text accompanying it with horrid fascination. Aude had married Thierry Léandre, up-and-coming French conductor, and the happy event had taken place—I gasped—six weeks ago. I collapsed on my bed, *six weeks, six weeks,* echoing through my mind like a hellish mantra. If I had come home after Christmas as I had planned, if I hadn't stayed in Spain because of Tiago, I could have stopped it.

"Good morning, Niels." Leah perched on the ottoman beside the sofa on which I sprawled. "How are you today?"

I regarded her with gummy eyes. "I can't believe how much it hurts." Since confirming the truth of Aude's betrayal—for all the fault that rested with me for losing her I still viewed it this way—I had been prostrated by a grief so painful that each breath was a knife in my heart, and my gut churned like a pack of mice had been let loose inside.

"Aude called us, you know. Twice. We didn't know anything more than she did the first time, and all I could tell her the second time was that you were on a ship somewhere."

"Yeah, well, it's hardly your fault."

Rune had followed my mother in. He sniffed my bare toes delicately then touched noses with a large gray tabby curled up against my stomach, another new addition to the household since my departure. Leah reached out to stroke the cat.

"I see you've made friends with Padmore."

"He's not as judgmental as your dog."

Leah smiled. "It's in their nature to be protective. Rune will come around." She glanced at the half-drunk cup of coffee on the side table. "Niels, you should eat something."

"I'm not hungry." I shifted my position. Padmore stood up, yawned, stretched, and jumped lightly off the sofa. He padded out of the room on black velvet paws, Rune following behind.

"Lying around and not eating aren't going to help."

"You think I should just forget about it? Act like everything's okay?"

"No, I know how much losing someone can hurt and how long it lasts."

"Who have *you* ever lost?"

Leah regarded me with a faint smile. "You, for a start."

I passed a hand over my eyes. "Sorry, Mom."

She rose from the ottoman. "But one thing I learned is that life does go on. How about a shower first, then some lunch."

I mumbled assent, aware of the staleness of my body and breath, the days-worth of bristle on my cheeks. "Give me half an hour."

At lunch, my parents left me alone to eat my soup and sandwich and talked of other things: Papa Luke and Mama Ris's anticipated return from Carmel where they had been visiting friends, Theo's new commission to paint a portrait of the retiring chief justice of the Supreme Court, the breakthrough Leah had that morning on a sticky part of the book she was writing. When I had set my empty dishes aside and filled my cup from the teapot, Leah turned to me.

"I had a call from your friend Jax."

I had emailed Jax and Polly shortly after returning to bring them up to date and give them my phone number, but hadn't spoken to them yet. "Why was she calling you?"

"Because you weren't answering your own phone." That was true—I hadn't plugged it in to charge since coming back from Whistler and wasn't even sure where it was.

"What did she want?"

"She's coming here later this week for an interview at the University of Victoria."

I perked up. "You mean like for a job?"

"That was my understanding." Leah paused. "I took the liberty of inviting her to stay with us while she was here. Not the most convenient setup given our distance from the campus, but I thought you'd want to spend time with her, and driving her around will give you something to do."

Something stirred in me, like warmth returning to a frozen limb. "Yes, I'd like very much to see her. Thanks."

"Oh, Nielie, I'm so sorry," Jax said. She was staying in Fox's bedroom and we were sharing an after-dinner glass of wine in the breezeway lounge.

"It's just, you know, we had an understanding. I thought we did, anyway." My grieving since getting the news from Aude's mother in Whistler had been dry-eyed, but within the ambit of Jax's warmth and sympathy I began to snuffle. I hunched over and gave my eyes an annoyed swipe with my handkerchief. "It wasn't like we hadn't been apart before. We'd go months sometimes without talking. I did tell her that I had to work something out and would be away for a while. Why didn't she wait?"

Jax rubbed my back. "I don't know, sweetie."

"If I had known I'd have stayed in close touch. Of course I would have. But I never thought this would happen, that she'd do such a thing. And I did try to get in touch with her—twice. But her phone number and email were both dead and you know we never got into social media much."

"It's tough, I know."

"I'll stop now."

"It's okay. Say what you have to."

I blew my nose. "Anyway, it's so good to see you. Tell me more about this interview thing."

"It's big, Nielie. Assistant professor position. Tenure track. I've made it to the interviews. Figure I'm a good fit and I'm hoping the whole diversity thing will work in my favor."

I smiled faintly. "You wouldn't mind being a token appointment?"

Jax laughed. "Hell, no. I'd deck myself out in rainbows if it would help. I'm trying not to get my hopes up too much, but it's such a sweet opportunity. Apart from the job, moving to the coast is really appealing. Polly's parents live here, and you too, of course. You *are* planning to stay now that you're back, aren't you?"

I sighed. "Jax, I haven't the foggiest idea where to go or what to do next. I need to talk to my grandfather about what I brought from Spain." I gave her a full account of Tiago's death, the circumstances around my abrupt departure, and what I had learned about his life.

"So this guy was a big deal in flamenco before he went to prison?"

"That's what his granddaughter said. And judging by how he could play, I believe it."

"And you studied with him?"

"In a way, yeah, although I didn't appreciate who he was at the time."

"Did he ever release any records?"

"Paula said he never recorded, had a kind of superstition about it."

Jax regarded me intently for a few moments. "So, you have tapes of performances by an unrecorded flamenco guitarist who may possibly have ranked among the top players of his time?"

"Yeah, maybe."

Jax drew back. "Jesus, Nielie. You could be sitting on a veritable treasure."

Chapter 25

I STILL WOKE EVERY morning to the soul-wrenching knowledge that Aude was lost to me, but now resolutely filled the day with distractions. First was a return to working out in my parents' exercise room. With each drop I sweated I purged myself of the sick broth of misery, anger, guilt, loneliness, and regret that roiled through me. When notice came that my belongings had arrived from Spain and were waiting to clear customs, I rushed to Vancouver and brought the collection of boxes and my guitar to Fin's house. I let the instrument adjust to its new environment after the stresses of its time in transit for a couple of days, carefully examining it when I removed it from its case. Apart from being badly out of tune—out of sympathy, perhaps—it didn't seem to have suffered much from the trip.

Fin and Dominique returned home around this time. My grandfather and I had spoken twice during their absence, but only in generalities. I braced myself for a grilling over how I had spent my time since we last met, what I had lost, and the new direction in which I had embarked—or lack of it. When I met them at the airport, however, he only embraced me and said that he looked forward to hearing all about my adventures. In this I detected Dominique's moderating influence—the Fin of old would have briskly shaken my hand then gone up one side of me and down the other before we had reached the car.

That evening I asked for a couple of hours of his time at his earliest convenience—my experience with Tiago and his legacy were not a matter for casual discussion over dinner. Fin replied with equal formality that he had a few pressing matters to deal with the next morning but would be entirely at my disposal in the afternoon. I found him at the desk in his studio listening to a voicemail. He jotted a note when it was done and motioned me into a chair with a smile. I set the box of cassettes on his desk and sat down.

"I have a story to tell you."

Fin leaned back in his chair and listened to my account, his fingers tapping a pattern on the armrests.

"Returning the gold jewelry was the correct thing to do," he said when I was done. "What do you think this Tiago's intention was in leaving you the guitar and cassettes?"

"It could be that I was the only person in the end to be interested in his music—none of his family appeared to be. Maybe he just wanted to be appreciated and remembered. But Jax thinks this stuff may be worth looking into further."

Fin stretched to pick one of the cassettes out of the box, read the inscription on it, and set it down again. "Yes, maybe. By the way, how did she fare with that job at UVic?"

"You know about that?"

"I gave her a reference."

I raised my eyebrows. "How did you come to do that?"

"I got to know her during your absence. I saw her a few times when I was in Toronto, went to a couple of her quartet's performances. She kept me posted on your exploits." He smiled faintly. "She also helped me understand you better."

I shut my mouth, which had fallen open in surprise. I didn't particularly like the thought of being dissected by Jax and my grandfather. "She's waiting to hear about the job."

"I hope she gets it. She's a fine musician."

While my mind boggled at their peculiar friendship, Fin

examined a few more of the cassettes. "First thing we should do is re-record the contents of these tapes before they deteriorate any further. There's an audio technician here in town who knows how to handle delicate media and can capture and clean up poor-quality sound. We'll get him to do it. He also can advise on how to properly preserve them."

"Preserve them?"

"As artefacts they may be valuable in their own right."

"So you think these may be of possible significance?"

Fin regarded me thoughtfully. "I know people in Spain. Let me make some calls."

Two days later I stuck my head through the door to Fin's studio. "Thought you'd like to know that I got a text from Jax saying she got the assistant professor position."

He looked up and smiled. "I'm glad to hear it. Maybe it will encourage you to stay out here as well." I said nothing. "Anyway, come in for a minute, Niels. I have some information back from Spain."

I entered and sat down in the chair in front of his desk. He flicked through the pages of the notebook in which he kept a record of his daily dealings.

"I spoke with a couple of friends and one of them talked to a couple more. Ah, here it is." He read briefly and raised his eyes. "An interesting man, your friend Tiago. Joachin—he played oboe for the Spanish National Orchestra for many years—is old enough to remember him well, even saw him perform a couple of times. He says that Tiago was an extraordinary guitarist, that he could have rivaled Paco de Lucia—they were around the same age—if he had continued. But he had a few, well, quirks. One was that he was a staunch traditionalist in respect of flamenco, didn't agree with the direction some of the artists were taking it, like introducing jazz influences. So, his potential to grow in his art wasn't clear."

I nodded. "Yes, at one time there were strong views on that within the community."

"He also mentioned the business about Tiago refusing to have his music recorded." Fin held up a finger and consulted the notes he had written. "Something to the effect that Tiago felt flamenco needs to be directly experienced to be authentic, and recording would gut it of its spirit and meaning and turn it into nothing but noise."

I smiled faintly. "Yeah, that sounds like him. Yet it didn't stop him from making those cassettes."

"He probably wanted to know what he sounded like to fine tune his playing. Or possibly capture his own compositions."

"Could be. An awful lot of flamenco is improvisation, and even set pieces can get very different interpretations, often by the same performers."

Fin nodded. "Joachin also said that Tiago was quite wild, beyond the drink and drugs that are common among artists to quite outrageous behavior. Like walking on roof ridges and riding a horse through Madrid traffic. And then, of course, that mad business with the British girl."

We were silent for several moments. I didn't try to exonerate Tiago.

"Joaquin said that the murders were horrific, but the silencing of an extraordinary talent was another great loss." Fin closed his notebook. "And you studied with this man?"

"Yes, if you could call it that. When I first asked him to teach me he said no—told me to come back when I knew how to play guitar."

Fin smiled. "Spoken like a true master. So did you?"

"Yes, I took lessons from others and worked on it for several months before I went back to Tiago."

Fin nodded his approval.

"But then I had only, what, six months playing with him?" I shook my head. "But what a time it was. He didn't instruct, per se. We played together, what he called *conversations.* He'd set the *palo*—the theme and rhythm—and we'd go back and forth, building on each other. And I observed him, his playing, closely. With all the other flamenco I had experienced by then I realized that he was more than good, but until his granddaughter told me I had no idea of his past." A great sadness gripped me. "He was important to me."

"And you obviously were important to him. So, what are you going to do with this legacy he's left you?"

I shifted in my chair. "I don't know. I guess we'd have to hear what there is first, but maybe create proper recordings of these performances? If there are still people who remember him, they may want to hear his playing."

"Joaquin was curious about why I was making enquiries about a long-forgotten guitarist. Of course, I didn't tell him about what you have—it wasn't for me to do so without your agreement—but I expect that he, and others, would be very interested to know that these recordings exist."

"Maybe some university or archive in Spain would want them. If he was that important in his time, some researchers might want to pick through his music."

Fin regarded me with slightly raised eyebrows. "Niels, just bringing this music into light would be significant enough, but the wealth of information you have would feed several avenues of research and I don't think interest should be limited to Spain. You have the basis here for a doctorate, at least. You're looking for something to do, aren't you?"

"Granddad, I'm hardly knowledgeable enough or equipped to process and interpret Tiago's recordings."

"Not yet, perhaps, but by doing it within a study program you'd develop the skills you need."

"But a doctoral program? I haven't even completed my undergraduate degree."

"That's easily fixed."

"Yeah, but you don't just go to a university and say, hey, I've got some interesting stuff, why don't you let me into your PhD program."

"Actually, that's not a bad way to approach it."

"But I don't want to go off somewhere for years and years." I stopped, surprised at the statement. Had I just made up my mind to stay here?

"You needn't go off anywhere. The UBC School of Music is very good."

"Yet you didn't want me to do my undergraduate degree here."

Fin waved away the comment. "You needed exposure to other influences. It would be different now. I know the director."

"I wouldn't want you to pull strings for me!" But I doubted I would need Fin's help getting into the program—my great-grandmother had been on the university's board of governors and my grandmother Alexandra, an eminent scientist, had been in the physics department. As a memorial after her death, my family had financed the construction on the university grounds of a small pavilion to serve as a place for quiet reflection, musical performances, and events. Fin was speaking. "Sorry, Granddad, I didn't hear what you said."

"I said of course I wouldn't pull strings or intervene in any way against your wishes."

I pushed back my chair. "Well, it's an interesting idea, but right now I really don't know what I want to do. Maybe my future isn't in music at all. Maybe I should pursue a career as a chef."

Fin began to speak but bit back his intended words. *Don't be ridiculous*, no doubt. Instead he said, "That's not the future I would want for you, but of course it's your life."

The audio technician was tied up on a large job and then

off somewhere so he was unable to meet regarding the cassettes until two weeks later. I decided to return to Counter Point for the interim.

"Do think about what I've suggested," Fin said when I told him I was leaving. Dominique had just brought him a cup of coffee. She was a tall woman with a cap of tousled salt-and-pepper hair, large brown eyes, and a swan-like neck. She and Fin became acquainted when he hired her from among the four architects considered to design my grandmother's memorial pavilion at UBC. Dominique's design was stunning: upon a small dark base that served as the entrance floor she had built a cubic structure sheathed in a material that conducted light. Set against the woods on the campus, at night it glowed mysteriously as though suspended in the air. She still advised on projects undertaken by the architectural firm she had created but was no longer involved in its day-to-day activities. It had given her time to develop her art—exquisite watercolors of building interiors and exteriors. I followed her back to the kitchen and we took coffees to the small atrium connected to it. She used it as a studio and showed me two pieces she had just completed inspired by their recent trip: a modern Finnish church and the interior of a Prague coffee house.

"Granddad has really mellowed," I said as we drank our coffee. "Talking about what I'm going to do—he's really pulling his punches. Your influence, maybe?"

Dominique regarded me with a slight smile. "It's more likely a result of the shock of your departure and absence. He took it hard. He feared that he had made the same mistake with you as he had with your mother and that you were lost to him for good."

I didn't speak for a moment. "I'm sorry about that."

"But you're back now, and that's all that matters."

"Darling . . ." My mother hesitated. "Is there a pressing need to resolve all this now?"

I had just unloaded to her about my confusion over my future.

"It's just that I feel so . . . discombobulated. And useless."

"I know the feeling. Take some time to regain your balance."

"But I need to decide what I'm going to do. I think Granddad figures my career as a musician is a non-starter—he proposes that I go the academic route."

"And that has no appeal?"

"To some degree, but I'm wary that Granddad may be trying to control my life again."

"Niels . . ." Leah paused. "There was a time when I rejected almost anything my father suggested out of principle. I've learned that what he says merits consideration, at least."

"Yeah, well. Then there's the matter of where I should live."

"You're welcome to stay here as long as you like. There's plenty of room—we wouldn't live on top of each other."

"Still . . ."

Leah sighed. "Darling, why don't you go and talk to Papa Luke."

That afternoon, I descended to Mama Ris and Papa Luke's cottage, positioned where Counter Point sloped down to the ocean. My relationship to them was complicated. My mother and Theo are half-cousins, a situation I didn't realize was unusual until the revelation in high school that Einstein was married to his cousin prompted guffaws and lewd comments from my classmates. As Fin's half-sister Mama Ris was Leah's aunt, but as Theo's mother she also was her mother-in-law. Leah had coined her and Papa Luke's pet names after her marriage to cover this dual relationship, and the rest of us had adopted them.

Mama Ris greeted me with a long, warm hug. "I am so sorry you had to learn about that business of your parentage, and I understand how upsetting it must have been. You were very much missed."

"I missed you all too."

She held me at arm's length and studied my face. "I like this new look of yours. It suits you well." Releasing me, she gestured to a set of French doors in the living room. "Luke is on the deck and looking forward to seeing you. I'm about to take him some tea. What can I bring you?"

"Tea is fine."

I went out to the deck, where Papa Luke sat in an armchair gazing out at the water, a leg propped on a footstool. As a young monk doing charitable work in the Andes, he had been sucked down a raging chute of water while helping people escape a flood. Miraculously he had survived, but his leg had been badly injured and he had subsequently walked with a cane.

"Niels!" he said with a wide smile.

He had aged in the years I had been away. In his late eighties now, his body sagged on its large frame and the planes of his broad, strong face were sharper. But his mane of white hair was still thick and his grip firm when we embraced. I drew up a chair to sit near him, feeling my breath slow as it always seemed to when I was in his presence. My fingers touched my left wrist, bare since the little punks in Seville had stolen the watch he and Mama Ris had given me.

Mama Ris brought out the tea tray. We took sips of our tea and sampled the lemon loaf that accompanied it.

"Now, tell me what's been happening with you," Papa Luke said.

I set down my cup. "I don't want to talk about the reason I left."

"I understand."

I began with my time in Halifax and on the container ships—what I had done and seen, the people I had met. "The year I was on the ships, on the water, it was like I was suspended in space and time. I felt detached, out of myself somehow, in another dimension. It was . . . I don't know, therapeutic. What I needed, anyway."

Papa Luke smiled. "Retreats take many forms."

We sat in the spring sunshine listening to the tide inhale and exhale in the little bay below. A seal appeared, bobbing and twisting in the water. A sapsucker landed on a nearby fir tree and went to work on its trunk. I tapped the staccato rhythm out on my knee. Papa Luke watched me curiously.

"It's kind of like a flamenco beat." I told him about Daniel and going to Spain and discovering the musical form. "The playing is incredibly complex. With good players, it's like they're weaving tapestries of sound."

"Would you play for me sometime?"

"Of course," I said.

I brought my guitar on my next visit. A light rain fell and Papa Luke was alone inside the cottage—Mama Ris had gone to Vancouver to see a sick friend. When I took it out of its case, Papa Luke leaned forward to examine it.

"That's a fine-looking instrument."

"The top is actually made of cedar from here in British Columbia, which is unusual. Tiago, my teacher, helped me find it. He said it suited me." I settled the guitar into position on my knee. "I haven't practiced much since I got back, so things may be a bit stiff to start."

I played a short, simple piece to loosen my fingers, then a more complex one. When I finished I explained *compás* and the different flamenco *palos*.

Papa Luke glanced at his watch. "I'm ready for a scotch. Will you have one and then join me for dinner? Ris left a casserole of some sort. There is plenty of it and I would be glad of the company."

While Papa Luke poured out measures of whisky into

heavy-bottomed glasses, I sent a text to my mother saying I would not be back for dinner. I put the casserole into the oven to heat and we settled down with our drinks.

"Tell me about this teacher, the one who helped you find the guitar," Papa Luke said.

I talked about seeing Tiago playing in the street, how his music had caught my interest, how I had slowly gotten to know him, and the jolt I had felt when I first held his guitar. I described my efforts to learn flamenco guitar well enough to engage Tiago's attention.

"I didn't know then that he had once been a virtuoso, but I understood enough to realize that he played exceptionally well."

A *ding* indicated the casserole was heated through. While I set the table, Papa Luke opened a bottle of Pinot Noir from a local vineyard in which my parents held a small stake after investing some capital to save it from bankruptcy. Over dinner I talked about the *gitano* wedding, Tiago's blistering performance, my own modest contribution to the evening. As we finished the bottle of wine I spoke hesitantly about my experience listening to Maria sing.

"Being transported by flamenco like that is called *duende*. I felt like I had been turned inside out and all kinds of dark, dark stuff was pouring out of me."

"A kind of catharsis?

"Yes, maybe. After, Tiago began to seriously instruct me in flamenco, like I had gone through some rite of passage."

We tidied up and withdrew to the comfort of the deep armchairs in the living room, watching the flames' contortions in the fireplace while we sipped cups of smoky tea. Papa Luke set his empty cup to the side.

"You refer to Tiago in the past tense."

"He died a few weeks ago." I described Tiago's decline, the last months of his life, and his final night out under the stars.

"It sounds like an extraordinary experience."

"It was. Tiago didn't welcome death but he went out to meet it. I hope I can face it in the same way when my time comes."

"Yes."

I glanced at Papa Luke, concerned that my comment had been insensitive. At his age the matter of death was probably not far from his mind. Sadness pierced me at the thought of losing this fine and gentle man.

"Having a person like Tiago come into one's life is a gift," he continued.

"Yes, but it had some downsides. It turns out he was a murderer, and because of him I lost Aude."

Papa Luke's eyebrows shot up. "A murderer?"

I told him about Tiago's killing the British woman and her fiancé all those years ago. "I didn't know this until after he died."

"Has it changed your sense of him?"

"I don't know. It's complicated."

"And how did Tiago cause you to lose Aude?"

The loss still sat heavily on my heart and I didn't answer immediately. "I had intended to come home after Christmas but stayed to see Tiago through his final days. If I hadn't stayed I would have been back in time to know of and hopefully interrupt her plans to marry that guy." I made an impatient gesture with my hand. "Oh, I know I'm at fault for not having kept in touch, but I did try. Anyhow, she's off married now and here I am."

Papa Luke studied me. "You have endured several hard losses in these last few years. Not the least of which was the loss of innocence."

There it was at last. I didn't shy away now. "Yes, that may have been the hardest. I don't know which part of it is worse, what those guys did to my mom or the fact that half of me is made up of one of them."

"Niels, you are not made up of halves or parts of anything. You are wholly yourself."

"Maybe, but I can't help but wonder if some of that awfulness lives on in me."

Papa Luke smiled. "I think any awfulness in you would have shown up by now. But tell me, will you continue with flamenco? It does sound like you have found your instrument and music. Or it has found you."

"I don't know." I shifted in my chair. "I'm not sure that a product of the sun and heat of Spain can thrive in the clouds and mist here on the coast. Western music—well, it's got a logic to it, an intellectual base, but flamenco music comes from feeling. And I'm not sure I can recreate the right feeling. So all the time I put into learning it . . ." I shook my head. "I don't know where to go with it now." I told him about Tiago's legacy, my flight from Spain, returning the gold, and now the question of the tapes. "Granddad thinks I should turn them into a research project to get a doctorate."

"An interesting idea."

"In some ways, but it would be a big commitment and I'm not sure it's what I want to do. Trouble is, I've no sense at all of what that is. Like I've cut lines all over the place and am completely adrift. It's not a comfortable feeling."

"Sometimes if you just relax and let things evolve, your new direction reveals itself in some way."

"Maybe," I said.

Fin called the following week to say that the audio technician was back and ready to look at Tiago's tapes. I returned to Vancouver and we took the cassettes over one morning. The technician's workshop was in a strip mall on Kingsway. A man in his forties with a closely shaved tonsure and rimless glasses opened the door to our ring.

"Mark," he said, shaking my hand. His tight black jeans and Nirvana T-shirt clothed a compact and tidy body. His shop had the stark character of a clean room in a high-tech facility. Long and narrow, it was filled with several workbenches and a phalanx of equipment, great boards bristling with buttons and switches, screens blinking like eyes, speakers of different sizes and every type of recording device. Mark took the box of cassettes from me and set them on a workbench. He drew on white cloth gloves, gingerly removed a cassette from the box, and examined it from all sides. After testing that the tape spun freely, he carried it to a piece of equipment connected to one of the boards and slid it into a slot. Removing his gloves, he pushed buttons and fiddled with sliders. A string of garbled sound issued from the speakers. Mark's fingers danced over the board and the sound resolved itself into the recognizable clamor of a nightclub threaded through with music. Continuing to work the controls, Mark slowly peeled back the ambient noise until only the music remained.

Despite the inexpert recording and the thin and scratchy quality of the sound, I recognized Tiago's distinctive edgy, punchy playing. It was like a wormhole had opened back to Andalusia. My breath caught, my heart leapt, and something like an electric current buzzed down my spine.

This is it, I thought. *This is what I want to do.*

Chapter 26

AND SO BEGAN SEVERAL wildly intense and wonderfully productive years of work.

I returned to Toronto to complete my degree. Fin was pleased with my decision to continue my studies but in a reserved way, feeling, perhaps, that overt enthusiasm might scare me off. We had a tussle over who would pay.

"I can do this myself. I have money saved," I said.

"In this family, we pay for our children's education."

"I'm hardly a child."

"Nonetheless. You may need your money for other things."

With Jax moving to Victoria, I rented a small service flat in the same building near the University of Toronto campus where I had briefly lived seven years previously. I got reacquainted with Celeste, whom Jax had left with a mutual friend. With the decision to return to my studies I was obliged to practice rigorously, eventually regaining most of my facility on the instrument, although the cellist with whom I had studied previously despaired that I no longer played with the same finesse.

I spread my studies over the summer and fall to include advanced courses in classical guitar and Spanish. On one of my visits home I requested and was granted a meeting with the director of the UBC School of Music. The director, an imposing woman who had offset her severely coiffed white-blond hair and charcoal-gray suit with dramatic florescent-pink glasses, received me with the flat smile and constrained air of someone discharging an obligation. I felt a prick of conscience at trading on my family connections and, not wishing to take more of her time than necessary, launched into my desire to pursue graduate studies at her school and the unique material on which my research would be based.

"Among the other work I'd be required to do, I propose to transcribe and publish whatever original music I find on the tapes and write a monograph about Tiago's life and position in flamenco history."

"You say this Tiago was a musician of note?"

"In his time, yes."

She leaned towards me over the desk, her eyes glittering behind the curious glasses.

"And you studied with him?"

"Yes, for a few months before he died."

"And he never formerly recorded his work?"

"That's what I understand. I'd have to confirm that, of course, but as far as I know the tapes he bequeathed to me are the only ones in existence."

She leaned back in her chair. "I see."

We spoke for forty-five minutes. The director asked penetrating questions and offered valuable suggestions. When her executive assistant entered in what was probably a pre-arranged interruption to remind her of another meeting, she waved him away without looking up. His second interruption was firmer. I took the cue and collected my things to go.

"What you propose would fit within the ethnomusicology stream and could be structured as an integrated master's and doctorate program. Assuming, of course, you meet the admission requirements." The director rose and smiled. "Which I doubt will be a problem." She walked me to the door and shook my hand. "Give my regards to your grandfather."

With no urgency to complete the task, Mark worked on Tiago's cassette tapes slowly and steadily, fitting them in around his other work. For each one he produced a digital file as free of other noise as he was able to make it. They varied considerably in quality. Four were complete duds. Seven of the tapes yielded beautifully crisp and clear music, offering the potential to create and release a recording of Tiago playing. The rest varied in quality. The arrival of a new file in my inbox was an event. I would close my eyes, and any scratches and flaws would recede as the power of Tiago's playing washed over me.

Fin brought some administrative order to my efforts. "You need to register your ownership of these materials with performance rights organizations, both here in North America and Europe. Talk to Hilary, she can help," he said, referring to his music manager.

"But it's Tiago's music."

"He is no longer here and you are his heir, so the music now belongs to you. And the transcriptions will certainly be your work, as well as recordings or performances you do."

"Still, it doesn't feel right."

"If it will make you feel better, why not assign a portion of the proceeds from licensing or sales by the publishing company you'll have to create to some appropriate charity in his memory?"

"Yeah, I could do that. Though I don't know who's going to be interested enough to license any of that stuff."

"You may be surprised," Fin said.

In the eight months between completing my degree in Toronto and starting the program at UBC—to which I was readily admitted—I returned to Spain for an extended visit. As a precaution I confirmed with Paula beforehand that returning Tiago's gold jewelry had mollified her uncle and I was no longer in his sights. It apparently had. Emilio insisted on my staying in Daniel's apartment while I was in Seville. "It's your home here," he said. Daniel joined me for a week and I visited him in Cartagena, where he was based.

My main purpose, besides reconnecting with Emilio, Daniel, and Paula, was to research Tiago's life and music. Prior to the trip I had searched online sources for information about Tiago but found little available, understandable given the time that had passed. I had better luck plumbing the archives of the major media outlets in Spain and found, in addition to articles about the murders and Tiago's trial, obscure pieces about his performances. I also arranged to speak to anyone who had known Tiago, starting with the members of his family and friends I already knew, except for his son—I declined Paula's offer to arrange for me to interview him. These people suggested other names and leads, and I traveled widely through Andalusia following them up. Fin also had provided introductions to people he knew in the Spanish music industry, who in turn directed me to other relevant people and sources. When the opportunity arose I attended workshops with some renowned guitarists, and through them found others to talk to about the music scene. And throughout it all I soaked up flamenco.

I was conscious of the moral issues surrounding the work of a criminal and had spent a few difficult days wondering whether even to proceed with Tiago's music.

"You will have to address the matter in your research, of course," Fin said, "but it's no reason not to do it."

To start, I wanted to let the relatives of the woman and man Tiago had killed know what I was doing. Through newspaper accounts and other research I had tracked down some of their nieces and nephews. When I contacted them, most shrugged at my plans—they had never known their aunt or uncle.

Two of the murdered couple's siblings were still alive. On my way home from Spain I stopped in England to speak to them in person. The sister of the man was in a retirement home. She smiled without comprehension and pressed tea and cake on me as I described what I planned to do. Tiago's girlfriend's brother, Henry, was a different story. I found him through his son, Martin, an Anglican clergyman. Martin accompanied me to the flat where his father lived. While he prepared cups of instant coffee in the kitchen, Henry scowled at me from under bushy white eyebrows.

"Are you asking for my permission to do this work?" he said when I had outlined my research.

"No, I am letting you know about it as a courtesy."

"Pfhaw!" His hatchet-sharp features twisted in disgust. "Why the bloody hell are you even bothering with this man?" He waved away the cup of coffee Martin handed him. Martin set it down on the table next to his father's chair, offered a cup to me, and sat down in an armchair with his own.

"He was a flamenco guitarist of note—"

"Ha!"

"And the tapes I have are the only recordings of his work. Before he died—"

"Good bloody riddance!"

"I studied with him for a short time."

"And you didn't mind that he was a murderer?"

"I didn't know it then. He was just an old man who played guitar. I learned about his past after."

"My sister was a silly girl. Spoiled, you know, always had her way, but she didn't deserve to die like that." His rheumy eyes glistened.

"No, she didn't."

"And you want to glorify her murderer? She doesn't deserve that either."

I didn't respond immediately. "Tiago's life ended in many ways then as well."

"Through his own bloody fault."

"Yes, and he spent a long time in prison. The old man I knew was not the young one who killed your sister."

"At least he got to live to get old."

"Yes."

Henry turned to Martin. "What do you think?"

"We're told to hate the sin, not the sinner."

"Pfhaw!" Henry rubbed his chin and glared at me. "Do what you want. I don't bloody care."

"The book I write about his life will provide a full and honest account of what he did."

"Humph!"

I set my cup aside. "I appreciate your receiving me. I'll leave you in peace now."

"Peace? Huh."

I rose and Martin made to follow. "It's okay," I said. "I can find my way out."

Chapter 27

"WHY DON'T YOU LIVE here?" Fin said. "There is plenty of room and you're often at Counter Point anyway. Dominique and I come and go all the time, and it would be good to have someone in residence."

I glanced up from checking out the "for rent" ads on my computer. We were sitting at the marble-topped table on Fin's back terrace with the September morning sun slanting over our coffee cups. I had spent the summer at Counter Point bringing order to all the material I had collected in Spain. While there I visited often with Jax and Polly, occasionally spending the night on the lumpy sofa bed in the den of their little townhouse. They had happily settled into their new home and jobs in Victoria—Jax at the university, Polly with a communications department in the provincial government. I was back in Vancouver now to start my studies at UBC and figured it was time to set myself up for the years it would take me to complete the master's and doctorate programs.

"I don't want to impose."

"You're not imposing," Fin said, "but I understand if you would prefer to be around younger people."

"It's not that, Granddad. I just feel that at my age I shouldn't still be living at home."

"Well, it's far better than some grotty rental accommodation. If you really want your own place, I'm sure we could find a condo among the holdings that's not occupied."

The "holdings" was the portfolio of real estate the family owned. I thought of the tall buildings and their sterile, cookie-cutter units with their cautious, color-coordinated interiors, precious balconies, and hard glass and metal shells. "Ah, no, I'd rather not." Continuing to live in my grandfather's familiar and comfortable house had appeal. "Are you sure it would be okay if I stayed here? Wouldn't Dominique mind?"

"She's the one who suggested it."

"I guess we could see how it goes. But I'd like to pay some rent."

"Oh for Christ's sake."

"I know—how about if I cook for you and Dominique?"

Fin shook his head, laughing. "Sure, why not?"

I lowered the lid of my laptop. "It's a deal."

"And you are perfectly welcome to, ah, bring friends over to visit, and stay, if you'd like."

I grinned. "Thanks, I'll keep that in mind." I didn't doubt that my grandfather would greet the appearance of a strange female at breakfast with perfect aplomb.

The living arrangement worked out well. As promised I baked bread and pastries and filled the refrigerator with dishes I thought Fin and Dominique would enjoy. Given our respective busy schedules, we often saw each other only in passing but ate together whenever we could.

"Well," Fin said, spooning up the last bit of duck ragù from his bowl, "it's good to know that something came out of all that time you spent working in kitchens."

The practicality of cooking and physicality of working out balanced the demands of my courses and hours of guitar and cello practice. When the coursework was completed I focused on the research. The wait proved beneficial—my studies had better prepared me to approach Tiago's music. Still, processing over eighty hours of recordings was a daunting task.

I began by separating out musical fragments resulting from either poor-quality sound or the tape reaching its limit. From what remained I identified fifty-five pieces that had an identifiable structure, as opposed to open-ended improvisation. Twenty-four of these were recognizable flamenco standards. I planned to transcribe the remaining thirty-one pieces then check them against the body of published flamenco works. If no matches were found I would treat the pieces as Tiago's own compositions.

Transcription of the compositions was complicated by gaps in the flow because of sound or media quality issues, or because the tapes included multiple versions of them. For the gaps I had to introduce my own bridging notes, and in the case of the multiple versions I had to judge which were the best, often knitting together segments from different performances. The more I transcribed, the more uncertain I became. Had I made the right choices? Was I doing Tiago's music justice? I appealed to Fin for help.

"If I can hear properly," he said gruffly. His hearing had deteriorated in recent years and he was adjusting to new hearing aids.

"You probably hear better with one ear than I do with both of mine." We entered his studio, which he had generously made available for my work. "Although I'm not sure it's kosher to have someone help me with my homework," I added as we sat down before the console.

"This is hardly homework. It's not unusual and, in fact, customary to consult with colleagues when you're working through music."

Colleagues? I glanced at Fin—he was not being ironic. He fiddled with one of his hearing aids, wincing as he adjusted it, and I felt a rush of affection for this complex, gifted man who was my grandfather.

The other component of my research was the book about Tiago's life and music. As I had with Fin, I appealed to my mother for assistance. She helped me sort through the materials I had gathered: the newspaper accounts, audio files, and notes from my many interviews; relevant research articles; and, perhaps most significant, the journal I had kept with entries after my sessions with Tiago. She also helped identify different approaches to the narrative.

"Which would be best, do you think?" I said.

"That's for you to choose."

It took me sixteen months to write the first draft. *Here it is—finally!!* I wrote in the email accompanying the digital file of the two-hundred-sixty-seven-page manuscript I sent to her. She promised to read it in time to discuss when I visited the following week. Pleased and proud of my efforts, I sat down across the table from her in the breakfast nook, ready for her praise. Her comments were sharp and without pity.

"Point of view is all over the place. Sometimes it's not clear whether it's yours, Tiago's, his family's, or anyone else's. And the text is too limp. Your subject was a passionate man. Your words should convey that energy. Start by making the language more direct. And his crime and punishment are muddled. He's good then he's very bad then he's good again. I assume that the book, as well as the work you're doing on his music, are predicated on the notion that a creative work exists and has merit independent of the character and actions of its creator, but this needs elaboration. Perhaps the whole book should be prefaced by a discussion of morality and art. And you need to put more of yourself into Tiago's story. Your relationship with him is one of the most compelling aspects."

I acknowledged the validity of my mother's comments with poor grace. She placed her hand on mine. "It's no small feat to complete a manuscript, so you should be proud of that. And there is a lot of good in what you've written. With a few iterations you'll have a solid book."

"A *few* iterations! Like more than one?"

She smiled. "Each one is easier."

Life was not all work. I returned to Spain at least once a year to catch up with friends and continue to chase down useful information. Back home I occasionally played cello with a chamber ensemble Jax had created. I also joined the local flamenco society which gave me the opportunity to play with the local dance troupe and meet and jam with visiting artists.

A friendship with a fellow student named Greg drew me into the local music scene. Two years younger than me, Greg had a halo of reddish curls and gold-brown eyes that constantly squinted behind round wire-frame glasses. He had dropped out of graduate school halfway through the first year, saying it wouldn't take him where he wanted to go. I wasn't surprised—bright though Greg was, his interests were too scattered. He played several instruments and his main passion was creating a streaming platform for the ambient music he composed. He did this in a loft over his parents' furniture business using banks of audio recording equipment, several computers, and every kind of instrument and noisemaker one could imagine. I spent many nights in his loft helping to generate sound and mixing the amorphous, atmospheric pieces he created. Thin and stooped, Greg looked chronically underfed and I often brought him home for a meal. If Fin were there, the talk inevitably turned to the use of synthesizers in music and the evenings often ended in Fin's studio playing around with his.

Greg, his friend Hess, and I formed a guitar trio. Hess, a high school science teacher, named it String Theory and found gigs for us playing an assortment of blues, jazz, and flamenco in local community halls, pubs, festivals, and country fairs. In the city I became known as the flamenco guy and picked up some session work. The city's recording studios attracted big-name artists and occasionally I was brought in to spice up a piece with a few flamenco licks. With Fin's advice to never turn down a chance to perform in mind, I played flamenco in a television commercial promoting a brand of hot sauce without blushing. The casting director who had found me for the commercial also got me a cameo role as a guitarist playing in a bar on a movie shot in the city. "Just come as you are," he said, eying my long hair, leather vest, and jeans.

Chapter 28

I NEVER DID TEST Fin's tolerance for strange women at the breakfast table, but that didn't mean there were none in my life. It took me a long time to accept losing Aude. The realization of it would catch me unawares and make my stomach twist and my heart flop. But, as my mother had said, life does go on.

When I was back at U of T, Caitlin, a voluptuous red-headed music teacher working part time on a master's degree, held a party to celebrate the end of the summer term. Most of the summer students were, like her, returning to jobs in the fall. Alcohol was consumed and Caitlin kept finding reasons for me not to leave. Long story short: we ended up in bed. She took charge and writhed on top of me, and when it was over pronounced herself well satisfied. I didn't tell her it was my first time.

On my way home early the next morning I stopped in a café for a large coffee to blunt the edges of my hangover. Sex with Caitlin had been pleasant but not the monumental event I had anticipated. I remembered the preparations I had made—the champagne, the irises, the brioche—for my first night with Aude that fateful New Year's Eve. Swallowing a mouthful of the hot, strong liquid, I thought, *Is that all there is?* Perhaps it helped to be attracted to the other person.

I was grateful to Caitlin for breaking the ice, so to speak. Inhibited, inexperienced, and determined to never let anyone break my heart again, I didn't initiate relationships with women. It helped that most of the ones to whom I was attracted were otherwise committed. I avoided those who were not. But occasionally a woman would signal her interest and, if I liked her enough, but not too much, I would respond. Over the years I had several short affairs, never letting the women get too deeply into my life. If they suggested coming over to my place I would say, "Sorry, I live with my grandfather."

"Aren't you sweet," one of them said, no doubt picturing me providing tender care to an ailing old man. Moving around as much as I did also kept things loose—I would head off on a gig or to Spain or just to Counter Point, and things would peter out.

My longest relationship was with Irina, a post-doctoral fellow from Georgia who spent a year at UBC through a scholarship that had been created in my grandmother Alexandra's memory and awarded annually to an outstanding young physicist from anywhere in the world. Fin always hosted a welcome dinner for the recipient and luminaries from the university. If I was in town I attended. As the only young folks among the guests at Irina's dinner, we were seated together.

"We will have coffee tomorrow, yes?" she said as the evening wound down.

"I'm away for the next few days."

At the door she pressed a piece of paper into my hand. "You will call me when you return?"

Amused, I did. The first thing she told me was that she was engaged and would marry on returning to Tbilisi where a position at the university waited for her. "But while I am here, it is okay that I have sex with you. Nikoloz, too, he can do what he wants before we marry."

Most men wouldn't have given Irina a second look, with her lanky figure, unremarkable features, and mousey brown hair.

She had the grace of a baby giraffe and I've seen bigger breasts on men, but she was smart and funny and positively acrobatic in bed.

"You must meet Nikoloz someday. He will like you very much," Irina said when I took her to the airport for her flight home.

"Who knows, maybe I will," I said and kissed her goodbye.

Despite having known that we had no future, I was at a loss after Irina left. A visit with Jax and Polly was the usual antidote when I got the blues so I invited myself over for the weekend. It turned out to be a celebration. After six years at the university, Jax had been awarded tenure. As we lingered over after-dinner coffees before I headed back to Counter Point, Jax and Polly exchanged looks.

"Now?" Jax said.

"No point in waiting," Polly said.

They turned to me.

"We have a proposition for you," Jax said.

I raised my eyebrows. "Yes?"

"More like a request." Polly's years working in public relations had made her sensitive to the nuances in language.

I opened out my palms in a giving gesture. "I'm at your disposal."

"You go ahead, Jax."

"Okay." Jax's dark-brown eyes held mine for a moment. "My getting tenure has brought quite a bit of security into our lives. Polly and I would like to start a family now."

I took a sip of coffee. "Oh, that's nice. Are you thinking of adopting?"

"No, we want to have children and we'd like you to be the father."

My eyebrows shot up into my hairline. "What?"

"You're the nicest man we know and, really, already part of our family," Polly said.

I stared at them, at a loss for words.

"You'll need to consider, of course," Jax said.

"You think? But do you really want someone with my genetics? You know what my biological father was."

"Oh, Nielie, rapists aren't born, they're made," Jax said. "You're not even remotely like whoever that man was. And to clarify, it would be completely without obligations of any kind on your part. We'd make that legal."

"And, ah, how exactly do you see this happening?"

"Oh, nothing awkward. We figured the turkey baster method."

"You mean . . . and you don't consider that awkward?"

Jax shrugged and smiled.

"So, which one of you would be the guinea pig?"

"Both of us," Polly said.

My eyebrows shot up again. "Like, to see which one takes?"

"No. We propose to both get pregnant at the same time and get it all done at once. Polly says she's ready to stay at home and raise kids."

Polly nodded. "Being the same age, the children would be good company for each other, and if they have the same dad they'll be true siblings."

"Timing?"

"Well, I'm not getting any younger," Jax said.

"Neither am I," Polly said.

"We thought to time it so that we'd have the babies around the end of spring term next year. I would get maternity leave and could probably start the sabbatical I'm due after."

"So, ah, that means that it—I mean, the turkey baster part—would have to happen in two or three months?"

They nodded.

"And if I don't do it?"

Polly wrinkled her nose. "There's no one else we know who we'd want to ask so we'd have to go to some awful sperm bank."

"I see."

Jax reached over and stroked my arm. "It's a big ask but do consider it, Nielie. It would mean a lot to us."

Polly stroked the other arm. "And it would be perfect because we love you so much."

My parents were having a late dinner when I returned to Counter Point.

"Have you eaten?" Leah said.

"Yes, but I could really use a drink."

I brought a glass to the table and sat down. Theo handed me the bottle of wine. I poured out a generous measure and swallowed a mouthful. He eyed me quizzically.

"What's up?"

I wiped my mouth with the back of my hand. "You're not going to believe this. Jax and Polly want to get pregnant and they've asked me to be the father."

My parents' mouths fell open.

"That's . . . interesting," Leah said.

Theo grinned. "So maybe they like men a little bit after all?"

I waved a hand dismissively. "No sex would be involved. Not with me, anyway."

"Ah."

I motioned to their full plates. "Look, I didn't mean to interrupt your dinner."

They resumed eating.

"But I wouldn't mind knowing what you think."

Leah swallowed and took a sip of wine. "Why don't we start with what *you* think? You must have had an initial reaction. Often they're the most valid."

"I was too shocked to think, really."

"Okay, but you didn't give an immediate and definitive refusal and now you're asking us what we think, so you must be open to the idea."

I twisted the stem of the wineglass back and forth. "It took a while to understand what they meant, and they don't expect me to answer right away."

"Why would you even consider it?" Theo said.

"Because they asked. It's important to Jax and Polly, and they're important to me. Like family. They said I'd have no obligations—they'd draw up a legal agreement to that effect."

"It's not that simple," Leah said. "If you decide to go ahead with this—and you really need to give it a good, hard think first—I'd suggest a legal agreement say that the extent of your involvement with or commitment to these children will be entirely at your discretion." She pushed her half-eaten meal away. "When would this happen?"

"Sometime in the next year." I glanced at Theo. "What do you think, Dad?"

He warded off the question with raised palms. "This is entirely up to you, Niels. But if you go ahead, be prepared for your life to change radically even if you don't have direct responsibility for those kids."

After a fitful sleep I woke early, trod quietly to the kitchen, and made some coffee. Rune padded in after me. The dog and I had become friends over the years.

"Go for a walk?"

Rune's ears shot up and his tightly curled tail flopped back and forth. I scribbled a note for my mother, put on Rune's harness, attached the leash, and set off along a trail that tracked the shore, leash in one hand and a large travel mug of coffee in the other. A short distance away the trail connected with a public seawall dotted with benches. I sat on one of these. "Down,"

I said and Rune slid to his stomach beside me. I drank some coffee and turned my mind to Jax and Polly's request.

I took stock. My research was going well, and if I completed it successfully—which I fully expected to do—I would be awarded my PhD next year. One of the final steps would be a public performance of some of the pieces I had transcribed. After, I would publish the transcriptions through the music company I had established. I also would record demos of my playing them, and possibly produce an album of Tiago's performances taken from the best-quality recordings we found on the cassettes. The university press had accepted my book on Tiago, much improved after seven—*seven*—rounds of revisions guided by my mother, for publication in digital and print-on-demand formats. Assuming that there would probably be more interest in the book in Spain, I used some of my university grant funds to have it translated into Spanish.

On the personal front I was about to turn thirty-one and was still living in either my grandfather's or parents' home. I shrugged—until I figured out where I needed to live there was no point in getting a place of my own. With Irina gone there was no woman in my life, but that was okay. It was full enough with my work, family, and many friends, and I would no doubt meet other women to provide diversion along the way.

To this point I had not given any thought to having children. It certainly wasn't going to happen in the foreseeable future, if ever. Polly and Jax seemed determined to go ahead, and the thought of them having to resort to a sperm bank made me cringe as well. Helping them out would make them happy and should not interfere with my life or plans.

Reasons not to do it? The state of the planet, perhaps. Would a child appreciate being thrust into a world rocked by floods, fires, pestilence, war? I put the question to the sea. It transitioned seamlessly to the cloudless sky at the horizon. A light breeze ruffled the incoming tide. Two blue herons stepped delicately through it, their heads darting into the water after prey. A man towed by a small terrier bearing a stick in its mouth that was twice its length came into view. Rune sniffed the air and, as the other dog approached, started to rise. "Leave it," I said. He sank down again. The terrier gave him a disdainful glance from the corner of its eye. The man, trailing behind, wished me good morning. I smiled and raised a hand in reply.

Despite all the chaos and anguish in the world, it was still beautiful and life was sweet. I rose, drawing Rune up with me.

So why not?

Chapter 29

I HELD UP THE empty mason jar Jax handed to me. "You want me to fill it?" I said, my voice rising to a squeak.

Jax laughed. "Of course not. It's sterile and should be, well, big enough for comfort." It was turkey baster time and I was deeply regretting having agreed to be part of Jax and Polly's pregnancy plans. "You can use our bedroom," she added.

"Yes, well, I'm glad not to have to do it in the hall."

"It's okay to be a bit nervous," Polly said.

"We'll be on the patio," Jax said.

I growled an incoherent reply and stomped up the stairs to their bedroom, the mason jar in hand. I could think of no circumstances less conducive to arousal. Perhaps conscious of this, Jax and Polly had set a porno movie running on the screen in their bedroom. It was lesbian porn and I was so intrigued by what the characters were getting up to that I forgot what I was there for. Eventually I got the job done and headed back downstairs.

"I'm, ah, finished," I called through the back door.

Jax and Polly rose from the Adirondack chairs in which they had been lounging in the August sun and came into the house.

"Here." I thrust the mason jar with its nose-pricking payload to Jax.

"Thanks." She and Polly regarded me expectantly.

"I guess I'm surplus to requirements now."

They both grinned. I shook my head and headed to the front door.

"Have fun," I said and left.

In late October Jax phoned to tell me that the turkey basting had been successful in both their cases and I was going to be a dad. "That's nice," I said. When I arrived for a visit a few weeks later, Jax sat me down at the kitchen table and pulled a bottle of scotch from the cupboard.

"Hey, you're not going to drink any of that, are you?" I said.

"I wish I could. No, it's for you."

"I'd rather have a beer."

Ignoring me, Jax poured out a good measure, added a bit of water, and slid the glass over. I took a sip. She sat down across from me.

"Drink up."

"What the heck, Jax?" I said, but obligingly swallowed half of it. Polly entered the room and sat on another chair at the table.

"Have you told him?" she said.

"Told me what?"

Polly smiled sweetly. "I'm going to have twins."

"It's not funny!" I said.

Leah pressed her lips together to contain her laughter. "No, of course not." Her eyes danced. "But it is, actually."

Theo smiled broadly. "You guys certainly didn't mess around, did you."

I had arrived home stunned with the news that there were going to be three babies. The humor of the situation struck me and my lips twitched. "I always knew there'd be more than one. I'm not sure why three feels so weird."

"Two was probably manageable but three takes it to another

level of complexity." Leah shook her head. "Those poor women are going to need some help."

"There's no way I can afford to buy Jax and Polly a house," I said.

My mother and I were drinking our morning coffees on the deck at Counter Point in the watery sunlight of an unseasonably warm December day. She zipped up her fleece top against a tentative breeze.

"It wouldn't be for them, it would be for the children. Their townhouse is not adequate for a family of that size. Especially if they get a live-in nanny to help, which I think will be necessary."

"The agreement I have with Jax and Polly says I'm not obliged to provide support."

"I know, but that doesn't mean you shouldn't. Providing a home would be the easiest and most effective way, as it would leave Jax and Polly with more money for the children's day-to-day needs and care."

"Okay, I see the sense of it, but the reality is that I just don't have enough money to do it."

"You wouldn't do it yourself. I discussed it with my dad and he has agreed to help. Consider it an advance on your inheritance."

"So you've gone and sorted all this out behind my back? Don't I get a say at all?"

"Yes, of course you do. I didn't mean to be devious or presumptuous, but I wanted to sound him out before raising the matter with you."

"It doesn't feel right involving Granddad in what is very much my own private concerns."

"They're not entirely your own private concerns. These children are my grandchildren and his great-grandchildren. By the way, Dad is absolutely thrilled they're coming along. As you know he'll be eighty in three years and, with the way things were going, he doubted whether you would have a family in his lifetime."

"Yeah, a bunch of budding musicians for him to mold."

Leah smiled. "Well, he does expect that at least one of them will have some talent. Anyhow, the house would be in your name but for the use of your children as long as they may need it. What do you think?"

I didn't answer for a while. "I never expected things would get this complicated. Was helping to make these kids a mistake?"

"It's too late to worry about that. And I for one am looking forward to their arrival."

On Easter Sunday the following spring, Jax unlocked the door to a nondescript suburban house with a double garage, picture window, white stucco siding, and half-timber trim. A red panel door with a fanlight at the top was the only decorative feature of interest.

"It doesn't make much of an architectural statement but it's only a few blocks from the university, has all the space we need, and is in good shape."

It was my first viewing of the house that had been bought in my name for Jax and Polly's children. Preparations for the submissions, oral exam, and performance that marked the completion of my doctoral work prevented me from being involved and it was Leah who had toured around with them to find a suitable place.

Jax waved to a carpeted staircase that turned on itself. "It's reverse living. Kitchen, living-dining room, and three bedrooms are upstairs. Door on the right is to the garage, laundry, utilities and all that stuff. This one"—she opened the door to the room on the left, revealing an empty space with a gray tweed fitted carpet and a window facing the street—"is your room for whenever you visit. Which I hope will be often, although you may want to wait until we get through the bawling-infant stage."

She closed the door and proceeded down the hall. "There's also a bathroom and another bedroom." At the end of hall she opened the door to a large space with windows to the backyard. "The family room. I plan to soundproof it so that I have somewhere to practice without disturbing anyone."

We left the room and headed for the stairs. Jax glanced up the stairwell, then at me. "Can we sit for a minute?"

"Sure."

She eased herself down with a sigh. Her navy suit jacket hung open over an untucked dress shirt. Her trademark tie, this one dotted with tiny elephants, draped over the bulge of her stomach. She smiled wryly. "I'm thinking thirty-nine is maybe too old to make a baby."

I sat down and looked at her with concern. "Are you okay?"

"Yeah, just really, really tired. Polly's even worse. She's enormous. We can't even hug properly anymore."

"Can I help in any way?"

"Oh, Nielie, you've helped more than enough." She gestured around her. "This is a godsend. We realized we'd need a new place but figured we'd have to go way out of town to get something we could afford." She gave him a troubled glance. "I hope you don't feel we're taking advantage of you or your family. That wasn't the intent when we asked you to be the dad to our kids."

I put my arm around her and pulled her close. "Don't even think it."

Her eyes teared up. She swiped them away and sniffed. "The worst part is that with my hormones all over the place I cry at the drop of a hat. Like, performing Dido's Lament last weekend—you know how sad it is. Fucking awkward it was."

"It will be over in a few weeks."

"Ha! That's when the fun really begins." She shook her head. "What the hell were we thinking, Nielie?"

"Who's this *we*?"

She laughed. "You know, I can't imagine being in this situation with anyone else. I wonder sometimes what would have happened if you hadn't seen my room-for-rent notice."

"There's a good chance I wouldn't have seen it. I only glanced at what you had put up on the board because you smiled and said hello to me."

"I had a mask on. How did you know I was smiling?"

"Your eyes."

"So on the strength of my smiling eyes you decided that you wanted to live with me?"

"I was so lonely and, seeing the notice, I thought, gee, it would be nice to have roommates. And you seemed a decent sort of person."

"It could easily not have happened." Jax's eyes teared up again. "Well, I for one am awfully glad the universe decided our paths should cross that day."

My phone lit up while I was listening to a demo I had just made in Fin's studio. I glanced at the screen intending to ignore it, but snatched it up when I saw Jax's number. I removed my headphones and answered.

"Hey, Jax."

"Congratulations, Nielie. You're a dad."

I frowned. "What? I didn't think you were due for another week or so."

"Not me. Polly had to have an emergency C-section."

I sat up straight. "That doesn't sound good. Is she all right?"

"Yeah, and so are the babies, thank god. A bit early, but they'll be okay."

A roar filled my ears and my heart thumped around in my chest. "Ah . . . what are they?"

I could hear the exhaustion in Jax's short laugh. "Of course. A boy and a girl. No names yet. They'll need to stay in hospital for a few days."

A boy and a girl. I rubbed my forehead. "Thanks for letting me know. Give Polly my love. And how about you? How are you doing?"

"Still on track, but *man* I'm ready for it to be done."

When we hung up I set the phone aside and looked around without seeing. Music still trickled from the headphones. I pushed a button to turn it off and sat, my mind blank. A shiver ran through my body. I raised a hand—it trembled slightly. To this point Jax and Polly's pregnancies had been distant affairs with no particular significance to me beyond that of events happening to friends. I had not owned any of the experience, not viewed myself as an expectant father, and technically was not considered one of the parents. Why was I reacting this way now? I gave myself a shake, drew a steadying breath, and dialed my mother's number to give her the news.

Jax safely delivered a boy ten days later. When they all were back home, Leah drove me over to meet the twins, Arkady and Anastasia, and Jax's son David. When I clumsily picked up the latter, his eyes widened with alarm and he let out a surprisingly robust howl.

"I don't think he likes me," I said, handing the damp, squirming, red-faced bundle back to Jax.

Her face softened as she accepted him. "I think he's protesting being ejected out of the comfort of my belly into a strange and daunting world."

On the way home Leah glanced at me and touched my hand. "You're awfully quiet."

"I think you should keep your eyes on the road and both hands on the wheel."

"Oh, don't you start," she said laughing, but returned her

full attention to driving. Theo often fretted about what he called her "tearing around" in her sleek steel-gray sportscar. "Still, you don't seem very happy about the babies."

My hands loosened their vise-like grip of my knees. "It's not about happiness. I don't know what I expected—I really hadn't given the fact of these progeny of mine much thought to this point, but now that they're here I feel, I don't know . . . alarmed and anxious and scared for them. Very glad I'm not responsible for their care. They're so tiny and helpless and it wouldn't take much for something to go wrong. How does anyone ever know what to do?"

Leah glanced at me again and in a quick motion pulled the car to a sudden stop on the side of the highway. Cars zoomed by, the vacuum created by their passing rocking the little sports car. She set the parking gear and engaged the emergency brake.

"What are you doing, Mom?"

She twisted in her seat and regarded me intently. "Niels, that is exactly how I felt when you were born, and I was all by myself. I didn't know the first thing about how to care for you, what was needed, what to do. And it's why I made the awful decision to give you up then. I think you still struggle with the fact of my having done that. I hope you understand better the reasons now."

I regarded her, trying to imagine being sixteen and alone and suddenly having the responsibility for an infant without the knowledge or means to take care of it. I probably would have made the same decision. And then eternally regretted it.

"Yes, I do understand."

Leah's eyes filled with tears. "And can you forgive me?"

I leaned over and kissed her cheek. "I forgave you a long time ago."

Chapter 30

A FEW WEEKS LATER I was heading to my car after having coffee with Greg when my phone buzzed.

"Hi, Mom." No one spoke. "Mom?"

"Oh, Niels." Leah's voice was heavy.

"What is it?"

"It's Papa Luke."

My heart sank. I had spent many tranquil hours at Papa Luke's side since returning home. In recent months a change in him, a kind of dematerialization, had become noticeable. That great heart of his was winding down, his doctor said. "Is he . . ."

"No, but he's on his way."

"Have you called Granddad?"

"Yes, he's ready to leave whenever you are. Ben and Beth are already here," she said, referring to Theo's brother and his wife.

"I'm heading home now," I said.

We caught the last ferry and arrived just before eleven that night. Papa Luke lay still as a boulder on the bed he shared with his wife in the room looking out to his beloved ocean. Mama Ris, wraith-like in her pallor, sat on one side holding his hand. Ben rose from his position on the other side, as did the others who were seated in chairs around the room. Fin and I went around and embraced everyone. He spoke a few quiet words to his sister. She nodded and pressed her face against his shoulder. I sat down beside the bed and gazed at Papa Luke, so still and silent that if it weren't for the slight rise and fall of his chest I would have thought him already gone. *How many deathbeds am I fated to attend?* I wondered.

"Hello, Papa Luke," I said softly.

A change in the rhythm of his breath—the inhalation held slightly longer than the one before—was the only acknowledgement of my greeting. I rested my hand on his and tried not to cry.

Shortly after, a new nurse arrived for the night shift. She conferred with the one departing and checked Papa Luke's vitals.

"I don't anticipate any major change for a while," the nurse said. "You should all try to get some sleep."

Mama Ris and Ben remained while the rest of us headed to the Big House. None of us slept well and we all were up early to resume our vigil. It was one of those June days when the weather didn't know whether it was coming or going: showers one moment, bursts of sun the next. Theo left at one point to collect Fox from the airport, where he was arriving on a shuttle from Seattle after a multi-leg overnight flight from New York.

To our parents' great joy, Fox had returned to North America to do his doctorate in applied microbiology at Cornell University. In the four years he had been there I had only seen him twice, as our school breaks coincided and I usually went away. His visits were still typically only two or three days long and he always brought a girlfriend with him—never the same one.

"It's like he needs them as a buffer between us," Leah said once.

On the two occasions when I was home, as a courtesy I had given up my bedroom in our wing for the guest room at Mama

Ris and Papa Luke's cottage to afford Fox and his girlfriend privacy, but it meant he and I never had a chance to visit on our own. As we waited for Fox I recalled with indignation his casual dismissal of Papa Luke as a new-age guru during that long-ago lunch in Seville, but when he arrived, white-faced and bag-eyed from the tiring trip, his grief was genuine.

The day dragged on painfully. Food was needed and I was happy to oblige with sandwiches for lunch and a pot of pasta for dinner. Restless, we sat and rose and ate and drank and then sat again. Mama Ris remained at the bedside, composed and straight-backed as always, but the effort of maintaining it showed on her face and in the slight tremor in the translucent hand that stroked her husband's. We took turns sitting on the other side, holding Papa Luke's hand and speaking softly to him. I told him about my studies, my music, my children. He rested his eternally kind, infinitely understanding eyes on me, but after a moment they shifted away to something in the distance.

The bedroom became stuffy with all of us in it and Theo set the French doors leading to the deck ajar. Dark clouds dimmed the sky as the long spring day wound down. We were all sprawled in chairs, speaking desultorily in low voices, when a great wind roared up and violently shook the house. The French doors flew open, banging against the outside wall, and then slammed shut. Startled, we looked at each other. The wind died as quickly as it had risen.

"Noooo," Mama Ris wailed.

The nurse hurried to the bed, bent over Papa Luke, and placed her fingers on his wrist. After a moment she raised her head.

"Yes, he's gone," she said.

We sat frozen in disbelief, then rose as one and clutched at each other in grief.

"Papa Luke was a colossus," Leah said. "It's not surprising that his spirit made such a spectacular exit."

It was the next morning and everyone except Mama Ris and Fin was gathered around the dining room table at the Big House picking at a late breakfast. After the undertakers had borne Papa Luke away, we had huddled together drinking scotch deep into the night, unwilling to let the final day of his life end. Talk turned again and again to the stunning moment of his death.

"Yeah, but it sure was weird," Fox said.

Theo scrubbed his face tiredly. "We should get organized. There's a lot to do."

Tasks were discussed and assigned: arrangements to make at the funeral home, a service to organize, people to notify, an obituary to write.

"How about I take care of the meals?" I said.

"Could you, darling?" Leah said. "That would really help."

I worked out several days of menus and went to the grocery store to load up on provisions. By the time I returned, unloaded, and did the prep for the evening meal it was after three. I stuck my head in Leah's office.

"Things are all set for dinner so I'm heading out for a walk. Would you like me to take Rune?"

The dog lifted his head at the resonance of the words *walk* and *Rune*. Leah stroked him.

"No. We were out earlier, and I need his company."

"I can keep you company."

"That's okay."

"So, you prefer the company of your dog over that of your son?"

Leah smiled. "No, I think my son would benefit from a break. Why don't you ask Fox to go with you?"

"Guess I could."

Fox was in the lounge outside our bedrooms working on his computer.

"I'm going for a walk. Want to come?"

"Oh, yeah. Give me a minute."

After typing a few more words he peered at the screen, his lips moving slightly, and hit a key. The computer dinged and he closed its lid and set it on a side table. "There. Ready to go."

We walked along the shoreline path, joined the public seawall, and continued to its end. From there we turned onto country lanes leading to the road that looped back to Counter Point. Initially we spoke stiffly about different things: our respective studies, travel, parents. By the time we reached the pub, where it was customary to stop after a walk, we had regained some ease with each other.

"Sorry to hear about your grandfather," the proprietor said when we entered the pub.

We thanked him, surprised at the speed with which the news had spread, and found an empty table. Thirsty after the long walk we drank our first beers quickly and ordered seconds. I had just raised the glass for a sip when Fox spoke.

"So, you got a couple of lesbos pregnant, huh?"

I slowly put down my glass. "I'm not going to sit here and have you disrespect my family," I said, rising. I fished some money out of my pocket, threw it on the table, and left Fox staring open-mouthed after me.

Dinner that night was a subdued affair. Mama Ris pushed the food around her plate, hollow-eyed and silent. Conversations were murmured and of inconsequential matters. Fox sat at the other end of the table from me. Busy with preparing and serving the meal, I ignored him. After, I accepted Ben and Beth's offer to clean up and went to my room. I was picking out a melancholy tune on my guitar when someone knocked on the door.

"Come!"

Fox stuck his head around the door. "Niels?"

"Yeah?"

"Can I come in?"

I hesitated then motioned him in. He held out a ten-dollar bill and some coins. "You left too much money for the beer."

"Ah, geez," I said, accepting the money.

Fox remained where he stood, head bowed and hands behind his back in exaggerated penitence. "I was a real shit today," he said.

"You think?"

"I don't know why I said what I did, Niels. Trying to be funny, I guess. Sorry."

"Huh." I wasn't going to let him off easy.

He produced a bottle of Australian Shiraz from behind his back. "Pax?"

"I don't have any glasses," I said discouragingly.

He held up a finger, slipped outside the door, and returned promptly with two wine glasses. I wasn't in the mood for a tête-à-tête, but before I could object he perched on the side of my bed, set the glasses down on the nightstand, twisted open the screwcap on the bottle, and filled the glasses. I set down my guitar and reluctantly accepted the one he handed to me.

"What do you want, Fox?"

"Just to talk. Like old times." Fox leaned to the side and ran his hand over the cover on my bed. "Remember how I used to come and lie down here sometimes? We had good talks then."

I sighed and waved a hand. "Knock yourself out."

He set his glass on the bedside table, shifted his bottom backwards, and swung up his legs. Lying with his arms folded behind his head, he contemplated the ceiling.

"So, what do you want to talk about?"

Fox twisted his head to look at me. "It's a shock, Papa Luke dying."

"Thought you didn't like that name."

"Yeah, well, I don't know what else to call him now." He picked up his glass and took a meditative swallow of wine. "Wish I'd spent more time with him but . . ." he made a vague gesture. "You know how it is."

"Yeah, you think they'll be around forever."

Fox nodded. "And coming back this time, it's hit me that I don't fit in here anymore. The way everyone's behaving, I could be a stranger. Even Dad treats me like I'm just someone visiting."

Trust Fox to make the situation all about himself. "Come on, Fox, cut them some slack. Everyone's mourning—Dad's just lost his father. And is it surprising you feel like a stranger? Taking off to Australia all those years ago, and then whenever you did come home it was always with some girl in tow and never for long enough to do more than say hello and goodbye?"

"Yeah, well, the whole Australia business—it's kind of your fault."

My eyebrows shot up in surprise. "My fault? How's that?"

"When you started looking for your dad it made me think about my mother."

"You've known that Fiona is your biological mother all your life."

"Thought I should spend some time with her."

"But you had before."

"Sure, I'd visited but never actually stayed with her, and Dad was always hovering. Wanted to really get to know her and my sister Madeleine."

"Leaving so abruptly, then staying away so long—it broke Mom's and Dad's hearts, you know."

Fox sighed. "Yeah, that was the whole idea."

"What?" I stared at him. "Why?"

He sat up and studied the floor, forearms on his thighs,

wineglass dangling from his fingers. I fought the urge to haul him up and give him a shake.

"You remember when I got COVID?" he said.

"Yeah."

"Dad was furious."

"What did you expect? You snuck out to see that girlfriend of yours when you weren't supposed to and got infected."

"Yeah, but it wasn't because *I* got sick that he got mad, but because Leah caught it from me. He was more worried about her than me."

"She was a lot sicker than you were."

"I know. But I figured it meant he loved her more than me."

My forehead wrinkled in puzzlement. "Of course, he loves her—she's his wife."

"Yeah, but he's *my* dad. I always thought I was first in line with him. It really hurt when he blamed me for Leah getting sick."

I studied him for a minute. "So that's why you took off for Australia?"

"Yeah. Figured I'd show them."

I shook my head. "Jesus, Fox. You certainly did. Was it worth it?"

He set his glass down, leaned back on his elbows, and sighed deeply. "Not really. First couple of weeks were fine, then one day Fiona said that before I went home I should see other parts of the country, like Melbourne and the Gold Coast. She hadn't understood that I intended to live with them and go to university there. She was always saying I should come out and stay. I believed her, but of course she didn't mean it. Things came to a head when her parents called to say they were coming for a visit. They live in a small town on the other side of the country, so it didn't happen often. Great, I thought, I'll finally meet them. But Fiona told me I had to leave." He sat up and gave me a twisted smile. Pain clouded his eyes. "Turns out her parents don't know I exist. She's never told them about me."

"What do you mean?"

Fox plucked at a knot in the woven bed cover. "I've always accepted that when Fiona and Dad split up, I stayed with Dad because she wasn't able to raise me. I never realized that she was keeping me a secret from her family, even after all this time." He shook his head. "It was quite a blow."

All my irritation fell away. Learning that your mother had not informed your grandparents of your existence might not be as earth-shattering as discovering your father was a rapist, but it wasn't far behind. "Fox, I'm so sorry."

"Yeah. I also discovered that Fiona's got issues—she's bi-polar." He grimaced. "Maybe explains some things in me. And Madeleine . . . I thought we'd have a chance to bond but she's almost ten years younger and spoiled as hell. She resented me being there."

"What did you do?"

He shrugged. "Did what I was told and left."

"Why didn't you come home then?"

He smiled without humor. "And admit I was wrong? I went to Melbourne and applied to the school of architecture at the university there. Another stupid mistake."

"Why a mistake?"

"I always thought I needed to do something creative like everyone else in the family, but it didn't suit. I totally crapped out the first year and they nicely told me not to come back." He shook his head. "That's when things really went sideways. It was a bad time."

I studied Fox, recalibrating my sense of him. "Do Mom and Dad know about all this?"

"Not the bad stuff. I don't want them to know that."

I set my glass down and leaned forward. "I never realized what you were going through. Why did you wait so long to say anything? All those years I tried to keep in touch you blew me off. Two-word responses to my emails if you replied at all. And there was never any time to talk when you came home."

"Yeah, well, some kind of pride, I guess."

"And that time in Seville—we could have talked then. You went to the trouble of looking me up. Why didn't you get in touch that evening?"

"I couldn't. That girl I was with . . ." His brow furrowed.

I remembered the fussy blonde. "Belinda."

"That's right. She didn't want to be left alone."

"I thought there were a bunch of you?"

He shrugged.

"You could at least have called. I waited and waited."

"Yeah, sorry." He glanced up at me from under his lashes. "Thing is, Niels, you'd changed so much I felt awkward. I'd expected my old geeky bro and here was this"—he waved a hand in my direction—"long-haired macho guy, all cool and confident."

I raised my eyebrows and touched my fingers to my chest. "Me, macho?"

We laughed and the restraint that had existed between us fractured and fell away.

"I'm really sorry you went through all that, Fox. Things obviously turned around at some point."

Fox nodded. "A good counselor. Had another go at university, general program. Included an introductory course in life sciences. Something clicked."

"You found your calling?"

He laughed drily. "Maybe. Not a cakewalk, though—fucking hard work. But it's kept me occupied, given me purpose." He glanced at me. "I'm going to talk to a biotech company in Vancouver before I fly back. Met the president at a conference. Might be a job there. What do you think?"

"That'd be awesome, Fox. Mom and Dad would be thrilled to have you so close."

"Don't say anything. It might not happen."

"Okay, but keep me posted."

He nodded and reached for the wine. "Hey, let's finish the bottle." He refilled our glasses and stretched out again on my bed. "You buggered off as well. What was that all about?"

Fox apparently was unaware of the crisis over my parentage. That story could wait. "Needed a change," I said. "Now, tell me about this company you're interested in."

Chapter 31

"HO, HO!" EMILIO WINKED and slapped me on the back. "You rogue!"

I smiled weakly and swiped the photo of Anastasia, fat-cheeked and grinning, off the screen of my phone. Despite my now fluent Spanish, I couldn't find the words to explain the turkey baster method of insemination and all he understood was that I had three children by two women.

I was back in Seville to perform at *La Bienal de Flamenco*, a month-long festival held every two years in September. I thought it a good place to present Tiago's music to the world, but the organizers didn't immediately accept my application. I had no profile there as a flamenco guitarist, and the simple show I had put together featuring me playing Tiago's works with Greg as my sideman was not of the scale typical of the festival. And no one seemed to remember who Tiago was. I mentioned this in passing during one of the video chats I regularly had with Emilio. It may have been purely coincidental, but a few days later I received an email from the festival organizers inviting me to participate.

I was given three slots during the festival, performing in a room in an eighteenth-century manor house that was now a cultural center. The room held only sixty-odd people, which was, I supposed, appropriate to the scale of the production.

I structured the program around six sets, each focusing on a stage of Tiago's life. Speaking in Spanish, I began each set with a vignette about him followed by thematic selections from his work: light and lively for his youth, assertive and sensual for his days of glory, dark for his crime and punishment, pensive for his twilight years, heartrending for his death, hopeful for the discovery and renaissance of his music.

My first performance was late in the evening and up against a concert by one of the festival headliners. The room was only half full and many were people I knew: Emilio and Mía; some staff from the tavern; Paula and Paloma with the men in their lives; Fatiha, who still lived above Paula's office; Ximenez; Paco and Maria; and a handful of other friends I had made. Daniel, now a *capitán de corbeta*, the equivalent of a lieutenant commander, was off on naval exercises in the Red Sea and had sent sincere regrets and pithy advice about facing audiences. The small, friendly group created a warm intimacy that smoothed away any jitters I felt. Towards the end of the show a round, bald, older man wearing dark clothing entered and slid into a chair at the back. I only noticed him because I had just ended a set and was about to begin the spiel that preceded the final one.

My next show was scheduled for late morning. Three-quarters of the chairs were occupied. At the end a few people came to the stage to speak to me or pick up one of our brochures. As I spoke with a publicist doing a writeup for the festival's newsletter, I saw the older man who had slipped in at the end of the previous performance leaving the room. In the light of day I noticed that his taupe suit and black shirt were stylish and expensive, and the aviator glasses he wore had yellow lenses.

My last performance was in the early evening. Thanks perhaps to the article about my act in the festival newsletter, the room was full with extra chairs squeezed in along the walls. Several people came up after to chat. I tried to keep it friendly but moving along—Emilio was holding a celebration at the tavern to mark the occasion and I was anxious to get there. As the last person left and I began to hurriedly pack things up, the man in the yellow-lensed aviator glasses rose from a chair at the end of a row near the front and came forward. I greeted him perfunctorily while closing the clasps on my guitar case.

"Martin Pérez," he said, extending a hand.

I descended from the low stage to shake it. "Niels Larsen. *Encantado de conocerte.*"

Today's finely tailored suit was pewter gray and his shirt plum purple. Seeing the network of wrinkles on Pérez's face, I placed him in his seventies and concluded that the odd glasses were likely due to an eye condition.

"I knew Tiago," Pérez said. "I mean, I knew of him. Was quite a fan—I aspired to play flamenco guitar myself. I attended three of his performances when I was young. They were electric." He cocked his head to one side. "You don't quite have his fire."

I shifted and shrugged uncomfortably, anxious for the conversation to be over. "Yes, well . . ."

Pérez raised a placating hand. "No, no—you are a very fine player. Tiago was a bit crazy. More than a bit. And his playing was so furious and tightly wound sometimes that you feared it would spin out of control. I remember holding my breath, willing him to keep it together." He shook his head. "Appalling how it all ended. And such a waste. But you actually studied with him?"

I explained briefly how I had come to know Tiago and the legacy of his tapes.

Pérez regarded me intently. "How extraordinary that they existed. He was famous for refusing recordings or tapings of any kind. And he left them to you. I congratulate you on reviving his work." He glanced at the stage where Greg had finished packing up and was waiting with folded arms for me. "But I am keeping you."

"No problem," I said politely.

He drew a card from the breast pocket of his jacket and handed it to me. "It turned out that I had no talent for playing flamenco guitar, so I became a promoter. I would like to find out more about your time with Tiago and how you teased out the compositions from those tapes. You have an intriguing story and some excellent music. I think there's a basis here for a show to tour, in Spain certainly, and possibly in Europe." He swept his hand to the side. "We'd flesh you out with an ensemble, add some flash." He tapped the card I was holding. "Phone my office, tell them I asked you to call and to find a time for us to meet in the next few days. You're not leaving right away?"

"No."

"Good. I'll see you soon then." He turned and walked down the aisle to the door with me staring open-mouthed after him.

"What was that all about?" Greg said. His knowledge of Spanish was limited.

"He's an impresario. Thinks that, with some beefing up, the show might have potential for a tour.

"Well, well," he said.

Internet research confirmed that Martin Pérez was a big noise in Spain. Before contacting his office to set up a meeting, I called Fin's manager, Hilary, for advice. A small, gaunt, wire-haired woman, she had taken care of the business aspects of his music since I was a child and occasionally helped me, "off the side of my desk," as she put it, with my own music publishing and performance arrangements.

I described my encounter with Pérez, then said, "I'm out of my depth here."

"Sure, I help you. You get the man to call me." Hilary's slow and sultry Jamaican-accented speech led people to underestimate her—at their peril.

"It's probably time you and I had our own contract," I said.

"Don't worry, we do that when you get back."

When we met two days later, Pérez expanded on his idea of a show based on Tiago's story and music to tour Spain. He proposed an ensemble, including a singer, dancers, some *palmeros*—the people who clap out the flamenco rhythms—and another guitarist. "You would be the lead, of course. Now your friend, he is fine, but I was thinking maybe a guitarist from here."

"It's okay, my friend isn't interested anyway."

"Count me out," Greg had said. "I've got too much else on the go, and besides, my playing is nowhere good enough for that kind of show."

Pérez figured the show could be put together and tour venues booked for the following spring. "And I think once we have the other musicians lined up we should do an album to release with the tour." He raised the copy of my book about Tiago that I had brought him. "And we'll find a Spanish publisher for this and release it as well. You have given me a lot to work with. I think we can create a production that will draw considerable interest."

I agreed in principle with the proposal and Pérez's organization kicked into gear. By the time I returned home two weeks later, one of his business managers and Hilary had knocked together a comprehensive agreement that covered licensing the music, the live performances, the recordings, book sales associated with the tour, and any audio, video, and merchandising products coming out of it.

Hilary tapped a copy of the document. "You'll do okay."

"If it goes well."

In truth, the speed in which the tour had become a reality unnerved me. I had never envisaged performing on this scale. And Pérez's comment that my playing lacked fire still stung. Could I even do Tiago's music justice? I signed and sent off the agreement to the person Hilary had dealt with at Pérez's company and was even more disconcerted when, apart from a short acknowledgement of receipt of these items, I heard nothing for almost two months. Had Pérez changed his mind or forgotten all about the tour?

In late November I received an email from Alma Rubio of Pérez's company requesting a video meeting. When we connected—morning for me, late afternoon for her—I saw on the screen a woman in her forties with strong, rather severe features, dark hair drawn tightly back from her face, and penetrating eyes behind glasses with tiger-stripe frames. She began speaking in tight, awkward English, and when I replied that we could converse in Spanish she agreed with relief. She apologized for the delay—they had been busy winding up several events—and thanked me for the book about Tiago and the demos I had made of his work, which she claimed to have read and listened to carefully.

"I am the producer for your show. I have some preliminary ideas to discuss."

"Yes?"

"In general we like the format following the stages of Tiago's life that your show at *La Bienal de Flamenco* was based on. But because it will be a bigger show with other players, you and the troupe will have to work out who does what in each set and choose pieces to fit. It should start with an ensemble, of course, like an overture. Then a segment representing his youth and prime, lots of color and life. The crime of passion segment should start rich and sexy, then become more dramatic and end in a violent climax."

I scratched down notes, trying to keep up with her.

"For the time in prison," she continued, "something with a hard, rhythmic start for the judgement, then anger, despair, and a long lament. After prison, in the ranch segment, something heavy, hypnotic to reflect his limited, routine life. Now the death scene—we see something not just sad but eerie and unearthly. If you can bring the same sensibility to the music as is in the description of that experience in your book, it will be extraordinary. And then, for the finale—what we call the resurrection of his music—another ensemble. How does that sound?"

I had stopped trying to write. *And they thought I could put this all together?* I cleared my throat. "It sounds fine. Like an opera."

"*Sí, sí,* a good story, lots of theater. Now, you are very much part of the story, but we think introducing each segment as you did before would interfere with the show's momentum. Perhaps you could just make some comments after the first ensemble piece, you know, to give context and set the show up. There will be another guitar and you will share the segments, but it's your show so you can choose which ones you play. We will start to look for suitable artists to make up the troupe. Martin is talking about late next spring and we need to pin them down soon."

In January I went back to Spain to set up for the months of work ahead. After returning home from *La Bienal de Flamenco* in the fall, I had fallen back into my patchwork of a musical life: touring with a local indie-folk band, contributing reverb cello sounds to one of Greg's electronic music recordings, providing backup to the local flamenco dance troupe on a two-night show, playing cello with Jax's ensemble at Christmas. The casting director who had got me the gig as the guitarist in a bar snared me a part in an artsy film about a woman contemplating suicide, where I was a mysterious guy playing cello on the shore near the woman's beach retreat. It required five sessions in different weather conditions, and in each I sat with my bare feet in the surf, dressed only in jeans and a sweater. I tried to make friends with the cheap, stiff instrument they provided but it turned out not to matter—for practical reasons they used an existing recording of the piece overlaid on surf and seagull sounds rather than recording the music I played. In the end the nice check I received was not worth the bad cold I caught.

I still rotated among my rooms at Fin's place, Counter Point, and Jax and Polly's house. I watched with a puzzled curiosity as the babies lengthened, fattened, and became more aware of the world they had entered, still unsure of what to make of these extensions of my being. As the plane arced through the sky on the way to Spain, I brooded over the two worlds I inhabited and the two families of which I was part—Emilio, Daniel, Paula, and Paloma had become almost as important to me as my own flesh and blood. *Where did I belong?*

Chapter 32

"YOU HAVE TWO MONTHS to put this show together, then we have two weeks for the technical and final rehearsals," Alma said. She spoke in Spanish and her voice echoed in the empty theater where we sat clustered on the stage. Dust motes glittered in the shafts of light emanating from the stage lamps. Martin Pérez's company owned the building which also included dressing, storage, and work rooms in the back and basement. The show would open here.

I regarded the people attending the meeting—my fellow performers as well as the technical and design crew—as curiously as they regarded me. Alma had introduced me as the brains and impetus behind the show, and despite my protests insisted on referring to me by the honorific "Doctor."

"I know you all have other commitments, so work out a schedule among yourselves," Alma continued. "You can rehearse in here if it's available. There also are a couple of back rooms you can use. Book the space as soon as possible." She gathered her materials together. "I want to see a skeleton of the show in two weeks and a solid program by the end of the month."

She and the technical and design crew left. The other members of the troupe turned polite, inscrutable faces to me: Dante, the singer; Adriana, the female dancer; Pyro, the male dancer;

Cruz, the other guitarist; and a couple, Hugo and Lucia, who would do *palmas*, be extra dancers, and take care of administration and logistics on the road. Researching their backgrounds I had learned that, except for Hugo and Lucia, who were middle-aged and part of Pérez's operation, they were all young, upcoming artists with a growing body of followers who could probably fill a hall on their own. My job was to build a show based on Tiago's story and music using the talents of these accomplished individuals and weave their performances into a smooth, integrated, and coherent whole. *You are so totally over your head*, I thought.

"You all received copies of the book, the sheet music, and the demos?" I said, continuing in Spanish.

Heads bobbed. Cruz studied me from under lowered lids.

"Ah, Cruz, is it? Did you get the stuff?"

"*Sí*."

"Okay. Let's figure out when we can get together. We've got a lot to do."

I arrived at our fourth day of rehearsal short of sleep and on edge. Alma would be expecting the skeleton of the show in a week and we had made little if any progress. My efforts to gain the confidence and control of the troupe had not succeeded. A kind of tribal dynamic had formed among the younger ones, the sarcasm in their use of "Doctor" undisguised. They had received the notional program I had proposed with moues and shrugs, but when invited to didn't offer their own ideas. When they thought I wasn't looking they exchanged glances, whispered, and concealed smirks behind their hands. Hugo and Lucia didn't join in but followed the proceedings with closed faces and hooded, watchful eyes. No one had accepted my invitations to go for coffee or beer after.

I got it to some extent—who was I, after all? A musician unknown in Spain, an academic to boot, whose main claim to fame was having brought the music of a long-forgotten musician back from the dead. Still, the success of the show depended on my turning this insolent lot into a harmonious, cohesive body. I was not Fin, who could reduce someone to trembling silence with a withering glance. But I had hoped that a positive approach, growing familiarity, and passing time would bring them around.

This morning I struggled to get their attention to pin down what pieces to include and where each performer would feature in the opening ensemble set. Dante jotted something down in a notebook balanced on his knee. Pyro and Cruz shared a joke. Adriana had pulled her phone out and begun to tap a message. I slammed my hand down on the small table holding my materials. Adriana jumped and the others turned startled faces to me.

"You guys are starting to really piss me off." I kept my voice level but spoke in Spanish slang. "You're supposed to be professionals and you're acting like school kids. If you've got a problem with any part of the show, let's hear it. If you've got a problem with me, let's talk."

Hilary had worked into my agreement with Pérez the right to veto the members of the ensemble they proposed. Exercising it would be hugely disruptive, but I was angry enough not to care.

"We're done for today." I gathered up my things. "You have my number if you want to talk. But you all need to seriously consider whether you're a fit with this show and are prepared to commit to it. If not, don't show up on Monday. If you do, I expect to get your best."

I slung my jacket over my shoulder and walked out.

No one phoned me after. I feared the worst and dreaded the call I would have to make to Alma with news of having fired some of the cast, considering the implications for the schedule. On Monday I arrived early at the rehearsal hall, set my materials out, and waited. Hugo and Lucia came in a few minutes later. Hugo winked at me as they went to their usual spot behind the chairs of the others. Dante came in next and gave me a neutral nod. "*Hola!*" called Adriana and Pyro, following closely on his heels. I gave them a relieved wave. Cruz had not arrived by the time the rehearsal was scheduled to start. *So that's how it is.* I stood and arranged my materials.

"Okay, let's begin."

Two minutes later Cruz sauntered in, gave me a sidelong look, and headed to an empty chair. I let him shrug off his hoodie and take his guitar out of its case before continuing, trying not to reveal my immense relief. When he was settled I drew myself up to my full height and regarded each of them briefly in turn.

"*Gracias por venir.* Now let's get down to work."

We didn't immediately become best friends but work on the program progressed rapidly. We pinned down the musical elements and corresponding acts for each segment, and worked out a system of cues to signal beginnings, endings, or shifts in the show's flow. The music would be a template—once stated, the dancer, singer, or guitarist who was the focal point would offer an interpretation of the piece. After the opening ensemble set, Cruz and I would back Adriana and Pyro in the happy, energetic segment dealing with Tiago's youth and prime. Cruz would disrupt this with an intense solo to create the lovers' triangle and lead into the crime-of-passion segment. Dante would end it with a wild, almost demented *cante*. Hugo and Pyro would open the punishment-and-prison set with a dance representing the trial and judgement accompanied only by hard rhythmic clapping and the tapping of their canes. Then Dante would launch into a lament over fate. I would back him and end the set with a melancholy guitar solo. Cruz and I would open the horse-ranch segment with a guitar dialogue against a *compás* that suggested hoof beats, which would transform into a subdued, almost ponderous dance duet by Hugo and Lucia. Dante would begin the death segment with a mourning *cante*, which would fade into my haunting guitar solo with Adriana performing a ghost-like dance in the background. The ensemble would come together for the upbeat and lively renaissance finale.

As things took shape I felt not only relief at the troupe's cooperation but genuine admiration of their talents.

Adriana was not a beauty, but the exquisite grace, powerful expression, and smoldering sensuality of her dancing would have made a piece of deadwood tingle. Pyro, though not as accomplished as Adriana, was fine-featured and slim and they sparked off each other in the duets.

Dante was a small man and seemingly made of knotted cords. So unexpected was the deep, raw voice that issued from him that it was almost a separate presence. When he sang, his hands, poking out from over-long cuffs, clawed at the air and his face contorted as though wracked with pain. Not finding anything he considered suitable from the existing body of flamenco *cantes,* he composed the songs he would perform in the show. After we had established the program format he came only occasionally to rehearsals, saying he knew what he had to do and when, and wasn't going to waste his voice and energy. We first heard the full force of his *cantes* when we were recording the album that accompanied the show, and the power and passion of them twisted my gut and raised the hair on the back of my neck.

Alma had chosen well when she brought Cruz on as the second guitarist. He made an imposing figure on stage with shaggy hair, heavy brows, piercing eyes, and full red mouth. Next to him I looked like a choirboy. He choked the neck, tore at the strings, and thumped on the soundboard of his guitar as though they were locked in mortal battle. *There is the fire Pérez wanted*, I thought. He was the obvious choice for playing the segments that dealt with Tiago's youth and the crime. My own more lyrical playing style suited the quiet, pensive segments. We played well together when required, but an unspoken rivalry shadowed our relationship and we never managed more than a crusty rapport.

The company gelled as a group as well, helped by the finely honed sense of timing and emphasis that comes from performance experience. In true flamenco tradition the members were generous to each other, sensing when to recede if someone else had something to say and needed the spotlight. At the beginning I wasn't sure I would measure up to them, but that ended when I played my first solo. Eyebrows rose and lips pursed in approval, and in time our rocky start was forgotten.

I tested the hard-won cohesion, however. Unsatisfied with the tone I was able to achieve with the guitar for the death-segment solo, I tried performing the piece on a cello. With its lower register and longer tones I was able to create the deep haunting sound that I sought.

"You can't play flamenco on a cello," Hugo said.

"Why not?"

"It's just not done. Your guitar piece is fine."

"I can do better on the cello."

"But how am I going to dance to it?" Adriana said.

"We will still have the *compás*."

"If you can't do that solo, let me," Cruz said, his eyes flashing.

I looked around the troupe. They raised their eyebrows and shrugged. I had no choice but to let him try. He snatched up his guitar and began to play, the sound bright and urgent. Dante, who happened to be in attendance, shook his head.

Cruz stopped and raised his hand. "No, no, I can do it." He went at it again, then again, never able to produce the desolate, elegiac sound needed.

"Give up, man," Dante said.

"I still don't think he should do it on the cello," Cruz said, pointing a chin in my direction. He didn't use my name if he didn't have to.

"Why don't we see what Alma says," I said.

Alma listened to me playing the piece first on guitar, then on the cello, and then again on the cello with *palmas* and Adriana dancing. When we were done we remained in our positions, awaiting her verdict. Her face had been expressionless throughout, so I had no idea where she was going to land. After several minutes she gave a short nod.

"It works. The sound is more profound. Catches the mood. I like it. Different—it will be a surprise to the audience, but that's not a bad thing."

Alma overlaid the show with her own verve and style, aided by the set and lighting designers. Martin Pérez dropped in a couple of times as the show took shape, speaking quietly with Alma as we rehearsed.

"It's coming together," was all he offered us directly in comment.

Adriana, Pyro, and Cruz visibly sharpened up when Pérez was present, sliding their eyes in his direction as they performed. Dante was as remotely polite to Pérez as he was to everyone else, but otherwise indifferent. I had come to like him a great deal, as much for the way he negotiated life on his own terms as for his extraordinary talent. He was the only full-blood *gitano* in the troupe—Cruz claimed a *gitana* grandmother and the others were entirely Spanish—and there was some indefinable quality in him that reminded me of Tiago.

"This is a good thing you've done," Dante said once, waving a couple of pages of sheet music, the only one in the troupe to acknowledge, or perhaps even recognize, the significance of my efforts to save Tiago's music.

Chapter 33

BY THE TIME WE were ready to hit the road we had been polished and packaged into an impressive production titled *Cae un Meteoro*: "A Meteor Falls." The Pérez organization had also unleashed a multi-dimensional promotional campaign for the tour. Vaults and archives were plumbed for old news stories about Tiago's musical career and subsequent infamy. Older people were reminded of his brilliance, to those younger he was presented as an anti-hero. Much was made of the discovery of his original music when no record of it was thought to exist.

"What would Tiago think of what we've done?" I asked Paula, showing her a sensational magazine article that played up on his notoriety. "Would he really want to have his past, the killings, his fall from grace raked over like this?"

She scanned the article and handed it back to me. "He would love it. I think more than anything he hated being forgotten."

By opening night I was so tired of the show and related kerfuffle that I wondered whether I could summon the energy and spirit needed for the performance. I sensed the same fatigue in the rest of the troupe. The curtains opened to a full house pulsing with expectation, and when the first chord was struck a shock wave of energy surged to the stage and lit us up like a string of light bulbs. There was the odd misstep, delay, or missed cue during the show, but nothing anyone but us would notice. The applause was loud and long when we took our final bows.

After the curtain went down and the hall cleared, the troupe and production staff gathered backstage, sweaty and exultant, around Martin Pérez to toast the successful opening with the bottles of cava he supplied. Other friends and associates wandered in to offer congratulations. Emilio and Mía, and Paula and her now husband, were among them. I had just introduced them to Pérez and Alma when I felt a light touch on my arm.

"Hello, Niels darling."

I turned, disbelieving. My parents stood there, smiling, and behind them Fin and Dominique.

"Mom!" In our video visits none of them had ever spoken about being here. "Why didn't you say you were coming?"

"We knew you'd be busy and didn't want to distract you. But we couldn't miss your big day. It was wonderful."

The others enclosed me in a circle of hugs and congratulations.

"The odd glitch, but otherwise well done," Fin said.

I laughed, knowing that from him this was high praise. "Only you would notice, Granddad."

"*Quién es?*" Emilio said, pressing forward.

I introduced him, Mía, Paula, and her husband and they swarmed my family with handshakes, backslaps, and cheek kisses. Observing it, I marveled at the collision of my two worlds.

Over the next six weeks we traveled to the main cities in southern Spain, doing four or five shows a week. Hugo drove the twelve-seater van in which the rest of us sprawled during the two-to three-hour trips between venues. The technicians followed in a larger van with all our gear. Freed of the confines of the rehearsal space and buoyed by the good reviews the show received, we were looser and easier with each other, except for

Cruz, who was too invested in being difficult and contrary to relax. Everyone took it as given and ignored him.

The halls in which we performed varied in size from a few hundred to over a thousand seats. The shows were all close to if not fully sold out.

"Martin knows our market well," Alma said when I commented on this during one of our regular phone calls. "It's a fine balance—you don't want a lot of empty seats but you also don't want a place too small where potential ticket sales are missed."

A little flurry of media attention accompanied the performances in each city. In Cordoba one of the national television networks did an interview with me. Tiago and the discovery of his music was the focus, but they were curious about the foreigner he had chosen as the heir to his legacy. The interview ran on a daily news-magazine broadcast out of Madrid, prompting a clamor for seats for the show. Martin Pérez was quick to add a second performance in Madrid when the venue was again available, three days after the first. Madrid was the last stop of the tour and I had arranged to fly home a few days later, thinking that would be enough time to wrap things up with Alma before leaving. With the change, my flight was now on the day after the second show. Alma asked me to delay my departure.

"No, I have to get home for my son's birthday." My video visits with Jax and Polly were filled with talk about the babies' trials and tribulations, little achievements, and charming antics. Any who were awake and not fussing were held up for me to see. They drooled and kicked and scrabbled with tiny fat fingers at my face on the screen.

"We really hoped you'd be here for the twins' first birthday," Jax had said.

"Sorry, I just can't do it. But David's, maybe."

"You have kids?" Alma said. "I didn't know you had a family. Then, yes, of course you must go home. We can do whatever is necessary in the days between the shows."

After the first show in Madrid, local crew, well-wishers, and friends of the other members of the troupe milled around the green room. I signed a few programs—still finding the requests strange and amusing—then extricated myself from the crush and headed to the dressing room, wanting nothing more than to change out of my sweaty clothes, remove my makeup, and head out for a cold beer and some food. I was drying my face with a towel when an achingly familiar, dusky voice said in English, "Niels Larsen—is he here?"

"*Allí*, there," a male voice said.

I lowered the towel and turned as in a dream to the door. "Aude," I breathed.

As though conjured by my voicing of her name, she appeared in the doorway clutching a purse in both hands like a shield.

"Hello, Niels."

We stared at each other for several moments. She was thin to the point of gauntness, the soft folds of her dress drooping on her angular frame. Her lustrous hair had been cut into a dense helmet around her head, a style that made too much of her long, straight nose and generous mouth. Her face was a mask of bones and skin, her ardent eyes the only life within the leaden flatness of her makeup.

I set down the towel and extended a hand. "Aude . . ."

Cruz and Pyro crowded in past her and she stepped back.

"Let's find somewhere else to talk." I led her into one of the wings. There was nowhere to sit so we stopped and faced each other.

"What are you doing here?" I said.

"I came to the show—I saw you on television. Could hardly believe it was you until they said your name. Thought I'd say hello."

"I mean in Madrid."

"Thierry, my husband"—her eyes flickered—"is the guest

conductor with the Madrid Symphony. We're here for a few weeks."

"How are you?" I said, concerned that her appearance marked an illness.

"I am fine, thanks." Her lips twitched in a smile. "You certainly seem to be doing well. That was a brilliant performance." When I had last seen her—over ten years ago, I realized with a start—she had spoken English with almost no French accent but it embroidered her words again.

I glanced around. "Look, I'm parched. Can we maybe go somewhere, sit down, get a drink?"

Her face settled into neutral lines. "Sorry, no. I have to go."

"So, what, you stick your head in, say hello, and bugger off? Really? Why did you bother to come at all?" I said, my voice sharp.

Aude bit her lip. "I wanted to see you, Niels. It's just that I can't stay right now. But maybe tomorrow?"

The short spike of anger subsided. "Okay. I'm tied up in the morning. How about lunch?"

"I can do that, yes."

"Where are you staying? I can pick you up."

"In an apartment a couple of blocks off the Plaza Mayor, but I won't be there then. It would be better if we met at your hotel."

I gave her the name and address of the modest establishment where the troupe and I were housed. "How about two?"

She nodded, extended her hand to me in farewell, drawing it back with an apologetic smile when I forgot to let go, and walked away.

Chapter 34

"JUST COFFEE FOR ME," Aude said.

"Okay." I turned to the server and ordered in Spanish. "The lentil soup and some grilled bread for me and coffee for the lady."

The server picked up our menus and left.

"Have you already eaten?" I said.

"I don't usually eat lunch."

"Well, maybe you should. You're awfully thin."

"And you're awfully direct." She smiled and met my eyes for the first time since our awkward greetings when she had picked me up at the hotel. Behind the unflattering hairstyle and the fancy suit she wore, I glimpsed the Aude I used to know.

After she had left the theater the previous night I had returned to my hotel room and collapsed into a chair, the delayed shock of seeing her again running like a charge under my skin. As the city lights dimmed and the streets emptied of people and cars, I sat staring out the window, my thoughts in a muddle. The joy I felt—and there was plenty—was clouded by the anticipated pain of inevitable loss. *Why, after all this time, had she bothered? Did she really think we could meet like nothing had happened?* It was only when the night began to lighten at the edges and traffic noise swelled to a steady hum that I fell asleep. Gazing at her now, I wondered again: *Why have you done this?*

"How is your family?" Aude said.

I cleared my mind. "Everyone's well, thanks for asking. My mom is as prolific as ever. She publishes literary works under her own name and mysteries featuring a female cop and a priest as sleuths under her married name. She says the serious writing is her work and the mysteries are her relaxation. And my dad is still doing portraits, but he's limiting them to a couple a year to give him time for his other painting. He's into an allegorical series right now that he says he doesn't fully understand but is enjoying."

"I always liked your parents."

"Yes, I like them too, and try to spend as much time at home as I can. And with Granddad. He's getting on, not accepting as much commission work now, but still active. And my brother Fox, remember him?"

Aude nodded.

"Surprised us by going into microbiology, of all things. He's with a biotech company in Vancouver. I don't understand his work well enough to describe it except to say that it involves the eating habits of some bacteria."

Our food and drinks arrived. Steam rose from my bowl of soup and the heady aromas of tomato, oil, and garlic wafted from the grilled bread. Aude swallowed hard and looked down at her cup of coffee.

"Have some bread at least," I said. "I'll get another plate."

Aude arrested my gesture to the server. "No, it's okay."

The facets of the diamond she wore flashed as she briefly rested her fingers on my hand. I picked up my spoon. "This business of not eating, Aude . . . are you okay?"

"I'm fine. It's just . . ." She bit her lip and gave me a faint smile. "My mother-in-law has fixed ideas about the correct appearance of the wife of an important conductor and they include being fashionably thin. If I reach for the breadbasket she smacks my hand."

I gaped at her. "That's ridiculous. Does she live with you?"

"Her husband died three years ago and left her alone."

I let the non-answer pass and began eating my soup. After a few mouthfuls, I said, "Does she choose your clothes as well?"

"I'd wear jeans all the time if I could so, yes, she advises me on appropriate attire."

"For the wife of an important conductor."

Her cheeks flushed but she held my gaze. "And who picks yours? What happened to the strait-laced guy I used to know, all neat and tidy in his tux and bowtie?"

"Sometimes I wonder about that too." I picked up a piece of bread. "Anyhow, how's it going with the harp?"

"Oh." She drew back in her chair. "I gave it up."

I raised my eyebrows. "Really? After all the years of study? I remember you saying once that it was all you ever wanted to do."

She twisted her spoon for a moment then looked up at me. "It turned out that there's room for only one musician in my marriage."

I opened my mouth to express outrage and stopped. Did I have any right to question, to comment? All those years when we had shared every thought and spoke our hearts—did they count for anything now? The soup curdled in my stomach and the smell of the grilled bread nauseated me. I set it down and pushed the bowl away.

"I'm done. I'll just get the check."

Aude's face creased into lines of remorse and she reached across the table. "Don't mind me, Niels. Please finish your food."

"It's okay. I'm not hungry anymore."

I signaled to the server for the bill and paid it. Outside the restaurant we stopped and looked at each other. I wanted nothing more than to return to the solitude of my hotel room to puzzle out this reunion and nurse the pain I knew the end of it would bring. I was about to say as much when I caught a mute appeal in Aude's eyes. Could she still read me as she had once been able to?

"There's a park a few blocks away that has a café with a shaded terrace," I said instead. "Why don't we go there and have a coffee. You didn't get a chance to drink yours."

Her grateful smile wrenched my heart. *She needs something from me.* Walking to the park we spoke without saying anything that mattered. At the café we found a table in the dappled shade of an acacia tree and ordered coffees. A couple of goldfinches chased each other among the branches, chirping and trilling in dispute. Laughing at their antics eased the stiffness between us. After the coffee arrived and we had completed the small ceremonies of stirring and tasting, Aude set down her cup and regarded me through eyes clouded with emotion.

"Niels, why did you go away and leave me?"

Ah, here it is. I gazed out over the ordered beds of multicolored flowers and shrubs that edged the terrace for a few seconds to collect my thoughts. Turning back to her, I said, "It was as I told you then, Aude. Something had happened and I needed to go away for a while to sort it out."

"Yes, I remember that, but I never expected it to be for so long. And the fact that you wouldn't tell me what the problem was hurt just as much. We'd never had secrets before."

"It was intensely private and challenged everything I thought I was. Until I had figured out what it meant I couldn't bear to face anyone. And it didn't concern me alone."

Aude's eyes searched mine, her forehead pleated in lines of puzzlement. "What could possibly have been so serious?"

"After all this time, why do you want to know?"

"Your leaving was a pivotal moment in my life and I need to understand why."

"For the record, I did try to get in touch with you."

"When? I don't remember that. When did you try to get in touch with me?"

"It was . . ." I frowned, trying to remember. "It was at the end of my first summer in Spain, a year and a half after I left, maybe a bit longer. But your phone and email were dead, nothing connected. Later, I tried to contact your parents but they had sold the guesthouse and I couldn't find out where they had gone to." I opened out my hands in an appeal for understanding. "Aude, we'd often go for weeks, even months, without being in touch before. I didn't think it would be a problem."

"Weeks, months, yes, but it was *years*."

"I never thought you wouldn't wait for me. Trust me, if I had I would've come home sooner. But I got caught up in flamenco and Tiago, and even after I finally decided to return, he got sick and I couldn't leave him."

"It would probably have been too late by then anyway," Aude said, almost inaudibly. "But I still don't know why you did it."

I studied Aude for a moment. With where we were now, did I still owe her an explanation? And how would my mother feel about my sharing what was her story too?

"Aude, what happened to us, I regret it very much. But we're both at fault—me for presuming too much on your faith in me and our relationship, and you for losing it. I'll tell you why I left if you tell me why you rushed into marrying another guy."

"I didn't exactly rush, but okay."

"Whatever. And I ask that you not repeat what I will tell you to anyone."

Aude raised her eyebrows in surprise. "Yes, of course."

"Remember that New Year's Eve party at my, ah, grandparents?"

"How can I forget it?"

"Yeah, I know. Anyhow, I met there, for the first time, my

supposed aunt. And she told me . . ." I swallowed. It was still difficult to put that dire news into words. "She told me that her brother may not have been my biological father as my mother claimed because . . ." I drew in a steadying breath. "Because he was one of three guys who had raped Mom."

Aude's eyes widened and her hand flew to her mouth. "Oh, Niels!"

"It totally threw me for a loop. I felt like I had a mark on my forehead, like a curse. I worried that I might have inherited that tendency to violence from whichever guy it was that fathered me, and I was too ashamed to talk to anyone about it, especially you. When I started the new semester it was clear after a few days that I wouldn't be able to do it. I no longer knew who I was or what I wanted to do with my life. I figured a complete break and change was the only way to figure it all out."

Expressions of horror, sadness, and what may have been understanding shadowed Aude's face. "I am so sorry, Niels. If only I had known . . ."

We sat for several minutes without speaking until the force of my revelation had dissipated somewhat. I drank the last of my coffee, now cold, and set the cup down.

"Anyhow, that's my story. Now your turn."

Aude pushed her own half-drunk coffee to the side. "I think I need something stronger."

I called the server over and ordered a beer for myself and a glass of wine for Aude. When the drinks arrived she emptied half the glass in one swallow. Setting it down, she straightened up in her chair and raised her chin.

"Okay. When I finished my degree I hadn't heard from you for over a year. I contacted your mother—"

"She mentioned that."

"All she said was that they hadn't heard from you either and that you were on a ship somewhere. My parents had just sold their place in Nelson. I was at loose ends, so I helped them pack and move and set up in Whistler. By then I was pretty upset about not knowing what was going on with you. And there were only bits and pieces of musical work in the offing, nothing that paid enough to live on anyway. I was facing having to get a job in a restaurant or something just to pay the rent.

"It was my mother's idea that I go to France—change of scene and all that. They financed the trip as a graduation gift. I went over, toured a bit, got a job in a hotel in Cannes, then at a ski station in the winter."

I regarded her with dismay. In all that time we had been on the same continent.

"*Maman* also asked me to look up Agnès, an old schoolmate. They became close friends after she saved Agnès from drowning while a group of them were swimming in the local lake. *Maman* was a competitive swimmer in her youth—you may not know that."

"No, I didn't."

"Yes, quite an athlete. She and Papa met at a national sports event where they were both competing—he was a gymnast."

"I thought your dad skied?"

"He did that too. Anyway, *Maman* attached great importance to her friendship with Agnès—she was the daughter of the local aristocrat while *Maman*'s father was only the town pharmacist. And with Agnès's son being a conductor, *Maman* thought I might get some leads for possible music work in France." She gave me a fleeting smile. "At this point, can I just say that the rest is history?"

"And that was all it took to forget me?"

Aude huffed something between a laugh and a sigh. "I was lost and hurt and sad. Thierry was older, impressive, exciting. He swept me off my feet. It was like a fairytale—the places I went with him, the people I met."

We fell silent. What would our lives have been like if I had not left her at her door that New Year's Eve? I wondered.

Where would we be now if we had spent that night together and continued down the path it would have set us on? We would probably be married, cobbling together a living teaching and performing as musicians do. Maybe we would even have children. Pleasant enough, but Aude would not have had her fairytale and I would have missed sailing the seas, meeting Daniel, and discovering Spain, Tiago, and flamenco. I would not have done all that I had or become the man I was now. And I would be loath to give up either.

I glanced at Aude. She was looking out over the beds of flowers, her eyes pensive. Was she wondering what our lives together would have been like as well? Was she weighing and measuring it against her fairytale? I studied her face, its lines still so familiar and dear. I thought of all the years we had known each other, of the quick and deep affinity that had sprung up between us and how our thoughts and dreams had seemed to come from one mind. In the strange balance sheet by which the universe meted out our lives, it seemed that she was the price I had to pay for a life I enjoyed and valued. If I could return to that New Year's Eve knowing what I did now about the cost of my decision to leave, would I have chosen differently? I did not know.

Aude checked her watch and exclaimed, "I have to go."

We rose and wound around the flowerbeds to the street. At the crosswalk she stopped. "I go this way." People jostled past and we stepped to the side. "Can I see you again?"

I regarded her, my mind still wreathed in disconcerting thoughts. Did I want to see her again? "I'm only here until Thursday. I fly out after our last performance."

"That's in three days. I can't tomorrow, but maybe the day after?"

"I have some business to tie up with the show. I don't know how long that's going to take."

"Why don't I call on Wednesday morning to see if you have time? I'd like to hear about all that you've done."

"Ah . . . sure, why not."

With a farewell nod she stepped into the stream of pedestrians and crossed the street. When she reached the other side she looked back over her shoulder and smiled, and the loss of her pierced my heart anew.

Alma arrived that evening from Seville. We spent Tuesday with the rest of the troupe doing a postmortem on the show and tour. After the other performers left she and I tied up business matters.

"I expect all you want right now is to be done and back home with your family, so this probably isn't the time to raise it," she said as we were packing up our materials.

I glanced up at her. "Raise what?"

"Martin would like to take the show farther into Europe—the capitals and other major cities."

"Would Tiago's story resonate outside of Spain? From what I remember he wasn't that well known abroad."

"Martin thinks the core of the show is solid enough, and with a few tweaks we can make the story more universal. He knows the market well—there are sizeable groups of flamenco aficionados looking for a good production."

"When?"

"Next winter, probably. It would take some time to set up."

"The same troupe?"

"If they are able and interested to do it."

"I don't know, Alma. As you say, it's a bit soon to consider. Let me think about it."

"If you really don't want to we could find someone else. You would still get something out of it—you own a good part of the show. We would much prefer that you continue, of course."

Although the accounting of costs and revenues would not

be concluded until after the final performance, Alma had given me an idea of what I could expect to earn from the current tour and it was considerably more than I had thought.

"Another tour has appeal. Give me a couple of weeks to get home and back to normal and then we can discuss."

That night I went with several of the troupe to a flamenco club off the beaten track that Dante knew. As often happened in these places, we ended up jamming with the local musicians until two in the morning. Aude called shortly after nine o'clock.

"Oh, Niels, I've woken you, haven't I?"

I rubbed my eyes. "It's okay. I need to get up."

"Can we still get together?" Her voice held a mix of doubt and entreaty.

"I have to be at the theater this afternoon for setup and soundcheck. Would coffee later this morning work?"

We agreed to meet at a café around the corner from my hotel. Aude was at a table when I arrived and rose with a smile at my approach. We shyly exchanged cheek kisses. Her scent, with its subtle undertone of rosemary, threw me back to our few occasions of intimacy—mostly inexpert necking. Expecting to have the whole of our lives for the rest, we had been in no rush to take it further.

"So glad you could make it, Niels. It's my turn to get the coffee. What would you like?"

"A cappuccino, thanks."

I watched her go to the counter and place the order. Her jeans, sailor-stripe T-shirt, and blazer suited her better than the matronly clothes she had worn at our previous encounters. She returned balancing two cups the size of small bowls on their saucers.

She set one drink down in front of me. "You liked cinnamon on your cappuccino. Hope that's still the case."

"Yes, thanks."

I took a sip of my milky drink and sighed inwardly. Why

had I agreed to come? Seeing this Aude-not-Aude, one minute so familiar, the next a shorn-haired shadow of the girl I had known, was deeply unsettling. I was glad—really—that we had the chance to talk about the circumstances of our separation. It had afforded me, if not exactly acceptance, a kind of resolution at my loss. But did we have anything more to say to each other?

Aude obviously thought so. "It was quite something seeing you playing flamenco, Niels. My Spanish is basic so I didn't understand much of what you said during the show. How on earth did you get here?"

As we drank our coffees I told her about going to Halifax, working on the container ships, getting to know Daniel, following him back to Seville, meeting Tiago. Aude chuckled at the chicken nuggets, quizzed me on my flamenco guitar studies, listened intently to the account of my epiphany when Maria sang by the fire at the *gitano* wedding, and laughed out loud at my fleeing to Morocco in my down-at-heel espadrilles with the box containing Tiago's legacy.

"It wasn't funny," I said, smiling. "I feared for my life. And when I got back home it was Granddad's idea that I go back to school and use Tiago's forgotten music as the basis for getting a doctorate—he probably figured it would make me employable."

As we talked color warmed Aude's cheeks and her eyes sparkled. All the time we had spent apart folded away into nothing. After I finished the account of my life, I said, "And how about you? If you no longer play harp, what are you involved in?"

Aude shifted in her chair. "Oh, this and that. I volunteer at a center for immigrants, help with language instruction. And I walk the dogs at an animal shelter when I can, although they make me sad. I'd bring them all home if I could."

"My mom would be the same."

She nodded. "Also, since my father-in-law died I spend a lot of time with Agnès. And of course I keep Thierry's life in order and often accompany him when he travels. In the winter

I ski. We have a small apartment at the Courchevel ski station and I spend as much time there as I can."

"No kids?"

She looked to the side for a moment then back at me. "No . . . no. And you?" She glanced at my left hand. "I don't see a ring, but that doesn't mean much anymore, does it. You must have someone, and a family maybe?"

I leaned back in my chair. "I have three kids. Anastasia and Arkady, one of the boys, are twins. And there's another boy, David."

Aude's mouth fell open. "Three!"

"Actually, it would be more accurate to say that I helped make three kids—they're not exactly mine."

Her forehead pleated in puzzlement. "I don't understand."

"Remember Jax, the woman I used to live with?"

"Yes, but I thought she was a—"

"Yes, she is, and married to Polly. When Jax got tenure at UVic she and Polly decided it was time to have a family. They asked me to help and I obliged. Their plan was to get pregnant at the same time and get it over with. Then it turned out Polly was going to have twins." I shook my head. "With three babies it's pretty chaotic, but they seem to be managing."

"So how do you fit in?"

"Not clear. I have no legal or practical responsibilities for the kids." I shrugged. "I guess we'll see how it evolves."

"How does all that work with the woman in your life? You're an attractive man, Niels. There must be someone."

"No, no woman. There was only ever you, Aude."

I had spoken without thinking. We stared at each other, wide-eyed. Spots of color bloomed on Aude's cheeks and I felt the heat rise in mine.

"I, ah, didn't mean to say that."

Aude looked down at her hands, clenched on the table. "It's okay."

We sat in awkward silence for several moments. I stirred. "I should go. It's time to get to the theater."

Aude nodded. I rose and touched her shoulder lightly. "Goodbye, Aude. Be happy," I said and left, willing myself not to look back.

Chapter 35

STANDING IN THE WINGS before the last show, the troupe members gathered their energy and concentrated their focus. Still shaken and miserable after leaving Aude, I wondered if I would be able to get through the performance. There was a slight commotion deeper backstage and we all turned to see Martin Pérez come forward.

"I was in town, thought I'd take in the last of what has been a splendid tour."

The others stood up straighter and their faces became more animated—we weren't often favored with his attention. He came to me and whispered, "We'll talk after."

I nodded. The stage manager signaled and we assumed our positions onstage. The curtain rasped open to anticipatory applause and Cruz struck his first exuberant chords. My fingers automatically plucked out a response and the music took me over. When the show was done and we had changed and packed our stuff for the crew to load into the trucks, we headed to a tavern a couple of blocks from the theater where we had booked a long table for the afterparty.

Pérez came to my side. "Let's walk together." We followed the others, falling slightly behind. "Alma says that you're interested in a possible European tour."

"Interested enough to discuss it further."

"*Bueno, bueno.* We'd start with a couple of stops in Portugal then Barcelona, which we missed this time. Then on to France: Marseilles, Nice, Lyon, and of course Paris. Then to Brussels and Amsterdam."

He continued listing possible stops but my attention had snagged on Paris. Maybe Aude would look me up again? I shook my head: *No, no.*

"And Central Europe—Hungary, Romania," Pérez continued. "A sizeable Romany population there."

At the tavern I held the door open for him. "How long would it be?"

"Longer than this one, of course. Greater distances to cover. Two, three months, maybe?"

"Let me close this tour off and then I can start to get my head around one through Europe. I'll get back to Alma in the next few weeks."

"Of course."

At the table Pérez accepted a glass of wine and went around, speaking briefly to each person with a squeeze of the shoulder or pat on the back. When the last members of the production crew arrived, he set down his untouched wine and shook their hands. Spreading out his arms in a gesture of benevolence, he said, "Enjoy!" and left.

"I think that's enough," I said across the table to Hugo as a fresh pitcher of wine was plunked down. It was ten to two in the morning and most of the group were flushed and boisterous with drink.

"I'll settle the bill." He rose and clapped his hands. "Okay folks, time to wind things up."

The rumble of disagreement that met his words quickly turned to plans to move the party to a club nearby.

"Are you going to join us?" Dante asked me.

"No thanks. I've had enough and still need to pack."

Dante blinked. "This is goodbye then?"

"Yes. I'll probably be gone before any of you are awake."

I went around to each one, exchanging hugs, handshakes, and promises to keep in touch as fitted our relationship. Saying goodbye to people with whom you had lived and worked for several months was difficult, and I was glad the time for leave-taking was short. When I came to Adriana, she said, "If you're going back to the hotel, I'll come with you."

We followed Hugo and Lucia, who had also declined to continue the festivities, out to the street.

"You were awfully quiet tonight," Adriana said.

"Just tired and a bit down. You know how it is when something finishes."

"*Sí.*" She slipped her arm around mine. "I heard rumors that the show may go into Europe."

Alma must have said something—it wasn't a secret, exactly. "Maybe."

"Would you be part of it?"

"Maybe. How about you, if you got the chance?"

She smiled. "Maybe."

Given the hour I accompanied Adriana to her room, which was on a different floor than mine.

"I guess this is goodbye." I bent to exchange cheek kisses.

She turned her face and gave me a lingering kiss on the lips instead. "I've been wanting to do that for a long time."

"You have?" I said in genuine surprise and allowed myself to be drawn into her room.

The urgent sense of needing to do something jolted me awake. I glanced at my watch—Papa Luke and Mama Ris had promptly replaced the one that had been stolen when I told them about the theft—and groaned: it was ten after nine. Light edged the drawn shades. I glanced at Adriana's bare back and tousled hair and eased myself out of bed. Collecting my scattered clothing I went to the bathroom, closed the door, and dressed as best I could in the dark. Before opening the door to the hall I looked back at Adriana. Leaving this way was shabby, but I didn't have time for what would likely be a prolonged goodbye. *I'll leave a note at the desk*, I thought, hurrying down the staircase.

Back in my room I quickly showered and dressed. My plane left at two o'clock and, allowing for the taxi ride and time needed to check in, sort out the special arrangements for my guitar, and get through security, I had less than an hour to pack and check out. I emptied drawers and threw items any which way into my suitcases, cursing myself for not having packed sooner. I was scooping up my razor, toothbrush, and toiletries when there was a knock at the door.

"Come back later," I called, assuming it was the room cleaner.

After a few seconds the knock sounded again. I hurried to the door, thrusting the items into my shaving kit on the way.

I swung open the door. "*Que?*"

Aude stood on the other side. Her hair was disheveled and her eyes sunken and red-rimmed. A beige trench coat hung loosely on her, the belt trailing, and a green scarf was looped unevenly around her neck. She gripped the handle of a small suitcase tightly. Her mouth twisted in an attempt at a smile. "Hi."

I stared stupidly at her for several seconds. "What are you doing here, Aude?"

"Take me home, Niels," she said.

PART III

Chapter 36

MOST STORIES WOULD HAVE ended there. But life is more complicated than that.

After five precious minutes of debate I accepted that Aude had left her husband and was determined to come back to Canada with me. Nonetheless, I tried again in the taxi to the airport.

"Aude, are you sure you want to do it this way? Wouldn't it be better if you stayed to sort things out?" She shook her head. "I don't mean go back to your husband if you don't want to, but there must be somewhere you can go, a friend maybe? It's going to be awfully difficult to deal with it from so far away."

"I don't have anywhere or anyone else to go to." She turned eyes brimming with tears to me. "Please, Niels."

At the airport we said little as we shuffled along in the line to the check-in counter. My flight itinerary involved a stop and plane change at Heathrow.

"I am sorry, you will have to sit separately on the leg to London," the agent said in accented English. She tapped away at her computer, leaning forward to scan the screen. "But . . ." She looked up with a smile. "I can get you seats together in business class on the flight to Vancouver."

"Fine," Aude said and handed over her passport and credit card. I choked and did the same to pay for the upgrade from my seat in coach.

Aude was silent as we made our way through security and tracked the long halls to our departure gate. When we arrived the flight was loading and we entered the queue, splitting up inside the plane to go to our respective seats. I stowed my small grip in the overhead compartment, stepped over the knees of the person already in the middle seat, and wiggled into my own. The events of the morning settled on me like leaden weights. *Am I the cause of this?*

When we arrived at Heathrow it took some time to get from the terminal at which we had disembarked to the one from which our flight to Vancouver would depart, but when we found our gate over two hours remained before the flight left.

"Can I get you a coffee, or something to eat?" I asked Aude.

During the previous flight she had tidied up her clothes and put on some light makeup but still moved as though in a dream. She looked around distractedly. "The airline should have a lounge nearby. Let's go there."

Flying coach, airport lounges were not something I frequented. Following directions from an agent at the gate we retraced our steps to a discrete door down the hall. The concierge scrutinized our boarding passes and waved us in. I led Aude to a table next to a window. She sank down in a chair and buried her face in her hands.

"Why don't I get us some food? You probably haven't eaten yet today, and I could sure use some," I said.

She straightened up and drew in a sharp breath. "Just some coffee."

Aude had taken off her coat and recovered her composure when I returned with soup and buns from a buffet in the lounge.

"I only wanted coffee."

"You'll feel better if you eat something."

She acquiesced and swallowed a few spoonsful of soup. After finishing my own I went back to the buffet and returned with coffee and pastries. I set a plate with a lavishly frosted slice of cake in front of her.

"You used to like chocolate."

She regarded it dubiously but forked up a morsel and held it in her mouth for several seconds before swallowing. "I can't remember the last time I had anything so decadent," she said and took another bite.

I finished my own pastry, set the plate aside, and drank some coffee. Aude was looking out the window at a plane that was taxiing to its gate. Her folded hands rested on the table. The diamond ring was gone.

"Aude, can you tell me why you're doing this?"

She turned and regarded me in silence for several moments before speaking.

"Niels, I was so naive when I married Thierry, so terribly naive. I truly didn't see beyond the wedding." Her voice was strained but steady. "It seemed so glorious at the time, so amazing that over other women he could have had—and there were several—he chose me for his wife. Recently I've begun to wonder why they did, in fact, choose me." She gave a short, dry laugh. "It is a *they*—Thierry and his mother are a unit. He's the only son and Simone, his sister, doesn't figure. At least she's happily married and doesn't seem to care.

"Anyhow, Thierry had just turned thirty when we met and I think they decided he needed a wife. Knowing them I figure they wanted someone malleable and compliant to fill the role. And I fit the bill: a little provincial girl who'd be so awed and gratified by the privilege of being married to a remarkable man and part of an important family that I wouldn't be too demanding or independent. Once I overheard Agnès say to a friend, 'The family is petite bourgeoisie, of course, but she is well educated, understands music, and speaks English fluently.' I was actually flattered. Agnès also said that, being an athlete, I was sure to be strong and healthy. She and her friend had a little laugh over that. I understand now that she meant I was good breeding stock."

"Come on, Aude. Who thinks like that anymore?"

"Huh. Believe me, it still matters. Early on we talked about having a family but not immediately. About four years ago Agnès took me aside and said that it was time to stop the contraceptives. I obliged. A few months later, when I was in Cairo with Thierry, I began to experience pain in my abdomen. Thierry said that as we were returning to France soon we should wait until then to seek medical help. I thought I would die on the flight home and went directly to hospital when we landed. The problem was an ectopic pregnancy—that's when it happens somewhere other than the uterus. It wreaked quite a bit of havoc, including a severe case of peritonitis." Her eyes blinked rapidly. "I was very sick."

She paused and drank some coffee.

"When I finally recovered the race to get pregnant started again." She gave a sad little smile. "Time passed but nothing happened. My doctor said that with the damage the pregnancy and peritonitis had done I may never be able to conceive. Thierry and Agnès wouldn't accept that, and since then I've been poked and prodded by countless doctors. I've had liters of blood drawn, swallowed hundreds of pills, been shot full of hormones, but nothing's worked. Thierry would seek out projects in cities that had clinics and doctors who were supposed to be able to perform miracles. None did. Madrid was the last one, a kind of Hail Mary pass. Last week they confirmed what all the others had said: I am sterile."

"I'm so sorry, Aude," I said quietly.

She was silent for a moment then sighed. "Thierry and Agnès want a dynasty, so I have no value to the family now. Not that they would ever say as much—they're much too polite— but the air is thick with their disappointment. And I've woken to the fact that my life has little meaning or purpose. Sharing in

Thierry's glory as his recognition and importance grew helped me rationalize giving up my own music and thoughts of a career. Now I don't know who I am or what I'm doing anymore."

She gave me a wry smile. "And then in the middle of all this turmoil I see you on television. When I thought about how I had come to be where I was, it all came back to your leaving me. I really wanted to know why. I went to the performance intending to seek you out. But the compelling guy I saw chattering away in Spanish and burning up the stage was nothing like the Niels I remembered. After, it took me half an hour to get up the nerve to go and find you."

"I'm glad you did."

Aude regarded me quizzically. "Are you? There were times when it seemed like you wanted to be anywhere but with me."

"It wasn't easy seeing you again. Or what had become of you."

"Yes, I got that. But it was so good, so cheering and comfortable, to just sit and talk with you. It reminded me of who I had been and what I had wanted and striven for all those years ago. And just before you left yesterday, you said something that really gave me a jolt."

I winced. "You mean about there being only you?"

She shook her head. "That wasn't it. I think we both know the Aude you felt that way about doesn't exist anymore. No, it was when you said *be happy*. It kept echoing in my head and I realized that I had not been happy for a long time.

"When Thierry returned last night I was bursting to talk but he brushed me off, saying it was late and he was too tired. I couldn't sleep for thinking. Seeing you, speaking to you, had given me a badly needed sense of perspective and the courage to act. When it started to get light I dressed and packed my bag, then sat and waited for Thierry to wake—we slept in separate rooms when he worked late, so as not to disturb me, he said. I knew you were flying out today and was about to leave a note and go when he finally got up. I made him some coffee, and while he drank it I prattled on about how unhappy I was, how useless and lacking in purpose I felt, how I needed to leave and make a fresh start. All through this he didn't speak, and when I finished repeating myself for the third time he just looked at me coolly and said . . ."

Aude's lips trembled and tears spilled from her eyes.

"He said: 'Perhaps it's for the best.'"

"Will you go to your parents?" I said.

Aude pushed the scrambled eggs on her plate from one side to the other with her fork. We had flown in from London and arrived at Fin's house the previous day. He and Dominique were away but I had found enough in the refrigerator to prepare a simple breakfast.

"No, not right away. They're going to be very disappointed in me, especially my mother. She has a lot invested in my marriage. I can't face that yet. I need some time alone."

"Where will you go then?"

"I don't know—a hotel perhaps."

"I'd offer you this place to stay but it's not mine."

"No, no, of course not."

I shook my head ruefully. "You'd think that at my age I'd have my own place, but moving around as much as I do I haven't bothered. I don't even know yet where I'd settle."

"That's the life of a musician, isn't it? Anyhow, don't worry about me, Niels. I'll figure something out."

But I did worry about her. She was not as distraught as she had been at the start of our journey—the benefit of distance and rest perhaps—but she still looked like a refuge from a war zone and didn't seem to have thought out any steps beyond leaving her husband. I checked myself, remembering the confusion and lack of direction around my own flight all those years ago.

She would need help. A thought struck me and I snapped my fingers.

"I have an idea. Let me make a call."

I went into the house, got my phone from where it had been charging in my room, and called my mother.

"Niels, darling! Are you back?"

"Yes, arrived last night. I'm at Granddad's. Listen, Mom, something very . . . interesting has happened." I told her about meeting Aude in Madrid and summed up her situation.

"Oh, my," Leah said.

"And she needs a place to stay for a while to sort things out. She's not ready to go to her parents' place yet. Look, is Mama Ris back in the cottage?"

"No. She's decided to stay at the apartment in the retirement complex that she moved into after Papa Luke died."

"Is anyone else staying there right now?"

"No. Aude would be welcome to use it."

"That's great. It's such a calming place, I think it would do her good. Would today be too soon to bring her? I'm coming over for David's birthday."

"Today would be fine. The cottage was spring-cleaned recently but I'll go and air it out. What time do you think you'll get here?"

We spent a few more minutes discussing arrangements and I went to give Aude the news.

"I couldn't impose!" she said.

"You won't, no one's using the place. If you want to come I'm heading over later today."

Aude and I caught an afternoon ferry to Vancouver Island. She watched the small islands we passed in silence, only saying once that she had forgotten how beautiful the coast was. I snoozed. On the way to Counter Point we stopped in the nearby town for provisions. My mother met us at the cottage.

When Aude was settled in, she thanked us but pleaded jet lag when Mom invited her to dinner.

Over the meal I elaborated on my reunion with Aude in Madrid and the circumstances that prompted her to leave her marriage.

Leah shook her head. "It sounds positively medieval."

"She always struck me as a very solid and level-headed girl," Theo said. "How did she get sucked into such a peculiar relationship?"

I shifted uncomfortably in my chair. "I'm partly to blame, I guess, leaving her the way I did and staying out of touch for so long. But I got the sense that her first years with him were happy."

"Will you stay with her here?" Leah said.

I shook my head. "I'm not what she needs right now." *Or maybe ever.*

Encountering Aude as she was now had altered my emotional landscape. As she herself had observed, the Aude I had enshrined in my heart and around whose absence I had structured my relationships with other women no longer existed. The present Aude had loved another man and been redefined by their relationship. Ripping herself out of it would take her somewhere else, perhaps even farther away from me. Maybe that was what I needed.

"Besides, I've got a lot on my plate right now," I continued.

"Why are you doing this then?" Theo said.

"Because she was a good friend once and she needs help."

Chapter 37

I RETURNED TO VANCOUVER after a clamorous visit with Jax and Polly—the babies now stumbling around like drunken dolls and uttering their first words—to discover that I was in demand. Hilary had assumed the role of my publicist, and through her vast connections in the music world had put out word of my work in Spain. A journalist with a local arts revue interviewed me and a piece of puffery appeared in the next issue.

"A sensation? Taking Spain by storm? Showing them how flamenco's done?" I said to Hilary. "This is embarrassing. I hope no one over there sees it."

She laughed and patted me on the arm. "Never argue with publicity."

The calls and emails started: a duet with a rock musician for his next album, spots at a major folk festival and the evening show at the local summer fair, guest artist with a flamenco troupe from Montreal, an invitation to be one of the judges at a kids' talent show. Greg had been anxiously waiting for my return to work with him on a new project and Alma had already started planning for the European tour. On top of everything else I needed to prepare a summer course on flamenco guitar at U of T. A former instructor who had followed my studies had proposed it earlier in the year. Curious about whether teaching might be of interest, I had agreed to do it.

I didn't keep in touch with Aude. When I spoke to my parents I didn't enquire after her and, perhaps because of this, they didn't offer any news. Seeing Aude again had accomplished what all the years of separation had not: it made me realize that I had to move on. With this came sadness, but it was a tender melancholy rather than the heart-shattered state learning of her marriage had reduced me to. I was in my second week teaching in Toronto when I received an email from her. "Just want to say how very grateful I am for all your help," it began, then went on to tell me that after nearly a month at Counter Point she had gone to stay with her parents, and was returning to France shortly to initiate divorce proceedings. I replied with a chatty note describing my activities since I had seen her and wishing her luck in sorting out her affairs.

The summer passed quickly. My flamenco guitar course went well and I discovered that, for the most part, I enjoyed teaching. At the end of August I accompanied Greg to an open-air ambient-music festival in a field near San Francisco, where I learned that not only had his music garnered him a following but my name was known to some from the credits he gave me for my cello, guitar, and voice contributions.

The itinerary and dates for the European tour of *Cae un Meteoro* were finalized, to begin in Lisbon in the third week of February. With everyone from the original cast except Cruz continuing on we didn't need to begin rehearsals until January, for which I was grateful, as I had numerous commitments in the fall. Among these was an offer from the casting director with whom I had previously worked to do a part in a film as a guy playing piano at a party.

"And you speak in this one," he said. "Three whole lines."

I accepted—these bit parts were easy money.

"Are you sure you don't want to take up acting seriously?" he continued. "The camera likes you."

"No thanks," I said.

I also received a query from a Spanish film producer wanting to buy the rights to my book about Tiago. It had received good reviews and been on the bestseller lists for several weeks there. I handed it to Hilary to deal with—she was quickly becoming indispensable in keeping me sorted out and managing the administration generated by my work, especially the collection of fees and royalties. These had jumped with airplay of the album we had made of Tiago's music, and as other musicians began to cover his compositions.

I received another email from Aude before Christmas. There was a light, almost breathless tone to it.

> *Sorry not to write sooner, have had crazy busy fall. Got work as a ski patrol in Whistler but needed to do training to update my certification. Enjoying it all. Living with parents, not the best arrangement but accommodation is scarce and expensive. Papa is fine but Maman still bursts into tears whenever she sees me.*

It continued with other snippets of news and ended with:

> *Enjoyed hearing about your activities in last email. Let me know how and what you're doing.*

A second email immediately followed.

> *Oh! Forgot to tell you something that happened back in France. On first meeting with Gilles, my* avocat *for divorce, I came out of office—it's on ground floor of his house—to find woman with flaming red hair pacing in the reception area. "Your voice, you sound just like I hear her in my head!" she said to me. Was quite startled. Gilles said, "May I present my wife, Suzi Beaufort." She grabbed my hand and started to*

lead me upstairs. When I looked to Gilles for help he said "Ma chérie, Aude does not know who you are or what you mean. Perhaps some explanation?" Turns out Suzi Beaufort writes mysteries and publisher wants to make audio recordings of her books but she's resisted because no one's had the right voice for main character—until me! Did one book there. Needed some instruction of course but I had done voice and performance at school. It went well and was very amusing and best of all I made some money. Suzi happy with result and I got contract to do four more. There is a recording studio in Whistler I can use and I will work on them over the winter. All great fun.

I was at Counter Point for the holidays, and at dinner that night told my parents about Aude's experience and contract to do the audiobooks for Suzi Beaufort.

"Yes, she told me," Leah said.

"She did?"

"We keep in touch. When she was here I visited her often to make sure she was okay, and we'd go for walks, or to town, or she'd come up for dinner. We became friends."

"I see."

My mother gave me a sidelong look. "Is that a problem?"

"Humph," I said.

Chapter 38

ADRIANA POUTED. "AND YOU left without even a goodbye."

With all the drama and confusion around Aude's leaving her husband on the morning I flew out of Madrid, I had forgotten to leave a note for Adriana at the hotel and didn't remember to send an email until several days later.

"*Lo siento*, Adriana. We had slept late and then I had to rush to catch my flight, and when I got home there were some things I had to deal with right away." It was a true if somewhat incomplete account.

"And then you didn't write after."

I sighed. As far as I understood the rules of engagement, a one-night stand didn't a commitment make. "Don't hold it against me. We're here now and have to get on with the show."

She ducked her head and gave me a coquettish look. "Of course I will not hold it against you. It is good to be back, *sí?*"

"Yes it is," I said and smiled.

The other returning members of the *Cae un Meteoro* troupe—Dante, Pyro, Hugo, and Lucia—greeted me as a long-lost friend, their initial resistance to my involvement in the show long forgotten. Jago, a guitarist in his early twenties, replaced Cruz. Jago had brilliant technique, his fingerwork was extraordinarily quick and precise, but it was at the expense of expression. Tiago would have said that his playing left the music behind.

Tiago's music was still the backbone of the show but his story was reduced to a footnote in the program. Although the narrative structure remained the same, changes to the music and dance components were made. There was less latitude for interpretation by the performers. Music was programed and the dance components more tightly choreographed. Everything became more extravagant, the set and lighting brighter, the music faster and louder, the dancing more visceral.

"It's lost some of its nuance and meaning," I said to Alma.

"Yes, but these audiences want glitz and flash, not subtlety."

I regretted the loss of authenticity but went along with it all—Pérez understood his market.

The tour followed a punishing schedule, thirty-two performances in twenty-one cities in eleven weeks. The distances between venues were greater than those on the tour through Andalusia and the theaters were bigger. Our bus was larger and more comfortable as well, but the hours on the road were still long. Occasionally we traveled through the night to get to the next destination. Our time in each city was short and consumed by setup, rehearsal in the new space, promotion with media and local flamenco clubs, and dealing with personal matters. We tried to fit in a sightseeing walk or bus ride around the city, but often all we saw of it were the streets around the theater and hotel and what we passed entering and leaving.

We each had our own way of dealing with the tedium. I listened to music, read, and wrote in my journal. Others played cards or carved or did needlework. Everyone was glued to their phones, and hisses and groans erupted when there was no service or a battery ran dead.

In the absence of other company, friendships flourished. I spent a lot of time with Dante—the most intriguing member of the troupe—and jammed with Jago. Hugo, two guys from the technical crew, and I worked out and we took turns finding a gym when we hit a new city. Nonetheless, disagreements and upsets happened. Hugo and Lucia, the tour managers and de facto elders, scolded or smoothed feathers. I provided guidance on the show—it usually needed only a light hand, as most issues were recognized without my having to point them out and sorted in our postmortems after each performance.

Despite the monotony and occasional contretemps, when the curtain rose the troupe came together and delivered spirited performances, buoyed by the irresistible flamenco rhythms. Most of the shows were sold out and the audiences appreciative. After a few repetitions of the roll-in, set-up, perform, pack-up, roll-out sequence, time lost dimension for me. Regular contact with the others in my life kept me from sliding into a state of complete detachment.

I had replied to Aude's Christmas note with one from Spain describing the planned tour. She wrote back not long after.

> *Full days here. Took a while to get back into form—feeling my age?!—but I can go full bore now. Just finished second audio book for Suzi (it's what I do in my free time) and hope to start third soon. Let me know where you are and how it's going.*

I wrote back the following week, repackaging pieces I had sent to others. Aude's response came a few days later—questions, comments, and details of her daily life and some of the people in it.

> *Spend as little time at home as possible. Papa's okay but Maman! It's like I'm in a time warp and back in childhood. Maybe menopause making her so cranky. Can't wait for spring to get out of here.*

I added Aude's name to the list of those to whom I sent my regular missives recounting life on the tour, and the frequency of our exchanges increased. But while my accounts to her were generic, hers became personal. Waking early one morning I checked my emails while still in bed, as was my habit. Aude's was the first I opened. I settled back for an entertaining read then sat bolt upright.

> *Had my first revenge sex. Australian guy. His idea of conversation is delivering catchphrases from movies he thinks suit the situation but not much need for talk anyway. Parents not happy about hours I'm keeping, Maman threatening to take back key to their house. Only a few more weeks.*

I stared wide-eyed at the screen of my phone. *Of course she will sleep with other men*, I reasoned, but my heart pattered with indignation. The irony was not lost on me that I was reading the note while in Adriana's bed. A boyfriend had delivered her to the tour bus when we departed Seville so I had no expectations that our night together would be repeated. On the second week out, however, she asked me back to her room when we returned to the hotel after the performance.

"Aren't you in a relationship with someone?" I said.

She shrugged. "He's not here."

In the spirit of "what goes on the road stays on the road," I had accepted her invitation. I glanced down now, concerned that she might see what I was reading, but she slept deeply, dark hair a nimbus around her head, her face still.

Aude's revelation of having revenge sex plagued me for days. Revenge against whom? And why did she think I needed to know? Was I supposed to be glad for her? She appeared to have reverted to the unreserved and unfiltered communications of our adolescence. I remembered her unabashed accounts of going out with other boys. What did this mean? And why did I care? Had I not accepted that we had no future and it was time to move on? Aude's actions indicated that she certainly had.

Chapter 39

"YOU KNEW THIS WOULDN'T last, Adriana," I said. "I'll be going home soon." She was tucked under my arm, her breasts pressed against my chest, her breath feathering my skin. It was the morning after our last night together. We had finished the tour in San Sebastian and would be driving back to Seville that day.

"Why don't you stay in Spain? You're here half the time anyway. We would make a good team: you play, I dance."

I stroked her hair. "We live in different worlds. And I should go now." I knuckled her chin up and gave her a lingering kiss of sincere regret. "*Lo siento.*"

Adriana's boyfriend was waiting for her when the bus arrived at Martin Pérez's headquarters in Seville. She received his embrace of welcome with a smile. While he loaded her luggage into a small car she went around and said goodbye to the rest of us. The other members of the troupe curiously watched us exchange cheek kisses and a hug. "Don't forget me," she whispered before letting me go.

I busied myself with my own goodbyes to avoid seeing her drive away.

I didn't fly home immediately. Among other things I wanted to spend time with Emilio, who had recently undergone prostate surgery after a cancer diagnosis, and visit with Daniel, who was taking a few days leave for the same purpose. I was glad of the distraction, as the post-tour malaise had gripped me hard. In the final weeks the troupe and crew wanted nothing more than to be free of the wandering and relentless grind of putting on the show. Re-entry into normal life wasn't smooth, however. Without the structure of a hard schedule and constant presence of others I was restless, unfocused, disoriented. And I missed Adriana. Walking in the streets, my head would snap in the direction of any lithe woman with long dark hair who passed by, and I seemed to hear her lilting laugh at every corner.

Daniel arrived at the tavern apartment on Friday evening. "Just like old times," he said, embracing me in greeting.

"Yes." Having hitched a ride on a navy plane flying to the nearby Rota naval base, he was still in uniform. "But you're not. The mustache is new."

He stroked it with his thumb and forefinger. "Thought it might make me look older."

"Geez, you're already quite formidable. I feel shambolic beside you."

He laughed and slapped me on the shoulder. "You look just like an artiste should."

It was too late to visit Emilio that evening so we caught up over a meal at the tavern. We had been speaking Spanish but Daniel switched to English. "I need the practice," he said.

I laughed. "Could be difficult—I've spoken mostly Spanish for the last few months."

We brought a bottle of wine back to the apartment and eased ourselves down into the old beanbag chairs to drink. After taking a sip Daniel put down his glass and stroked his mustache as he had done several times during the meal. I was contemplating telling him that the mannerism was fussy and spoke of diffidence and missed what he said.

"Come again?"

"I have some news."

"Yeah?"

"You're the first to know. I haven't told family yet."

We regarded each other for a moment. He was trying not to smile too broadly.

"You've either received a major promotion or you've met someone," I said.

"Not a promotion."

"Huh! Who is she?"

He grinned. "Her name is Adela. She works at a medical lab in Cartagena. We met at a friend's house."

"You never said anything."

Daniel shrugged. In our communications he rarely mentioned his female friends.

"Serious?"

He grinned again. "We're getting married."

"Well! Have you set a date?"

He mentioned a day in September. "You will come, I hope. I want you as my best man."

"Yes, of course. I wouldn't miss it."

He chattered on about Adela and their plans until it was time to go to sleep. I took the bed in the alcove as I always did, even when alone in the apartment. Lying sleepless I thought about Daniel's news and wondered why I didn't share his joy. Was I jealous of his happiness or afraid of losing this man who was almost a brother? I shifted into a more comfortable position with a sigh. Regardless, things between us would change.

The next morning I passed the bathroom on my way to make a cup of coffee. The door was open and Daniel, wearing only pajama bottoms, was leaning forward against the sink and staring intently in the mirror. I backstepped.

"Everything all right?"

He glanced at me. "I'm wondering about the mustache."

"You don't need it."

When he joined me in the living room twenty minutes later with a cup of coffee in hand he was clean-shaven. "Better?"

"Yes."

"Adela wasn't too enthusiastic about it either." He took a sip of his coffee. "We talked so much about me and her last night. How about you? Any women in your life?"

I spilled out the story of Adriana.

"And you just let her walk away with her man?" Daniel said.

"Yeah. I never thought I'd miss her this much. I liked her an awful lot."

"But maybe not enough, huh?" Neither of us spoke for a moment. "And the other one, your girlfriend from long ago, the one you took home from Madrid? What's happened to her?"

"Oh, yes, Aude. She's in Canada, working through a divorce, getting on with her life. We keep in touch." I grunted. "The things she says in her emails. She told me about sleeping with a guy—revenge sex, she called it. Like when we were young and she'd tell me about the boys she was going out with as though I wouldn't mind."

"So you do mind? Even though you were carrying on with Adriana?"

"Well . . ."

"Maybe you still have feelings for Aude."

I pondered that for a moment. "She's been a big part of my life. Even when we were apart. So yeah, I still have feelings for her. I just don't know what they are."

We spent the next four days with Emilio, taking him out for lunch, going on drives, sometimes just sitting and talking about nothing. He was listless and subdued, the effort it took for him to respond to us apparent.

"I've never seen him so down and discouraged," I said to Daniel over a drink after leaving Emilio. "It's like someone's let the air out of him. The prognosis is good, isn't it?"

"Yes, he should be fine. But you know, this surgery, it cuts at the heart of his sense of being a man."

"You wouldn't think it mattered so much at his age."

Daniel shook his head. "I don't think that ever changes."

We had time for morning coffee with Emilio before I borrowed his car to drive Daniel to the airport for his flight home. He shook his finger at me in parting.

"I'm counting on you for September."

"I'll be there."

With a final wave he headed down the corridor to the security check, head high, back straight, stride firm. How different we were, I mused, yet there were few people to whom I felt closer.

During my time in Seville I spent an afternoon wrapping up tour business with Alma. Martin Pérez stuck his head through her office door at one point.

"A good tour, yes?"

I gestured at the pages of financials Alma and I were reviewing. "From the looks of it."

"They want the show at *La Bienal de Flamenco* this year. Two nights."

"Oh?"

"You'll come?"

"It happens I'll be here in September, so yes, I will do the show. But that will be it, I think."

"You wouldn't be interested in a tour in America?"

"Is there a market for the show in the States?"

Pérez shrugged. "Haven't taken anything there. Thought you might know."

I shook my head. "Anyway, not something I'd want to do."

I also visited with Paula and Paloma. While on the tour I had received a text from Paula containing only a link to a news item. Opening it, I learned that her uncle had been killed in an apparently targeted hit. I responded with cautious condolences. She didn't reply. Neither of us raised it when we met on my return. We focused instead on setting up the foundation to provide scholarships to promising *gitano* youth, funded by the share of royalties for Tiago's music I had assigned for this purpose. There were now sufficient earnings to start. Paula would complete the necessary paperwork to get it established and explore possible cultural grants from the Spanish and European governments.

"We should be able to get some private donations as well," I said.

"Yes, maybe, but I wouldn't know how to go about getting them."

"Emilio may have some ideas."

When I raised the matter with him Emilio perked up somewhat. "Yes, the welfare of *gitanos* is getting attention right now and some people and companies might want to be seen doing something good in the area. That Pérez guy for a start—he's made a lot of money off Tiago's music. I'll put in something as well, of course, and I can think of a few others who might."

I had a sudden inspiration. "We're going to have to have a proper board of directors for the foundation. Would you like to serve on it?"

"The lovely Paula is involved?"

"Yes, she's a big part of it."

Emilio wiggled his eyebrows provocatively. "Then how can I say no?"

I smiled. The surgery didn't seem to have affected him that much.

In the middle of this I received an email from Aude. The last I had received was the one informing me of her Australian lover. He was nowhere in evidence in this one.

Suzi Beaufort sent me draft of English translation of first book in her series. I told her that in translation the female character—it's written in first person—sounded different than in French. "Can't have that!" Suzi said. "Fix it and do the other translations." Well! A bit out of my depth but thought I should talk it through with someone before saying no.

She went to see my mother. On Leah's advice, and with assurances of her support, Aude decided to give it a try. For the one which had already been done it was just a matter of changing language and tone. To prepare for the rest she had started some crash courses in writing and translation. She was heading to France shortly to work out arrangements.

I was reading her email lying in bed. Her last sentence brought me upright.

Met your children yesterday. They're lovely.

I stared at the words then grabbed my phone and began to dial my mother's number. I stopped just before it connected—it was past midnight there. I got up, showered, dressed in a slapdash manner, had too many coffees, and fumed my way through the day. At what was precisely seven thirty in the morning back home I dialed my mother's number again.

"Niels! Hello. How nice. Just give me a minute, I'm walking Rune and I need to clean up after him."

I waited, listening to sounds of steps, plastic rustling, dog feet scraping the ground, and a metallic *thunk* as the doggie bag landed in a garbage bin.

"There. How are you, darling?"

"I'm fine. Look, Mom, what's this about you taking Aude to see my kids?"

She took a moment to answer. "I didn't take Aude to see

your children. Aude came along with me when I went to visit *my* grandchildren."

"Still."

"Why does it bother you?"

"Just because," I mumbled.

"Look, Niels, I don't know what's going on between the two of you, but I don't think I should have to temper my interactions with Aude to suit your sensitivities. Is that the only reason you called?"

"Of course not," I lied. "How's everything going?"

My last piece of business before flying back to Vancouver was a meeting in Madrid with the producer who had bought the movie rights to my book on Tiago, arranged at his request.

"Your agent asked if there might be a role in the film for you," he said.

I raised my eyebrows. It was not something I had discussed with Hilary. "The thought hadn't occurred to me. I'm obviously too old to play myself and wouldn't be at all suitable to play Tiago."

He leaned back in his seat. "You could play the part of a flamenco guitarist. There will be several needed."

"Thanks, but no."

He smiled, not quite hiding his relief. "But you will, I hope, act as an advisor to us as we put together the film."

Seeing no reason not to, I agreed.

Chapter 40

"JUST ONE NIGHT?" JAX said.

"Yeah, well, unfortunately I'm all booked up," I said.

Jax, Polly, and Dina, their nanny, were feeding the children, who were seated in highchairs around the table. I was on a stool at the kitchen island drinking beer.

"We haven't seen you for almost half a year and all you could spare us is one night?"

"Look, I'm sorry, but Hilary managed my bookings while I was away. I really wasn't expecting much to happen, so when she asked for guidelines on selecting gigs I told her to do what she thought best. When I got home I found my calendar pretty well full."

"And then you're off to Toronto for the summer?" Jax continued.

"Yeah, I'm doing that course again."

Anastasia smacked the food remaining in her bowl with her spoon, sending bits of green pea flying. "Don't do that, please," Jax said. She took the spoon, scooped up some food, offered it to the little girl, then withdrew it suddenly. "If you want to teach, why go all the way to Toronto? You could teach here." Anastasia's mouth had opened in anticipation. She frowned and grabbed at the utensil. "Sorry." Jax offered the spoon again.

"Well, they asked me. No one here has asked me to teach."

"Victor Bakula is going on sabbatical this fall and we're looking for someone to fill in. You could do that."

"I can't. I'm going back to Spain in September."

"Back to Spain? Again?" Her eyes glittered behind the lenses of her dark-framed glasses. "Niels, we barely see you anymore. You're drifting away. I really fear that one day you'll meet a dark-eyed beauty there and be lost to us forever."

Adriana inevitably came to mind and I glanced briefly away. Jax set down the spoon.

"You already have, haven't you?"

At the sound of her raised voice the three children turned to me, its target. Arkady glanced at me, then quickly away. He was a shy little boy with cornsilk hair and Polly's black-rimmed silvery-blue eyes. Anastasia's eyes were blue-green and her hair a jumble of gold-brown curls. She scowled at the apparent cause of her mother's distress. Solid little brown-eyed, brown-haired David eyed me with open curiosity.

"Daniel's getting married so I'm going back for his wedding and to do the Tiago show at *La Bienal de Flamenco*. And I'm getting drawn into planning the film they're making from my book."

"Yeah, well, just don't get too deeply rooted there," Jax muttered.

Polly rested her hand on Jax's arm. "Honey, you're nagging a bit." She turned to me. "What Jax is saying is that we really miss you, Niels."

The rest of the visit continued in the same tone and I left with a heavy heart. What was causing the discord, I wondered. Expectations? Resentments? Had I changed? Had Jax? If I could have stayed longer it may have shaken itself out. Jax was a cornerstone in my life and losing that bond was unthinkable.

I had hoped the summer teaching gig would give me a breather to clear my mind, but my Toronto friends quickly drew me into projects and festivals and the partying associated with them. I had a pleasant little fling with a jazz singer named Zhara, and ended it more confused than ever about women and love and what I wanted in that department. Adriana still haunted me. Did I really not like her enough, as Daniel had said, or was it that I had not allowed myself to? Suddenly weary of it all, I bowed out of a trip with Greg to an ambient-music festival in Colorado and returned to the West Coast before heading to Spain. As a gesture to Jax I arranged to meet with the head of her department about covering some of Victor Bakula's courses during the winter semester. Mostly I just wanted to rest.

Leah stuck her head through the doors that opened to the deck of the Big House where Theo and I were lingering over morning coffee. "Niels, do you have anything planned for today?"

I glanced up. "No, not really. Why?"

Chatting on the phone, she went back into the house without answering. A few minutes later she came out with a cup of coffee and sat down beside us.

"What was that about?" I said.

"Aude called. She's about to buy a condo—she's written an offer, in fact—but wanted to have someone come and do a reality check with her before her agent presents it. I can't because I'm taking Mama Ris to an eye appointment so I said you would."

I sat bolt upright, sloshing coffee on my bare knees. "What?"

"You said you had no other plans."

"I know but really you should have been more specific," I sputtered.

Leah eyed me. "Are you avoiding her?"

"No. I'm not."

"Then what's the problem?"

I exhaled in exasperation. "There's no problem, but you could have asked first."

"And what would you have said?"

"I don't know! Probably that I haven't the slightest idea about how to evaluate a condo."

"She's not looking for someone to do a technical assessment. She made her mind up very quickly. She's only seen the place once and that was yesterday, and she just wants a second pair of eyes in case she's missed something."

I harrumphed and slumped back in my chair. "Why on earth is she buying a condo here?"

"You'll have to ask her that yourself."

Theo had been following the exchange and was smiling broadly.

"What are you laughing at?" I said.

"Me? Nothing. Nothing at all."

"So when am I supposed to show up for this?"

"Eleven." Leah handed me a piece of paper. "Here's the address."

"That's, like, in a couple of hours! I haven't showered or anything yet and it's a long drive."

"Then I guess you'd better get a move on."

I fumed while I showered and shaved and stomped out of the house without saying goodbye. *Why are they pushing me at Aude? What business is it of theirs anyway?* Halfway to Victoria I blushed at my overreaction. *Why does it bother me so much?*

I was still pondering the question as my car's navigation system directed me to turn onto a street that climbed a short rise. Aude was leaning against a small Japanese SUV parked on the right where the hill crested. I pulled in behind it, cut my motor, and got out. Aude straightened up and came towards me with a smile.

"I appreciate your coming, Niels."

"No problem."

We touched cheeks in greeting and I stepped back to look at her. Gone was the crop-headed stick insect I had left at Counter Point the previous year. Her hair floated around her shoulders and her cheeks were round and smooth. Fitted jeans showed off her long muscular legs, and a T-shirt in the dark green that suited her coloring so well was molded to her breasts. I had forgotten how generous they were. But for a tautness around her jaw and some fine lines on her face she could have been the girl I left at her door that fateful New Year's Eve.

"You look great," I said.

Her cheeks pinked with pleasure. "So do you." She motioned to a woman hovering by a white late-model luxury sedan. "This is Diane, the agent who's helping me."

Diane came forward with a polished smile and extended a hand. She outclassed both of us in a stylish black and cream ensemble embellished with chunky gold jewelry. I shook her hand and raised my chin to indicate the buildings lining the street, older, run-down houses intermixed with newer builds and low-rise apartment buildings.

"Not the greatest neighborhood."

Diane's eyes grew wary. "It's in transition. A good time to buy." She gestured to the three-story building we stood next to. "Shall we?"

I turned and regarded it. It was finished in smooth dark-gray stucco panels and had a silver metal roof. Each floor had three inset loggia balconies. Diane led us to an entrance and tapped a code on the keypad next to the door. The lock released with a *clack* and she motioned us inside. A modest foyer ended at an elevator and angled staircase in the building's core. There were two doors off the hall on the left and four doors off the right hall.

"We're on the top floor," Diane said. As we followed her up the stairs she explained that the building was two years old and the vendor was the original owner of the unit for sale. At the door on the left facing away from the street she fiddled with a lockbox, withdrew the key, opened the door, and motioned us in. "Please."

We stepped through a small vestibule into an airy space that looked northwest over rooftops to the Gorge Waterway. The whole effect was light and airy: tall windows, sleek lines, pale wood, stone accents. I followed Aude through the rooms: a good-sized kitchen with mid-range appliances and ample cupboards; a combined living and dining room; two bedrooms, one larger with an ensuite bath; a second full bath and a room for laundry, utilities, and storage. Back in the living room Aude looked at me anxiously.

"What do you think?"

"I think it's quite wonderful. I wish I could find a place like it."

She smiled, relieved. "Yes, I knew right away it's what I wanted, but it's good to have someone else confirm it."

We did another walkaround, Aude pointing out some of the features she particularly liked, then we left. Diane locked up behind us. Outside, I stood to the side as Diane briefly conferred with Aude. She set papers on the hood of her car, which Aude flipped through and signed. When she was done Diane slipped the papers into a folder, shook Aude's hand, got into her car, and drove away.

Aude came towards me with a tremulous smile. "I guess it's just fingers crossed now. It really helped to have you here, Niels. Can I offer you lunch as thanks?"

Aude tore off a piece of crusty baguette, dipped it in the aromatic broth, and ate it. "Oh, that's good."

I had followed her vehicle to a narrow-fronted bistro named Jules located nearby. We parked and met up at the door. "I've never eaten here," she had said. "Hope it's okay." The interior décor was spare: wide-plank fir floors, bentwood chairs at square wooden tables, black and white photos of cityscapes on white walls. *Moules frites* was one of the daily features and we both ordered it. The mussels arrived in cast-iron pots along with a cone of shoestring french fries and a basket of sliced baguette.

"Good to see you eating again," I said.

Aude paused in the act of plucking a plump mussel out of its shell and looked at me levelly. "You saw me at a very bad time, Niels."

"Is it all sorted?"

"Yes. The settlement is what allows me to buy the condo." She smiled. "It was quite generous. Gilles, my lawyer, learned that Thierry had impregnated another woman while I was still with him and was able to use that to good advantage. They married soon after the divorce came through. He has a daughter now and is no doubt working on a son."

"How do you feel about that?"

She considered briefly before responding. "For like two minutes I felt very angry and bitter and stupid, but now just very, very relieved to be out of that marriage, out of the clutches of Thierry and his mother." She shuddered. "I have nightmares about being back there. Never, ever will I let someone control me like that again. What I regret most is all those lost years, and they *are* lost. I have a lot of ground to make up."

We ate in silence for a while. I swallowed a mussel and wiped my mouth. "So, why Victoria?"

"I want to stay on the coast but can't afford Vancouver, and really it's too big. And I have friends here. You remember Clara, my roommate? She runs one of the city choirs. Married with a one-year-old. I've been staying with her. And Colin Jeffries? He was in the same year as me, plays bass."

An old boyfriend? Maybe a love interest? Annoyingly, my chest tightened. "Don't think I met him."

"Maybe not. Colin plays with the Victoria Symphony, but he also helps his wife run her kitchenware shop. And of course there's your mother. She's been invaluable in helping me get into the translation business. I learn more about writing from an hour with her than from the courses I'm taking."

"Yeah. She helped me turn what would probably have been a dry academic book on Tiago into something of a thriller. So, where do things stand with the translations?"

Over chocolate mousse and coffee Aude told me that she now had contracts to do translations for the five other books in Suzi Beaufort's mystery series, as well as recording the audiobooks. "I've really found the protagonist's voice. I'm not sure what that means—she's quite quirky. And I'll do the audiobooks of the translations as well." Her work on Suzi Beaufort's books had led to a contract to record another author's books with the French audio-recording company, and possibly more. "And I'm going to look into doing work with companies recording English books." She gave a half-laugh. "What a curious direction my life has taken."

Our meals finished, Aude paid the bill and we left. Outside she said, "Do you have to go right away? As we were driving here I saw a sign for a trail that goes along the Gorge and thought I'd check it out. Get to know the neighborhood."

"A walk would be good."

We backtracked to the trail entrance and set out.

"All we've talked about is me. What's happening with you, Niels?"

I had not been in touch since sending her my last tour newsletter and brought her up to date on what I'd done since—musically, that is. We followed the trail along the Gorge to the end and sat down on a bench. Heavily laden blackberry bushes covered the bank down to the waterway. Below us a raft of ducks wove among each other, and farther out a couple of kayakers in red life jackets swept past, their paddles slicing rhythmically into the water.

"And this fall?" Aude said.

"Back to Spain shortly." I talked about what I'd be doing there—Daniel's wedding, the Tiago foundation, the movie based on my book about Tiago, the final performance of *Cae un Meteoro* at *La Bienal de Flamenco*. "Closes the circle for me—it was my small show performing Tiago's music at the last *Bienal* that got it all going."

"Your life seems to be centered in Spain."

"Well, my profile as a musician is higher in Spain than in Canada and I continually turn down work. I've also got some very good friends there. I could easily make a life in Spain, but my ties here are strong too. Time is passing and Granddad and my parents are getting older." I shifted on the bench. "I'm pulled in both directions and right now all I feel is tired . . . of the pace I'm keeping, of people coming and going in my life, of constantly moving around and living out of a suitcase, in a hotel or someone else's house. I need to settle down, get my own place, but the question is where."

"I'd think your children are a consideration as well."

"Yeah, well, I'm still trying to figure out how I fit in with them."

Aude glanced at me curiously. "What's to figure out?"

Her phone buzzed and spared me having to respond. "Hello? Oh, I see . . . yes . . . yes . . . that would work." She glanced at her watch. "I could be there in about half an hour." She ended the call and turned to me with shining eyes. "They accepted my offer. They only want to bring forward the completion date, which is even better for me. I have to go and initial the changes and then it's done."

"Congratulations."

We rose and headed back down the path to where our cars were parked.

"Do you want to get together after to celebrate?" I said.

"Would love to, but I'm heading to Whistler. Taking the ferry from Nanaimo to Horseshoe Bay then up from there. It's

Papa's sixtieth birthday this weekend and everyone's coming for the celebration."

"That's a long way to go."

She smiled. "Another reason to be in Victoria."

When we reached her vehicle she unlocked the door and turned to me. "Thanks again, Niels. Everything you've done . . . I owe you an awful lot."

"You don't owe me anything."

She leaned forward and kissed me on both cheeks then lightly on the mouth. Before I could get my arms around her to do it properly, she slipped into her SUV and, with a little wave, drove away.

Chapter 41

"HOW DID IT GO?" Leah said when I returned home after seeing Aude.

"Fine. Nice place, and the seller accepted Aude's offer. She's pleased."

"Good."

To my relief my mother left it at that. I wasn't ready to talk about how I felt about seeing Aude, happy and healed and determinedly making up lost ground—I had not yet figured it out myself. She was much restored to the Aude of our youth, but I sensed a kind of forcefield around her now and new steeliness in her core. Natural defenses, perhaps, after what she had gone through.

I saw Jax and Polly and their family briefly before leaving for Spain. They had just returned from staying at a lakeside cabin and, what with unpacking and settling the children, all they could manage was a hurried and distracted visit over coffee. I left saddened by how our ties had frayed.

"And that woman called again," Hilary said.

I was in Vancouver closing off some business with her before my return to Spain. I glanced up from scanning the arrangements she had made for the trip on my tablet. "What woman?"

"The one who had phoned last spring." Hilary flipped back

through her notebook. "Yvonne Grisham. I guess you didn't call her back?"

I had had no desire to reconnect with the people I had thought were my grandparents. "No, I didn't."

"There was a message this time." She leaned forward to better read her notes. "She said she understood your reluctance to talk to her but asked that you call as a kindness to an old woman." She glanced up. "Don't suppose you still have her number."

I shook my head. Hilary scratched it out on a piece of paper and handed it to me. "Anything I should know about?"

"No," I said. After a moment's hesitation I accepted the paper and thrust it into the pocket of my jeans.

"Yvonne, hey!" the barista, a slight young man with thinning ginger hair, called when she entered the café, one of a local chain on the main floor of a condominium development on West Broadway. I calculated that she would be in her seventies now, but an old woman she was not. Her hair was certainly white but it was elegantly cut and framed a youthful face, and she wore a white shirt loose over jeans and a colorful chunky necklace. She smiled and waved at the barista, surveyed the room, and came towards me. At her approach I rose from the table.

"Thank you so much for agreeing to see me," she said, extending her hand.

I nodded and shook it.

"What can I get you?" she said.

"Just a black coffee."

Yvonne went to the counter and I sat down. While the barista filled her order they talked animatedly about a ceramics exhibition about to open. Yvonne assured the young man she would attend and carried our drinks to the table. Close up, the lines etching her face became evident.

"A friend of yours?" I said, accepting the cup.

Yvonne sat down across from me. "I come here often." She made a gesture towards the ceiling. "I live upstairs."

I blinked at the news but didn't probe.

"I really do appreciate your coming, Niels. I know it was a lot to ask. And especially since you are probably very busy." She smiled. "I saw the article about you in that arts magazine and have followed your career since. Very impressive. Congratulations."

I inclined my head in acknowledgement. "Why do you want to see me?"

She studied her cappuccino for several moments. Looking up, she said, "First of all, let me say how . . ." She paused and drew in a sharp breath. "I don't even know what the right word is. Appalled? Sickened? Dismayed?" She shook her head and her lips flattened into a tight line. "What my son did to your mother was beyond reprehensible and I am so very, very sorry. And then what my daughter did, what she said . . ." She grimaced and glanced away.

"Yeah, it was pretty upsetting."

"I can imagine. When I finally found out what she knew and what she had said to make you abandon us, I was devastated. The news ended my marriage. No great loss, it was already pretty hollow. But when Don defended what Brad had done, you know, 'boys will be boys,' and 'she probably asked for it,' I decided that a nice house and a comfortable life weren't worth having to live with a man like that."

I shifted impatiently in my chair. "Why do you feel the need to tell me all this?"

"Because I want to apologize for what my family has done. And because Rebecca was wrong in saying that any one of those boys could have been your father. My son was your father."

"And you know this how?" I coughed out a laugh. "The way my hair grows? Hardly definitive."

Yvonne regarded me somberly for a moment then drew something out of her pocket and slid it across the table. I glanced down and drew back: it was a photo of me. I looked up.

"What is this? Where did you get it?"

Yvonne tapped the photo. I bent to study it more closely. It was a picture of a man taken from the waist up. He leaned against a mudbrick wall, arms folded, squinting in the sunlight. He had on a creased khaki shirt with the sleeves rolled up and a small dark-blue bandana was tied around his neck. Like me, he wore his dark hair long and loose, and his brow, nose, and mouth were mine. But he was not me.

"Who is this?" I said, my voice unsteady.

"He's my brother Philip. We called him Pip."

I stared at Yvonne for a moment then turned away to gaze unseeing out the window. The truth exploded in my mind like the snow in a shaken glass globe then slowly began to settle. After several minutes I turned back to her.

"Why did you never show me this, tell me this, before?"

"I would have in time. We had so little of it before you left. But the resemblance was apparent to me from the first time I saw you and it is even more marked now that you're older." She gestured to me. "There are differences, of course. His face was narrower than yours and he was shorter and whip thin—you're more robust. But there's something about how you hold yourself and your disposition that's so like him. He was gentle and sensitive, a sweet guy. I adored him."

"He's not here anymore?" I said quietly.

Yvonne shook her head. "Pip was an idealist, wanted to save the world. Purpose fueled him. He became a doctor and spent several months a year abroad with the *medicins sans frontières*. He was in some godforsaken place in Africa with some colleagues, stopped at a checkpoint. He had gotten out of the vehicle to show the guards their transit papers. A kid who could barely hold his rifle shot him. No one knew why, maybe a misinterpreted gesture, or the gun just went off. They couldn't save him. He's buried out there somewhere."

She sighed deeply. "That was over forty years ago. The grief blighted my life for many years and my family, especially my children, suffered for it. It could be why Brad became what he was. And then *he* died." She shook her head. "A parent should never lose a child. I didn't know the truth about him then, but even if I had, he was still my son. With all that loss I could never give Rebecca what she needed, so it's not surprising that she chooses to live on the other side of the world."

She smiled faintly. "Then you came along and it was like Pip had returned. You're all that I have left now, Niels."

Chapter 42

I GOT ON THE flight to Madrid happy to leave behind all the emotional turmoil churned up by my visits with Aude, Jax, and Yvonne.

"How do you feel about it?" my mother said after I had texted her a copy of the photo of what would be my great-uncle Philip and phoned her to discuss it.

"I'm not sure. I'm still getting used to the idea. I was quite comfortable with not knowing which one of those guys was my father, preferred not to, in fact. The resemblance is clear, though, don't you think?"

"It is."

"But you always thought it was Brad, didn't you? The hair business, right?"

"There also was the matter of it being his house, *droit du seigneur*, and all that."

I was struck by how casually my mother and I were speaking about what had been done to her, a subject we had never discussed before. "One thing that's sort of comforting is that behind the awfulness of Brad there is some good in that family," I said.

"I suppose so."

"You don't sound very enthusiastic, Mom."

Leah sighed. "Yvonne's done a bit of a number on you,

Niels. Think carefully about what if any obligation you assume in respect of her."

My return to Spain was like walking into a warm embrace. In Seville I took up residence at the tavern apartment and was relieved to find Emilio back to his old self after the ordeal of his surgery. The *Cae un Meteoro* troupe reassembled for rehearsals with many hugs and laughs and stories. Our two performances played to full and enthusiastic houses. They were a valediction for me—I would never do the show again. My eyes teared without embarrassment as we took our bows after the last one.

I didn't know what to expect of my reunion with Adriana. She greeted me at the troupe's first gathering with the same embrace she gave the others and whispered, "*Esta noche*?" I decided not to overthink the invitation and went home with her. Our encounters lacked the tension of our parting the previous spring. About to embark on a tour of South America, her horizon had shifted, and when she departed her goodbye, though affectionate, carried a note of finality.

I had thought the position of advisor in the production of the film based on my book about Tiago a nominal one, but ended up spending several days with different departments involved in making it. My comments on the script were sought. It was built around the bones of my story but otherwise didn't resemble my book much, for which I was unexpectedly grateful. Numerous fictional elements were introduced to add texture or increase dramatic effect. I could have pumped up the drama by telling them about my wild flight from Seville with the toolbox in hand and Paula's uncle's henchmen on my heels, but I figured that, for her sake, the matter of the gold and her uncle's threats should remain secret. In the film, tension around my character's possession of the mysterious toolbox comes from customs agents threatening to destroy the cassettes in a search for drugs.

The customs were in the United States because my character

was rewritten as an American. The scriptwriters had the good grace to apologize—sort of—for the change, saying audiences would recognize Los Angeles as a hometown more readily than Vancouver. Confusingly, the actor cast as the American me was British. He was better looking than me, pretty even, with a boyish face and blond hair flopping down over big blue eyes. I spent a few hours with him discussing his character and providing pointers on playing flamenco.

"How did you come to be at loose ends in Seville, anyway?" he said, wanting to better understand my state of mind and motivations then.

"I had lost someone," I said, and wondered after whether I had been referring to my biological father, Aude, or my old self.

For the film they made the Paula character younger and hotter—inspired no doubt by the kind of women who appeared in *gitano* music videos—and hinted at a love interest between the fictitious her and me. Paula groaned when I told her about the budding and very beautiful actress they had chosen for the role.

"How can I show my face beside her?" she said.

The Paloma character was still a doctor but made into a brother, sexy *gitano* twins perhaps thought to be too distracting.

Our characters were correctly secondary to that of Tiago. His had been well written, capturing the arrogance, passion, complexity, and pathos of the man with neither apology nor sentimentality. Three actors were needed to play him at the different stages of his life. A venerable flamenco guitarist who also acted played the old Tiago I had known. He had an enigmatic quality and sly wit and I thought him well cast. He quizzed me on small details about Tiago: how he wore clothes, ate, walked, held his guitar, lit his cigarette. We spent several memorable hours talking and jamming, and parted promising to keep in touch. I spent almost no time with the actor who played the middle-aged Tiago who, upon leaving prison, gets work as a ranch hand, ignored and forgotten with only the horses in the stable as his audience. He was a closed, remote man and had no doubt concluded that, not having known Tiago at that stage of his life, I had little to offer him. Neither had I known Tiago in his youth, but the film's director drew me into the consideration of possible actors to play the role. While there was enough of a resemblance between the other two actors, they could not find one who could credibly play Tiago in his youth as well as decent flamenco guitar.

"He's the best of the lot," the director said, gesturing dismissively at the screen on which had just played the audition video for the candidate they were considering. "But even with makeup and prosthetics he's still not the right shape and a bit limp on the guitar."

I stared at the image on the screen. "I think I may know someone who is close enough in appearance and plays wild flamenco."

"You!" said Cruz when he arrived for an audition later that week. I told the casting director not to mention my role in suggesting him, in case it put him off, but agreed to sit in on the audition. "I thought it was because I was in the first *Cae un Meteoro*."

"It is, because that's where I saw what you can do."

He stood nonplussed for several seconds. "It's very generous of you," he said. *All things considered*, he might have added.

"It's not a done deal, Cruz. You have to be able to act too."

It turned out that all he needed to do was recite the lines, his natural arrogance, fierce guitar work, and shoe lifts for added height taking him the rest of the way. Would he remember my help when he became a star?

The film didn't dwell much on the long and laborious process involved in extracting Tiago's music from the tapes—they were miraculously all clear and clean and the individual tunes nicely intact. The film's conclusion matched reality, however.

An impresario discovers my character playing Tiago's long-lost music and mounts a show around them. The show ends with a production in the spirit of *Cae un Meteoro* featuring a medley of Tiago's music. For the finale the three Tiagos appear ghost-like on a stage floating above the main one and all play together. The director thought it would be a nice touch if I also appeared in the finale, playing a duet with my fictional self. I agreed.

Daniel's wedding was a joyous affair, three days of partying with old and new friends in Malaga, Adela's hometown. She was a quiet, self-contained woman with tawny hair and light-brown eyes. She greeted me affectionately, like an old friend.

"*Perdóname*, I have heard so much about you from Daniel that I feel I know you. You must visit us often."

I liked her immediately and immensely and shared, without reservation or envy now, Daniel's happiness. They ended their honeymoon with several days in Seville and insisted I stay on at the tavern apartment while they were there.

"You two might be comfortable sharing the place, but I sure as heck wouldn't be," I said to Daniel, and moved into a small hotel nearby.

Adela left Daniel alone to spend time with Emilio and me, insisting there were things she preferred to do on her own. My regard for her grew even more.

Early in October I received an email from Aude announcing that she had taken possession of her condo and was busy setting it up.

> *Was at estate sale looking for furniture and instead found forty-seven-string pedal harp. Limited provenance and the crown and pillar need some TLC but otherwise in decent shape. She is sitting by the*

window now like a grand lady with her hands folded in her lap, either inviting or mocking me.

I sent her a chatty account of my activities in Spain.
When R U back? Aude replied.
Not sure, I wrote.

Not wanting to return home to a full schedule I had asked Hilary to keep my calendar for the fall open. When people knew I was back in Spain, several opportunities for work arose and I accepted a few. Ensconced in the tavern apartment amidst good company, and with the gigs to keep me busy, I saw no reason to rush home.

This might have continued indefinitely but for a small epiphany. I was at a meeting in Paula's office concerning the Tiago foundation we were establishing. Emilio, Dante—whom I had convinced to sit on the board—and Soledad, Paula's former secretary who had agreed to take on the administration of the foundation in her retirement, also attended. Much progress had been made. The foundation was now a legal entity. A trust fed by royalties assigned to it from the use of Tiago's music, a large contribution from my family's charitable foundation, government grants, and private donations that Emilio had shaken out of the business community had been established. Principles and procedures for the selection and awarding of scholarships and a public relations plan were being developed. We anticipated being ready to grant the first scholarship in the spring.

I stayed behind to chat with Paula for a few minutes after the meeting was over and the others had gone. When I left her office I stopped in the street to zip up my jacket against the brisk November breeze. As I did so I glanced up at the window of what had been Tiago's apartment. I recalled sitting there talking to Tiago, drinking wine, playing guitar. What a bold and felicitous course he had set me on. What had he in mind when he willed those cassettes to me? Had he hoped then that I would bring him and his music back to life?

And what would my life have been if I had never met him, never learned flamenco, never received the gift of his music? I reflected on the original impetus that set me on the twisted path that eventually intersected with Tiago's—the unnecessary pursuit of a phantom and the bitter, life-changing truth I found instead. I recalled the conversation when I told Tiago about my awful parentage. "A man has many fathers," he had said. My thoughts leapt to the three children I had so casually fathered. No obligations, Jax and Polly had said. But a blood-bond automatically created one. "They are family," Paula had said to explain all that she had done for Tiago and her uncle, however difficult or distasteful. As Arkady, Anastasia, and David were mine.

I do not ever want them to have to come in search of me.

The breeze now carried a sprinkling of rain. I turned up my collar. It was time to go home.

Chapter 43

"HOW ABOUT IF I come over and make you guys dinner?" I said.

"If you like," Jax said.

"And maybe stay for a few days? Would that work?"

"It's your house."

"Don't be like that, Jax."

Silence then a sigh. "Sorry, Niels. We'd love to see you, and of course you're very welcome to stay for as long as you'd like."

I arrived late on a Friday afternoon loaded down with a fresh salmon, several bottles of wine, and various other bits for the dinner. I prepared it while Polly and Dina bathed and fed the children. Jax arrived home in time to give David his last few spoonsful and read them a bedtime story. Dina usually ate separately from Jax and Polly. In honor of my presence she joined us for dinner, so the conversation was light and mostly involved my talking about Spain. At the end of the meal Dina slipped away while Jax, Polly, and I cleaned up. Jax finished loading the dishwasher and turned it on.

"Why are you opening more wine?" she said.

I turned from wiping down the stove to see Polly plying the corkscrew on another bottle. "I'm going to bed. This is for you two. You need to talk." She kissed us both goodnight and left Jax and me staring at each other.

Jax shrugged and took a couple of glasses out of the cupboard. "Let's go to the quiet room."

I picked up the wine and followed her downstairs to the family room. It had been lined with acoustic tiles to create a soundproof space for practice and contained a wall unit filled with books and scores, a table, several straight-backed wooden chairs and music stands, a hard-edged sofa covered in a gray tweed, and a coffee table. We sat down on the sofa and I poured out some wine.

"Cheers," I said. We clinked glasses and I took a sip. "Polly thinks we need to talk. I do too. You've been awfully tetchy the last few times I've been here."

"Humph."

"Is it me? Have I done something?"

"You overrate your importance," Jax said into her glass.

I reeled back as though she had struck me. "I see." I started to rise. "Maybe I should just go then."

Jax's lips trembled and she burst into tears. She shakily set her glass down and buried her face in her hands. I eased back onto the sofa.

"What's going on, Jax?"

She fumbled in her pocket, found a tissue, wiped her eyes and nose, and rested her head against the back of the sofa. Tears leaked out of her closed eyes. After a couple of minutes she roused herself and blew her nose.

"I'm sorry. I'm being a real bitch, aren't I."

"Something's obviously very wrong."

She was silent for a long moment then exhaled a heavy sigh. "I feel like a fraud and a failure, Nielie."

"What? Where's this coming from?"

She raised a hand and let it fall. "I'm coming up short on everything: being a proper parent, my job, music."

"How's that?"

Her shoulders slumped. "First of all, Polly's doing all the

heavy lifting with the kids." She brushed away her own protest. "I know, I know, we understood that's how it would have to be, and she said she was ready and happy to be the main mom to them in the early years. She's totally fine about setting aside her own career, and always so fucking calm about everything. You know what Polly's like. I on the other hand can't wait to get out of the house and away from the constant demands and commotion." She glanced at me. "You have no idea what it can be like. It's so nice to be able to escape to my office, to my classes, to the world of adults. But it makes me feel like a real shit and so guilty that sometimes I just want to scream.

"And the kids—I think they'd rather be with Dina, not me. They're more used to her because I'm just not around enough. But like, I'm the dad and I have a job, and I should be practicing and performing, but I can't seem to find the time I need to do that either because I feel that I should spend whatever free time I have with the kids. But not keeping up professionally makes me feel inadequate and like I'm falling behind. It's a fucking vicious circle." She shook her head. "I don't know how men do it. None of the guys I work with who have families seem to be struggling like I am."

Her forehead wrinkled in puzzlement. "Funny, I've never put it together like that before."

"Have you talked to Polly about this?"

"No. I think I've only just figured it out."

"So why does she think the problem is between you and me?"

Jax's cheeks reddened. "Well, I've said a few things about you abandoning us, shirking responsibility and all that."

"Regarding the kids, you mean?"

"It's unfair, I know. We did say you'd have no obligations."

"But you think I do?"

She grimaced. "I don't know, Nielie. You've been away so

much and I think I was looking for a target for frustrations I didn't really understand. I truly am sorry."

I cleared my throat. "I think I have obligations too."

"Really?"

"It didn't matter so much when they were babies, but they're growing up and starting to become their own little selves. I think they should know who their dad is. I don't want them to go through what I did, first not knowing my mother for so long and then the whole stupid business about looking for my biological father."

Jax regarded me with raised eyebrows. "Well!"

"What do you think? Could we make it work somehow?"

"Yeah, sure, absolutely."

"It wouldn't confuse things even more for you?"

Jax regarded me intently. "No, no, I don't think so. It may even help, I mean, spread things around a bit. If there are three of us maybe I won't feel so much pressure. What do you have in mind? Do you want to move in?"

I laughed drily. "Don't think I'm ready to go that far."

"Where would you live then?"

"That's another thing—I need to settle down somewhere. I've been living in hotel rooms and other people's houses for as long as I can remember. I want to get my own place and it might as well be here in Victoria. Then I can see you guys often."

"No more Spain? I thought everything was happening for you in Spain."

"Yeah, there's a lot there and it could go on, but I'm ready for a change, a new direction. I've been riding on Tiago's music for almost ten years now and I think it's run its course. I'll always have a connection to Spain and go back, just as I'll go to Vancouver and other places I need to for work. But not as often or for as long. Home base will be here."

"Well, that's interesting. So what now?"

"I'm not entirely sure. I think I'll take a break to start, catch my breath. I've been going constantly for years. Then explore some new stuff. I've got the teaching gig at the university here this winter. And Granddad has composed several pieces for guitar. I've resisted working with him, haven't wanted to trade on our relationship, but it would be nice to do something together." I smiled. "I think he takes me seriously now."

Jax flashed me a sidelong look. "He's always taken you seriously. He's awfully proud of what you've done."

"In his own way."

"He's different talking about you with others, you know."

I shrugged. "Anyhow, there's always work with Greg and other musicians I know. Flamenco—well, it was part of what I went through after . . . you know . . ."

"That was quite a trip, wasn't it. But look at where it took you."

"Yeah, but I don't want it to define the rest of my life. It's time to turn the page."

Chapter 44

"I DON'T KNOW WHAT I regret more, opening that other bottle of wine or staying up until three," I groaned.

Jax and I were nursing sore heads with hot black coffees the morning after our talk.

"I for one am getting too old for this shit," she said. She glanced up at me from under her brows. "What *I* regret, Nielie, is saying that you weren't important to me."

I reached across the table and squeezed her hand. "Forget it. Are you feeling any better about things today?"

"I think so. As they say, the biggest part is identifying the problem. Not sure I can change much but I see it differently now." An attempt at a smile became a wince. "Just knowing you'll be with us helps."

The following Monday Dina woke with a severe toothache. Polly managed to arrange an emergency appointment with the family's dentist for her.

"Can you mind the children?" she said to me. "I don't want to bother Jax at work if I don't have to."

"Yes, of course."

She settled them down in the living room with a bin full of toys. "Dina has a sore tooth and Mama is taking her to get it fixed. Your daddy will take care of you."

The three children turned expressionless faces to me then dug into the bin of toys. In the three days I had been there they had paid me no more attention than what they would have to a tree that had sprung up in their midst. I sat down on the sofa with my laptop, intending to deal with some business and respond to emails, but found myself watching them instead.

I had formed preliminary impressions of their characters. Arkady, or Kady, as he was known, was a dreamy little soul who said little and seemed off in his own world. Anastasia, who they called Tasi, was the opposite. Self-assured, articulate, and opinionated, she bossed everyone around. She reminded me of my mother. David—Davy—was a solid little guy who held his own against Tasi's tyranny and devoured the world with enormous brown eyes. Not much seemed to escape him.

They started off playing separately. Kady had arranged a collection of random objects—a bright blue coil, a brown sphere made of mesh, a little plastic figure, a red disk, a wooden car, a green block with holes in it, a card with two apples and the number two printed on it—in a semi-circle in front of him. He changed their position from time to time, murmuring under his breath. Tasi had taken three stuffed animals and was performing a little dance with them accompanied by snatches of song. Davy was arranging colored pieces of different shapes and sizes into patterns on a magnetic board.

After a while Tasi abandoned the stuffed animals, plunked herself down near Kady, and reached for the red disk. Kady waved a frantic hand. "Don't touch them! They are necessary."

Perhaps as startled as I was to hear Kady speak, Tasi got up and went over to Davy. "What is that?" she said, pointing.

"A dog."

"It's a cat."

"No, it's a dog."

"I'm going to make a cat." Tasi sat and began to fiddle with the pieces.

Davy ceded the magnetic board and colored pieces to her and pulled a barn-shaped hinged box out of the toy bin. He dumped the contents, chunky pieces shaped liked farm animals, on the floor and began to fit them into matching cutouts on the barn box. Tasi watched him for a minute. Abandoning her cat she came over and began playing with the farm game. Davy rose, returned to the magnetic board, and resumed constructing his dog.

Well played, I thought, smiling. A few minutes later Tasi stood up. *Which one are you going to bother now?* I wondered. She ignored her brothers and came over to me. The barrette holding back her hair had slipped and she regarded me solemnly through curls tumbling over her face.

"I have to pee," she said.

My life experience to that point didn't include helping a female to urinate, but I managed.

"Wash my hands now," Tasi said when I had drawn up her pants and she had depressed the flush mechanism.

"Of course." I held her up to the sink while, with exaggerated care and an abundance of bubbles, she soaped and rinsed her hands. Setting her down I brushed the curls off her face and reset the barrette.

After checking that neither of the boys needed the bathroom, I sat back down on the sofa and regarded the children again. A shiver—anticipation? fear?—ran through me. These little people were my future and I had much to learn.

With tending the children and feeding everyone lunch I was not able to deal with business or my emails until later that afternoon. Among the newly posted emails was one from Aude.

Hi Niels. Where R U?
In Victoria, at Jax's, I replied. *Was going to call.*
Her follow up came shortly after.

> *Great! There's something that might interest you. Met other residents at condo meeting on the weekend. John one of the guys is planning to sell his place. He's a widower and moving to Hawaii to be with a woman he met on vacation there. When we looked at my place you said you wished you could find something like it. John's is one bedroom and den and looks to downtown rather than the Gorge. Otherwise much like mine. If you're interested I can arrange viewing.*

I sat back, my mind racing. Having made the decision to settle here I would need a place to live, and with what I had earned in the last couple of years through royalties, selling the rights to my book, various fees, and residuals, I could afford to buy one. But in the same building as Aude? Was she just being helpful or was she sending me a message? Living that close together, we would inevitably see more of each other. Did she want that? Did I? But as my mind sorted through the pros and cons, the various implications and possible outcomes, my fingers were quietly typing: *Yes I'm interested and would like to see it.*

She replied a few minutes later.

> *John's available anytime with a bit of notice. How about coming late afternoon Wednesday or Thursday and staying for dinner? Kind of a housewarming.*

Wednesday would work, I wrote.
Wonderful! 5:30?
OK see you then.

A tap on the little arrow sped the message on its way. I leaned back and smiled hugely. I would bring Aude a bouquet of irises and a bottle of champagne, a big one this time. And brioche too. I would bake Aude some for breakfast.

THE END

Acknowledgements

I ENJOY WRITING ABOUT places and things that interest me. Learning more about these subjects is one of the best parts of the process and the Internet is an extraordinary research tool. It allowed me, for example, to walk the decks of a container ship and attend a *gitano* wedding without being there. I consulted print sources as well, and would especially like to note *The Art of Flamenco* and *Lives and Legends of Flamenco* by D.E. Pohren, and *Gypsies and Flamenco* by Bernard Leblon.

My thanks to Iminah Kani for telling me about her experience as a student of flamenco guitar, Alex Nichol for describing the life of a musician, and Christopher Cameron for his instructive comments on the musical aspects of the book. Any errors in presenting these elements are entirely mine.

I also would like to express my gratitude for the friendship of the late Cliff Jones, and for his stories about and valuable insights into the music industry.

About the Author

Elaine Kozak came to writing after several fascinating careers. She designed and sold information-retrieval systems, worked on policy and agreements to expand international trade, and, with her husband, planted a vineyard and established an award-winning winery. This last experience inspired Elaine's first book, a vineyard mystery titled *Root Causes*. She followed it with *The Lighthouse*, a family saga set in New Mexico. A question about one of the characters in *The Lighthouse* intrigued her, and she wrote *Rhapsody in a Minor Mode* to answer it. Elaine now lives in Victoria, Canada.

Manufactured by Amazon.ca
Acheson, AB